W9-CQJ-909

FAKING
REALITY

Also by Sara Fujimura

Every Reason We Shouldn't

FAKING REALITY

Sara Fujimura

TOR TEEN

A Tom Doherty Associates Book

New York

FAKING REALITY

A Tor Teen Book
Published by Tom Doherty Associates
120 Broadway
New York, NY 10271

www.tor-forge.com

Tor® is a registered trademark of Macmillan Publishing Group, LLC.

Library of Congress Cataloging-in-Publication Data

Names: Fujimura, Sara, author.
Title: Faking reality / Sara Fujimura.
Description: First edition. | New York : Tor Teen, 2021. |
"A Tom Doherty Associates book."
Identifiers: LCCN 2021009140 (print) | LCCN 2021009141 (ebook) |
ISBN 9781250204103 (hardcover) | ISBN 9781250204127 (ebook)
Subjects: CYAC: Reality television programs—Fiction. | Dating (Social
customs)—Fiction. | Best friends—Fiction. | Friendship—Fiction. |
Japanese Americans—Fiction.
Classification: LCC PZ7.1.F84 Fak 2021 (print) |
LCC PZ7.1.F84 (ebook) | DDC [Fic] —dc23
LC record available at https://lccn.loc.gov/2021009140
LC ebook record available at https://lccn.loc.gov/2021009141

Our books may be purchased in bulk for promotional, educational, or
business use. Please contact your local bookseller or the Macmillan Corporate
and Premium Sales Department at 1-800-221-7945, extension 5442,
or by email at MacmillanSpecialMarkets@macmillan.com.

First Edition: July 2021

Printed in the United States of America

0   9   8   7   6   5   4   3   2   1

To Akiko and Fumio Fujimura
for opening your home and your hearts
to this American girl since the very beginning.
The American branch of the Fujimura family tree might be
far away, but we are strong because of your loving roots.
どうもありがとうございました。

FAKING REALITY

Chapter

1

"Can I get you anything else?" My favorite waiter at Matsuda puts down a bowl of edamame and a steaming cup of green tea in front of me.

I slide my shades off and let my guard down. I can be myself again because the cameras aren't allowed to follow me in here—or at school.

"You could join me." I give him a flirty smile.

"Duh, it's Wednesday. My future girlfriend is on TV. Like I'm going to miss that."

As I set up my tablet, Leo grabs a tray filled with all the decorative shōyu bottles from the restaurant's tables and a giant jug of soy sauce to refill them. I scooch over in my favorite booth so that Leo and his tray can join me. The opening strains of *Kitsune Mask*'s wailing guitar echo around the otherwise empty restaurant. Leo and I do our usual dance, which includes flailing arm movements—at least until my hand hits the tray and knocks over one of the decorative bottles, spilling shōyu everywhere.

"Dakota!" Leo lightly chastises me before jumping up to get a rag. "Pause it. I'll be right back."

My eyes follow after him. Leo Matsuda. My best friend for over a decade. The person whose lips send arcs of electricity through my body. Well, at least in my dreams, they do. In reality? I don't know. I'd be happy to take one for the team and find out though.

I shake last night's version—which included some intense action on the Matsudas' living room couch—from my brain and return to the Friend Zone as Leo comes back with a rag and a plate of karaage.

"Ojiichan said to give these to you." Leo puts the plate filled with five Japanese-style chicken nuggets in front of me and mops up the spilled shōyu.

"Dōmo arigatō gozaimashita, Ojiichan!" I yell a thanks toward the kitchen door. "Put it on my tab!"

"Hai, hai," *Yes*, yes, Leo's grandfather yells back, though we both know he isn't keeping a running total of all the times the Matsudas have fed me for free.

"If we suddenly get busy in the next hour, can you run the cash register? Mom and Dad are at the bank, and Aurora has marching band until seven." Leo sits back down beside me and wipes his hands on his waist apron.

"So the karaage is a bribe, then?"

"Pretty much."

I take a bite of the lightly spiced, deep-fried chicken. "Totally working."

"Now then. My future girlfriend. Jay Yoshikawa."

"Leo, Jay Yoshikawa isn't a real person, and Ava Takahashi who plays her is married. Not to mention that she's twenty-five and you're sixteen. So, ew."

"Shut up and let me dream."

"Wait, I forgot to put the subtitles on."

Leo doesn't need subtitles for the Japanese parts, but I do. His lack of Japanese writing skills got him stuck back in Japanese II with me learning the basics, but Leo's Japanese speaking skills are advanced, especially when he talks about food. Though I guess that's a given when you work in your Japanese grandfather's restaurant. Meanwhile, Ojiichan talks to Mrs. Matsuda in English—though he doesn't need to—to work on his language skills. Her years teaching English in Japan with the JET program after college have given her some mad skills. I aspire to get to that level. Maybe I could go to Japan on the JET program one day too?

I'm not going anywhere until my contract with HGTV is up though. They own me for the rest of this season. Then I will be free. Free to be me. Free to do whatever I want without having it possibly documented on film. I can leave my sunglasses off and my barriers down all the time. I can tell Leo how I feel about him.

"You okay, Koty?" Leo tips his head to the side and gives me a quizzical look.

"Yeah, sorry." I push play and let Leo slip away into his favorite show. One of the few things that is just for him in his overcrowded life.

As we watch the show, I cut my eyes to the side occasionally to watch Leo. Yeah, he has it bad for Jay Yoshikawa. Maybe one day he'll look at me that way too.

"Can I have some edamame?" Leo says when the show breaks for a commercial. He opens his mouth. I shoot a couple of soybeans into his mouth. One pings off his upper lip and onto the table. "Hey, in my mouth and not up my nose, please."

"Learned your lesson from the last time?"

"I was four. Give me a break."

Our favorite show comes back on, and Leo's attention goes back to it. Jay is just about to crush this week's creeptastic yōkai as her secret identity Kitsune Mask when Mr. and Mrs. Matsuda burst through the front door of the restaurant.

"It's fine, honey," Mrs. Matsuda says. "Everything is going to work out fine. We'll swap things around a bit. That will help boost traffic."

"Hey, kids." Mr. Matsuda looks over his shoulder and gives his wife a pointed look. She drops the conversation.

"Hey, Mr. Matsuda. Mrs. Matsuda," I say as Leo refills the last of the shōyu bottles.

"Anything else you guys want done before what I hope will be the dinner rush?" Leo slides to his feet and balances the tray on his arm with his usual grace.

"No, honey. I'll call you if I need you." Mrs. Matsuda kisses the top of Leo's closely cropped head. "Do some homework so you won't have to stay up so late again tonight." Leo groans. "Okay, you can finish your show first."

Leo flits around the restaurant putting all the shōyu bottles back on their tables while humming our latest jam. I nod along, as YouTube sensation Rayne Lee's song "One Last Kiss" has been on my mental radio all day long too. After depositing the tray on the counter, Leo oversings the chorus while doing a dance-y walk across the restaurant. He pauses in the middle of the floor to do the video's signature four finger snaps before finishing his strut to our table. I laugh. Nobody at school gets to see this side of Leo. These one-man shows are only for me.

"You are such a dork," I say as Leo slides back in the booth with me.

"Can't help it. Rayne's song has been stuck in my head all day long."

As soon as I push play again, a couple comes into the restaurant. Followed by a family of six. Leo's free time is over for today, and now he has to do his part in the family machine. My heart hurts for him. And for me.

"Tell you what. After I'm done, I'll leave my tablet in the back with Ojiichan. You can watch the last ten minutes tonight when you get home or if you have a slow spot during dinner."

"Thanks." Leo's dimpled smile makes my heart melt.

I clear my throat. *Get back in the Friend Zone, Dakota.* "Anytime."

◊　◊　◊

"This is awesome, Patrick," Mom says to her college friend—and frequent guest expert on the show—via Zoom. "I knew you would know. You were always Dr. Henderson's favorite for a reason." Mom waves at me over the top of her computer monitor. "Let's do this all again on . . ." Mom looks at Stephanie, our show's talent coordinator, who gives her the answer. "Tuesday at one thirty p.m. Same convo without the personal stuff. And be sure to move to your left about six inches more so we can get your business logo in the background. Great. See you soon."

Mom takes off her headset and swivels her chair around. "How was school today, Koty?"

"Eh." I shrug.

Stephanie moves a pile of research books off the only other chair in Mom's cramped home office and pats it until I sit down. Ugh. There will be work-work coming any second now.

"Tea break?" Stephanie says, confirming my suspicions.

"Yes, please, Steph." Mom slides off her reading glasses and rubs her eyes. "Let's break open that goodie box from Cadbury's."

While Stephanie heads to the kitchen, Mom rolls her chair over to the circular table and peers at Stephanie's open laptop.

"So next Monday, break out the flannels. We're going up to Mc-Guthrie Farms to pick out our Christmas tree for the holiday special."

Sweat pools in the back of my tank top after my short skateboard ride home from Matsuda. "Do I have to wear a winter coat? All that faux fur around my sweaty face is going to be itchy."

"Yes."

"C'mon, Mom. It's still eighty degrees up north, I bet."

"Seventy-five," Mom corrects me. "But we're going to wear the coats and enjoy McGuthrie's famous hot chocolate and think cool thoughts. After all, we are professionals. Unless, of course, you've changed your mind about buying a car."

"Hot chocolate and winter coats in August it is."

"That's my girl."

Leo refers to the way my family lives four or more months in the future because of our shooting schedule as the "McDonalds' Alternate Universe." For example, we filmed our traditional McDonald Family Thanksgiving with turkey, matching sweaters, and the air conditioner turned down to arctic levels before heading over to the Matsudas' house for a belated Independence Day barbecue.

"Can't we go on Saturday or Sunday instead?" I say. "I don't want to miss school."

Mom raises an eyebrow. "Because of school or because Leo's only day off is Monday?"

"School." But when Mom's laser stare penetrates me, I add, "And it's Leo's only *afternoon and evening* off. We still have to go to school. We wanted to watch a movie after our JCC meeting."

"I'll see if Stephanie can move it back to the weekend, but you know that comes with the extra crowds. Which is more important to you? Your personal space while filming or an afternoon with Leo?"

Hands down, a free afternoon with Leo, but I pretend to think it over. "I'm getting better with the crowds. Just promise that if someone brings up last year's Homecoming that we are out."

"Of course. I know that's still a sore spot for you."

That's the understatement of the century. A sore spot is an embarrassing moment that your friends rag you about for a few months. A sore spot isn't having your social blunders made into gifs and memes that circulate the internet. And then there's the *SNL* skit that cemented the moment into pop-culture history. My heart rate doubles, and the prickling sensation returns to my chest.

"Dakota. Deepen your breaths." Mom's hand on my arm slows my downward spiral. "We are *not* going there. Not today. Not ever again. Come back to today. Tell me about what you did after school. Tell me about Leo. What was he wearing?"

In any other context, that last statement would be somewhere between wildly inappropriate and completely gross, but I know what Mom is doing. I picture us sitting in the booth. Leo wears a T-shirt the same color as the cooked edamame shells. I focus the lens on Leo's face as the bean misses his open mouth and ricochets off his upper lip. The lips that keep ending up on mine in my dreams. When I open my eyes, Stephanie stands next to us with the tea tray and a concerned look on her face.

"How are you doing now?" Mom says.

"A little better. Dr. Berger's techniques help," I say.

Stephanie puts the tray on the table and serves us like she's a waitress in a cluttered, nerdy teahouse. "Try the square ones. They have dark chocolate in the center."

I'm convinced this is why Mom *gently persuaded* the production company to pick Stephanie as our talent coordinator. Stephanie and Mom share a mutual love of afternoon tea. They dissect PBS's *Masterpiece Theatre* on Monday mornings like other people discuss

The Bachelor. They are also both graduates of Oxford University, though a good twenty-plus years apart. You want to push either of their buttons? Put a tea bag in a mug of water, nuke it in the microwave, and refer to it as tea.

"Steph, can we see if McGuthrie Farms is willing to move our shooting date to the weekend instead of Monday?" Mom helps herself to one of the heaping pile of chocolate-covered biscuits—"Do not call them cookies"—in the center of the table.

Stephanie raises a quizzical eyebrow. "Are you sure you want to do that, Dakota?"

"Yes," I say.

"Okay then. I'll make it happen." Stephanie taps a quick note on her laptop before placing it on the bookshelf next to some antique-looking fabric samples.

I thought my contented sigh was Mr. Inside Voice, but apparently it wasn't because Stephanie says, "Are you ever going to ask Leo out on a real date?"

"No." I nibble on a biscuit. "At least, not until my contract is up and the cameras are gone."

"Good plan," Mom says. It's one thing for people to make a bingo game out of your unintentionally overused catchphrases, but the Great Homecoming Disaster cut my parents—especially Mom—deeply too. "One last season, then we can all try something new. In fact, I was thinking about going back to Oxford for a visit this summer while Dakota is in Japan on her school trip. Solo."

My face must telegraph my concern because Mom adds, "It's fine. Your dad and Uncle Ted are already talking about some big fishing trip up in Alaska around the same time. It will be a great chance for everybody to disconnect from our previous life and try something new. Maybe grow a little bit. Definitely a chance to refresh and recharge."

"If you need someone to carry your luggage while you're at Oxford." Stephanie raises her hand. "I volunteer as tribute."

"Tell you what, Steph. You decide where you want to go after we wrap the show, and I will make it happen. Airfare, hotel, the whole nine yards. You deserve it after all the network nonsense you've helped us navigate over the years."

"I would love that, Tamlyn. Where to go, though?" Stephanie taps her lips with her index finger.

Mom's phone pings. "Doug is finished. He wants us to come next door and see it."

"He couldn't take a picture and show us?" I shake my head and chug the last of my tea.

"Humor him." Mom puts a few cookies on a decorative napkin. "Here, bring your dad some biscuits."

"Wait. Before you two go." Stephanie quickly tidies the table and rearranges it a bit. She takes a bite out of one of the cookies and places it back on the plate. She opens up the camera app on her work phone and frames the shot.

"Please don't put me in it," I beg. "I've got a huge zit on my forehead."

Stephanie shuffles the tea set around. "Both of you *caress* the fine bone china teacups. Yep, that looks good. I'll load it up and tag Cadbury and Noritake in thanks. Don't forget, Koty, you need to post today too. Got to keep The Network happy."

"Can you send me a picture and caption? I have a ton of home-work tonight."

"It's supposed to be your feed, Dakota. Phil wants authenticity. And *spark*." Mom mocks Phil's jazz hands "spark."

Stephanie and I look at each other and let out derisive snorts.

"Tomorrow, we talk about the spin-off digital series, okay?" Steph-anie says and I groan. She ignores me and loads our tea stuff back on the tray. "Tamara Weatherbee is pressing Phil about this. He's not a fan of our new EP but he has to play nice with her. At least until he either takes her job or lands an executive producer job at another production company. Tell me what *you* want, Dakota, and I'll see if we can get The Network to give a little more with their take."

I don't know what to ask for in return for doing their YouTube-wannabe show. Thanks to my generous contract with HGTV, I can buy anything I want . . .

Okay, there are two things my money can't buy: a car and my way out of Leo's Friend Zone. At least, the first one I can solve after I pass Drivers Ed at school and receive a full driver's license issued by the State of Arizona.

ο   ο   ο

Dad slides his safety glasses up when we come through the door a minute later. His salt-and-pepper hair sticks up at a bunch of weird angles.

Dad throws his hands out wide. "Tah-dah!"

"They're just fancy cookies, Dad."

"I was referring to the state of the newly refurbished and installed banister behind me." Dad pats the banister proudly. "But, I am equally excited that you brought me a snack."

"Patrick said the beat-up refrigerator we found down in Tucson was mid-1930s like I thought." Mom pats some of Dad's silver horns down. "I'm going to research it a bit more before we film on Tuesday. Let's pull out the icebox versus high-tech—at least by 1930s standards—refrigerator angle in the next episode. It's unique, plus it will give Patrick's business a bump. He and Phoebe are expecting their third grandchild in the spring, so they could use the extra cash."

"Well, now I feel old." Dad double fists the cookies.

"Whoa, slow down there, Santa," I say, and Dad winces at his latest internet nickname.

"Hey, Santa is fine." Mom plants a kiss on Dad's cheek above his now fully white beard. "Santa is a positive thing."

"So, you're saying that I can now refer to you as Mrs. Claus?" Dad says.

"Absolutely not." Mom pats at her hair. "Why? Are my roots showing?"

People routinely think my parents, who are both sixty-two, are my grandparents. Nope. Go back to Season 4, Episode 12: "A Christmas Miracle." It's the episode that Mom revealed that at forty-six, she was going to be a first-time mom. She had planned on being quiet about it. After the tabloids kept mistaking Mom's horrible morning sickness—which made her look gaunt and pale on-screen—as cancer, they decided to put the rumors to rest.

Producers couldn't have scripted a more emotionally charged plot arc than Mom collapsing at a book signing and going into premature labor. Me being born eight hours later and spending an overly complicated three months in the NICU was ratings gold. As fans helped pay for my outrageous medical bills—by continuing to watch our show—my parents still feel an obligation to put more of themselves out there for their True Fans than most people would. That's why they agreed for me to be on TV with them. So I could play the role of the Miracle Baby. Then the Miracle Child. Then the Awkward Adolescent. And thanks to last year about this time, the Angsty Teenager.

Now I'm ready for this role to be over. I want to be Just Dakota. I don't know who she is or what she wants though.

Strike that. There is one thing I definitely want. Only I can't have him. Yet.

"Let me prep for shooting tomorrow, and then I'll go shower." Dad slides Mjölnir, aka his favorite hammer, back into the loop on his tool belt. "Since it's my night to cook, I vote we get takeout from Matsuda and binge-watch something."

Never one to turn down dinner from Matsuda, I say, "Or we could eat at the restaurant and then come home. I have a kanji test tomorrow in Japanese to study for and an essay due too."

"Do you want me to quiz you on the kanji? That way I can practice too. I wish I started studying Japanese *before* I was an adult, but my mother—and especially my grandmother—didn't want us to. She wanted us to leave our Japanese side behind and become one hundred percent American."

"Well, that's biting me in the butt right now." Granted, I barely squeak under the Asian bar at only one-quarter Japanese, but it's still a part of me. A part of my history. "If we eat at Matsuda, then I can ask Mrs. Matsuda to check my Japanese essay at the same time."

"Dakota, we are not asking Jen to check your essay while she's working," Mom says.

Part of me wonders if Mom's resistance to her closest friend checking my work has more to do with the fact that a zero-percent Japanese person knows more about Japanese language, culture, and food than her fifty-percent Japanese self does. But Mom has never lived in Japan, and Mrs. Matsuda did for years.

"Only if they're not that busy," I say.

"Fine. I have a couple of more emails to do, but I'll be ready to go by six, Doug." Mom kisses Dad's cheek again. "I love it when it's your night to cook."

"I'm not that bad!" Dad says.

"Weren't you the person Food TV specifically called to be on their *Worst Cooks in America* show, the celebrity charity edition?" I say.

"Maaaaybe. By the way, I see right through you, Dakota Rae. You want to go to Matsuda so you can see Leo," Dad says, and my heart trips. "I know we've been working a lot lately. You miss your friends. Why don't you invite Leo over? Order some pizzas. Spend some quality couch potato time together."

I guarantee that the version of couch potato time with Leo that passes through my brain is 100 percent different than what Dad's thinking.

"Yeah, I'd like that. A lot."

Chapter

2

"Tell Mom and Dad that I had an extra sectional rehearsal today." Aurora intersects Leo and me outside Japanese class after school the following Monday. "I'll be home by five . . . no, six."

Leo puts his arms across his *Kitsune Mask* T-shirted chest. "I'm not lying for you."

"You're not, Favorite Matsuda Child." Aurora checks her hair in her phone's mirror. "You are repeating bad information. One day, when you finally get a life, I'll do the same for you."

"Um, ow," I say as Aurora breaks off our trio without even a goodbye.

"I can't wait for you to leave for college," Leo says to her back.

"You and me both." Aurora makes a beeline for her boyfriend, Jayden, at the end of the hall.

I follow Leo into the classroom for JCC—Japanese Culture Club. We take our usual seats next to Nevaeh, whose hair sports a new hot pink streak today.

"Mina-san," Iwate-sensei says in a warning tone to try to focus our members—a ragtag group of anime-obsessed teens mixed in with a few students who have some Japanese blood flowing through their veins. After everyone settles down, Iwate-sensei continues, "Let's talk about Homecoming. Cooper-san, tatte kudasai."

Nevaeh stands up on command and comes to the front of the room. "Okay, weebs, Homecoming is coming up in a little over a month. We need to pull something together for the annual carnival. Something easy because seven of us are in marching band and won't be able to work much the night of the Homecoming Carnival.

"I still have some of the traditional Japanese festival games in my garage." Jax stops and puts an index finger up. "Wait. Maybe not. I think the citrus rats got into that box too."

"Ew. Get back to us on that. Let's come up with another idea. Cinnamon Roll Prince." Nevaeh points a bedazzled finger at Leo. "You know I want you to be president of the JCC next year. Give me a good idea."

Leo pulls at the neck of his T-shirt. "We could sell Japanese food. Low-cost stuff so it can compete better against the higher-priced food trucks' stuff."

"Yes! See, I knew you'd come through."

"Mina-san, you can't sell food without a food handler's certificate. Gomennasai." Iwate-sensei gently shoots down our idea. "Keep going. I know we can work together to find a good idea."

"Aurora and I both have a food handler's certificate from working in the restaurant," Leo says.

The wheels in my mind begin to turn in true Dynamic Duo fashion. Leo comes up with the good—okay, and occasionally bad—ideas, but I'm the one who brings them to life.

"We could sell pre-packaged, closed food." I look at Leo before handing the mental ball back to him. "Maybe the Matsudas could buy some Pocky and Ramune and a few other simple snacks through their food distributors at wholesale prices for us?"

"I can definitely ask," Leo says.

"Great. Find out and get back to us on this ASAP," Nevaeh says and then moves on to planning our next event, a Japanese movie night at a local, indie movie theater. It's even on a Matsuda Monday night.

Leo looks at me and whispers, "Want to go?"

I shake my head no. I don't go on outings. HGTV would insist on documenting it, and I'm not sure our middle-America, forty- to sixty-year-old, white, suburban Super Fans are quite ready for genderfluid Nevaeh. I would be happy to broaden their horizons, but I don't want ignorant comments or rants directed at my friend. It's taken a while, but most people at school are used to Nevaeh's unapologetic personality and pronouns. But that's this small world. The bigger world hasn't always been as kind to Nevaeh. Plus, I learned my lesson last Homecoming. I don't mix HGTV Dakota and High School Dakota. It's safer for everyone that way.

"You should go," I whisper back, but Leo shrugs.

The meeting rolls on about other things that I can't participate in until Iwate-sensei retakes the floor.

"One last reminder before we go. Those of you going on the Japan trip with us this summer"—Iwate-sensei gestures at the giant poster on her classroom wall—"the first payment of the three is due on the Monday of Homecoming week. That will be your nonrefundable deposit."

o o o

Leo and I walk out the front doors of school after the meeting and drop our skateboards on the ground.

"Do you have enough? For the deposit?" I say.

"Not yet." Leo blows air out of his puffed cheeks. "Last weekend was slooooow. I even told Aurora to go home so I could up my tips—don't look at me like that, she was cool with it—and I'm still over five hundred dollars short."

"Then let me give you the difference." When Leo balks, I say, "*Loan*, not give you the money then. You have to go. It's our Tanabata wish."

Back in early July, I designed an interactive display inside Matsuda to celebrate the Japanese holiday of Tanabata, the star-crossed lovers' holiday on July 7. Along with the traditional bamboo and tanzaku—bookmark-like papers people write their wishes on—I created a Milky Way on the ceiling of the restaurant out of my family's entire collection of Christmas twinkle lights. A local food critic even did an article about it. This gave the restaurant a much-needed boost since business is always slow during the broiling summer months. That's when Leo and I wrote the GO ON JAPAN TRIP wishes on our tanzaku and hung them up.

One small problem—the Matsudas think that Leo and I want to go to Japan after our *senior* year. Not this year.

"Did you come clean to your parents yet?" I say.

"No. But I'm going to. Soon. Probably. If I can't make the deposit, then I'm not going to be able to go anyway. Why create unnecessary drama for myself?"

"Okay, once it is a definite go—and it will be—then you have to tell them. Iwate-sensei isn't going to let you go if she finds out you forged your dad's signature."

"I didn't forge his name. Dad signed it. He just wasn't paying attention to what he was signing. That's why I specifically asked him during monthly inventory."

"That's sneaky."

"Sneaky but effective. You still coming over?" Leo says as we roll away from school.

"Of course. It's Matsuda Monday. Plus, I'm looking for some inspiration for my art class project. I've got nuthin' right now."

"Want me to set up a still life for you or something?" Leo ollies his skateboard onto the metal handrail of the stairs in front of our school and slides down. Meanwhile, I take the wheelchair ramp.

"Show-off," I say when I catch up to him.

"Or if you need a model, here I am." Leo flexes as we roll down the sidewalk next to each other.

"Awesome. So, can I tell Mr. Udall you want the human modeling job next month? It pays fifty bucks a class." I can see the cash signs in Leo's eyes. "We can't do nudes at school, but you are okay modeling in basically a Speedo, yes?"

Leo hits a deep crack in the sidewalk and stumbles off his board. As always, it only takes a few steps before Leo gets his feet under him again. He doubles back to get his skateboard and hops back on. "Never mind. I'm going to pass."

"C'mon. It's an easy $250. At least do my class. Plus, it's not like I've never seen you in a Speedo before. We were on the same summer swim team that one time."

Season 12, Episode 23: "BBQs and Belly Flops." My first and last attempt at being on an organized sports team. It's one thing to suck at a sport. It's another thing when all of America sees you suck at it.

Leo does an exaggerated shiver. "We were eight, and Beth Roberts called me 'Chunk' all summer. I still have bad flashbacks about that."

It's true. Up until about eighth grade, Leo was the slightly overweight kid with glasses. Then puberty finally kicked in, and, *bam*, he shot up six inches in one year. He still wears his glasses instead of contacts occasionally, but overall, Leo went from Zero to Hero by the time we started high school. Unfortunately, I'm not the only one to notice his transformation.

"Beth is in my art class. Come show up in the Speedo and let her kick herself a few thousand times."

"I'm desperate for money. But I'm not *that* desperate."

The Speedo fantasy stays stuck in my brain all the way to Leo's house. I blame the Tanabata display I did for Matsuda for creating this problem. Because when Leo and I hung up our tanzaku, we did a pinky promise. What Leo dismissed as static electricity, shorted a fuse in me. The fuse that has always insisted Leo Matsuda is only my friend.

o   o   o

"Tadaima!" Leo yells when we step through the front door of his house.

"Okaeri!" Ojiichan's welcome echoes down the hallway.

"Hungry?" Leo says after we leave our shoes and skateboards at the door.

"Always."

I follow Leo into the kitchen and park myself on a barstool at the counter my dad installed for the Matsudas, back when Leo and I were babies. We've always been Matsuda's best customers, but this low-level "weekend project" build turned our parents into friends too. Soon after, Leo and I became Toddler Time buddies. We were not instant pals though. Leo's skull probably still has the dent from when my toy backhoe collided with it. On purpose even.

While Leo goes upstairs to drop off his school stuff, I pull my drawing supplies out and spread them all over the island. I have to come up with something today. Anything. I flip through pages upon pages of abandoned ideas. I knead my gum eraser while I rack my brain. Leo's fluffy, gray cat Maru strolls into the kitchen for a snack. When she sees me, Maru drops her tail, flattens her ears, and takes off in the opposite direction.

"You will love me"—I yell after her—"one day."

"What?" Leo says, appearing from around the corner.

"Your cat is still salty about the Great Painting Disaster."

"Yeah, if I had to be shaved to get all the paint out of my fur, I'd be salty too."

"You looked fierce, Maru," I say when the cat peeks her head around the corner. "Like a lion."

"One day, she'll forgive you." Leo moves Maru's food bowl closer to her. "What's your assignment?"

"For the first part, we have to do a two-dimensional drawing. That's due tomorrow. The second part is building that 2D drawing into a 3D piece of art. We don't even have to stay in the appropriate medium. Like I could draw a pirate ship and then make it out of cake instead of wood."

Leo pulls a bag of rice crackers wrapped in seaweed out of their cupboard and pours it into a decorative glass bowl. "Too bad Sasha isn't here. She could probably help you create anything out of sugar."

Five years older than Leo, Sasha has been more of a babysitter than a friend to me. She's always been kind to me, even when Leo and Aurora were on her very last nerve. Honestly, I think she likes me better than Aurora. Then again, maybe I would feel the same if I had to share a room with my sister.

"Is Sasha coming home for a visit soon? Maybe I could talk her into helping me make some kind of sugary masterpiece."

"She's supposed to be here Homecoming weekend. Not for the

game, but so Mom and Dad can sign over the car and a couple of other things now that Sasha is twenty-one."

"I thought it was Aurora's car and then yours next year?"

"Not anymore. Sasha talked Mom and Dad into giving it to her. Warning: There may be a WWE-worthy smackdown between my sisters when Sasha gets here."

"At least get it on video." I pop some rice crackers in my mouth. "Don't forget, we have to ask Ojiichan about the wholesale Pocky and Ramune."

"Right. I will." Leo opens the refrigerator and pulls out a liter bottle of Mitsuya Cider. He pours the ginger-ale-Sprite-ish kind of soda into two small glasses and slides one across the counter to me. "I was thinking on our way over here. Since I have a food handler's certificate and everything, what if I tried cooking something super simple at the Homecoming Carnival? Like, on my own so I can make some extra money? What do you think?"

"I think it's a great idea. What would you make?"

Leo sits on the barstool next to me and bites his lower lip in thought.

"What about ramen?" Leo's deep brown eyes light up as the cogs in his brain start turning. "We still have all the equipment in the storage shed left over from the restaurant's kitchen rebuild three years ago. Dad wants to put it in a food truck one day."

"What if you made a small, free-standing booth instead? Like what I saw the last time I was in Japan."

"Leo-kun, kochi kitte," Ojiichan yells from his bedroom off the kitchen. As always, Ojiichan pronounces his name so that it sounds like something between Leo and Rio.

"Hai!" Leo yells back, both of us understanding that Ojiichan wants him to come to his room.

While Leo helps his grandfather with whatever, I sip my soda and gnaw on my 2B pencil.

I think back to my family's trip to Japan when I was nine. Season 13, Episodes 1 and 2: "Summer Fun in the Land of the Rising Sun." It was mostly fun, if a bit overwhelming. Nobody knew who we were in Japan, so on the days that we weren't filming our two-part special, Mom, Dad, and I wandered around the streets of Nagoya freely.

That's one of the reasons why I want to go back to Japan. I want to be part of the group of teenagers from my school putting their limited Japanese skills—except for Leo, of course—to work and learning about our bigger world. Though the official itinerary hasn't been set yet, we would be coming through Nagoya right around the time when the Tanabata Matsuri—the Star Festival on July 7—is happening in nearby Ichinomiya. I hope we can go.

A spark of an idea hits my brain. I pull up that episode of our show on my phone and fast-forward through it. *Aha*. Finally inspired, I sketch. I slip so deep into my creative zone that I yelp when a hand suddenly touches my shoulder.

"Sugoi," Ojiichan says in surprise at my sketch.

"Did you ever go to the Tanabata Matsuri outside of Nagoya, Ojiichan?"

"Of course. Many times." Ojiichan sits down on the barstool on the other side of me and pulls my sketch pad toward him. "This brings back many memories."

"For me too. I was probably too young to appreciate our trip to Japan, but some things are cemented in my brain. Things I want to do with . . . my friends from school when we go to Japan in July with Iwate-sensei." I fast-forward the video a little bit until I can find the scene I was thinking about. I show it to Ojiichan. "What's this?"

"You look kawaii, Dakota-chan." Ojiichan chuckles. "But it looks like you don't want to eat the ikayaki."

"Yeah, squid-on-a-stick is not my favorite thing. No, I was talking about what the man beside me is making."

"Oh, that's yakisoba. You can find it often at matsuri. I make it here sometimes for my family. Yaki means grilled or fried. Soba is buckwheat noodles." Ojiichan tips his head from side to side. "But they are different noodles. Not the usual soba noodles. I will make you some."

"You don't have to."

"I want to." Ojiichan pats my head. "For my bonus grand-daughter."

"Add it to my tab."

"Hai. Hai."

I sketch faster, my muse finally talking to me again. Only, I change the little girl in the picture. She still wears the expensive, rental yukata and obi—the summer-style, cotton kimono and wide cloth belt—but nobody is insisting that she eat squid on camera. It's not that I hate squid. It's because the showrunner insisted on the squid. I wanted yakisoba, but they said it was too messy for me to eat on camera. I draw a plate of yakisoba in Revised Nine-Year-Old Me's hand and sketch a genuine smile on her face. I have a good, solid draft sketched out by the time Ojiichan finishes cook-ing the yakisoba. Leo sits next to me after completing whatever chore Ojiichan gave him.

"That looks good." Leo points at my sketch.

My mouth waters when Ojiichan slides two plates of yakisoba in front of us. "No, *that* looks good."

"Itadakimasu," *Thanks for the food, let's eat,* Leo and I say in tan-dem, and Ojiichan nods.

Leo hands me a pair of Pikachu chopsticks from the container that lives on the kitchen counter. We dig into the mounds of noodles with pork pieces, cabbage, carrots, and onions, covered in a rich brown sauce.

"And tastes good. Thank you, Ojiichan," I say.

"Hai, hai." Ojiichan waves away my compliment. "Oh, my tele-vision show is on now."

"Ojiichan, you know we can record it for you to watch anytime," Leo says as Ojiichan serves himself a plate of yakisoba and places it on a tray with a pair of chopsticks and a can of Japanese beer.

"It is my Monday vacation. I can eat good food, drink beer, and not wear pants," Ojiichan says. "In my room, of course."

"Thank you for that, Ojiichan." Leo turns to me. "Because he only wears pants when you're here. Otherwise, Monday is Boxers City at the Matsuda House. Yikes."

Ojiichan gives the back of Leo's head a light baka slap as he passes him. Leo laughs and slurps another mess of saucy noodles.

"Though your design is awesome, Koty, I think it would be too hard to do in sugar. Even with Sasha's help."

"Yeah, I agree. Some people have already started building out their pictures in clay or papier-mâché or balsa wood. I don't know. That's kind of basic, don't you think?"

"Doing the whole street would be too hard, but what about focusing on only one element? Like the yakisoba booth. Buy a pancake griddle at Goodwill, build a box around it, paint it red, add some poles and a canvas sign. Boom. Done. One yakisoba stand. The only thing that might be a problem is making the food part to scale, but I'm sure we have stuff around here that you could repurpose and size down. What?"

"Have I ever told you how amazing you are?"

"Yeah, probably the last time I saved your bacon on a school project." Leo bumps his shoulder against mine.

"If Mr. Udall signs off on my design, will you come shopping with me to find all the supplies?"

"Of course. It's not like I have a social life."

The truth stings. "Yeah, but do other people have Matsuda Mondays and get to watch the newest episode of *Kitsune Mask* every Wednesday?"

I realize how pathetic that sounds as soon as it comes out of my mouth. Unfortunately, that's all I've got right now.

"Maybe we can try a little harder this year? Maybe I could finally find a girlfriend," Leo says, and my heart cracks.

"Yeah," I say without conviction.

When the cameras are off of me for good, then I'll come out of my self-imposed bubble. Until today though, I didn't realize that what was protecting me might also be smothering my best friend.

"What if instead of going smaller with the project, I went bigger?" I wash my plate and chopsticks and put them in the drying rack.

The last of Leo's noodles fall off his chopsticks as the spark from my idea ignites in his brain. "What if you build a yakisoba stand from the old griddle we have in storage? The potential-food-truck one. Could you make it functional?"

"Of course. This is not my first rodeo. I just need to ask Dad how to do the energy source."

Building from scratch is Dad's domain, but Mom and I have basic power-tool skills too. Season 16, Episode 7: "Like Father, Like Daughter." When I was twelve, Dad walked me through renovating my bathroom. Along with cosmetic things like repainting the walls, we also built a custom-designed counter for my bathroom and switched out the old toilet for a dual-flush, water-saving one.

"I wonder if Mr. Udall would give me extra credit if you made yakisoba for us during class?" I say.

"You're still thinking too small, Koty." A smile pulls across Leo's face as he uses the phrase that has gotten us grounded more than once for what seemed like a good idea . . . until it wasn't.

"You want to make this a functional build for the Homecoming Carnival, don't you?"

"You get an A on your project, and I make some much-needed dough. It's a win-win."

"Not gonna lie. I think it's a great idea. *If* it works. But what if my building skills aren't good enough. I don't want you to miss out on—you know what—because I failed you."

Leo puts a hand on my arm. "They'll be good enough."

"I hope you're right."

"I'm always right."

Chapter

3

"Dad, I don't want cameras on this," I say after Mr. Udall signs off on my "ambitious design."

"Yes, we have to. Plus, I want to. My baby is all grown up and doing her first solo build-out." Dad sniffs dramatically. "I'm so proud I could burst."

"Daaaaad." Okay, part of me wants to commemorate this event on film. Not so much for me, but for my parents. I'm going to leave for college soon, and this is our over-the-top version of a family scrapbook. "Okay, but if I say something cringey or hit my thumb with the hammer or anything meme-worthy, we cut it."

Dad grabs me in a tight hug. "Of course, Koty. This is simply going to be an empowering episode about a girl and her toolbox. I will attempt to keep my commentary—and the beavers—to a minimum."

To keep our show at the network-required G-rating, Dad has come up with some ridiculous work-around swears. For example, instead of bleeping Dad every time he uses his most famous catchphrase, HGTV trots out a cartoon beaver in a hard hat with a sign that says HOT DAM! Though the trolls mock him relentlessly for it, Dad's charity raises tens of thousands of dollars each year thanks to the cheesetastic beaver joke—whose likeness you can buy on T-shirts, coffee mugs, temporary tattoos, etc.—so he keeps on doing it.

"Give me just a minute more," Dad says as he finishes setting up in his workshop. Well, his studio workshop, which will eventually become the build's kitchen. Not his small, cluttered, real workshop in our backyard.

Stephanie fixes my unruly hair and hands me a tube of lip gloss.

"And, when you're ready," Phil says when the lights are finally set.

I walk into the shop and put my turquoise toolbox on Dad's workbench with an audible clunk. Dad looks up from the plank of wood he's measuring.

"What's up, Dakota?" Dad says.

"I want to build something," I say, like this idea has suddenly erupted in my brain instead of having been under advisement for the last two weeks. "Can you help me?"

Dad slides off his bifocals—which also doesn't help the whole Santa nickname—and looks at me with his slate-blue eyes with laugh lines all around them.

"I'm so proud." Dad sniffs dramatically. "What are you thinking about exactly?"

"Remember when we went to Japan when I was nine? I want to build a yakisoba stand for L—my friend for our school's Homecoming Carnival."

Dad and I freeze and count to five.

"Cut," Phil says. "Great. We'll pull some footage from that episode and then maybe have you do an on-the-fly interview about yaki-whatta. Let's do a cutaway shot from above looking down at Dakota's plans. Wait. Dakota, go get your nails fixed."

"I'm not getting a manicure before I cut wood, Phil."

Phil, our fifty-something showrunner, isn't a bad guy. Sometimes, our "visions" for the show don't align. Specifically, Phil wants us to be more *Keeping Up With the Kardashians* than *Fixer Upper* with a nerdy, historical twist.

He shrugs. "Take it off then. America doesn't want to see your chipped nail polish."

Stephanie appears out of nowhere with a nail polish remover packet. I don't know how she does that. I call the black, crossbody bag she wears at shoots the "Magic Handbag" because if you need something, Stephanie's got it. Duct tape? Steph's got it. Aspirin? See Steph. Dental floss to get the hunk of spinach out of your teeth after lunch? Yep, Steph again.

Phil glances at his watch. "Doug, why don't you cut most of the wood while we're waiting."

"No!" I yell over my shoulder as I scrub my nails. "It's my school project. I'm being graded on it. No Hollywood Magic allowed."

Phil lets out an irritated sigh.

Nail polish removed. Safety glasses on. We are ready to film again.

"You know what I always say, Koty," Dad says into the camera after we do the yakisoba stand bit again.

"Don't eat yellow snow?" I say, and the new guy on the camera crew snort-laughs. Phil gives him a withering look.

Dad and I look into the camera and say in tandem, "Measure twice, cut once."

That one's on the bingo card along with HOT DAM! and a few other unintentional catchphrases people like to print on T-shirts and make into memes.

I pull the miter saw down, cutting the piece of wood in one smooth step. Though it isn't exciting, they continue to film cut-aways as I do the same task over and over until I have a nice pile of perfectly cut wood. No catchphrases uttered. No lost appendages. Just a girl and her miter saw.

"Cut!" Phil glances at his watch. "I thought the griddle part was going to be delivered today."

"I got it." Leo's voice echoes across the room.

Everybody looks back to see Leo and his dad coming through the door. They carry the griddle top between them. Phil snaps his fingers at the new camera guy who starts rolling.

"Hey, Dakota." Leo gives me one of his dimpled smiles that melts my heart. "Where do you want this?"

"Hey, I don't want to be on TV," Mr. Matsuda says.

"It's a cameo. Sixty seconds tops." Phil gestures for the camera to swing back to Leo. "We'll do the appearance release afterward."

"I said no," Mr. Matsuda says.

"But don't you want America to meet your handsome son?"

"Absolutely not."

"Fine." Phil makes a cut sign to the camera guy. "Let's break for tonight, people."

"Put it over here, Kenichi," Dad says as Phil and his crew turn off the lighting and pack up.

Mr. Matsuda and Leo lean the griddle against the workbench.

"We're going to use all new hardware for safety's sake," Dad says to Mr. Matsuda. "It shouldn't be too hard to convert from gas to propane. And I'll have Dakota put in some framing or brackets inside the base to keep the griddle stationary."

"Wait. Is that going to require a blowtorch?" Leo's brown eyes sparkle.

"Yeeeees," Dad says, his eyes sparkling as much as Leo's. "Only it's an acetylene torch, not a blowtorch."

"That'll work."

"Hey, pyros, it's my project." I point at myself. "Mine."

Dad blows air out of his cheeks. I know he's tired.

"Let's eat dinner first, and then we'll do Welding 101. I want you to walk into filming confident in your skills."

"Can I learn too?" Leo gives me a small shove to move over.

"If you switch your shoes," Dad says. "We have a couple extra pairs of work boots in the hall closet. And grab a pair of safety glasses while you are in there too."

"Not tonight, son," Mr. Matsuda says. "We have the romance writers group coming in at five thirty. You and Mom need to serve it up as fast as we can make it."

Leo sighs dramatically.

"Ah, the fun of working in the family business." Dad pounds Leo on the back. "Tell you what, bud. Next time you're over, I'll do a reprise of Welding 101 with you. If your dad is okay with it, of course."

Mr. Matsuda nods, and Leo's smile returns.

"You have a second, Kenichi?" Dad says. "I want to show you my latest hobby—kombucha brewing. Tamlyn and Dakota don't like kombucha, so I need someone with distinguished taste buds to give me an objective opinion."

As our dads walk off toward the house talking about SCOBY and the finer points of fermentation, Leo helps me clean up the shop for the day.

"So, you think after I have the basics down, I could weld together some armor?"

"Armor?" I say.

"Yeah."

"Like the Silver Samurai on *Kitsune Mask*?" I joke and then realize that is exactly where he's going with this. "So, if you're going to be the Silver Samurai, does that mean I get to be Jay Yoshikawa and kitsunebi you into next week?"

"You think you could pull off Jay's white leather jumpsuit?"

Leo holds out my turquoise-handled hammer. I yank it out of his hand. It clunks into the bottom of my toolbox.

"Of course you could." Leo wisely walks back his last comment. "It's just hard for me to see you like that."

"What is *that*?"

"You know." Leo pulls at the neck of his T-shirt.

I cock my head to the side and wait for him to elaborate.

"You're my dude," Leo says. "Jay is—you know—hot. You're not."

"Not today." An indignant fire lights in my stomach. "You don't wear a Speedo while serving people dinner. I don't wear tank tops and booty shorts when working with power tools. Don't push your outdated gender conformity ideas on me."

"Wait. What?" Leo genuinely looks confused. "All I'm saying is that I don't think of you that way. I think of you as like my least annoying sister."

That hurts even worse. Because the more I try to keep things platonic between us, the more I don't want to. It's like pushing on a bruise to see if it still hurts. It does.

"Dakota?" A wrinkle of concern forms between Leo's eyebrows.

I walk toward the door with Leo two steps behind me.

"I'm hangry and annoyed with Phil." I flip off the overhead lights and lock up the build, which includes setting the alarm. "Ignore me."

Leo and I walk the twenty steps over to my house.

"Can't beat the commute," Dad jokes every time an interviewer asks him about my family's final historic build in Phoenix. At least for the show. Mom and Dad will probably continue to restore old homes until neither of them can hold a hammer anymore.

"I wish it was Matsuda Monday," I say as we climb the front steps to my house, which is twice the size of Leo's with half the number of people living in it. "Mom's even making carne asada tonight."

Leo sniffs the spicy, beefy air as he follows me inside. "So. Not. Fair."

I remove my work boots and put them and my safety glasses in their designated spots in the hall closet. "I can bring leftovers tomorrow. We can swap lunches like we used to."

"Tempting."

Leo follows me into the kitchen. As soon as Leo's butt hits the barstool, Dad and Mr. Matsuda come out of Dad's man cave.

"We should head out, Leo." Mr. Matsuda tosses his car keys to Leo. "Wish we could stay longer, but duty calls. We'll catch up soon, Doug."

Leo looks back over his shoulder as his dad herds him out the door. "Ja mata ne."

"Later."

The bruise still hurts.

o   o   o

Later, I text Leo the picture Dad took of me during our Welding 101 lesson. It's a close-up of me with my welding helmet down and my thick leather-gloved hand wrapped around the acetylene torch. Sparks explode like fireworks out of the two pieces of metal I'm connecting together.

ME
Whatcha think? Too hot for my IG page?

Soon after, I receive a picture back. Leo wears sunglasses and holds Sasha's crème brûlée mini blowtorch in his oven-mitted hand.

LEO
Too hot. Might need to dial it back to your usual girl-next-door look.

I send him back a laughing emoji, but he never expands on his assessment. Life in the Friend Zone. More like life in the Bermuda Triangle.

Chapter

4

"Tell Mom and Dad that I'm coming. I needed to talk to a teacher after school for a few minutes," Aurora says when she intersects Leo and me after the final bell.

"I'm not lying for you." Leo brushes past his sister. "Besides, maybe *I* have plans tonight and *you* need to work for me."

Aurora snorts. "Riiiiiight. You and Koty have a hot date of watching *Kitsune Mask* or something?"

Leo and I wince in tandem. As usual, Aurora's assessment is painfully accurate. Unfortunately, on multiple levels.

"When you're finally busy having a life instead of trying to win Favorite Matsuda Child all the time, let me know, I'll cover for you," Aurora says to our backs. "Until then, help a sister out, okay?"

Leo makes a rude hand gesture in the air but never breaks his stride.

"I'm not trying to be Favorite Matsuda Child, by the way. I just am." Leo drops his skateboard outside of school. "It's called putting your family above yourself."

"I know. You have a big heart. You always have." I head down the wheelchair ramp on my skateboard.

If HGTV were filming us right now, Phil would cut to a montage of all the times Leo has helped me over the years. Like the time he bandaged my scraped arm when our unsanctioned tree-house-building idea went horribly wrong. And when Leo offered me his favorite stuffed animal—a giant cow aptly named Mr. Ushi—when we found out the same arm needed a cast because it was broken, not just scraped. Or the time when I was ten and Leo bawled right alongside me as we buried my beloved calico cat, Lita. And last fall, when he talked me down ten seconds after the *SNL* sketch about me ran on TV.

Leo shortens his strides so we can roll beside each other away from school.

"Aurora's right," I say. "You deserve to have a life outside of school and the restaurant."

"Just because I'm not making out in the hallway and lying to my parents about it doesn't mean I don't have a life," Leo says, and my brain has to go there. "And I like watching *Kitsune Mask* with you. It's the thing I look forward to all week. Okay, that sounds pathetic, I get it, but having a girlfriend requires both the time to go somewhere and the money to do something. Neither of which I have at the moment."

"Hey, Leo. This isn't 1950. *Date* is a very subjective word. Also, what if the potential girlfriend wants to take *you* out? You gonna be all macho about it, or you gonna say 'thank you' and get over yourself?"

"Wow, Koty. Did I miss the memo that it's Dump on Leo Day?"

"We're not dumping on you. We're hitting you with a series of truth bombs. Now whether you listen to us and do something about it is a different story."

Leo grumbles because he knows I'm right. So he changes the subject. "How's the build going?"

"Good but slow. Dad insists that he has to be there when I'm working with power tools. Phil and the crew hover, waiting for me to lose a finger or at least pound my thumb or something cringey and meme-worthy."

"And have you?"

"Nope. Super boring."

"Good." Leo jumps off his skateboard when we get to the stop sign at the crossroads. He stomps on the end of his board with his Vans, making the board flip up effortlessly into his hand. I try to do the same, except my board flies off at the wrong angle, whacking me in the knee instead.

Leo stifles his laugh with a cough as I swear and rub my knee.

"You're getting better. You'll be sliding down the school's hand-rail soon."

Yeah, Phil has already voiced his opinion on me skateboarding. Not only the potential danger of a broken arm or concussion, but that he wouldn't be around to capture the wipeout on film. And then there's the whole fight with him about "softening" my look. I am not a Kardashian or Jenner. I wouldn't wear false eyelashes and three-inch heels to the grocery store or a yoga class, or even if I suddenly had the urge to go to a club. I am a jeans-and-T-shirt kind of girl despite the trendy outfits that brands keep sending me for potential OOTD posts.

"Listen, I get what you and Aurora mean about the sad plane of existence I seem to live on. What if I insisted that I needed to come by this afternoon to check on how the yakisoba build is going? Just for an hour or so before the dinner rush hopefully kicks in. It's the truth. And if your dad wants to give me a Power Tools 101 lesson, that would add validity to my story."

Date *is a subjective term.*

"I would love that. I mean, Dad would love that."

"Cool. Ja mata ne."

I watch Leo roll away before launching my skateboard in the opposite direction. Except instead of smoothly hopping onto my board like Leo does, I have to retrieve mine from the ditch first. As I roll home, my stomach bubbles at the thought of having more Leo Time than usually allotted this week.

o   o   o

Stephanie puts her index finger to her lips when I step into the build after depositing my school stuff and changing into my work gear. Mom is in front of the camera today. They've talked her into wearing a dress with sensible shoes instead of her usual high-waisted jeans, plaid button-down, and work boots. She still wears her signature bedazzled safety glasses—thanks, nine-year-old me—perched on her French-braided head though. That's an essential part of the Halloween costume. They even sell HGTV-branded bedazzled safety glasses at Party City. I don't get a cut for my cheesy but incredibly profitable idea. Not to mention that I stopped wearing bedazzled safety glasses after Season 13, thank you very much.

"This final season, we're doing a build close to my heart." Mom taps her heart with her temporarily manicured hand. "While Doug deals with the contemporary termite problem, which has put us weeks behind schedule, I found a key piece of information recently in my research." Mom pulls out an old photo. "And as we've never shied away from some of the uglier parts of American history, I want to share it with you."

Mom flips it over, and the camera op steps in closer to film it. "The good. The bad. The ugly. Next time on *If These Walls Could Talk,* we uncover how this house"—Mom points at the picture before opening her hands up to the ceiling—"became *this* house. Until then . . ." Mom looks directly into the camera and puts her index finger to her lips for two beats before turning her head to cup her ear. She looks back into the camera, "History's talking."

Mom freezes with a smile on her face until Phil yells, "Cut."

Mom puts the photo down on the makeshift table next to the giant, period-appropriate chandelier she is restringing. Mom flew all the way to Idaho last weekend to buy the handblown crystals at an auction.

"Are you sure you want to do that last bit?" Phil says. "It's a little . . . heavy."

"We've been over this, Phil." There is a fire behind Mom's eyes. "Yes, I'm sure. Very sure. We're not going to skip over an important part of my family's history—including the Akagis being sent to a Japanese internment camp during World War II—because it might make a small percentage of viewers uncomfortable. We can't learn from history if we're too scared to talk about it."

I step over the cables littering the floor and come behind Mom to look more closely at the picture. It's the same two-room adobe house surrounded by fields of alfalfa that Mom showcased at the beginning of this season. Her mother's family, the Akagis, came to Phoenix in 1915 to farm vegetables on the land we're currently standing on. Because of his race, my great-grandfather Kajuio Akagi wasn't allowed to own the land his family worked. After the Japanese dropped a bomb on Pearl Harbor, he wasn't allowed to live on this land either. The whole Akagi family, including my then eleven-year-old grandmother, was shipped off to the Poston Japanese internment camp until the war was over.

Though we studied Japanese American internment camps in school briefly—and I once famously ended up in the principal's office over it in the sixth grade—we never talked about the Arizona angle, despite our state having two of the camps. Nor did we talk about how much anti-Japanese sentiment the Akagis and others faced here in Phoenix well after the war was over.

It's still here, though it stays hidden under a rock most days. Occasionally, it bubbles to the surface. I've seen it flung at the Matsudas. Mom somehow gets a pass—or at least a more condescending version of it—because she's famous. Meanwhile, I look so white that people sometimes forget and let their ugly show.

"Yeah, you should definitely talk about it," I tell Mom. "So many people want to sweep it under the rug even though it's still happening today."

Mom throws an arm around me. "That's my girl. I'm going to make a history major out of you yet."

"Let's not get ahead of ourselves, Dr. Akagi." That's my mom's real name, by the way, since my grandparents weren't legally married when she was born. Asian people like Obaachan weren't allowed to marry white people like Grandpa in the 1950s.

When my parents started the show twenty years ago, somebody talked Mom into dropping her earned title and using dad's last name. They said Dr. Akagi sounded too "uppity and unrelatable" to their target audience.

"Maybe that's what I could do after this season. After Akagi House is ready to open to the public for tours." Mom wraps her hand around Obaachan's locket necklace and looks off into the room. "Maybe I could be a guest lecturer and finally put my Ph.D. to use in an academic setting."

"Sounds like a good idea. Just not *my* college because that would be awkward."

"Oh, we'll see." Mom steeples her fingers together and gives me her best archvillain look.

"Dakota, you're up next," Phil interrupts us. "We need to film some wild lines for the HGTV Gives Back spot. With sincerity, not snark this time because we're tweaking it to reference the Hurricane Darius relief campaign. Also, I want to get more footage of you today painting the yaki-whatty stand."

"Yakisoba," I correct him.

"Yes, that. Where's Doug?"

"I can do this part without him. I'm not going to lose a limb spray painting."

Phil walks away chuckling like I'm kidding. *What the actual Phil?*

o   o   o

"Turn it a little more to the left, Doug," Phil says. "Wagner is one of our sponsors this season."

Only I can see Dad's eyes roll as he adjusts the spray paint gun in his hand to show the sponsor's logo.

"Okay, we're set," Phil says and motions at the camera op.

"When you are using this type of sprayer," Dad says like there are only the two of us in the room, "having a steady hand is the hardest part. You want a light, even coat. Too much and it will cause drips down your project."

Something moves in my peripheral vision. Leo, in his favorite *Kitsune Mask* T-shirt, leans in the doorway. Phil nods his head. I realize that I'm smiling. Like genuinely smiling.

"Hey, Dad, you know what inspired me to build this for my art class?" I say, and Phil looks ready to fall over from my sudden candidness.

"What's that, Koty-Kat?" Dad says, and the fans watching at

home get another bingo square for Dad calling me by my nickname.

"Remember the summer we went to Japan when I was nine? We went to the Tanabata Matsuri—the Star Festival—outside Nagoya. There were all of those cool food vendors. Our hosts insisted on dressing Mom and me up in yukata."

"That was a fun trip, wasn't it?" Dad says wistfully. "I remember a squid on a stick in the equation somewhere."

Phil points at his PA, who scribbles something in her notebook. Probably, *Find that picture of Dakota to plug in here.*

"Yeah. But right beside the squid-on-the-stick vendor was a guy selling these saucy, brown noodles. They smelled so good, but I never got to try them. For some reason, that has always stuck with me, but now I get to bring that memory to life. I guess it's true what Mom says about keeping your eyes open and finding inspiration everywhere."

"I think this is going to be your best project yet, Koty."

I pull up my respirator, and Dad does too. He watches as I add several smooth layers of red paint to my giant box. If Phil is waiting for some other words of wisdom from me, that was it. Probably for the rest of the season. Finally, he gets bored.

"And cut," Phil says, though I keep painting.

"Dad, you don't have to keep standing here. I know it's hurting your back."

"True." Dad stands up straight and kneads his back. "You can come in now, Leo. I think we're finished shooting for today."

I stop spraying and remove my respirator.

"I wanna learn how to use the sprayer." Leo claps his hands together like he's five.

"Okay." Dad chuckles at Leo's enthusiasm. "Those shoes got a steel toe?"

Leo's face falls. "No."

"Dad, we're not going to touch anything but the sprayer, I promise."

"You stand in this area, and this area only, understand, bud?"

Dad makes an invisible rectangle with his index fingers. Leo nods. "And don't touch anything else. I'll be back in a minute to give you a tutorial."

I put my free hand on my hip. "Dad, how many hours have I spent painting everything but the box in the last two days? I could do a whole show about it."

Leo perks up at this spark of an idea. "I think it would be cool if you had your own DIY show. Maybe not a full show like this. Something simpler."

"HGTV has been trying to talk me into a scripted spin-off digital series. But what if I did unscripted short episodes on things that teens and college students would want to know for real life? Like how to hang a shelf or retrieve a ring that went down the drain or fix a hole in the wall because you were horsing around with your BFF and his elbow went through the drywall. Ahem."

"It was an accident." Leo shrugs, but I'm sure he's remembering how we got grounded after our indoor game of Spider-Man and Spider-Gwen—leaping off the Matsudas' living room furniture—went horribly wrong. Leo raises his hand. "I'll be your guinea pig. I mean, if you can't teach me how to do something, then other teens won't be able to do it either. You should do a webisode about welding. That'd be cool."

"That's a hard no to the welding, but if you want to practice painting with Dakota today"—Dad hands Leo his safety glasses and respirator—"knock yourself out."

"I feel like an extra in a Star Wars movie." Leo mimics Darth Vader's breathing and voice in his respirator. "Luke, I am your father."

"Dork," I say as Dad follows the last of the camera crew out of the room that transformed from a laundry room to Dad's workshop and will eventually become Akagi House's parlor.

"Wait." Leo digs his phone out of his back pocket. "I get to post this on my Instagram page, yes? 'Cause, c'mon, I look cool."

"Here." I take the phone and hand him the spray gun instead. I back up to frame the shot while Leo holds the spray gun like it's a weapon.

"We have to do one together. I won't post it. It's just for me."

My heart flips. I step in close to Leo and put my arm around his muscular shoulders. I angle the camera to get my best side.

"Pull the respirator up," Leo says. "It's funnier that way."

That's right. I'm the least annoying sister in Leo's world.

After a couple of shots, Leo slides his phone into his back pocket, and we get to work. I put my hand over Leo's.

"Hold it at a perpendicular angle, like this, about ten to twelve inches away from your project. Sweep from left to right to stay with my original painting pattern. Pull the trigger to start the spray before you hit the object and keep it going until you are past it. Gentle. Even. Strokes. Too close. See, it's beginning to drip. Don't worry. Before I add the next coat, I'll sand the drip down a little." I leave my hand on top of Leo's as we finish the first layer of bright orangey-red lacquer to the back.

"Can we keep going?" Even with his respirator on, I can tell from his eyes that Leo is smiling. The Full Dimple.

We're halfway through the next side when the paint starts to spit.

"It's probably a loose connection letting air in." I double-check all the pieces, but the paint gun continues to sputter.

"Want me to go get Mr. Doug?"

"No, I got it. We're probably out of paint." I take a peek. "Yep, all we need is a quick top-up."

I put the top part of the sprayer on the newspaper. Leo cranes his neck to watch as I take the paint cup over to the workbench to refill. I pour the rich red paint into the cup and wipe off the extra on the lip. A moment later, I have it hooked back up and ready to go.

"This looks amazing." Leo nods his head. "I know we were just joking about your DIY show idea earlier, but what if you did it for real? It'd be cool. I'd subscribe."

"You'd be my only subscriber."

"Not true. America loves its DIY Princess. Some of them a little too much."

A chill travels up my spine. I know we aren't the only TV family who has hired an IT expert in the vain attempt to block some of the creepy to downright scary things grown men think are acceptable to send to girls. It's like whack-a-mole with these idiots. At the same time, I'm *required* to have a digital life. And that's not even HGTV talking. That's my classmates asking me why I'm not on the latest social media app to keep up with all that's hot and trendy.

"Koty?" Leo has a crease between his eyebrows. "You getting weird stuff again?"

"Yeah. On the daily. Low-level 'Hey, beautiful, just wanna talk' stuff but still. Block and delete."

"On behalf of the guys who *don't* do this, I'm sorry." Leo puts his arm across my shoulders. "I would punch them in the face for you if I could."

I slide out from under his arm. "I don't need you to fight my battles for me."

"I know. Can I at least hold them while you go all *kitsunebiiiiii* on them?"

"Yes." I bump Leo's hip with mine. "But not today. Today, I want to paint."

"Me too." Leo makes grabby hands at the sprayer. "I want to fly solo on this side."

Leo hums Rayne Lee's "One Last Kiss" as he paints.

"Looks great," Leo says when he's done.

"Don't jinx us." I take the spray gun from Leo. "We still have to get the fuel line changed over. I wonder if Dad would let me skip school tomorrow. Maybe we could film a touching father-daughter moment in the middle of Lowe's."

"I wanna come." Leo takes off his safety gear and puts it on the workbench next to mine.

"Get your parents to sign the appearance release, and I will gladly take my BFF to the hardware store with us."

Leo sighs. "Not going to happen. I mean, I get it. Mom said she felt so powerless after the-event-that-shall-not-be-named. She cried. You know she claims you as the baby of our family. She doesn't want anything like that to happen to my sisters or me."

"Yes, there have been some huge—and I mean HUGE—negatives to this life, but there have also been some big positives."

"Like a fully funded college account, a trust fund, and being able to easily afford the Japan trip?"

I wince. Leo's assessment isn't exactly wrong.

"I was referring to our annual Giving Back episodes. Hands down, helping rebuild the burned-out home of the recently widowed woman with four kids was my favorite build of all time."

"I liked that episode. Especially when the girl got to help you redo her bedroom."

I don't usually ask for favors from The Network, but I wanted this girl's room to be epic. Why? I couldn't do anything about her family's new life without their dad, who had died in a helicopter accident overseas. But I could create a comfort zone for Leticia filled with all the things she loves, like bees and art supplies. Her family still sends us a Christmas card each year along with a giant box filled with jars of honey and honey-based items from their family's apiary.

"Sometimes, I think about taking a gap year after high school and going abroad to help build houses. I know my welding skills are still meh, but I install shiplap like a boss."

"Your painting skills are lit. But you talk too much, and I have to leave in five minutes to go wait tables. So . . ." Leo rolls his hands. "Can we do another layer yet?"

"Not yet. I can show you how to clean the sprayer though."

I go to the temporary utility sink to wash out the nozzle. The paint cup refuses to cooperate with me. I grit my teeth and grunt, but it won't budge.

Leo appears behind me. "Here."

"Wait! You have to—" The paint cup turns easily for him, but not without splattering us both with red paint first. "Release the pressure first before you take it off."

"Oops." Leo looks down to see that his favorite *Kitsune Mask* T-shirt has a spray of red paint across it like he knifed someone. "Kuso!"

"Quick, wash it out before it sets." I don't care about the red paint on the shoulder of my long-sleeved T-shirt with the *If These Walls Could Talk* logo on it. I have a whole rainbow-colored stack of them in my closet.

Leo pulls off his shirt and scrubs at the splatter like he's removing incriminating evidence.

"How bad is it?" Leo holds out the shirt to me.

I try to keep my eyes on the shirt only. I fail spectacularly. The weight set Leo bought last winter was definitely a good investment. My eyes trail down . . .

"Koty."

"Hmm." My eyes snap back up to squint at the wet fabric. "I think it's okay, but it's kinda hard to tell in here."

"I gotta go anyway."

Leo leaves his shirt off as we go outside. And I am not sad about this. He retrieves his skateboard, and I follow him to the sidewalk. I hold the edge of the T-shirt out in the bright afternoon sunshine.

"I'm sorry." I run my finger across the now light pink splotches. "I'll buy you a new one."

"Why? It wasn't your fault."

"I know, but I feel bad."

"The paint gun got you too."

When I tip my head to look at the damage on my shoulder, Leo steps toward me. I instinctively put my hand out to keep my personal bubble intact. Which means my bare hand is on Leo's bare chest. A bolt of energy crackles to the pit of my stomach. And not like the time when I was four and crammed a metal washer into an electrical socket—even worse. Leo must not feel the same jolt because he doesn't move at all. Instead, his left hand gently cups my face and tips my head back to the other side. My eyes are instinctively closing when he suddenly spits on the fingers of his right hand and rubs at what is most likely paint next to my ear.

"Mom says Mom Spit is more powerful than 409. I can't promise mine is, but it did manage to get the paint off your cheek. You've got a blob in your hair too if you want me to try to get it out."

Stuck somewhere between disgust and a swoon, the muscles in my mouth have forgotten how to work. Leo takes that as a yes. He rubs at a spot of hair above my ear.

"Sorry. I think I made it worse." Leo presses on the side of my head.

"It's okay. I'll fix it later."

Leo looks down at my hand, still on his chest. "Koty. You're making things weird."

I pull my hand away and press the damp shirt into Leo's chest instead. "You're making it weird. Especially with the 409-spit thing. Gross. I want to go wash my face with Lysol now."

Leo flicks me in the arm. Hard. "Boys stop having cooties around fifth grade, just so you know."

I flick him back. Hard. "And yet you've never had a girlfriend. Hmmm?"

A wrinkle creases Leo's forehead. I kick myself.

"I'm working on it." Leo slides his wet, stained shirt back on. "There are over two thousand people at our school. Surely, there is *somebody* out there for me."

"There is. I know it." Though I would rather have my eyebrows ripped off with duct tape than see Leo Matsuda making out in the hallway with somebody else.

Leo's phone pings six times in a row. "I gotta go. Ja mata ne."

"Yep, later." I watch Leo skateboard away.

When I turn back around, I see the new camera op—the one who snort-laughed at my yellow snow joke—standing next to Phil's trailer with his phone pointed in our direction. He immediately turns his back and puts the phone to his ear. Icy fingers grip my heart.

It's fine, Dakota. He's not the paparazzi. Breathe.

Chapter

5

It's finally the Monday of Homecoming week. I turn in my Japan trip deposit and prepare to take the build for a test drive.

"The meat is already defrosting at home. You can use our oil. What else do we need besides yellow onions, mushrooms, cabbage, and carrots?" I say as Leo and I wheel our shopping cart around Fry's after school.

"He shoots." A plastic baggie of green onions flies through the air. And completely misses the basket. In one smooth move, Leo scoops the bag off the linoleum and plops it back into the basket. "He scores. Sorta. That's it. I have the noodles and sauce in my backpack."

"Can we get gummy bears?"

"Are you buying?"

"Yes."

"Then, in that case, let's get two bags. One for us. One for Aurora. Maybe that will help with her extra salty mood today."

As if she can somehow hear us from the parking lot, Aurora group texts us from the car: HURRY UP!!!!! I'M DYING OUT HERE!!!!

Leo and I pull up to the cashier and dump our goods on the conveyor belt. When I lean back to grab a pack of gum, Leo has a weird expression on his face.

"Can you move?" I say. "I want a pack of gum."

"What kind?" Leo stands like a wall.

"Do they have the cinnamon kind?"

Leo rotates his upper body instead of moving to the side.

"Dude, what are you doing?" When I push him to the side, I see it—the tabloid.

DIY Sweetheart's Second Chance at Love

"Don't look." Leo steps closer to me.

"What the—" Aurora says from behind Leo with an open bottle of Pepsi in one hand and the tabloid open in the other. "I know this is you, Leo, despite the bar across your eyes."

Leo yelps and turns around. Aurora holds up the tabloid. The air whooshes out of my lungs as I focus in on the full page dedicated to me and my nonexistent love life. Like even if the tabloid isn't straight-up mocking me, it can still invade my privacy and get a pass.

Aurora closes the tabloid and throws it on the conveyor belt.

"We're not buying this." Leo snatches it back off and crams it backward on the display.

"Mom's going to see it at some point." Aurora puts a hand on her hip and cocks her head to the side. "Trust me. The best defense is a good offense."

"No. Let's go." Leo grabs my shoulders and turns me around. He gently pushes me through the checkout lane and pulls out his wallet. He even doubles back for a pack of cinnamon gum for me.

Meanwhile, I stand there shivering with rage. I will not explode in the middle of Fry's. That's *exactly* what they expect me to do. Want me to do.

"Thank you," Leo says quietly to the cashier before grabbing our bag. He puts a hand on my lower back and herds me out the door.

"You two need to chill." Aurora follows us out of Fry's a moment later with a copy of the tabloid tucked under her arm. After we're all in the car, Aurora opens up the tabloid. "I get it. You had your privacy invaded. That sucks. But look at you guys." Aurora points at the picture, but Leo and I still don't look. "Look. Y'all are cute. Which is gross on multiple levels, but objectively speaking, it could have been much worse. Laugh at yourselves and then let it go."

Leo gives her a withering look.

0 0 0

Mom is waiting when Aurora drops Leo and me off at my house a few minutes later. She has a copy of the tabloid too.

"I'm guessing from your expressions that you've heard about the tabloid problem." Mom follows us through the shortcut between the build and our house to the backyard.

"Yeah." I drop all my stuff on the weather-beaten picnic table I built in the fourth grade.

Mom places the folded tabloid beside my backpack and pulls me into a hug. "The camera operator who took these photos was fired so fast his head is probably still spinning. And Dad and I insisted that Phil enforce the non-disclosure clause in the guy's contract to the letter." Mom releases me and squeezes Leo's arm. "I'm sorry, Leo. Even though it doesn't name you specifically, I'm going to call your parents and apologize. I know how your parents, especially your dad, feel about your privacy."

"Thanks. You guys deal with this stuff all the time, but it feels weird to me. Violating." Leo shakes his head. "But I'm not going to let it ruin my day. It's time to focus. The Homecoming Carnival is Thursday. Time to take this baby for a spin. I've been making yakisoba in the restaurant for the last week—thanks to Ojiichan making it a special—but I'm excited about doing it for real. 'Cause if I'm going to screw it up, let's do it now."

I pull the tarp off the yakisoba stand with a magician's flourish. "Ta-dah!"

This pulls a small smile from Leo.

"You're not going to screw it up. We got this." I wish I could say that I was confident in my welding abilities, but I'm not. I turn the propane on and hold my breath. I push the ignition button and hear the telltale whoosh as the gas meets the spark. Whoosh. Not boom. Whew.

"Now, we're cooking with gas . . . well, propane." Leo puts his hand a couple of inches above the griddle and nods that it's heating up. "I'm going to go wash my hands and prep the vegetables. Back in a sec."

Mom drops her head. "And I'm going to go call Jen."

I fiddle with the build while they're gone. Finally, I can't stop myself. I grab the tabloid.

> After last year's Homecoming disaster, which broke our hearts, it looks like America's DIY Princess has found romance again. Sources say that this boy is a student at Dakota's school and that the pair is inseparable. Mystery Boy even comes over to help Dakota with her builds sometimes, though we have to wonder what kind of DIY project requires one to be shirtless? Could Mystery Boy be the one to mend our favorite fifteen-year-old's broken heart? We sure hope so.

It's a little grainy, but the camera op got Leo's good side. From this angle, my Cinnamon Roll Prince looks long, lean, and chiseled.

"You couldn't resist, could you?" Leo's voice travels across my backyard.

I stuff the tabloid under my backpack and go back to fiddling with the build. Leo sets the tray of supplies down and ties a piece of white fabric around his forehead. The sign of someone hard at work, according to Ojiichan. It also helps absorb sweat when you are cooking outside in Phoenix, where summer doesn't end until late-October sometimes.

"You want me to help?" I say, and Leo scoffs. "I know how to cook. Sorta."

"You could go see if the meat is defrosted yet. Our moms are talking about the—you know—so Ms. Tamlyn may have forgotten about it."

"Back in a sec."

Leo was right. I can hear Mom in the kitchen talking on the phone to Mrs. Matsuda as I come up the backstairs to the house. I crack the back door open. Mom stands at the microwave with her back to me.

"I know, Jen. Unfortunately, they are growing up, and when they hit a certain age, the narrative changes. Welllll. Maybe, but keep that to yourself because she would kill me. And if Kenichi asks, they are definitely just friends. At least for now. Who knows? It could simply be hormones or puppy love or a phase." Mom pops open the microwave and pokes at the pork inside. "I've got to run. It could be nothing, but I wanted you to hear it from me first. Let's not make a big deal of it and hope it goes away. Okay. I agree. Bye."

Hormones? Puppy love? A phase? As much as it burns me, there is a truth to Mom's assessment. Is it specifically Leo causing all the weird things going on inside me, or would it happen with whoever was in my inner circle? Is this hormones or feelings by default or something even bigger and scarier?

Mom turns around with the plate of pork in her hands.

"I was coming to get that." I come fully into the kitchen, pretending like I didn't hear her on the phone. "Leo is ready to cook."

"Give me another minute." Mom dumps the pork on a chopping board and cuts it into bite-sized pieces. "Is your dad back yet?"

"I don't think so."

Mom puts the pork pieces into a clean bowl. "Okay, let me get my laptop. I can finish up my designs outside."

"Mom, Leo and I don't need a babysitter." I grab the bowl as Mom washes her hands. "We're making yakisoba, not welding."

"I know, but the tabloid thing got me thinking. Maybe we should—"

"Mom! I'm fine. It's fine. We're fine. It's no different from some of the other creative editing Phil does with the show sometimes. Other people want to corrupt the story or make it more dramatic or whatever their personal agenda is. I can't control it, so I'm choosing to let it go."

Okay, do I totally believe this? No. But, I'm trying to use the tools my therapist gave me and take control of this situation as best I can.

"That's a good plan, Koty. You guys cook and text me if you need a hand. But . . ." Mom leans over and grabs the small fire extinguisher from the corner—the one we had to replace after my fried chicken experiment went sideways last month. I give Mom a look. "I know. Humor me."

I drop the fire extinguisher on the picnic table next to my backpack. The tabloid is still there but turned the other side up now.

"I was about to send out a search party for you." Leo pours a little bit of water on the griddle. It immediately bubbles and steams. After the water disappears, he drizzles vegetable oil all over the stove and uses a metal spatula to coat the griddle's surface.

I put the container of pork next to the other chopped up ingredients. "Is that enough space? It kinda has to be because I don't have time to do a rebuild."

"It'll work. I'm going to bring a camp table to put behind me. Otherwise, I think the cooler is going to be too close to the heat of the griddle." Leo wipes beads of sweat from his upper lip onto the shoulder of his T-shirt. "Do I get tuneage while I work?"

I pull up "The Leo Mix," which he put on my phone specifically for occasions like this. I crank it up. Leo bobs his head as he creates his noodle masterpiece. He dumps the pork pieces on the griddle first and moves them about with the spatula. Soon after, he adds the perfectly uniform slices of yellow onions and carrots. The onions sizzle and begin to brown—caramelize, Leo corrects me—almost as soon as they hit the hot griddle. He adds a layer of cabbage and then the green onions and mushrooms. Leo does a goofy shoulder dance as our current favorite slow jam echoes around my backyard.

"One last . . . kissssss," Leo sings the chorus into his spatula.

The hormones in my blood steam up as much as the water on the griddle. But is it hormones? As a test, I plug Aurora into the equation. Yes, Aurora could probably hit the high note without straining into falsetto. But she wouldn't cough and laugh at herself if she cracked the pitch as bad as Leo just did. So, I try Nevaeh in the equation instead. They would have hit the high note and maybe even a good chunk of the vocal run into the stratosphere Rayne Lee does, before pretending to pass out. I would have still laughed, but the thought doesn't make bubbles appear in my stomach. That is until I look at Leo again. Is this just biology? Or friendship turned up to eleven? Or love?

"I don't know," Leo says, and I snap to attention, afraid that he's read my mind. "The heat might be up too high. Can you turn it down a notch?"

I do as Leo begins to flip and blend the yakisoba noodles into the mixture on the griddle.

"What?" Leo catches my eye.

"What what?" I say.

"You keep looking at me weird."

I scoff. "I'm trying to learn how to make this dish so I can recreate it for my parents later on our pancake griddle."

"Oh, okay." Leo squirts most of the bottle of the rich, brown yakisoba sauce on top of the pile and mixes it around. "So it has nothing to do with the tabloid article? You gotta admit, that weight set I bought last winter seems to have paid off. Either that or somebody photoshopped the picture before it printed."

I don't even know how to answer that. I'm pretty sure it is a trick question.

My phone pings. Nevaeh's text comes with a screenshot of the tabloid picture. My stomach drops.

NEVAEH

Is that Leo in the pic?

ME

Yes. Keep that to yourself.

NEVAEH

Ummm. Too late. You 2 are hot gossip in the group chats.

ME

?!?!?!?!?

NEVAEH

Not everybody thinks it's Leo though.

"Nooooo." I look over at Leo. "The picture. It's all over the—"

Before I can finish my sentence, Leo's phone sounds like it's caught in a pinball machine. To his credit, Leo delivers my plate of yakisoba and a pair of chopsticks without stopping to check his phone. Leo plates up his portion of yakisoba and puts it to the side before pouring water all over the griddle. Once he's scraped off all the slightly burnt bits and the griddle is clean again, Leo turns off the propane and joins me on the bench of the picnic table.

"You don't want to see the latest disaster?" I nod at Leo as his phone continues to ping.

"Would it make you feel better?"

"No."

"Can I at least turn it off before my phone overheats and my pants burst into flames?" Leo stands back up and pulls his phone out of his back pocket.

I hold up the mini fire extinguisher. This pulls a laugh out of both of us. When Leo sticks his butt out in my direction, I tap it with my foot.

"Hey, now." Leo turns off his phone and slides it into his pocket like this is no big deal to him. He calmly sits back down and digs into his yakisoba.

"What do you think?" Leo points to the yakisoba to make sure we are on the same page again.

"This is . . . yummm." I slurp up a mess of noodles.

One piece flips out and smacks me in the chin. Leo points at my face before licking his thumb and hovering it close to my chin.

"Gross." I lean away from him and wipe at my face.

"Made you laugh though." Leo bumps my shoulder with his.

"You always do." I bump him back. "Sometimes, even intentionally."

Leo nods at the build. "I hope this works. I need to make $200 by Friday. And that's $200 profit because I still have to pay Ojiichan for the raw supplies."

"Don't worry. This idea is fool-proof."

"Didn't we say that about the tree house idea?"

"Okay, that was a bad idea. I can see that now. But this one?" I nod at the yakisoba stand. "Is solid."

"I hope you're right. And Koty, don't worry about the picture, okay? Just keep your head down, and it will soon blow over. Seriously, nobody is going to care five minutes from now."

Chapter

6

"Five minutes? Riiiiight," I say as Leo and I walk down the hallway at school the next day. I'm used to people staring at me, but Leo looks like he has a permanent sunburn.

"Is it true?" Lindsay whispers from her seat behind me in Japanese class. "Is this really Leo?"

"What makes you think that?" has been my standard answer all day.

"Matsuda-san. Tatte kudasai." Iwate-sensei gestures at Leo to stand up and holds out her dry-erase marker toward him. "Please conjugate *hanasu*."

Leo stretches his arm up to conjugate "to talk" above where Jax conjugated "to wash" already on the board. Lindsay isn't the only person in class who suddenly looks into their lap at their phone and then at the long, lean guy at the front of the class.

"It was Leo, wasn't it?" Lindsay whispers. "So, are you guys going to Homecoming together?"

"No comment and no."

"Does he have a date?"

I look back over my shoulder at Lindsay and lie, "I don't know. That's his business, not mine."

"Hmmm." Lindsay sits back and looks at Leo.

I don't know why I suddenly feel stabby at the mere thought of Leo going to Homecoming with someone. And it's not just Homecoming. Or even Lindsay.

"Yoku dekimashita, Matsuda-san." Iwate-sensei nods her head at his conjugation. "Now, you pick someone to conjugate 'to sleep' for us."

Any other day, Leo would pick me. Leo always picks me. I always pick him. I want him to pick me today. I also don't want him to pick me today. As if he can read my mind, Leo looks me in the eyes but hands the marker to Lindsay. I sit on my hands so I don't strangle her.

What is wrong with me?!?!

Leo sits down in his seat in front of me. The red continues to creep up from the collar of his T-shirt until it disappears into the back of his closely cropped, dark brown hair.

◦   ◦   ◦

"Maybe we should eat lunch separately today to help things die down?" A still beet-red Leo says after class.

My stomach falls. We've been lunch buddies since kindergarten.

"Yeah. I'll be in my usual spot because I refuse to let them win." I can tell from his face that Leo took that as me calling him a coward, so I clarify. "It's my drama. Not yours."

We split up at the door to the cafeteria and I make a beeline to our usual table. I slip my earbuds in and work on my kanji worksheet like it's the most important thing in the world.

As always, Neveah sees right through me. They sit down next to me and pull one of my earbuds out. "Hey, you okay?"

"Perfect," I say though the three bites of tuna sandwich I forced down my throat are currently lodged behind my sternum like cement. Neveah cocks their head to the side. "Honestly, I'm just okay, but I'm used to this. Sorta. You should check on Leo though. He looks ready to spontaneously combust."

"On it." Nevaeh gives me a one-armed hug—because they are allowed to hug me—before flitting off.

Five minutes before the bell, a still-red Leo slides in next to me. I remove my earbuds. My barriers melt like sand in the rising tide.

"This has been the weirdest day ever. I might have a social life." Leo smiles. The Full Dimple Smile. "Lindsay asked me to Homecoming. Of course, I can't go thanks to Aurora already taking off, but then the words 'How about we do something else sometime' flew out of my mouth before I could stop them. And guess what? Lindsay said yes. Is that awesome or what?"

Or what.

I mute the stabbiness in my heart and scrape up a truth. "I'm happy for you, Leo."

"Now let's find somebody for you."

"Yeah. One day. Once the show is over." I pack up my mostly uneaten lunch. "I'm not feeling well. I'm going to see if Mom will check me out."

I want to go home and tear something apart. Like, myself. I want to rebuild me into something new. Someone new. But who and how?

This will be my toughest project yet.

"This is going to be a disaster." Leo paces back and forth in front of our delivery truck as Ojiichan micromanages our dads on the Homecoming Carnival plans. "Why did I think this was a good idea?"

I grab him by the arm. "Leo. Stop. Breathe."

"What if Cholla Vista High School isn't ready for yakisoba? What if it's too weird? Iwate-sensei already gave me an extension on the trip deposit. Tonight is pretty much do or die time."

"It's a good idea. Trust me. People may come to the JCC's side of the booth first for Pocky and Ramune, but then you can woo them with the smell of your awesome noodles. *You* are going to be great. And if things get desperate, take your shirt off and announce to everybody that you are the guy in the tabloid picture."

"First, that would be a health code violation. Second, Ojiichan would baka slap me into next week. Third, I thought we were trying to get people to forget all about that."

"Yeah, we are, but I also don't want to go on the Japan trip without you. I'm not kidding, Leo. If you're not going, I'm not going. At least not this summer."

"But you'll lose your deposit."

"Don't care. Either we both go, or neither of us do. Hey, I don't make the BFF rules. I just follow them. To the letter."

"Leo!" Sasha, still wearing her school's official pastry-chef-in-training uniform, rushes out the front door of the restaurant with a big tray in her hands. "Don't forget the manju."

Underneath a layer of plastic wrap, a huge cookie sheet is covered with dainty, white, egg-sized confections decorated to look like sleeping bunnies.

"These are amazing!" I squeal.

"Try one." Sasha pulls back a corner of the plastic wrap.

"I don't want to eat the merchandise. Also, I most definitely want to eat the merchandise." I bite into the soft, white, sweet rice outside to find anko—sweet red bean paste—on the inside.

"This is soooo good," I say.

"Oooh, may I have one?" Dad says from over my shoulder. Sasha holds the tray up to him. "I see you got a heaping helping of the Matsuda cooking gene. Did your grandpa teach you how to make these?"

Ojiichan and Sasha look at each other and scowl.

"No. Google did," Sasha says flatly. "I have an exam on Wednesday, so I have to practice this weekend. Which means the restaurant is having a special on manju all weekend long."

Sasha pulls the plastic wrap over the manju and hands the tray to Leo. "Do *not* drop them."

"Here, take this with you too." Mrs. Matsuda hands me the blank Specials board and a baggie with chalk markers inside it. "Maybe Dakota can work some of her magic."

It's true. I've been doing doodles and designs on the Specials board for years now. It started as a joke. Like every time I was in the restaurant, I would sneakily add a cute drawing to the Specials board just to see if anybody noticed. Except for the time Leo double-dog dared me to make a drawing of a steaming pile of poo, my designs have always gone over well. I even do Japanese holiday-themed designs now.

"Okay, you guys have fun tonight." Mrs. Matsuda looks at Leo. A smile crosses her face. "My baby, the entrepreneur. I'm so proud."

Leo ducks around his mom before she can hug him.

"Ittekimasu." *I'm off,* he says.

"Itterasshai," she replies, but adds a stern warning, "Ki o tsukete ne."

"Hai, hai."

"I'm serious, Leo." Mrs. Matsuda yells after him. "Be careful."

Once we are tucked in the middle of the Matsudas' minivan, I notice the little bit of white mesh fabric peeking out of the top of Leo's happi coat sleeve.

"What happened?" I tug the happi coat's sleeve farther up his arm. A bandage circles his arm up near his elbow.

"It's nothing. I had the heat up too high. Hot oil splattered me."

"Did the hot oil splatter your neck too?" I run my fingertips down the side of Leo's neck to the dime-sized splotch on his skin. "Or did your 'chat' with Lindsay about the pricing of the Ramune and Pocky go that well yesterday?"

I quirk an eyebrow at Leo.

Leo scoffs. "Why? You jealous?"

I elbow him in the ribs. "No." *Yes. Horribly.*

"Hey, watch the manju. There's easily a hundred dollars' worth of merchandise here. Which Sasha gave me for free, by the way, even the materials. She knows about the Japan trip, but promised to keep it on the DL."

I pull out a chalk marker and write manju in hiragana on the Specials board. "Three bucks apiece?"

"Yeah."

I add a chibi drawing of Leo in the corner, complete with the happi coat and white cloth around his forehead.

"You have to be on the board too," Leo says. "This was a Dynamic Duo idea after all."

In the opposite corner, I draw a chibi version of myself in a yukata holding a plate of yakisoba in my hand. I write *Oishii desu!*—It's delicious!—in hiragana in a speech bubble above Chibi Dakota's head. Leo gives me a satisfied nod.

"Ikimashō," *Let's go,* Ojiichan says as he gets into the driver's seat of the van. He signals our dads riding together in the delivery truck.

"I hope this works," Leo whispers.

o   o   o

I'm glad Homecoming is in early October this year. Phoenix continues to hit over ninety degrees during the day, but at least the temperatures are bearable at night. Still, all five of us are sweaty by the time we get the booth unloaded and set up on the track inside the football stadium.

"Looking good, Dakota." I turn around to see Mr. Udall. "And you must be Dakota's father. Nice beard."

"I am. And likewise." Dad shakes Mr. Udall's hand. Whereas my dad's completely white beard against his white skin makes him look like Santa, Mr. Udall's shorter, silver-flecked black beard against his dark brown skin makes him look like Idris Elba.

"Dakota got a double dose of creative genes from your family." Mr. Udall nods as he walks around our setup. "I've given my students this assignment for twenty years now, but Dakota is the only one who has ever turned it into a life-size model."

"Life-size *working* model," Leo says, as the pilot light makes a *pop*. "Come back in about ten minutes, and I'll have the first batch of yakisoba made. It's on the house, even."

"You don't have to bribe me, Leo. Dakota is already getting an A on this project." Mr. Udall makes small talk with Ojiichan and our dads.

Meanwhile, Leo sends me back to the van to retrieve the case of Pocky from the cooler. When I get back, our fathers are still hovering.

"We got this, Dads." Leo takes the case of Pocky from me. "If we run into trouble, we have Ojiichan."

"Proud of you, Leo." Dad pounds Leo on the back a few times. Unfortunately, it's always my dad who encourages Leo first.

"Don't turn the heat up too high. The oil will splatter." Mr. Matsuda adds his version of encouragement. "We'll be back at ten fifteen to load you back up."

"Hai. Hai." Ojiichan waves the dads away. "Leo-kun is fine."

Ojiichan places a picture frame—which contains the restaurant's business license along with his, Aurora's, and Leo's food handler's cards—on the back table.

Leo looks at the time on his phone. "You too, Koty. Go. I'm fine."

"I feel bad." I rearrange the Pocky and Ramune display for a third time as Leo washes his hands. "As usual, you're the one working while everybody else is having fun. I feel like you're Cinderella—or Cinder-fella—who never gets to go to the ball."

Leo shrugs. "I have a goal to meet. Failure is not an option."

"Gambatte, Iron Chef Matsuda." I put out my fist for him to bump, but he doesn't.

"I don't want to rewash my hands." Leo puts out his elbow for me to bump instead.

When Ojiichan spots Aurora and Jayden, he puts two fingers in his mouth and lets out an ear-splitting whistle followed by, "OI! AURORA-CHAN!"

Aurora looks mortified, especially when Ojiichan gestures at her to come to our booth. Jayden starts to come with her, but she shakes her head. He goes off with some of their drumline friends instead.

"You are the future businesswoman." Ojiichan gestures at Aurora to come even closer. "What do you think of the booth?" Before Aurora can answer, Ojiichan adds, "And who is that boy?"

Aurora shoots us a panicked look. Leo and I stifle a laugh and busy ourselves reorganizing his supplies for the hundredth time.

"I think it looks good, Ojiichan." Aurora puts my Specials sign on the other side of the mobile cash register. "I know people are going to love it."

"Good."

"The manju needs to be up front, though. Nobody is going to see them back there," Aurora says and Ojiichan grumbles. "What? You don't think Sasha made them to your standards?"

"No, they are good." Ojiichan still doesn't move them to the long table next to the cash register. "Very good."

"Then put them out." Aurora swoops around him and grabs the smaller decorative tray, which holds about twenty of the manju bunnies and a pair of wooden tongs under a protective layer of plastic wrap. "And smile, Ojiichan. You aren't in the kitchen tonight. You are the host. Look friendly and inviting. More teeth, please."

"What is it with Americans showing their teeth? I look like a mad dog." Ojiichan pulls his lips back, and his forced smile does look like a rabid dog's.

"Yeah, that's disturbing. Go for friendly then. Like you are talking baseball with Mr. Doug. Eh, good enough." Aurora squeezes her grandfather's arm. "Now, I'm going to get back to my friends. And *that boy* is Jayden. We're going to Homecoming together. Ask Mom about it later."

"Hmmm," Ojiichan says as Aurora walks away. "Oi, take Dakota-chan with you. She is under my foot."

Yes, it hurts my feelings when I see Aurora hesitate. Last year, she would have immediately grabbed my elbow and insisted that I come along. This year, I feel like a continuous third wheel with her. The regret must show on my face because Aurora checks herself.

"Of course." Aurora has lied so much recently that I can't tell if she is telling the truth or not. "Just because Leo is boring doesn't mean you have to be too."

Aurora waves at Jayden and the three other drumline guys standing next to him. She links her elbow through mine.

"Who knows," Aurora says as we walk away. "Maybe your future boyfriend is here tonight."

I look over my shoulder at Leo, who is already preparing his first order of yakisoba for Iwate-sensei. I feel a twinge of guilt about Leo's half-truth to Iwate-sensei about why his parents hadn't told Ojiichan about the Japan trip yet. That Ojiichan would lose face for not being able to afford to send any of his grandchildren on the annual trip. She doesn't press the issue. Instead, Iwate-sensei must be highly praising Leo and his yakisoba stand based on the amount of culturally required deflecting Ojiichan is doing.

"C'mon, Koty." Aurora suddenly pulls me to the left. "Let's go buy tickets for the games before I have to work my shift at the dunk tank."

o   o   o

The fourth and final hour of the carnival is my JCC timeslot with Nevaeh. Ojiichan sits on a stool with his arms crossed, while Tori and Jax run the JCC part of the booth. He taps his foot impatiently.

"You should go eat some cotton candy, Ojiichan," I say. "At least go throw some snowballs. You know, have some fun."

"You should go to the marching band's dunk tank. Aurora will only be there for another fifteen minutes or so," Leo says, and Ojiichan perks up.

"I was the pitcher on my high school baseball team." Ojiichan rotates his right shoulder as he walks away from the booth. "Aurora should be worried."

"I'm glad he's getting out," I say after I insist Tori and Jax leave early to go witness and, more important, video the event. "You and Ojiichan both work too much."

When Leo turns around, I slide a twenty-dollar bill out of my back pocket and into Leo's tip jar.

"I saw that," Leo says, his back still to me.

"I don't know what you're talking about."

"Take it back."

"Make me."

"Later, because otherwise, I have to rewash my hands and we're getting low on water."

"So, how are sales?" I say, though I know the answer based on his expression.

"Maybe yakisoba and manju are too weird for Cholla Vista High School. Yeah, all the JCC members have come to buy something, but at this rate, I'm going to be lucky to break even." Leo's shoulders slump. "Bye-bye, Japan trip."

My heart sinks too. "So, we'll go on the Japan trip next year instead. We're only sophomores. We have two more chances."

"Yeah, but they rotate cities, so in theory, you could go on four different Japan trips during your high school career. This year, they are going to Nagoya as their big city."

"I like Nagoya, not that I remember that much from before, but I'm sure Kyoto or Hiroshima or Yokohama would be fun too."

"No, I need to go to Nagoya."

"Why?"

Leo looks around to make sure Ojiichan isn't around. "I want to go to the Matsuda Manju Shop."

"That's cool. Does Ojiichan know the owners?"

"Ojiichan was supposed *to be* the owner since he is Number One Son. Instead, he married Obaachan against her family's wishes, and then moved to Arizona to open a restaurant. So pretty much, the American limb has been completely cut off from the rest of the Matsuda family tree. But they found us, thanks to Sasha's wagashi posts on Instagram. Mio-san, my second cousin, studies at a pastry school in Japan and reached out to see if we were related. When Sasha asked him, Ojiichan totally shut her down. That's why they were so weird earlier. But if I go on the Japan trip this year, maybe I can help reconnect our family. I want to go to the Matsuda Manju Shop in person."

"*We*," I say. "We have to go to the Matsuda Manju shop in person. I have spoken."

A group of students passes right by us. One of them looks like she's going to stop, but her friends pull her back into motion.

Leo lets out a defeated sigh. "Or maybe we can go to Nagoya after graduation instead. I just worry. It's not like Ojiichan is getting any younger."

"Sorry I'm late." Nevaeh runs up to the booth, their holographic boots sparkling in the football stadium's lights. "Your grandpa dunked Aurora three times in a row. I had to post about it. Also, I gave your booth a shout-out."

"Thanks. I need all the help I can get."

"I know how we can boost traffic," Nevaeh says.

"How?" I say, because if anybody knows how to get attention, it's Nevaeh.

"Give 'em a little fan service."

"HGTV isn't allowed to film on school grounds, Nev."

"Not those fans. Local fans." Nevaeh pulls out their phone and shakes it. "Start the buzz. Give 'em a little razzle-dazzle."

Part of me is desperate enough to agree to whatever Nevaeh suggests. "Only if Leo is cool with it."

"Fine." Leo blows a sweaty lock of hair out of his eyes. "Just don't be weird."

"Yeah, no promises on that." Nevaeh pulls the scrunchie out of my ponytail and fluffs up my shoulder-length hair. "You need lipstick, Dakota. These lights wash you out."

Nevaeh sells two bottles of Ramune to a couple of freshmen and then upsells them two boxes of Pocky before returning to critique my look. "There you go. Next up. We're having a fire sale. Buy a plate of yakisoba and get a manju for free. Dakota, go grab a big stack of cups from the Band Boosters' free water table. Tell my stepmom I need them. She'll be cool with it. Part of the problem here is that people don't know what you're selling. So, your lovely assistant, Dakota, is going to give away samples. Leo, what are you standing around for? Get to cooking. We've got forty-five minutes to get this night turned around."

Nevaeh is finishing up their live post by the time I get back with the small plastic cups.

"You guys know you want a piece of this." Nevaeh stands behind the griddle with Leo talking into the phone's camera. "And I'm talking about the noodles here, peeps."

Leo looks over, gives the camera one of his boy-next-door smiles and a peace sign.

"You only have forty minutes left, so put down the cotton candy and get over here." Nevaeh comes back out from behind the griddle. "If we sell out, Cholla Vista High School's DIY Princess Dakota McDonald is going to reveal just who she was kissing in that tabloid picture. Live."

I'm glad the camera was on Nevaeh because I trip over my own feet at this announcement. I fake a flirty smile to cover up the existential horror I feel inside.

"Tick-tock, people. Nevaeh out. Peace!"

Leo scowls from behind the griddle. "That was low, Nevaeh. Seriously."

"No, Nevaeh's right. As Aurora says, sometimes the best defense is a good offense. And we're desperate here, Leo."

"Okay. Fine." Leo shrugs. "But I'm *not* taking off my shirt. Understood?"

"Got it," Nevaeh says. "Now Koty, here's your part . . ."

o   o   o

"How many plates do we have left, Matsuda?" Nevaeh yells over from the small crowd swarming around the portable cash register.

Leo does a quick count. "Twenty-nine."

"Only twenty-nine plates until the truth comes out." Nevaeh could be the next P. T. Barnum. "Now, who's first? You want a drink to go with this, right? And dessert. Come on. You gotta have dessert."

"Sugoi," Ojiichan says in surprise when he returns to the booth twenty-five minutes later with a big bag of cotton candy and a dripping Aurora behind him.

"How many now, Matsuda?" Nevaeh yells over the crowd.

Leo counts. "Twelve!"

"Only twelve plates left, people. Better hurry up." Nevaeh wipes off the *19* written on the Specials board and writes *12* instead.

I grab a clean towel from the pile and walk behind the griddle.

"Look this way." I press the towel against Leo's sweaty face and then his neck.

"Hey, hey, hey! Make that *five* plates left," Nevaeh yells. "Five more plates until the truth comes out!"

After a quick sidebar, Aurora steps behind the cash register, and Nevaeh races off. A minute later, they're back with three tall, tanned guys with closely cropped, dark brown hair. Nevaeh organizes them side by side next to the cash register.

"Two plates left. *Two!*" Aurora shivers from behind the cash register until Jayden puts his drumline jacket around her shoulders.

I'm shaking as bad as Aurora. The yakisoba I ate earlier sloshes around in my stomach, threatening to reappear. I look at Leo, who is cooking as fast as he can. This is for him—both in the short term and the long run. I can do this for my BFF. I can help him get to Japan.

"One last plate. It's nine fifty-nine. Is the secret going to be revealed tonight or not?" Nevaeh weaves through the line of guys.

I'm not going to pretend that everybody understands or accepts Nevaeh at school, but they are known as someone who is always fun. I wouldn't say Nevaeh is part of the popular crowd, but somehow they move through multiple social circles with ease. Or maybe they truly are the next P. T. Barnum, bending reality to become whatever they want it to be.

Nevaeh pulls me to the side and gives me a quick once-over. They whisper, "If you want our Cinnamon Roll Prince to go on the Japan trip, then you're going to have to take one for the team tonight."

I gulp.

"Sold!" Aurora yells. "That's the last one!"

Nevaeh pulls their phone out and livestreams. "*They*dies and Gentle*thems*! Welcome. Thanks to your generous support, our friend Leo Matsuda has sold all twenty-nine plates of yakisoba before the end of the Homecoming Carnival, so you know what that means." The crowd hoots.

Nevaeh flips the camera around and hands their phone to Aurora to keep livestreaming. "I think you all know the tea. But in case you've been living under a rock, let me bring you up to speed. Cholla Vista High School's favorite—and only—celebrity, Dakota McDonald, was recently, ahem, *featured* in a tabloid. Tonight, we're going to unmask the mystery guy."

Nevaeh puts a bottle of Ramune in my hand and gently pushes me toward the line of tan guys. I don't know what in the world Nevaeh bribed them with for this humiliation.

"Is it Taylor Dixon?" Nevaeh gestures at Taylor like he's a new car, not a guy wondering how he got himself into this hot mess. "Or is it Kyrese Montgomery? A bunch of you seem to think it is Dante Soto. Which one will Dakota give her heart—and this commemorative bottle of Japanese soda—to?"

Taking a page from Nevaeh, I weave in and out around the guys.

When I get to the end of the line, I pause. Cameras come out. I look at Leo, giving him one last chance at an out. Instead, he nods.

"Wait. Hold up." Nevaeh puts their hand up in the air. "Plot twist. We are missing a candidate. Red rover, red rover, send one Leo Matsuda right over."

Leo hands the last plate of yakisoba to Aurora and turns off the griddle. He wipes his hands off on his apron and comes to the line. Phone cameras follow me back down the line until I am standing in front of Leo. A redness creeps up his neck. I hold out the Ramune out to him, but the crowd remains silent. They expect more. They want fan service.

I rise up on my toes and kiss Leo on the nose. The crowd is mixed. Leo grabs me in a sweaty bear hug and swings me around. After my feet hit the solid ground again, Leo leans in and plants a kiss on my forehead. That gets the crowd going.

"I knew it!" Jax's voice cuts through the crowd. "Pay up, Tori."

Nevaeh takes their phone back. "There you go, Cholla Vista High School. The secret is officially out. It's Cinnamon Roll Prince Leo Matsuda with our DIY Princess Dakota McDonald in the picture. I think it's a match made in heaven. Don't you? Thanks for playing along. Nevaeh out. Peace!"

Leo opens the bottle of Ramune, pops the marble, and chugs. He leans forward and whispers in my ear, "Can I die now?"

"Not until after the Japan trip," I whisper back.

Ojiichan munches on his cotton candy with a confused look on his face, but doesn't say a word. Neither does Leo. When our dads return to load up the delivery truck, Aurora announces that she has to "help with the marching band's dunk tank" and is unnecessarily vague about her plans on getting home.

Finally, Leo falls into the minivan with an exhausted sigh. Ojiichan looks over his shoulder and asks what's probably been on his mind for the last thirty minutes.

"What is this?" Ojiichan opens his hand at me, and then Leo.

A nervous chuckle sneaks out of my mouth. "Acting."

"Honto ka?" Ojiichan raises a bushy, salt-and-pepper eyebrow at us in disbelief.

I don't understand 99 percent of the Japanese words that come out of Leo's mouth, but I can read his body language. He denies everything, including why we did the stunt. My heart squeezes. As much as I want to protect him from the paparazzi, part of me also desperately wants Leo to know how I feel about him. This was *not* the way to do it though. HGTV can't film on school property, but that doesn't stop other students from filming me. We may have hit the short-term goal—all the plates sold, plus Leo's full tip jar—but I wonder if I've completely ruined the long-term goal.

"Hmmm," is all Ojiichan says when Leo finishes.

"Can we go home now? I'm hot. I'm tired." Leo sniffs at his shirt and winces. "I'm gross."

Ojiichan gives Dad and Mr. Matsuda a wave out the window, but he also leaves the windows down all the way back to the restaurant to help ventilate the sweaty, porky smell circulating around the van.

o o o

"Do your accounting while we get the truck unloaded," Mr. Matsuda tells Leo when we arrive back at the restaurant. "School is going to come early tomorrow."

"I'll put the little bit of leftover stuff in the refrigerator." I want to go home, but not yet. I tug at the light, but bulky, cooler.

"Here. Switch with me." Leo's voice is flat as he hands the portable cash register and tip jar to me. "You don't know where the stuff goes anyway."

Leo and I have had dips in our friendship before. Like when we were seven, and Trevor, his next-door neighbor, razzed him about having a girl as a best friend. For three whole days, Leo and Trevor refused to let me play soccer with them and the other boys on the playground during recess. My mom got involved when she caught me drawing a picture of Leo with a large pile of poo for his head. The next day, *any* girl who wanted to play soccer at recess could play on any team she wanted. Trevor had to let me be on his team, but I still never got to play.

I stood on the sidelines watching my best friend play for a good solid week before the teacher finally noticed and insisted "all our friends are allowed to play, or nobody will play."

So Trevor put me in the goal. When the teacher wasn't looking, he slammed me with ball after ball. Day after day. Trying to make me quit. But I wouldn't. Not even when the ball Leo kicked knocked out my front tooth. Granted my tooth was loose to begin with, but the collision of Leo's soccer ball with my face sped up the process.

Leo felt so bad afterward that he offered to go play Spider-Man and Spider-Gwen with me on the jungle gym instead as an apology. We did end up doing that about a month later, but not until after I caught or deflected three of Trevor's zingers in a row. I have to give props to Stephanie—former star goalie of the Lincoln Valley High School varsity girls soccer team—for some intense coaching to make that happen. My point made, I did a mic drop and ended my playground soccer career to go play Spider-Gwen with Leo, which was what I wanted to do in the first place anyway.

I put the money on the table in the kitchen and join Leo in the walk-in refrigerator.

I squat down next to him. "Are you mad at me?"

"No."

When he doesn't look at me, I put my hand on his arm. "Leo."

Black clouds swirl behind Leo's brown eyes. I have screwed this up so bad.

"You're allowed to be mad. Even at me. I know you don't like to be in the spotlight, and Nevaeh did it in the most embarrassing and personal of ways."

Leo stands up. He has a death grip on the small plastic baggie of chopped onions.

"Yeah, it was embarrassing. Especially because now people think we're a couple, and we're not." Leo's assessment stabs a dagger straight into my heart. "You and Aurora rag on me all the time about not having a social life or a girlfriend, but it's crap like this that keeps setting me back. Did you see Lindsay's face? She probably thinks I was playing her."

It's like the soccer ball hits me in the face all over again. Only this time, it's my heart that falls out instead of my left front tooth.

"I'm sorry." I blink back the tears in my eyes. "I'll get out of your way. Figuratively and literally."

"C'mon, Koty, don't be like that. I just need some breathing room. You suffocate me sometimes."

"Got it. And don't worry about the buzz. I'll tell everybody tomorrow that we aren't a couple. That it was all a publicity stunt. No, even better, I'll tell them that it was completely one-sided and that I am insanely jealous of Lindsay, who you actually have a crush on. You took pity on me tonight and played along."

I turn on my heel to make a hasty retreat. Leo grabs my wrist to keep me from leaving.

"Dakota." Leo does a double take when he turns me around. "Okay, wow, you're gonna have to break this down for me."

I wipe a tear from my cheek and command the other ones to stay put. At least until I get home. I stare at him. No words forming.

"So, there was some truth to the stunt tonight?" Leo says. My silence answers the question. Leo's eyes open wide. "Oh, wow. This is . . . wow. Can I think about this a bit?"

"No. Because if you have to talk yourself into liking me back, then you . . ." My voice cracks as the truth flows out. "Don't."

"You know I love you, Dakota." Leo drops my wrist. "But not the way you want me to. I'm sorry. From the bottom of my heart. You're my best friend. I don't ever want to lose that."

"I know. Me too." I wipe at another tear that refused to obey orders. "That's why I didn't want to tell you. But we don't lie to each other. We never lie to each other."

"I feel like such a jerk."

"Why? It's not your fault. Or mine."

Leo shakes his head, still stunned at my declaration. "We can still be friends though, right?"

"Yeah." It's not a lie. I want to be Leo's friend, though I may need some distance for a while until my shattered heart pieces itself back together.

"Good." Leo pulls me into a hug. "And thank you. Between sales and the tip jar, I know I made the Japan trip deposit tonight, plus some. Yep, one more in the long line of your awesome ideas."

"You're welcome." I give Leo a tight hug and then push him away. "Since we don't lie to each other—you stink. And I mean literally."

Leo laughs and takes another step backward. "Oyasumi."

"Yeah. Good night to you too." I leave my heart and my dignity behind in the Matsudas' walk-in refrigerator.

Chapter

8

"We are not a couple," I clarify for Lindsay as we leave Japanese class the next day. "Despite what it may have looked like yesterday."

"Is that why Leo was sitting on the opposite side of the room today?" Lindsay glances back over her shoulder at Leo who is talking to Jax.

Not gonna lie. It stings. "Yeah. Leo said he needed some space."

Lindsay cringes. "So, you're saying that if I started dating Leo, you wouldn't come at me?"

I need to get out of Leo's way. Let him take a step forward. Why does it have to hurt so much though?

"Of course not." Well, it's a half-truth.

"I'm going to ask him then." Lindsay pulls out her phone.

We are barely halfway down the hallway toward the cafeteria when Lindsay's phone pings. She lets out a defeated sigh. I wish I could say I were a big enough person not to feel smug about that. But today is not that day. A surprised, muted squeal follows the sigh, and suddenly I don't feel so smug anymore. Leo runs up from behind us and puts a hand on each of our shoulders.

"Is that okay?" Leo says, nodding toward Lindsay's phone. "I work all day on Sunday."

"Sure. I've been wanting to see that movie." Lindsay's smile lights up the entire hallway.

Leo has a matching smile. "Awesome. I'll pick you up on Monday about five then."

I roll my third wheel all the way over to Leo's and my usual lunch table, where I sit alone for the rest of the period. The Friend Zone suuuuucks.

◦ ◦ ◦

Leo and I continue to give each other space for the rest of the day. It's so weird that even Aurora notices.

"What is with you two today?" Aurora says.

"Nothing," Leo and I say at the same time.

"Bull—" Aurora says.

"Can I have some personal space?" Leo cuts her off. "I am all sistered out right now."

"Whatever, Leo." Aurora shoves Leo and then links her elbow through mine. "Koty, my sister from another mister, think you could *volunteer* to work Sunday's lunch shift for me so I can spend the night at Nevaeh's house after the Homecoming dance tomorrow night?"

"No, Aurora." Leo drops his skateboard on the ground and puts a foot on it.

Ignoring Leo, Aurora bats her eyelashes at me. "You can keep my half of the tips."

"Sorry, I have plans on Sunday. Maybe another time. I gotta run. We're shooting today."

I drop my skateboard and hop on. Life throws me a bone, allowing me to make a swift and smooth exit.

Aurora's voice echoes down the sidewalk as Leo rolls in the opposite direction. "What did you do to Dakota?"

◦ ◦ ◦

"Just in time for tea, Dakota." Stephanie stands in the hallway with a large box in her hand.

Stephanie digs through the packaging and pulls out an expensive-looking decorative tin. When she pops open the top, a sweet, buttery, sugary smell wafts through the hallway. My empty stomach roars enthusiastically. I put my hide-in-my-room plan on hold and follow Stephanie to the kitchen, like my cat Lita used to follow me when I opened a can of tuna.

"Having a bad day?" Stephanie puts a chocolate-dipped short-bread cookie on a rose-patterned china plate and hands it to me.

"I've had better. And worse."

Stephanie adds another cookie to my plate. She pats the stool. That's never a good sign.

I slump down on the stool and let out a sigh. "Okay, hit me."

"You know how your sixteenth birthday is close to the final, live send-off episode? The Network wants Phil to lean into the DIY Princess idea and throw you a Sweet Sixteen *extravaganza*." Stephanie adds jazz hands on "extravaganza" to mock Phil.

"Pass."

"I haven't even told you the whole idea yet."

"Still pass."

"C'mon, Dakota. Listen to me for a sec. What's your favorite car right now?"

I sit up straight. "Shut up."

"Don't be rude." Stephanie hands me a cup of tea. "Doug said that he's going to restore the broken-down '69 Ford Mustang fast-back currently in your garage after he retires in May. Since Ford is one of our major sponsors, they asked if you and Doug want to participate in their 'History Restored' campaign next spring. You get a retro-inspired but state-of-the-art, customized Mustang for your birthday, Doug finally gets around to his passion project, and The Network makes a tidy sum on the ad-sales integration with Ford. Win-win-win."

I admit it. I can already see myself driving the Mustang.

"Wait, I know there are strings attached." There always are.

"You have to agree to the Sweet Sixteen party idea in all its tacky glory. Doug agreed to do the 'History Restored' campaign, but his part and your part are two different things. He said he'd support whatever you decide."

"Hmmm. Can I think about it?"

"Of course." Stephanie's phone pings.

As Stephanie texts away, I slip into a cookie-induced daydream.

I'm flying down US 60—doing the speed limit, of course—with the top down on my brand-spanking-new, cherry-red Mustang convertible, my hair flying wild in the wind. I'm getting my jam on, thanks to the killer sound system custom installed in my ride. I lean over and high five—

The wheels fall off my fantasy. Ever since Leo got his full driver's license in August, we have talked about the convertible dream, though his version contains a dog in the backseat and himself in the driver's seat. Now that I'm on the verge of making it a reality, the one given thing might now be the least likely one. I nibble on another cookie and imagine the fantasy with a chocolate lab that we don't own in the passenger seat. Nope. I try Aurora in the passenger seat instead. And then Nevaeh. Better, but not quite the same.

Stephanie taps on my arm, breaking my bubble. "Do you want to hear the fine print about the Sweet Sixteen party to help you decide?"

"Yeah."

"At least half of the episode will be a highlight reel of your life from birth on, minus the you-know-what. In between the 'Growing Up with Dakota' clips, fans will see you prepping for the big party. There will be heart-tugging scenes with your parents, followed by product placements. We'll give America one last peek into your life before you close the door."

My stomach tightens even as my heart lightens. Should I give viewers some fan service—the most G-rated version, of course, because this is HGTV—then take my car and drive off into the literal sunset? Stephanie is on her second cup of tea before I decide.

"Okay, I'll do it."

"Fantastic!" Stephanie claps her hands together. "I'm thinking about pitching Chez Versailles for the venue. We can squeeze a lot of people in there."

"Wait. I do have friends, but not enough to fill Chez Versailles. Probably not even ten percent. Maybe twenty-five percent if you count people who follow me on social media, but we've never had a conversation in real life."

"Hmmm. We're going to need it to be at near capacity. Not to worry. By the time we're done, it will be standing-room only."

"We are *not* going to hire actors to pretend to be my friends. Couldn't we pick a much smaller venue with fewer gilded mirrors and crystal chandeliers and have an *intimate evening with Dakota* with my JCC peeps and a few others instead?"

Stephanie's phone rings.

"No. It needs to be somewhere between gloriously tacky and utterly ridiculous." She pats me on the head. "I need to take this."

Stephanie dips out of the room, mouthing the name of the person she's talking to to Mom, as they pass each other. Mom lasers in on the opened tin of cookies.

"How are you feeling, Koty?" Mom pours herself a cup of tea and joins me at the kitchen island.

"Jumbled." It's the best answer right now.

"Are we talking about the Sweet Sixteen party idea or whatever happened at last night's Homecoming Carnival that Phil is mad about not getting on film?"

I cringe. "You heard about that?"

"Not from your father, mind you. Thankfully, Steph gave me a heads-up before Phil came in this morning." Mom sips her tea. Fitting. "Phil asked me to work on the Matsudas so that he can get you and Leo on film together."

"There is no Leo and Me."

Mom pulls up a picture on her phone and shows me—a sweaty Leo kissing me on the forehead. "Not according to today's TMZ special report."

The hot tea in my stomach freezes over. I knew it was a high probability based on the number of phones out last night. Part of me wouldn't have even minded if the disaster in the walk-in refrigerator wasn't such a fresh wound.

"Publicity stunt, Mom. Leo's business was bombing. Nevaeh and I wanted to help him."

"Now that the cat is out of the bag, at least you and Leo don't have to hide your true feelings anymore."

That cuts me even worse. "We are not a couple. Like I said, Mom. It was all a publicity stunt."

"Oh, but I thought . . . Oh. *Oh.*" Mom puts her hand on mine. "Want to talk about it?"

"Nope."

"Okay, but I'm here for you. Anytime. Or Dad. Okay, maybe not Dad. He totally didn't read the room correctly last night, or he chose *not* to. He still thinks you and Leo are five."

Stephanie pokes her head back into the kitchen. "They're ready for you, Dakota. Phil needs you to do a couple of voiceovers and pickup lines, but that should take no more than thirty minutes tops. Come back to the office when you're done. I want to go over the potential sponsor list with you for the party."

Since I've already established that I am not above a publicity stunt for personal gain, I feel slightly less conflicted about selling out my dignity for a car. But it's not just *a car*. It's a cherry-red Ford Mustang convertible I can drive around long after the TV show is done.

I pull up a new fantasy: Me rolling up to school solo. It's not quite the same, but it's growing on me.

"Will you come with me, Mom? I might need some backup when I refuse to elaborate on what happened last night."

"Of course." Mom squeezes my hand.

I finish my tea and put on my mental armor. Though I don't want to share my truth about Leo, I also don't want to continue the lie we created last night. The lie that my best friend is in love with me too.

Chapter

9

"If I threw a ridiculous party for my sixteenth birthday, would you come?" I ask Nevaeh when they pick me up for the JCC movie night at the local independent theater. Now that all the sponsors have officially signed on, I'm allowed to talk about the piece of news I've been sitting on for the last three weeks.

"Like you really have to ask me that," Nevaeh says, their turquoise-tipped bangs flopping into their unnaturally violet eyes.

"You wanna be my date?"

"You're not my type."

"As friends, Nevaeh. You can wear an over-the-top ball gown. Or a tux with sequined accessories. Shoot, wear your kilt-and-wings combo. I don't care. I just want you to be there with me."

"I will. Not as your date though. Because you are going with our Cinnamon Roll Prince." Nevaeh holds up their hand in front of my face. "I have spoken."

I scoff. I haven't had more than a two-sentence conversation with Leo in the last three weeks. Matsuda Mondays, gone. *Kitsune Mask* Wednesdays, gone. Even lunchtime hanging, gone. What twists the knife in my chest even more is every time I see Leo, he has a big, sappy grin on his face. I want to hate Lindsay, but I can't. She makes my best friend deliriously happy, even if she makes me miserable. So instead, I've been self-isolating.

After I numbed my aching heart by binge-watching all three seasons of *Tanabata Wish* in one week, I started rebuilding. The first step was getting the professional-grade, handheld video camera I received from HGTV out of the box and reading the directions. Well, at least for the first five minutes. Then I started playing around. *Dakota is a tactile learner, but she still needs to learn how to follow instructions,* my fifth-grade teacher once famously said. I'm not dyslexic like Dad, but I still have a hard time following written instructions. If you *show* me, though, I can pick stuff up quickly.

"I learned how to use the editing software you recommended," I say to change the subject. "I want to tweak the ending a little bit more, but I should have my first demo video done by the end of the week."

"Cool. Can't wait to see the final product."

I twist my dirty hair up and pull my baseball cap over the top of it. Nevaeh's wardrobe might be odd sometimes, but they always leave the house with an intentional look. Meanwhile, I look like I just rolled out of bed in my yoga pants and an oversized sweatshirt. Then again, I did.

"Also, glad to see you aren't still growing mushrooms in the Emo Corner of Woe after the whole Homecoming Carnival thing," Nevaeh says.

It takes me a few beats before I can squeeze out, "I'm happy that Leo is happy."

"Yeah, you're going to have to work on your acting skills, my friend."

"No, really. Lindsay is very sweet." That is the truth, as weird as it sounds coming out of my mouth. "It's complicated."

"No, really, it's not."

"Noted." I crank up Nevaeh's sound system, so we can't talk about Leo anymore.

o   o   o

"Hey, I didn't know you were coming tonight," Lindsay says when she intersects us at the door of the indie movie theater.

"Nevaeh said the JCC had to guarantee twenty-five seats to get the discount for the club, so here I am. Number twenty-five." I decide to leave out how much coaxing Nevaeh had to do to get me out of my room tonight.

The tiny theater is already three-quarters full. Iwate-sensei waves from the other end of our row. I match my ticket to my seat. I'm on Lindsay's left. Of course I am, because the universe hates me. Wait. Is this Leo's seat? For a hot second, my heart leaps at the idea that Leo and Lindsay might be broken up.

"Where's—" My question breaks off as Lindsay jumps to her feet.

"Back in a sec," Lindsay says. "Don't let Jax eat all my popcorn while I'm gone, Koty."

Jax stands up so Lindsay can scoot down our row. As soon as she's gone, the lights go down. This theater has fancy, high-tech chairs. I slip my shoes off and slide my seat backward until it's like I'm in our home theater. I put my box of overpriced popcorn and accompanying soda on the removable table between Nevaeh and me and offer them some. I've seen *Howl's Moving Castle* a dozen times, so I close my eyes to listen to the Japanese instead of reading the subtitles. We're five minutes into the movie before Lindsay comes back.

"Sorry," Lindsay's voice cuts through the dark.

I look down the row to see Lindsay holding the hand of a tall boy with closely cropped hair. Of course, he's holding her hand. They're dating. Dating people do that. And much more. Ugh. I take a sip of soda to wash that idea out of my mind.

"Sorry," Leo says as Jax moves farther down the row.

"It's okay, babe." Lindsay sits down.

I choke on my soda. I pull my baseball cap down, trying to obscure my identity. Out the corner of my eye, I see Lindsay whisper something to Leo. A second later, they remove the tray between them and recline their chairs. Lindsay pulls her feet up and wiggles closer to Leo. His arm wraps around her shoulders. I pull my right hand up to block my peripheral vision. It doesn't matter. My brain fills in the blanks. Especially during the quiet part of the movie when I can HEAR THEM KISSING.

I jump to my feet. "Sorry. Excuse me."

I don't care that I have to interrupt more people by leaving through the left side of the row. I have to get out of here. I hang out in the bathroom for several minutes before I get a text from Nevaeh.

> **NEVAEH**
> Are you sick?

ME
Sorta. Need fresh air. Meet you outside after the movie.

> **NEVAEH**
> Text me if you need me to drive you home.

ME
I'm okay. Just need some headspace.

I walk out the front door and sit on the wall between the movie theater and the hair salon next door. And breathe. Just breathe. In. Out. In. Out. I shake the invented visual of Lindsay and Leo kissing out of my mind. It wasn't a kiss on the forehead. That's for sure. Not with that amount of noise. Gag. Breathe in. Breathe out. In. Out.

I sit in the cool late-October air and scroll through my feed to pass the time until the movie ends. That is until I hit Lindsay's picture from earlier today during lunch—a selfie with her arms around a genuinely smiling Leo. Ugh.

My stomach growls. I kick myself for retreating without my expensive popcorn and soda. As I round the back corner of the movie theater, the smell of doughnuts tickles my nose. Diagonally across the parking lot behind the movie theater, BoSa Donuts is doing brisk business.

I'm standing in line contemplating if I should order a dozen to bring some home when Ojiichan comes out of the bathroom. I duck my head and busy myself on my phone. Instead of leaving, though, Ojiichan sits at a table with a cup of coffee and a plain cake doughnut already on it. He pulls out his phone. Kudos to Aurora, who convinced Ojiichan to finally give up his dinosaur of a flip phone so that he could read current, baseball-themed manga from Japan on his smartphone.

"I'd like a dozen, please," I scoot down the counter, so I don't have to raise my voice. "Three bear claws. Three butterflies. Three apple fritters and . . ." Out of habit, I almost order three cinnamon rolls. Nope. Can't do it. Not tonight. "And three maple bars."

I peek over my shoulder. Ojiichan is deep into his manga reading and coffee drinking. I pay for the doughnuts and sweep right past him out the door without him noticing. I power walk to the front of the movie theater again and hop onto the wall to enjoy my dinner.

I am three doughnuts in when I hear a high-pitched whistle. I look up from the cat videos on my phone.

"Oi! Dakota-chan!" Ojiichan yells out the open passenger window of the Matsudas' minivan.

There has been no parking available in front of the theater for the last thirty minutes. But because the universe particularly hates me today, a parking spot directly in front of me suddenly opens up. Of course it does. Ojiichan slides the van into it and waves me over to him.

"The movie is finished? Am I late?" Ojiichan says.

"No. I wasn't feeling well, so I came outside. The movie is still playing for another ten minutes or so."

Ojiichan unlocks the van door. "Come inside. It is cold."

When I start to make excuses, Ojiichan leans over and opens the door for me. I reluctantly climb in.

"Ahhhh," I say when my frozen butt cheeks hit the heated seat.

"I know. It makes my back happy."

We sit in silence for a few minutes before Ojiichan says, "You don't come to the restaurant after school anymore. Why?"

"I've been busy." To make that not be a complete lie, I add, "I've been filming some short web videos recently. Basic home improvement skills for teens. Easy things that I forget not everybody knows how to do. Like how to paint your room." I pick at some of the turquoise paint stuck in my cuticles from repainting my bedroom this past weekend.

"I remember when you taught Aurora how to paint her room."
Ojiichan chuckles.

"Yeah, I added a part in my video about securing the area from
pets during the job." I laugh too. "Maru still heads in the opposite
direction every time she sees me."

Sort of like me with Leo.

Ojiichan takes off his cap and runs his hand through his thin-
ning, gray hair. "Dakota-chan, did you and Leo-kun have a fight?"

"No." *He bodychecked me into the Friend Zone.* I have to know,
"Why? Does Leo seem sad?"

"No. He seems happy," Ojiichan says, and my heart drops. "But
he seems different."

"Yeah. I agree."

"You seem different too, but not so happy."

"I think we are becoming too different to be best friends anymore."

"Oh no. That makes me sad." Ojiichan puts a hand on top of
mine and pats it.

Ojiichan is not the touchy-feely type. That's more of an American thing. So his hand-patting releases the sob that has been stuck in
my chest for the last three weeks.

"Dōshita?" *What happened?* Ojiichan asks in alarm.

"I miss Old Leo. I want my best friend back." I wipe my watery
eyes with my sleeve and sniff. "Hazukashii. Gomennasai."

"Hai, hai." Ojiichan waves away my apology for being so embarrassing.

A sudden knock on my window makes Ojiichan and I both
jump. Nevaeh waves from the other side. I lower the window.

"You okay, Dakota? Konban wa, Matsuda-san." Nevaeh does a
head dip at Ojiichan.

Ojiichan dips his head back.

"Yeah. Sorry. I wasn't feeling well all of a sudden. I needed some
fresh air." I point at the box on my lap. "And doughnuts."

"And maybe some personal space from the *show* going on beside
us?" Nevaeh cuts their kohl-rimmed eyes to the side.

"That too."

"Where is my grandson?" Ojiichan looks around as the last of our classmates tell Iwate-sensei goodbye and head to the parking lot behind the movie theater.

Leo suddenly strolls around the corner, his hands tucked in his front pockets and a dreamy look on his face.

"Any chance you could catch a ride home with the Matsudas tonight, Dakota?" Nevaeh says. "I promised to drive Jax home, but he has to be back before ten."

"I don't mind being late." I catch Leo's eye through the windshield. It bursts whatever Lindsay-inspired bubble he was in.

"Hai, hai. I will do it." Ojiichan decides for me. He taps the horn and yells out my window, "Oi, Leo-kun!"

Leo's love-induced stroll turns into a sprint before Ojiichan embarrasses him even more. Leo climbs into the middle row of the van out of breath as Nevaeh says their good-nights.

As we pull away, Leo says, "Hey, Dakota. Haven't seen you in a while."

"Yeah. I've been busy working on some new projects." I tap my middle finger on top of the box of doughnuts to discharge the awkward energy pulsing through my body.

"Oh, good. I was beginning to think you were avoiding me or something," Leo jokes, but there is an edge to his voice.

"I wasn't avoiding you." I continue to tap.

"I know I said I needed some personal space, but you didn't need to ghost me."

"Like I said, I've been busy." My frantic tapping causes the corner of the doughnut box to cave in.

Ojiichan glances over at me with concern. He says something to Leo in Japanese, but all I understand is "she."

"Why don't you come over sometime," Leo says with semi-sincerity. "We'll hang and catch up on *Kitsune Mask*."

"I know you're . . . *busy*."

"I'm not *that* busy." Leo's look via the rearview mirror pierces me. "Seriously, come to the restaurant with me on Thursday after school. We'll talk. Catch up."

"Please come, Dakota-chan," Ojiichan says. "I will even make your favorite, karaage."

"Karaage isn't her favorite, Ojiichan," Leo says. "Miso-katsu is."

"That's right. You know Dakota-chan the best."

My frozen heart begins to thaw a little. "Okay. Maybe for a little while."

I open up my slightly crushed box of doughnuts and hold them out to Leo.

"No cinnamon rolls tonight?" Leo takes a maple bar. "I thought they were your favorite."

"They are." Both the literal pastry version and the too-pure-for-this-world anime hero version of the word. "But I'm trying to branch out more."

We ride in silence, which is a foreign concept for Leo and me. Ojiichan routinely chastises us with a gruff "Urusai!" because Leo and I usually talk too much, too fast, and too loud. As we enter my neighborhood, I want to bring back some of our old life.

"If I threw a ridiculous party for my sixteenth birthday in April, would you come?" I hold my breath as I wait for Leo's answer, which is no longer a given anymore.

"Ridiculous like everybody has to come wearing a Venetian mask ridiculous, or you're going to ride into the party on an elephant kind of ridiculous?"

"If Phil has his way, both of those suggestions would be considered tame."

Leo's laugh thaws my heart.

"Of course. I wouldn't miss it," Leo says. "But only if you promise I get to ride the elephant too at some point."

"Duh, of course."

"I'm holding you to that."

Leo keeps looking at my box of doughnuts, so I offer him another one. "So, did you see that Ava Takahashi is going to be on a panel at San Diego Comic Con this year?"

"She is? I wanna go." Leo begins to thaw too as I fill him in on all the latest industry gossip.

I know things are going to be awkward for a while, but maybe we've turned the page to a new chapter of our friendship.

Chapter

10

Thanks to Phil's boss, executive producer Tamara Weatherbee, I get to film whatever I want now for my weekly *DIY with Dakota* digital exclusives on HGTV's website. Because according to her, my style is "authentic and engaging, and will bring in a younger demographic."

Take that, Phil! Since I'm not allowed to monetize my videos like Jax does with his gaming videos on YouTube, Stephanie talked HGTV into giving me a different kind of payout. Viewers can see their clicks and views adding to the fundraiser thermometer at the top of my channel's landing page. Once I hit the goal, HGTV Gives Back donates $10,000 to a charity of my choice.

"Do you need me for anything else?" I ask Phil after Dad and I finish filming the segment with the large stained-glass window in the staircase area, between the first and second floor of the build. Not only did I help install it, but I also helped local stained-glass artist Mr. Tang create it to Mom's historically accurate specifications.

"No, you're good. Enjoy your Thanksgiving break." Phil gives instructions to our field producer about our next shoot. "You need to talk to Stephanie about the party before she leaves."

"I will." I pick up the shoebox filled with the other stained-glass designs I made in one hand, and my video camera in the other. I think my fans are going to enjoy the webisode I filmed with Mr. Tang about how to make a mini stained-glass creation for your bedroom window. I can't post it until March when the corresponding episode airs, but I plan to give away my Spoiler Alert pieces as Christmas presents to Iwate-sensei and a few of my friends.

Well, except for Leo. His nine-tailed fox design will be a New Year's present because the Matsudas are culturally Buddhist and don't celebrate Christmas.

"I'm not so sure about this, Stephanie. She might not be ready for it yet." Mom's voice comes out the cracked door of her home office as I head up the stairs to edit my new footage.

"Give her a chance, Tamlyn," Stephanie says. "Now that the whole Leo thing seems to be behind her, maybe Dakota is ready to try something new. No strings attached."

"There are always strings attached."

"It's a boy in a tux. A boy who can stay squarely in the Friend Zone before, during, and long after the event."

"I wish things would have worked out with Leo."

I stop halfway up the stairs.

"I know." Stephanie sighs. "They are so cute together, but I guess it's not meant to be."

I still haven't given up hope that one day Leo will change his mind, but we've only watched *Kitsune Mask* together once at the restaurant since the JCC movie night. With Thanksgiving next week and finals around the corner, I doubt that's going to change. I keep declining Leo's invitation to sit with him and Lindsay at lunch. Maybe it's time to rip off the Band-Aid and move on with my life.

I come back down the few stairs and knock on Mom's door. "I'm done filming for the day. It's my turn to make dinner. Would you like fish sticks and tater tots, or the Dakota McDonald Special: Tomato soup out of a can with a grilled cheese sandwich?"

"Soup and sandwich." Mom slides off her bifocals, which Phil hates her wearing on camera. So she does anyway and every time she can, because Phil doesn't complain when Dad wears his bifocals on camera. "Koty, can you come in here, please?"

"Stephanie, Phil said you needed to talk to me, before you leave for Thanksgiving vacation."

"I do." Stephanie moves the wallpaper sample book off a chair for me. "A Class Act Tuxedo Company wants to be one of the sponsors for your sixteenth birthday *extravaganza*, but they want prominent product placement."

Mom rolls her desk chair over to join us at Stephanie's circular worktable. Stephanie puts a large envelope in front of me. I pour out the contents of the already-opened envelope. Along with a letter addressed to my parents, a thin catalog falls out that says PROM SPECIALS.

"But prom is the week *before* my party." Not that I'm going, but the last time I spent time with Aurora almost a month ago, she was already talking about it.

"At your high school, because Arizona schools go back to school so early in August. Most East Coast and Midwest schools don't go back to school until after Labor Day, so their proms are usually in mid-May or later."

I tip my head from side to side. "I'm open-minded. I'm happy to wear a tux to my party. Maybe Nevaeh and I could have matching black tuxes with sparkly pink cummerbunds and bow ties?"

"No, sweetie—though that is an intriguing idea—no, they want to put your dad in a tux instead of a nice suit." Mom looks at Stephanie for support. "And they want you to have a date to the party who could wear one of the tuxes from their prom line. Someone who would allow the cameras to film him trying on a couple different designs from their latest prom collection."

"I'm sure Nevaeh would love it."

"No, honey. They want you to have a real date for the party."

Fire runs through my veins. "Then tell them Nevaeh is my 'real date.'"

Mom looks at Stephanie, who is suddenly interested in the pile of papers in front of her. Mom puts her hands over mine.

"*I* think that Nevaeh would be an awesome date. But Phil wants to bring someone else in."

"What kind of archaic, heteronormative garbage is this?"

"Hold on, Dakota. Phil wants to bring in a boy who is already in the business. Somebody who isn't afraid to be on camera. Somebody who knows how to handle the notoriety that comes with this life and is okay with possibly being in the tabloids."

"I'm not going to have a repeat of last year's Homecoming." I sit back in my chair and cross my arms.

"Dakota, listen," Stephanie says as I continue to burn. "They just want to give you some arm candy for the event. You don't need to have any kind of relationship with this boy before or after the event. He would be a special guest. A *special* special guest that you would have a dance or two with. Really, no different than working with Mr. Tang last week."

"Yes, it is. I wasn't required to hold hands with Mr. Tang."

"For the record, I wouldn't mind holding hands with Mr. Tang. Alas, he is married, so . . ." Stephanie makes an explosion sound. "My current love-life situation summed up."

"What do you think, Dakota?" Mom presses. "I always want you to push yourself outside your comfort zone, but only you know where the line is between uncomfortable and damaging. Whatever you decide, I will support one hundred percent."

"It might help you get over Leo," Stephanie says, and I cringe. I hate that I am such an open book to her. "Hey, it's okay. Your secret is safe with me, Dakota. I am unfortunately quite familiar with life in the Friend Zone. But you have to move on eventually, instead of pining away for years about it. Trust me on this."

"Okay, but I want to pick the guy. And I want to do a test date before the actual event. I want to at least have *something* in common with him before going into the event."

"That's my girl," Mom says. "Now back to reality. I'll make dinner tonight so you can put in more time on your homework. I've seen your grades slipping since you started doing the digital series on top of our usual shooting schedule."

"It's fine, Mom."

"No, it's not. Getting a good education is important too, Dakota." Mom might have a Ph.D., but Dad never went to college.

I will probably fall somewhere in between. "I know."

I smirk, remembering Drivers Ed today when Coach Klein busted on Jax for aspiring to be a famous YouTuber one day.

"How you gonna make a living doing that, son?" Coach Klein said, looking down his nose at Jax.

"Same way as Dakota, I guess," Jax said with a completely straight face while pointing at me. "How much money did you make from your *DIY with Dakota* videos last week, Dakota?"

"Depends. Do you mean from the advertising revenue, merchandise sales, or fan donations?" I said seriously, even though I'm limited to just my clicks-for-charity right now. Even after our show ends, my contract with The Network won't allow me to do anything for another year to eighteen months. But after that . . . hmmm.

Jax got detention for his "Oh, snap!" comment, and I picked up twelve new subscribers. Not a bad day of work, really.

"You work on homework, and I will work on finding you the perfect date, okay?" Stephanie says.

I nod. Time to pull that Band-Aid off.

Chapter

11

By the Monday after Thanksgiving break, the Band-Aid is officially off. Not only do I accept Leo's invitation to sit with him and Lindsay at lunch, but I even agree to come to the restaurant to watch *Kitsune Mask* on Wednesday. Granted, it's because Lindsay's violin lessons have suddenly moved to Wednesday afternoons, but I'll take it. I want to find a new normal with my best friend.

"Are you working this afternoon?" I ask Aurora when we run into each other after the final bell on Wednesday.

"Wellllll . . ." Aurora says.

"Yes, you are," Leo comes up behind us. "Mom and Dad know that marching band is over. Has *been* over."

"I can't wait for winter drumline to start," Aurora grumbles. "Why, Koty? What's up?"

"I need help picking a date."

"You're kidding?" Aurora's double-take mirrors Leo's.

"Nope. I'm trying to find the perfect date for my Sweet Sixteen *extravaganza*." I do the jazz hands too because "party" no longer accurately describes the ridiculousness that this event has snowballed into. "I was planning to get Nevaeh's opinion during lunch today, but they have a stomach bug."

"You don't want my opinion?" Leo says, though I can't tell if he's joking or not.

Aurora lets out a derisive snort and hooks her elbow through mine. "No, this job requires an expert. Now, tell me more."

I look over my shoulder as Aurora leads me away. Leo continues to stand in the middle of the hallway, his head cocked to one side as he filters my news.

o   o   o

"I thought we were going to watch *Kitsune Mask* today," Leo says after we all greet Ojiichan.

"We will. I just need to do this with Aurora first because Stephanie wants my list before five." I slide into my favorite booth and dig the file folder from Stephanie out of my backpack.

Aurora delivers two glasses of melon soda and a plate of cookie-sized black sesame sembei to my table before sliding in next to me. As I crunch away on the rice crackers, Aurora pulls the file to her side of the table. Inside, forty young actors from across the US compete to be my date to the most ridiculous party of the decade.

"This is so wrong." My stomach clenches in shame.

"No, it's not. It's awesome." Aurora pulls the top picture off the pile. "This one is going in the Awww Yeah pile."

That one and 75 percent of the pile.

"Well, that narrows it down," I say sarcastically when she's done.

Aurora takes a swig of melon soda and mimes wiping her brow. "I wouldn't do this for just anybody, you know. On to Round Two. Trust me. This is a good problem to have."

"What's a good problem to have?" Leo appears beside Aurora. "I'm done topping up all the shōyu bottles like Ojiichan asked. No thanks to you, of course."

"Guess you won Favorite Matsuda Child yet again, dear brother. Congrats." Aurora gives Leo a dismissive flick of her hand. "Begone. I'm helping Koty find her Prince Charming."

Leo ignores his sister's command and slides in on the other side of our booth.

"This isn't an episode of *The Bachelor*, Aurora." I can feel the heat in my cheeks. "I'm not trying to make a love connection. I'm looking for someone who is comfortable on camera and has more personality than a potato."

"Phil wants a fake romance to boost ratings?" Leo says.

Aurora gives Leo a scathing look. "Rude."

There is a truth to Leo's comment, but I'm not going to dignify it. "A tuxedo company is one of our big sponsors. They want my date to model some of their spring line for the party for an online and print campaign."

"But they're still buying you a date for your party?" Leo says. Aurora must have kicked him in the shin under the table because he winces and adds, "*Hiring,* not buying."

"Same difference. Yeah, I know it's pathetic, but it'll make things easier in the end. If things aren't a match, I never have to see or talk to him again after the party."

"Ooooor, if things are a match, you can walk the red carpets together." Aurora's eyes light up. "And give your designer gowns— because you wouldn't dare wear the same dress twice—to your favorite sister from another mister."

"You might have to fight Nevaeh for them."

Though I doubt that any of the guys in this folder are red-carpet-level actors, part of me enjoys watching Leo's conflicted reaction.

"I can't wait." Aurora squeals and grabs my arm.

I feel a twinge in my heart. I'm glad to have my closest friend's attention back, even if it is only for an hour on a random Wednesday afternoon, but I wish I didn't have to do something so dramatic to get that attention in the first place.

"Time to narrow down the pile." I push the Awww Yeah pile back to Aurora and tuck the others back in the folder. "Round Two."

On the top of the pile is the headshot of a very cute guy, probably of Southeast Asian descent.

"Yaaaasss." Aurora picks up the headshot and flips it over to read the guy's acting history and stats. He goes back into the new Awww Yeah pile.

"So, we're not going to watch *Kitsune Mask*?" Leo says.

"This might take longer than I thought." I hand Leo my iPad. "Why don't you watch it without me this week? I'll watch it later tonight, and we'll discuss at lunch tomorrow. Okay?"

"Go enjoy your fantasy girl in another booth." Aurora adds another headshot to the Awww Yeah pile. "Koty and I have work to do."

"And wear headphones while you watch it. I don't want any spoilers."

"Okay." A wrinkle creases Leo's forehead, but it doesn't stop him from accepting my iPad and sliding out of the booth.

I find it suspicious that Leo sits at the table closest to us, but I don't call him out on it.

"Ahhh, the pile isn't getting much smaller," Aurora says when we get to the end. There are still over a dozen guys in the Awww Yeah pile.

"He has to be more than a pretty face," I say. "I need somebody with a personality I can click with."

"Got it. First friend." Aurora gives me a sassy wink. "Then boy-friend."

Leo immediately looks back at the tablet when I catch his eye. It's bad for the restaurant—but good for me—that business is dead today. We're down to five choices by the time *Kitsune Mask* ends.

"You missed out, Koty. This episode is wild." Leo hands the iPad back to me.

"No spoilers." I slide the iPad into my backpack.

"I have to say that Jay Yoshikawa was looking hot hot hot." Leo pulls at the collar of his T-shirt.

"I'm sure Koty will be happy to pass along your fanboy compli-ments to Ava Takahashi when she's walking the red carpet with one of these up-and-coming actors." Aurora points at the table.

I know it's a low blow, but I can't help myself. "We need an ob-jective opinion, Leo. What do you think of these five guys? Which would be your Top Three choices as my date?"

Aurora crosses her arms and sits back in the booth. "Oh, I can't wait to hear this."

"Can do." Leo drags Aurora out of the booth by her elbow and takes her spot. "I'm not impressed by 'a smoldering smile' or a 'jaw-line that could cut glass.'"

Leo confirms my suspicion that he's been listening to Aurora and me the whole time. Aurora sits down across from us.

"Since you think you can do a better job than I can, what kind of guy would be perfect for Dakota?"

"Ummmm," Leo says.

"See." Aurora crosses her arms.

"Give me a second to think." Leo looks around the restaurant. His forehead creases in concentration. "Dakota needs someone loyal. Someone who will keep her safe."

"Well that settles it. I should bring a German shepherd as my date." I flick Leo in the arm. "You get to put him in the tux, though."

Leo flicks me back. "I'm just saying that looks are nice, but it's what's on the inside that counts."

"Says the guy who told me not two minutes ago how 'hot hot hot'"—I pull at the collar of my T-shirt, mocking Leo—"Jay Yoshikawa looked this week. Double standard much?"

"That's different."

"How?"

"Because she's a fantasy." Leo taps on the headshot closest to him. "These guys are reality."

"It's TV. Everything is a fantasy, even what they pass off as reality. You know that."

Leo flips over all five of the guys' headshots and reads the backs.

To her credit, when a couple comes into the restaurant, Aurora jumps up and seats them. I don't bother Leo as he continues to read and reread each headshot until he slowly pulls them into a ranking. Finally, Leo picks them all up, taps them on the table, and hands the pile to me.

"Actor Number One and Number Two were a tie on paper."

"What broke the tie then?" I look down. Actor Number One is definitely Asian. Actor Number Two is racially ambiguous.

"He's Asian. Representation matters." Leo taps his fist on his chest. "It says he speaks some Japanese." Leo scoffs. "We'll see."

"You're not coming on the date with me."

"I could. We could double-date. That way, you could get a second opinion."

"Good idea, but not with you and Lindsay," Aurora says as she passes by with a tray filled with ocha and edamame for the customers.

"I'm going to have to agree with Aurora on this one," I say.

I'm a decent-enough actress that Leo can't see that eating lunch with him and Lindsay—who insists on holding Leo's hand the entire time—still hurts. Still, it's better than losing him altogether.

"Are you sure?" Leo tips his head to the side. "Aurora tends to be somewhere between brutally honest and I-have-no-filter. What if he's Mr. Right, but Aurora scares him off?"

I wince because Leo is right. "And then there's the whole paparazzi problem. How can we even do a test date if there will be cameras in our faces? Maybe I should stick to video chats."

"You could have your date here."

"Because *that* wouldn't be awkward," I say.

"Awkward but safe."

"Leo's right for once." Aurora shares an I-can't-believe-we're-agreeing-with-each-other look with Leo.

"Okay. But I want Aurora to be my server."

"We'll see." Leo wiggles his eyebrows at me.

"Never mind. I'll stick to video chats."

"Seriously, Koty, come here as a test." Leo puts his hand on my arm. "Let me—us—help you find someone who deserves a girl as awesome as you are."

As much as I want to yell, "That guy is sitting next to me!" I don't. Instead, I put my hand over Leo's and say, "Thanks."

The front door of the restaurant opens, and a family of six comes in.

"I gotta run. I made the first payment for our trip thanks to the Homecoming Carnival, but I still have two more payments to come up with."

"Well, what are you sitting around for? Go." I gather my stuff. "Tomorrow. Lunch. We chat."

Leo greets the family with his boy-next-door smile that continues to melt my heart. I look down at this Jake guy who can speak a little Japanese.

Maybe he's the one I've been waiting for. Maybe he's the one who will help me move on, for real.

Chapter

12

Operation Kill-Dakota-with-This-Ridiculous-Party rolls on at full speed through December. Though I tried to put the date off until after the holidays, Stephanie scheduled it for Saturday instead. My stomach lurches thinking about it. I try to distract myself by being hyper-focused on the little stuff, like my clothes.

"Understated elegance," I tell Nevaeh at lunch. "Not, I'm going clubbing after the date is done. No foil eyelashes. No wigs."

"What? I think you'd look hot in my pastel pink wig." Nevaeh twists my hair up one way and then another. "Or what about the long, white wig? A little silver glitter eyeliner. You could borrow my white leather coat with the faux fur around the neck. Now, *that* would make a statement."

"Yeah, if the statement is: I'm cosplaying Jay Yoshikawa." Leo slides in across the table from us at lunch.

Nevaeh nods their head. "I like where you are going with this, Cinnamon Roll Prince."

"That was sarcasm, Nevaeh," Leo says. "Not that you couldn't pull off a white leather jumpsuit, Koty, but maybe that wouldn't make the best first impression."

"I want to be memorable, but in a good way." That said, if wearing a white leather jumpsuit and a white wig would move me out of the Friend Zone, I would drop my burrito right now and have them shipped to my house today. Is it too early to be thinking about Halloween?

Leo pulls a nondescript, plastic box out of his backpack, and a nutty smell wafts across the table. Leo and another one of his sad PB&J sandwiches. I understand why Ojiichan is offended by Leo's daily lunch choice, especially with the amount of delicious

Japanese leftovers always available in the Matsudas' home fridge. Leo stopped bringing a bento in fourth grade after kids mocked both his "weird" lunch and his matching Super Sentai–themed bento boxes and chopsticks. He's been the King of PB&J ever since. I even offered to swap lunches with him to make both me and Ojiichan happy. Nope.

"Hey, babe." Lindsay slides in next to Leo and puts her tray down. As Principal Docker is standing two tables over, Lindsay refrains from greeting Leo with her usual over-the-top PDA, like they haven't seen each other in years instead of five minutes ago when Japanese class ended.

"We're helping Koty pick out her outfit for her date tomorrow night," Nevaeh brings Lindsay up to speed.

"Oh, I want to help. Plus, I think I have a better sense of your style than these two." Lindsay swings her corn dog at Leo and Nevaeh.

"Here are the two outfits I—okay, Stephanie—picked out."

Nevaeh snatches the phone out of my hand as soon as I pull up the pictures. "Are these Starr Shibutani? I love her stuff!"

"I want to see." Lindsay pulls at Nevaeh's hand until they put the phone in the middle of the table.

"Hey, look, you have kneecaps." Leo says.

It's true. Look Number One includes a short, flirty floral-print dress with a tobacco-colored leather jacket and matching ankle boots. Stephanie talked me into curling a few pieces of hair to "frame my face" and wearing more makeup than my usual routine.

Lindsay nods. "Soft. Feminine. Approachable. I love it."

"A little pedestrian for my taste, but you've got a girl-next-door vibe going on here." Nevaeh looks at Leo. "Your thoughts, Cinnamon Roll Prince?"

"Erm, you look pretty." The way Leo says it sounds more like a question than an answer.

I side-eye him. "Thanks for that rousing vote of confidence."

Nevaeh slides to the next picture. "Oooh, now this one's got some sass. The earrings are basic though."

This time Leo leans in to see the picture better. Stephanie paired black, fitted cropped pants and a black blouse with white polka dots. I added the jean jacket and black ballet flats from my closet. Stephanie pulled my hair into a high ponytail, winged my eyeliner a little, and gave me some red lips.

Leo raises an eyebrow but gives me a generic, "You look pretty here too."

"What he means is that you look retro but still modern. Very on point for the TV show, but without looking dated and costumey." Lindsay nods appreciatively. "I agree with Nevaeh. The earrings are off."

While Nevaeh and Lindsay discuss the finer points of earrings, Leo swipes the photos back.

Leo points at my phone. "This one is my favorite."

I look down. I'm wearing the Dakota McDonald special, which means a black tank top with a soft, fleecy plaid overshirt, faded jeans with both knees ripped out—by accident, not as a fashion statement—and work boots. I have no makeup on, and a scrunchie keeps my collarbone-length hair pulled up into a sloppy bun.

"That was my *before* look, Leo."

"Oh." Leo looks down at the photo and then back up. His stare zaps me to the pit of my stomach. "I stand by my choice. You look kinda cold and uncomfortable in the other two pictures. You look warm and comfortable in this one. I'm no fashion expert, but maybe find something that makes you feel comfortable and confident."

Nevaeh fake cries. "My work here is done."

"Speaking of being comfortable in your own skin." I take my phone back. "Can I post a picture of your hands?"

After the whole Wings Controversy before fall break, Nevaeh has made it their mission to discover all the other loopholes in the student dress code. Today's act of rebellion: body art. Students aren't allowed to have tattoos that show. Even ones made with Sharpies like Nevaeh did back in early November. But henna is not a tattoo.

"I talked Diya into doing my henna early because we have so

many family members to do before the wedding," Nevaeh says, as I take an artistic shot of our hands together for my Instagram account. Mr. Dockert sees us. Sees Nevaeh's intricately decorated hands. "I dare somebody to write me up today for it. My stepmom would be down here in a hot second."

Mr. Dockert looks away.

o   o   o

"My, *somebody* is trying to make an impression." Mom walks into my room without knocking first, a vase of roses in her hand.

"Mom! I was filming." I lean forward and turn off my camera.

"And *somebody* sounds like a diva."

"Sorry. I've been trying to record this segment all afternoon. Why is talking about wall studs so impossible today?" I put my black-and-yellow stud finder, which I nicknamed Bumble Bee sometime around third grade, down on my desk. "But notice . . ." I gesture around my room. "I cleaned my room before recording. No more Mom Shame."

"Fantastic. Now these lovely flowers won't look so out of place in the usual pigsty."

"Roses? Fan-cy." I take the flower arrangement from Mom and read the tiny card. "*To Lovely Dakota. I can't wait to see you tomorrow. Breathlessly, Jake.* Breathlessly? Am I expected to know CPR or something for this date?"

"It's a little over-the-top, but sweet."

Okay, I'm impressed. The last time I received flowers from a boy was for my thirteenth birthday. I was having a *huge* pity party for myself because not only were my parents out of town on business on my actual birthday, but I also caught a nasty stomach bug and had to bail on my plans with Leo. Pretty sure that Stephanie—whom my parents paid to basically be my live-in nanny for the weekend—is never going to have children now. I've scarred her for life.

That Saturday, as I was alternating between lying on the cold tile floor wishing I were dead and driving the porcelain bus while revisiting the Ghost of Pizzas Past, the doorbell rang. A few minutes later, Stephanie's hand reached around the door. She put a little basket filled with daisies on the floor next to me, followed by a bottle of Gatorade and a sleeve of saltine crackers. There was a note inside the basket.

Happy Birthday, Koty! Get well soon so we can go to the movies together.

~Leo and Mr. Ushi

"I'm glad you're feeling more enthusiastic about this, Koty." Mom brings me back to the present. "But keep your head on straight. Not all boys are like Leo. I'm not saying to keep your barriers up, but be careful with your heart. The rest of your body, too. Maybe now would be a good time to have Part Two of The Talk."

"No, it absolutely would not." I plunk the vase on top of my desk and pick up my stud finder. "This *date* is going to be two people eating dinner and talking. That's it. If it somehow morphs into something bigger . . ." Why does my brain decide to torture me with an image of Leo and Lindsay and their "octopus arms" right now? I shake my head. "We'll talk. I promise. But now, I have a tutorial to film on how to hang a shelf."

"Stephanie said your web show is taking off. Who knew?"

I point at myself. "I did."

"Proud of you, sweetie." Mom kisses the top of my head. "I'll let you get back to it then."

After I finally get a good take, I stop and wander to my closet. I slide the door open, and my over-stuffed closet barfs out its contents all over my floor. It takes a few minutes of digging, but I finally find it.

The daisies are long gone, but I put the basket with Leo's note still tucked inside it on my desk, next to Jake's bouquet, and put my stud finder inside it too.

Chapter

13

"Are you sure about this?" Dad says when we pull up in front of Matsuda thirty minutes before my test date with Jake Yong. I nod. "If things go south, text me from the bathroom. I'll make up an excuse that I need you to come home ASAP."

"Thanks. But I got this. I'm on neutral ground—a paparazzi-free zone—here. I feel, maybe not comfortable, but at least safer."

Dad gives me a hug like I'm leaving for war. I hug Dad back. I know he's as conflicted about all of this as I am. You hand my Dad a gizmo from 1954, and he can opine about it for hours. But his words are measured on everything related to my growing up. Though there are days when Mom jokes that she can't wait to be an empty nester—usually when I'm salty about something like the state of my room—Dad always counters with him being fine if I never move out. Yeah. That's not going to happen either.

"Irasshaimase!" Mrs. Matsuda doesn't look up from the table she's cleaning when I first come inside. Then she does a double-take. "Sugoi! Dakota-chan, kirei dayo."

"Thank you." I accept her compliment that I look pretty though Iwate-sensei taught us that culturally you're not supposed to.

"You're early. Somebody is sitting in your booth right now. Do you want to pick another spot?"

"Not yet, I wanted to say hi to everybody before Jake gets here." And get a pep talk from Aurora, but Mrs. Matsuda doesn't need to know that. "Is it okay if I go back?"

"Of course. We had a big rush thirty minutes ago, but things are slowing down again."

As I head back, Aurora comes out of the kitchen with a tray full of different types of noodles. Though she can't stop to chat, Aurora gives my outfit a quick look and a nod of approval as we pass each other. I open the kitchen door to find a sweaty Ojiichan lecturing Leo about something.

"Hai. Hai. Wakarimashita." Leo rubs his temples and agrees to whatever Ojiichan is scolding him about.

I knock on the opened door. "I just wanted to say hi and thank you for letting me come here tonight."

Ojiichan tips his head at me as he plates up somebody's miso-katsu next to a pile of finely shredded cabbage. "Of course, Dakota-chan. You are family."

"So?" I put my arms out to the side and do a tight turn. "I took your fashion advice."

I paired the black fitted pants with a more modern black-and-gold top, a pair of tall black boots, my jean jacket, a little more makeup than usual, and my hair up in a half-do.

Leo nods. "You are missing one thing."

"What?" I look down at my outfit. "Is the purse too much? I told Nevaeh it was over the top."

Leo pulls the *Kitsune Mask* pin off his pine-green waist apron. "For courage."

When Leo's fingers slide underneath the fabric of my jean jacket to attach the pin, his knuckles lightly graze the skin of my exposed collarbone. A bolt of electricity races to the pit of my stomach. My breath catches when Leo's long fingers tuck a lock of escaped hair behind my ear.

Leo clears his throat. "Kirei dane. Ne, Ojiichan?"

Ojiichan glances over from plating the fourth miso-katsu dinner and nods at Leo's assessment that I look pretty. Leo goes to the sink to wash his hands.

"Girls stopped having cooties around the fifth grade, you know," I tease Leo, though he's just following health code rules.

Leo looks over his shoulder and gives me a wink. "I know."

"Thanks for the pin." I hold the kitchen door open for Leo to pass through with the heavy tray perched on his shoulder.

"It's only on loan for tonight. To help you channel your Inner Jay. Fierce. Confident. Sassy. So don't lose it."

"Gotcha." I watch Leo walk away, nimbly dodging Aurora, who almost backs into him.

When my booth is finally open, I grab an empty tray and pile up all the used dishes. I take them into the kitchen and hand them over to Mr. Matsuda, who is back from his break and loading up the dishwasher for probably the hundredth time today.

After cleaning my hands, I grab a towel and dry some of the plates fresh out of the dishwasher. The wet heat warms my cold hands. I dry and stack in silence until Aurora comes in.

"Koty, what are you doing?" Aurora unloads her tray of dishes and tucks the two empty trays under her arm.

"I don't mind drying dishes. Plus, I've got time to kill."

Because Mr. Matsuda isn't a particularly chatty person and often listens to podcasts while he does this mind-numbing job, drying dishes is a way to settle my brain. It's practically a form of meditation for me. I dried a LOT of dishes after the Great Homecoming Disaster.

"Well, stop before you melt your makeup off. Actually, finish that load so I don't have to do it, and then stop. I'm going on break, Dad." Aurora ducks out the back door for a few minutes of regular teen life.

Leo comes through the doors with another tray piled high with dirty dishes. "I wiped down your table, Koty, if you want to go get ready for your date."

I put the last two tiny shōyu plates in their pile. Mr. Matsuda and I have never had a lot in common, but there is one thing we agree on: One must keep the bowls, plates, and teacups in a specific order and stacked to a certain height. In fact, at rock bottom of my downward spiral last year, Mr. Matsuda insisted that I needed to come do inventory and reorganize the dishes with him because "my children don't do it right."

I realize now that the task was more about my mental health

than crockery organization. That it was his way of showing concern for me.

"Dōmo." Mr. Matsuda nods his head at me with a thanks when I hang the towel up to dry.

"Dō itashimashite." *You're welcome,* I nod back at him. I let out a cleansing breath and thank him too. "Dōmo."

"Anytime, Dakota-chan."

I stop for a quick makeup and hair check in the bathroom before settling into my favorite booth. My phone pings.

NEVAEH
You got this!

I send them a goofy selfie back. And then another one. And then a third.

"Right over here," Mrs. Matsuda says.

I'm in the process of taking a duck face selfie when Mrs. Matsuda delivers a tall Asian guy to my table. He quirks a manscaped eyebrow at me. I slap my phone facedown on the table and jump to my feet.

"Oh, hey. You must be Jake. I'm Dakota. Of course I'm Dakota. Yeah. Have a seat."

I am so cringe. Worse, Jake's hand still floats in the air. I jump back up and shake it. Across the restaurant, I can see Aurora shaking her head. Jake slides off his leather jacket to reveal a form-skimming, baby blue button-down shirt underneath. He unbuttons the cuffs of his sleeves and rolls them up. A waft of piney scent drifts across the table. Whether it is his cologne or the hair wax in his perfectly styled hair, I'll never know.

Aurora cuts Leo off on his way to our table. "Hi, I'm Aurora, and I'll be your survivor . . . server . . . I'll be your server tonight. Can I get you something to drink?"

Before I can answer, Jake says in a deep, rumbly voice like thunder, "Seltzer water. Do you have Perrier or at least La Croix?"

"No, but we do have Phoenix's best tap water that I can carbonate for ya." Aurora laughs at her joke, but Jake doesn't.

"I'll have ocha," I say.

"Me too then," Jake says.

When you are on a date, eye contact is important. At least, that's what the article I read this afternoon said. But where is the line between paying attention to your date and being weird and awkward? I look into his deep brown eyes for a count of three before flinching and looking away.

"You know a lot about me from my headshot, but I don't know that much about you. Besides what I've seen on TV, of course." Jake puts his left arm on the table. A large, expensive-looking watch encircles his wrist.

I have to wonder if the watch is as much a prop as Nevaeh's designer purse is for me. Because I mean, come on. You can use your phone to tell time like everybody else does. Then again, I let Nevaeh talk me into this purse because, according to them, "You are not a kangaroo, Dakota. Why do you walk around all the time with your pockets filled with crap?"

Before I can answer Jake's question, Aurora reappears with our ocha. "Do you know what you'd like, or do you need a few minutes?"

"A minute," Jake says, though I already decided on miso-katsu while I was still in the parking lot with Dad.

I pretend to look over the menu, which I have memorized. Leo cuts off Aurora so that he can clean the four-top next to our booth. Leo can get a table cleaned and reset in under one minute. I know this because we timed him one day when business was slow. Tonight he is working at snail speed. Eavesdropping much?

"I wonder how authentic this food is." Jake's low voice has a too-cool-for-you vibe. "I mean, I do live two blocks away from Little Tokyo in LA, so my standards are pretty high."

Though Jake can't see it, Leo rolls his eyes. To his credit, Leo keeps the snark out of his voice when he asks, "Do you have a question about something on the menu?"

"Is the chef really Japanese?" Jake says.

"Yes, he immigrated to the US from Nagoya in 1968."

"Is all the sushi locally sourced?"

"No." When Jake looks down his nose at him, Leo adds, "You're in Arizona. We're a landlocked state. If you give me a black light and about ten minutes, I could make you our secret, off-menu scorpion sushi. Fresh and locally sourced. Only the VIPs know about it."

"Scorpion sushi?" Jake says like he is seriously considering it.

I look at Leo, and it takes all of my limited acting skills to keep a straight face. Leo lets the question hang for a beat before he cracks a smile.

"Totally kidding. Plus, the scorpions are hibernating. Our specialty is Nagoya-style miso-katsu. It's like tonkatsu, only with a rich, red miso paste sauce on top of the deep-fried pork cutlet."

"I don't want anything fried." Jake's eyes skim over the menu again. "I'll have a double order of the yakitori chicken—light on the sauce. And no rice for me. Can I have double the salad? With the dressing on the side. And miso soup with extra tofu. I need the extra protein for this new training regimen the movie studio has me on. I have to pack on twenty pounds of muscle in the next six weeks before we start shooting."

I don't know how Leo reads the ridiculous order back with a completely straight face. "And for the lady?"

"She'll have—"

I cut Jake off. "I'll have the miso-katsu meal."

"Any special requests from the chef?" Leo fights unsuccessfully to keep the corner of his mouth from pulling up.

"Nope. As is. I heard the chef has won the Phoenix Phoodie Phestival's Asian Cuisine Award four times in a row. I trust his judgment." I look up at Leo. "Thank you."

As Leo walks off, Jake yells, "I forgot. No pickles either."

I sip my ocha. This is not going well. "If you are filming a movie soon, are you going to be available in late April?"

"Yeah. The director and I are close. He'll let me take a few days off. Being the lead of the movie has its perks."

"Why in the world would you want to take this low-level job then?"

Okay, so that wasn't my Mr. Inside Voice like I thought because Jake flinches.

"It's an indie film. Uncle Dan—I mean, the director—said it could be the next big thing if we can find a good distributor. If we can get it into some of the bigger film festivals that will help."

"Can I be honest with you?" I say, because at the rate we are going, Jake and I aren't going to make it to dessert much less anything else. "You can be real with me. We're auditioning for a guy who looks good on camera—and believe me, you do—but who doesn't take himself too seriously and can have fun even though we are technically working. This party is going to be a complete circus, so I want my date to be chill and fun."

Jake's voice suddenly comes up half an octave. "Can we start again?"

"Yes." I put out my hand. "Hi, I'm Dakota McDonald."

"Jake Yong. Nice to meet you."

Jake holds my hand for a few seconds and looks me deep in the eyes. *Wooooow.* I don't get the electric zap that I feel when I look at Leo, but now there is some kind of chemistry bubbling between us.

Suddenly, I can see us walking into the crowded ballroom, filled with rose-gold balloons. I have on a ridiculous rose-gold dress with yards of tulle and an enormous tiara perched on my perfectly styled updo. Meanwhile, Jake is doing his best impersonation of Prince Charming in a white tux with a rose-gold cummerbund and bow tie. Girls swoon right and left from Jake's perfectly straight, brilliantly white smile. Jake looks at me from under his heavy, dark lashes. His lips brush my cheek when he says . . .

"My agent says this gig pays $5,000 plus travel expenses."

I shake my head to release the sugarcoated fantasy from my brain. "You'll have to talk to Stephanie about that. I'm in charge of auditions."

"You have other guys auditioning?"

"Of course. Like I said. I'm looking for someone I have chemistry with. It doesn't even have to be romantic chemistry. I'm not looking for a boyfriend. It's more like a friend with benefits."

When Jake raises an eyebrow at me, I clarify, "Benefits like you get paid and get to keep the tux."

"I could do that for you."

"We'll see." I sip my tea.

"Did I tell you how beautiful you look tonight?" Jake's hand reaches across the table to take mine.

"Thank you," I say as Jake's thumb gently rubs across the outside of my hand.

Leo clears his throat. I let go of Jake's hand like it's a snake.

"Ohashi o tsukaimasu ka," Leo asks Jake.

"Huh," Jake says.

"Are you going to use chopsticks?" I translate.

"Chopsticks, of course. We are eating Japanese food. It would be a crime to eat it with a fork."

"Two pairs of chopsticks then." Leo doesn't hide his snark this time.

"I'm impressed." Jake nods his head at me. "If you give me a script written in phonetic Japanese, I can do it. Like for anime voice-overs. But now I kind of wish I would've gone to Japanese Saturday School like my mom wanted me to when I was a kid."

"You're part Japanese?" I say.

"Yeah, half Korean, half Japanese. Though I've never been to either country."

"I'm one-quarter Japanese. Unfortunately, the little Japanese I know comes from my high school Japanese class. But I'm working on it."

Jake looks down and snorts in disgust. He puts the tsukemono on what is supposed to be the shōyu plate.

When Leo comes back with our chopsticks, Jake pushes the tsukemono at him. "I said no pickles."

I slide the little plate stacked with a few of Ojiichan's neon-yellow daikon and shriveled green cucumbers toward me. "I'll eat them. I love tsukemono."

"My apologies," Leo says between clenched teeth. "Is everything else to your high standards?"

Jake looks at his meal and then mine. "Hmmm, we could use more tea."

"Yes. Thank you. Itadakimasu," I say.

Leo gives us a curt nod of his head before leaving, which is better than the baka slap he's probably dying to give Jake. I'm also not surprised when it's Aurora who comes back with the tea a few minutes later.

"How's everything over here?" Aurora flashes Jake a flirty smile.

"Everything is wonderful. Thank you," I say.

"It's okay," Jake says, and Aurora's smile dampens.

"Right then." Aurora does an about-face and storms off.

"The movie I'm making with my uncle is really cool. I play the role of a spoiled, arrogant, trust-fund, prep-school boy who will stop at nothing to reach his dreams of becoming a rock star or maybe an A-list actor. We haven't decided yet. It depends on how my guitar lessons go."

"Sounds like a real creative stretch for you."

Not only does Jake completely miss my sarcasm, he actually agrees with me. "Yeah. Uncle Dan says this could be my break-out vehicle. We're going to record an album and everything to go with it. I'm writing all the songs—well, the lyrics at least—for the soundtrack. I find all kinds of inspiration in the everyday world. Like today. I was lying on my bed at the hotel watching dust motes swirl around in the sunlight." Jake chuckles before continuing his monologue. "Finding words to rhyme with 'mote' is a challenge, though. So I decided to . . ."

Ten minutes into Jake's monologue on the existential meaning of dust, I'm ready to poke myself in the eye with a rusty spoon. I almost sob in relief when Aurora appears at our booth again.

"The chef insists that dessert is on the house, since Dakota is a VIP." Aurora tries one more time to save this disaster of a date. "Our special house dessert is ice cream mochi in strawberry, matcha, and vanilla flavors. Which would you like?"

"I don't eat dessert," Jake says. "I have to keep my carbs ultralow if I want to get my abs cut enough in time for my movie."

As I've probably consumed all of Jake's carbs for the month with my dinner alone, I say, "Can I take a rain check?"

"Are you sure?" Aurora knows that I love the matcha-flavored ice cream ones.

"Very. But thank you. We're ready for the check, please."

It's Leo who takes the bill from his mom and brings it over. He looks Jake directly in the eye and holds the bill out to him.

"Will you be paying in cash or with card tonight?"

Jake looks at me. "I thought this . . . Never mind."

When Jake digs for his wallet, I pull the bill out of Leo's hand. "I'm paying tonight."

Well, technically, the production company is, after I bill them. I pull out my credit card and hand it and the bill back to Leo. After Leo returns with my card, Jake watches as I fill in the receipt.

"That's not fifteen percent." Jake points at my math.

"I know. It's thirty." The production company's accountant can presume that I can't do percentages too.

"My, aren't you generous." The way Jake says it doesn't sound like a compliment.

"Food service is a hard job." I sign my name with a flourish.

As we pass Mrs. Matsuda on the way out the front door of the now-empty restaurant, I dip my head and thank her for the meal. "Gochisōsama deshita."

Jake and I stand outside in silence for an eternity before his Uber arrives. "Do you want to share the ride? I'm happy to take you home first."

"My car will be here any minute." And by "my car," I mean my dad and his brand-new Ford pickup truck. "You can send Stephanie, our talent coordinator, your Uber receipt and she'll make sure the production company reimburses you."

"Great. I will."

I am so done with this guy. "Thanks for coming out tonight. I have some more auditions to do, but Stephanie will get back to you soon."

"Awesome." Jake takes my icy hands in his equally icy hands. "I feel like we had a connection in there."

I'm not sure which date he was on, but I disagree. "You're really . . . something."

"You are too."

When Jake leans in to kiss me, my hand instinctively shoots out. He lets out a little *oof* when the heel of my palm collides with his chest.

"Too early?" Jake says.

"Way too early."

"Okay then. Next time. They made me the lead in the movie for a reason, you know."

"Yeah, I'm sure they did." I open the car door for him. "Night."

I fight the urge to shove Jake inside like I'm taking him down to the police station for crimes against polite society.

"Talk to you soon, beautiful." Jake puts his hand up to his ear and mimes, "Call me."

I slam the door closed. Jake gives me a flirty wave as they pull away.

"Thaaaaank yooooou!" I yell as they drive away.

Ugh. I stomp through the parking lot and throw open the door of the restaurant. Aurora's cackles echo through the empty restaurant.

Aurora puts her hand on a table for stability because she is laughing so hard. "Baka dayo!"

"Aurora!" Mrs. Matsuda says, though I agree that Jake's an idiot.

"C'mon, Mom, this guy is definitely on the Top Ten list for Jerkiest Customers Ever," Aurora says as Leo joins us. "And when he leaned in for the good-night kiss and Koty's like, 'Naaaaw, dude.'" Aurora imitates me protecting my personal space and snort-laughs. "I thought I was going to pee my pants."

"We're not going to let you pay for tonight, Dakota." Mrs. Matsuda opens up the cash register.

"Yes, you are, because the show is reimbursing me."

"Not necessary, but thank you." Mrs. Matsuda holds out an

equal number of bills in each hand for her kids. Aurora immediately snatches her tip, but Leo looks at the money.

"You earned it." I take the money from Mrs. Matsuda and hand it to Leo. "Can I take Ojiichan up on his offer of the matcha ice cream mochi now? I wanted dessert, but that would have meant more monologues on dust motes and ketogenic diets and other topics that make me want to bang my head on the table."

This pulls a smile out of Leo. "Let me bus these last two tables and take the trash out. Then I'll join you for dessert."

I help Leo bus the tables so that we can get to the ice cream part faster. I let him do the garbage solo. We're close. But not that close.

"I want to hear all about this later, Koty." Aurora sprints through the restaurant while putting on her coat. "But Jayden is here."

Mrs. Matsuda pokes her head out the kitchen door and yells, "You still have an eleven o'clock curfew, Aurora!"

"What? Eleven thirty, Mom? Thanks! Got it. See you at home." Aurora ducks out the front door before her mom can correct her.

I slide into my favorite booth and take a deep breath. What a night. A second later, Leo comes out of the kitchen.

"Compliments of the chef." Leo presents the ball of matcha-flavored ice cream wrapped in a thin layer of pounded sweet rice, like he's handing me a bouquet of long-stemmed roses. "We here at Matsuda like to take care of our VIPs. Even when they bring in dates who apparently missed the day they taught basic manners in kindergarten."

"Seriously. I mean there is oblivious, and then there is straight-up rude. Please tell me that non-reality-TV dates don't look like that." I take a huge bite. The slightly bitter matcha blends with the sweetness of the soft mochi covering.

"Mine definitely haven't." Leo bites into his strawberry ice cream mochi.

Part of me can't bear to hear about Leo's dates. Part of me is dying to know, and this might be my only chance to ask without it being too weird.

"Okay, enlighten me on what a *real* date might look like then."

"First of all, I would have picked you up at your house."

"That's a nope for me. I don't want strangers knowing where I live."

"A thirty-second Google search answers that question," Leo says, and I flinch. He knows we have security cameras and alarm systems on our build and the house for a reason. "Okay, presume that I passed the 'I'm not a serial killer' test in a public setting first, and you are okay with me coming to your house. I would show up with flowers. Is that too much?"

"Depends on what kind of flowers they are."

"Since this is a fantasy situation, let's say tulips because roses might be too presumptuous." Leo crams the rest of his mochi in his mouth and licks his fingers. "Or if you are going with the realistic I-work-for-tips-only version, whatever is on sale in the flower section at Walmart."

"I like flowers, but I think it's a little old-fashioned to expect them. A single flower hand cut from your mom's garden would have the same effect on me as a huge bouquet."

But only if you *don't* sign it: *Breathlessly, Jake.*

"Really?" Leo mimes taking notes. "Steal flower from Mom's garden for Lindsay."

I hope Leo can't see my cringe. I asked for this, after all. "Okay, flower accepted. Now what?"

"Fantasy version: I pick you up in my dope, cherry-red Ford Mustang convertible. Reality version: I pick you up in my family's minivan. I would spray the van with Febreze and remove any old protein bar wrappers from underneath the seats prior to the date, though."

"If I just spent thirty minutes obsessing over my hair, I wouldn't want to ride in your convertible. At least not without a heads-up first. That said, if the date goes well and you want to go to Lookout Mountain Park to star-gaze, a convertible would be the better pick for a romantic moment." I can't help myself. I have to go there.

"Naw, trust me, the minivan is a much better choice." Leo waggles his eyebrows at me.

"Can we not?"

"You brought it up."

"Okay, back up to the beginning of the date. We get into a nice, sensible, but still sporty hardtop car and go . . ."

"Fantasy date: Anywhere I'd have to Google the pronunciations of the food on the menu before we got there. Reality date: Here. Again, the works-for-tips problem."

"Dude, the last time I ate at one of those types of restaurants, I asked my parents to stop at Sonic for a corn dog on the way home. Again, outdated ideas. Plus, it sounds like a place Jake Yong would take me to in an attempt to impress me. I'd come here."

Leo sits back in the booth. "Even if there were other paparazzi-free areas available to you?"

"Yeah. Sure, I want to dine local and support the people I love, but for real, Ojiichan's food is ichiban, the best. Even if I could eat anywhere I wanted, I would still use this place as my litmus test. Like, if you don't love miso-katsu and ice cream mochi as much as I do, then there is no way we're going to make it to a second date."

"Agreed. Lucky for me, Lindsay likes both." A sweet smile pulls at the corners of Leo's mouth.

The look stabs me in the chest. Leo deserves to be happy, and Lindsay does too, but why does it have to hurt so much? I clear my throat and try to be a better best friend.

"You know what would melt my heart, and I bet Lindsay's too?" I say. Leo sits up straight. "Cooking for her. Gotta love a man who cooks."

"Speaking of outdated ideas. If I said I loved a girl who could cook, you would be all over me about the patriarchy—besides, all the men in my family cook. We own a restaurant. Duh."

"Okay, true. It's a double standard that needs to go. So, let's just say I would be impressed by anyone who cooked for me. And if it were a person I had a romantic interest in, they would get bonus points."

"Agreed. And the good thing is that I can do this, and it wouldn't cost me a cent. What should I make? Something impressive but easy. My cooking repertoire is still pretty small."

"Depends. Will there be kissing involved later? If so, then curry and rice or anything that has a lot of green onions or garlic in it would be a bad choice."

"Lots of kissing at Lookout Mountain Park while stargazing and—"

"TMI." I wave my hands next to my head to wipe away the image in my brain.

"What do you think about going to the Japanese Friendship Garden downtown? On a free First Friday Night, of course. Romantic or Try Hard?"

"Romantic, especially if it is close to Otsukimi. You could bring some ocha. Maybe have Sasha make you some moon- or rabbit-themed manju since it is the Moon-Viewing Festival. You could bring a blanket and have a small picnic beside the koi pond. Talk about romantic. I'd be like, *bam.* I'm dead. RIP."

Leo's laugh echoes around the empty restaurant. "Can you plan all my dates from now on? In fact, Lindsay would probably rather date you than me. Not only do you have great ideas, but you also have the time and money to pull them off."

"Yeah, I'm not out to steal your girl."

A pained look wipes away Leo's smile. He leans in and lowers his voice. "Aurora is right. How are we ever expected to have any kind of social life or significant other when our dating time is all of thirty minutes—an hour if the restaurant is having a bad night—before curfew on weekends? It's not fair."

One good thing about your moms being BFFs is that curfew rules become negotiable. Just as the restaurant is a safe zone for me, my house is a safe zone for Leo. A place for him to relax and be a typical teen, instead of just a cog in the family machine.

"After Aurora moves as far away from us as she possibly can next fall, guess whose social life is going to take an even bigger hit?" Leo runs a hand through his wavy hair and lets out a frustrated sigh. "I'm afraid I'm going to lose Lindsay before we even have a fighting chance. Ojiichan is on me all the time about being on my phone instead of paying attention to the customers. Can't see her. Can't talk to her. Can't text her. Full boyfriend fail."

Leo leans over and gently bangs his head on the table a few times before tucking his arms under his chin like a pillow. He mumbles into the table, "I'm so tired."

I can't stop myself. I reach across the table to stroke Leo's hair. He's let the top part grow out since the summer, and now his dark brown hair has natural waves. Leo looks up at me. My heart threatens to exit stage left. Of all the boys in the world, why does my heart continue to want the one I can't have?

I pull my hand away. "I like your hair longer."

"Ojiichan doesn't. He keeps threatening to cut my hair himself."

"Just clean up the bottom, but leave the top longer." I rake my fingers through his hair to pull some of the waves forward and to the side. "Aw, yeah. Give 'em The Full Dimple Smile and, *boom*, bigger tips."

Leo wraps his fingers around my wrist. "You're making things weird, Koty."

"I am not." Okay, I am. I pull my wrist away from his grasp and sit back. "I'm giving you fashion advice. And you're giving me dating advice since you're the expert."

"Yeah, right. Speaking of dating, I promised Lindsay I would FaceTime her after work." Leo digs out his phone.

"Yeah. Sure. Sorry. Dad should be here any minute. I'll wait outside and give you some privacy."

"No, it's fine. Wait inside the front door." Leo slides out of the booth. He heads to the opposite side of the restaurant, taking my heart with him. He's on his phone with Lindsay before I even get my coat on. My heart cracks a little more when I hear him say, "Hey, babe."

Dad flashes his headlights from the parking lot. I take a deep breath, push my feelings down, and poke my head into the kitchen. Ojiichan puts away the food while Mrs. Matsuda does the accounting for the day. Mr. Matsuda dries the last of tonight's hundreds of dishes.

"My dad is here," I say. "Thanks again for tonight."

Mrs. Matsuda slides off her purple reading glasses. "Anytime, honey. You and Doug be careful going home."

"Oyasuminasai, Ojiichan," I say.

"Hai, hai." He and Mr. Matsuda both give me a short wave.

As I travel across the darkened restaurant, I hear Leo's whispers. I don't want to interrupt him on his version of a date. I unlock the front door and let myself out.

"So, how did the date-slash-audition go?" Dad says when I slide into the pickup. I give him a look. "That good, huh? Okay, back to the drawing board. Besides, it's not like this was a real date. We'll find the perfect person, don't worry."

I know who the perfect person is. He's currently leaning out the front door of his parents' restaurant and waving at me.

"Yeah, maybe," I say.

Chapter

14

Though one would argue I should be studying for finals, which start on Friday, instead, I spend my rare free afternoon obsessing over my upcoming second date. I'm texting Nevaeh my twentieth or thirtieth wardrobe choice when Stephanie taps on my open bedroom door.

"Hey, kiddo, I have some bad news." Stephanie pushes over the heaping pile of clothes on my bed and sits down. "Date Number Two canceled."

"Why?" I smooth the fitted sweater dress over my curves.

"Because he got picked up yesterday by Warner Brothers for a new action hero show for kids. He flies out to New Zealand to start filming right after the holidays."

"Aww, Tyson genuinely seemed like a nice guy. At least from his reel and the few texts we've exchanged." Granted, everybody fronts on social media, but now all the red flags I missed on Jake Yong's page are suddenly crystal clear. Live and learn.

"Oh wait, it gets better . . . or worse. Potential Date Number Three is off the list too." Stephanie digs her hand through the clothing pile until she finds the perfect jade-colored jacket to layer over the top of the dress. "He was caught shoplifting last weekend. For the third time. Yep, don't need *that* in the tabloids. So, I had an idea. How do you feel about somebody local but from a different school?"

"Nope."

"Hear me out. Alex is a friend of my niece's. He was at her birthday party last weekend. Polite. Clean cut. Good student. Talented baseball player. Naturally funny. Just turned eighteen, but still a senior. Not a professional actor. Not even a hobby actor. Would you be interested in me setting something up with him?"

"I don't know." I flop down next to Stephanie. "At least with the actors, they know what they are getting into. It seems less icky."

"It's not icky. Most high school seniors I know would jump at the chance to earn an easy $5,000 to go toward their college funds. Do a test date. If Alex passes muster, we'll see if Phil will do a screen test on him."

"Is he cute?"

"Since I am old enough to be his mother, I will say, yes, Alex is conventionally attractive."

I stand up and survey my outfit. Nevaeh would wear this outfit on a date without blinking an eye. Probably with wings. But maybe I could wear it too, only with some cute boots and the jade-colored jacket. Maybe I could give this mystery guy a chance. Surely he couldn't be any worse than Jake Yong.

"Okay. I'll do it."

"Awesome. I'll see if Alex is available sometime over winter break and get back to you."

Chapter

15

The calendar might say it's December 23, but here in the McDonalds' Alternate Universe, Dad and I are wearing short-sleeved T-shirts because it's April. It doesn't snow in Phoenix, but we've got the portable heaters running full-tilt in the build, at least until it's time to film.

"Last shot, folks." Phil takes a chug of coffee, his sixth cup of the day. "Then, we'll call it a wrap for this year and take a long, much-needed break."

I don't know why Phil specifically looks at me during "much needed." So we had a *spirited discussion* this morning about his latest ratings-booster idea that I should arrive at my birthday party in a horse-drawn carriage shaped like a pumpkin. What the actual Phil?! No. Just. No.

"We need everybody to settle," Phil says.

Phil's PA cuts the heaters off. I drop my jacket into Stephanie's outstretched arms. Mom takes her mark while crew members hand Dad and me our matching cordless drills.

"When you're ready." Phil nods at Mom.

"While Doug and Dakota finish installing the chandelier in the dining room," Mom says while walking in front of the stepladder I'm straddling, "I have the fun job of stocking our 1930s kitchen. What a lot of people don't know is that this now-suburbanized area of Phoenix was once mostly farmland. Akagi House—back when it was still the Jansens' stately ranch home in the early 1900s— once sat on 140 acres of alfalfa. Danish immigrants like the Jansens weren't the only ones to come to this area to farm, though."

Dad and I pretend to install the chandelier until Mom is in the kitchen, and we are out of the camera's shot. I climb back down the ladder and quietly peek in the door to see Mom go full-on History Nerd for the folks watching at home.

"There was a small community of Japanese Americans and their Japanese immigrant parents farming in this area too, including my grandfather who started his journey from Hokkaido in 1900 and eventually settled in Arizona in 1915," Mom continues one of the mini-history lessons that she's known for. "My Japanese grandparents would've never been able to afford or legally own such a grand house like this. That's why we chose to call this rebuild Akagi House instead of Jansen House in honor of *all* the immigrants who came to Phoenix in search of the American Dream."

Jordan the Camera Op swoops in for a close-up of the hand-refurbished kitchen table and the period-specific antique vase Mom discovered recently at an estate sale. Mom pulls one of the purple tulips out of the vase as Jordan opens back up to the full shot.

"One thing that would've been in our 1930s Phoenix home: flowers. Obaasan Akagi, my maternal grandmother, wasn't the only one taking advantage of Phoenix's mild winters for gardening. The Nakagawa Flower Farm on Baseline Road near South Mountain took off after World War II, despite the anti-Japanese sentiment still present in this area. The acres upon acres of flowers were once a popular tourist stop. The flower fields are history now—and the land made into single-family homes—but we are going to keep fresh flowers in Akagi House to honor the Nakagawas' entrepreneurial spirit even in the face of adversity. Stay tuned. Next week, I head slightly northwest to Glendale to find another staple of our 1930s Phoenix home: strawberries." Mom picks a strawberry from the tray a PA is holding off-screen and holds it up in front of her. "Next time, on *If These Walls Could Talk*."

Mom takes a bite out of the perfect specimen of a strawberry and chews until Phil yells, "And cut."

Mom puts the strawberry back on the plate. Now that Mom is done filming, Dad and I can finish installing the chandelier for real.

"Ready?" Dad says, not to me, but to the PA whose actual job description is: the guy who breaks Dakota's fall if she loses her balance on the ladder or falls off the scaffolding. On days when things get boring, I wobble on the ladder to make sure he's still awake.

"Yes, Mr. McDonald." Toby, aka Dakota's spotter, grabs the base of my ladder as I climb back up it.

"Cut power," Dad says. All the lights except the one running on the generator go out. "Make sure you use extra safety precautions when doing electrical work, Dakota."

I flip my safety glasses down. Toby hands the cordless drill with the Phillips-head bit up to me. Though we filmed the setup multiple times already, the lighting wouldn't be good enough for us to install it in real time.

"Gotcha, Santa." I push the chandelier's electrical wires to the side so Dad can screw in his part.

Dad talks me through hooking up the electricity and finishing the install. He talks to me the same way whether cameras are rolling are not. Dad tugs on the chandelier to test its stability before turning the power back on. I wobble on the ladder for real with the amount of wattage suddenly in my face.

"Now for a little TV magic," Dad says to me before yelling over his shoulder. "We're ready, Phil."

We film it in two sections, but it will look seamless to viewers.

First, a close-up on Mom at the chandelier's light switch. "Ready, Doug?"

Then, a medium shot of Dad and me still on our ladders—with Toby out of view, of course—as we pretend to have just finished installing the chandelier.

"Let there be light!" Dad says with an arm flourish.

We pretend to be surprised when the chandelier lights up perfectly. Viewers get another bingo space because Dad says, "Let there be light!" every time he installs a light fixture of any kind. It's been twenty years since he first made the-joke-that-refuses-to-die, and yet Phil doesn't try to change him. Maybe because it's one of the many Dougisms printed on T-shirts and sold on the HGTV website.

"Cut!" Phil says. "That's a wrap. Enjoy your vacation, everyone. See you back here on January eleventh bright and early."

"Hey, Dakota, can you come over here?" Stephanie yells across the set. I notice a tall, tan guy standing behind her.

Toby hands my cordless drill off to someone else on the crew so he can spot my descent down the ladder. I tip my safety glasses up on my head like sunglasses and smooth out the sides of my hair. I wish I could double-check that the massive zit on my chin is still adequately covered with makeup, but there's no time. Stephanie holds out my jacket for me to slide on.

"You must be Alex Santos," I say to the guy standing behind Stephanie. Her assessment was correct. Alex is conventionally attractive. Maybe not as polished and Instagram perfect as Jake Yong, but he definitely has a more relatable vibe.

"I am. Ms. Stephanie has told me a lot about you. But still . . ." Alex nods at my ladder. "I'm impressed."

Alex immediately loses a point.

"Ms. Stephanie says that you paint too. Now I don't want you to see my car. You'll be able to see all my painting sins that others can't see."

Okay, he gets the point back.

"You like to paint cars?"

"Just my car. It started out of necessity after a slight mishap in the school parking lot. The dumpster was fine. The back panel of my Toyota . . . not so fine."

Stephanie gives him a hard look. "And my sister lets Vanessa ride in the car with you?"

"It was my first and only accident, I swear, Ms. Stephanie. I'm vain and didn't want to drive around with a dent in my car. The upside: I'm pretty good at car painting now. Though that's because it took me a dozen tries and a hundred hours on YouTube to figure out how to do it. If I knew Ms. Stephanie worked on your show, I would have hit her up for the connection a long time ago. Like, *before* I tried to fix the problem with spray paint."

"Spray paint?" I've never attempted painting a car, but even I know that's not going to work.

"Like I said, now I'm afraid to show you my car. Can I deflect by saying Ms. Stephanie showed me the booth you built for your school's Homecoming Carnival? That was lit."

"Since we're done shooting, I'm going to duck out. I will follow up with you later, Dakota, before I leave." Stephanie pulls a pair of safety glasses out of the Magic Handbag and hands them to Alex. "I had Alex come in boots, just in case you wanted to show him your workshop *or something*."

"This isn't the workshop?" Alex looks toward the back of the build.

"Sorta. Watch your step." I lead Alex over the tons of cables littering the build's floor toward the front door. "This one is for the show. Our personal one is in the backyard."

We take the shortcut to my backyard and walk over to the small building at the back. Since I was ten years old, the front corner of Dad's cluttered home workshop has been my space. Mom even made me a sign: DAKOTA'S FAB LAB. My bedroom might be one step up from a disaster zone most days, but the Fab Lab is an oasis of cleanliness and orderliness in the rest of Dad's borderline hoarder zone.

"Tah dah." I pull the old bedsheet off the project I've been working on when I'm not busy with my videos or feeling the gaping hole of not having Leo around like the good ole days.

"It's. Something." Alex nods his head at the elaborate dollhouse mansion that I'm building by hand.

"It's a custom build for someone else." It will eventually go to the Raising Hope Women and Children's Shelter across town, but The Network won't let me share that piece of information yet. Again, it started as a simple assignment for Mr. Udall's class and then snowballed into something much bigger. Stephanie even talked The Network into paying for all the high-end materials since I will eventually showcase the project on *DIY with Dakota*.

"Oh, okay." Alex sounds relieved.

"My mom built me a ridiculous dollhouse when I was five. I thought the . . . client's kids would like a similar one."

Alex picks up the handmade bed I made yesterday and rotates it. "If you need someone to come do a test run for you, let me know. My little cousins would lose their minds over this."

Mom reminds me weekly—sometimes daily, when the trolls are particularly nasty—not to base my worth on other peoples' reactions to my work. Still, I let Alex's words expand in my chest.

"Thanks."

Alex gasps and points at my other recent projects. "These are all your designs?"

"Yeah. I've been playing around with a couple of different things with varying results." I lead Alex to the painting section of the Fab Lab. "Doing the nails for Nevaeh was the hardest. But the skateboard was pretty easy. I still need to seal it before I can ride it again."

"You skateboard too?"

"Yeah. I'm not very good at it—there's a reason why I usually wear pants—but I'm getting better."

Alex looks at me. The corners of his mouth pull up into a smile. "Ms. Stephanie wasn't exaggerating. You are cool."

Again, my worth is not based on what others think of me, but the positive attention is nice. Especially after some troll ripped my last video, commenting that my voice was "so annoying that HGTV should hire me a voice coach."

I decide to cut to the chase. "Would you like to go out on Saturday night for dinner? My treat."

Alex startles. "You don't have to pay for me, but yeah, I'd love to. Could we push it back a little though? I'm going to Tucson for Christmas. Woo! I bet you are going somewhere awesome like Paris or the Bahamas."

"Nah." Though I have visited both of those in the past. "We're going to be homebodies this year."

"How about New Year's Day?"

"That day, I have plans. How about the Saturday after New

Year's at seven thirty p.m. at Matsuda? I hope you like authentic Japanese food."

Alex pulls out his phone and repeats back the details as he adds it to his calendar. "I can't promise I'll pronounce it correctly, but I like trying new things."

My phone pings.

DAD
It's my turn to make dinner. So I ordered it. Will be here shortly.

"I've got to go." I wave my phone in Alex's direction without elaborating. "But I'd like to see your car."

"Promise not to judge me?" Alex says as we head out of the workshop.

"I think anybody who has the guts to try something new deserves a little grace." I lock up the workshop and slide my safety glasses off. Alex hands his safety glasses back to me. "There are plenty of people who have never held a hammer, or in your case a paint gun, who are happy to point out everything you are doing wrong. It happens to me all the time, so I would be the last person to do that to you."

I shiver as a cold wind—well, at least by Phoenix standards—whooshes through my backyard. Alex pulls the sleeves down on his Desert Bloom High School sweatshirt with the giant burgundy-and-gold scorpion underneath the letters. I gasp when I finally see Alex's car parked on the street behind Phil's trailer.

Alex bites his bottom lip. "It's that bad?"

"What? No." I walk around the outside of Alex's car. When he said Toyota, I thought he meant your standard, four-door Old Man–mobile. This is not that car.

"It's as old as I am and has over one hundred thousand miles on it, but I kinda love my Celica. Toyota doesn't make them anymore, which added to the fun of trying to fix it. Lucky for me, it was the body that needed fixing and not the engine or something."

I do a second circle around the silver car with the spoiler on the back. "I can't tell which side you redid."

Alex hams wiping his brow. "Whew."

I look Alex over one more time. A tiny spark arcs between us, despite my barriers being fully up. I nod. "You passed the test."

"Awesome. I look forward to seeing you the Saturday after New Year's, then."

"Me too." Yep, he's miles ahead of Jake Yong at this point.

"Can I pick you up, or would you prefer to meet there?"

As I feel my chest expand instead of contract, I decide to take a chance. "You can pick me up here. Thanks."

"Will do."

Alex slides into his silver car and fires it up. He rolls down the passenger side window and gestures for me to come closer.

"So my mom doesn't kill me, would you give something to Ms. Stephanie for me since I forgot earlier?" he says, and I lean in to accept a potted mini rosebush. "Please tell her that Mom says thanks and that she's bringing Derek to Ms. Stephanie's New Year's Eve party. Yeah, that feeling when your divorced mom starts dating again. Awkward. I have to give Ms. Stephanie props for her matchmaking skills though. Derek is still better than any of the other guys from the dating apps Mom's tried."

I step back from the car wondering if Stephanie is secretly matchmaking here too. I guess there's only one way to find out. "See you soon, Alex."

Alex slides on his stylish shades and cranks up the music on his mediocre sound system. When his car pulls away, I notice the Matsudas' van peeking from behind the giant dumpster filled with old flooring currently sitting in our driveway. Leo skillfully maneuvers the family van into the narrow spot between Phil's trailer and the dumpster.

Leo slides out of the van with a confused look on his face. He holds up an insulated bag and says, "Dinner is served."

"You guys are doing door-to-door service now?"

"No. I was headed this way anyway, so I offered to deliver to our best customers." Leo tips his head at my rosebush. "You want me to carry this in for you since your hands are full?"

"Sure. Thanks." Part of me feels obligated to explain the flowers. Part of me wants to let Leo wonder.

I don't say a word as Leo follows me into the house. Leo silently unloads the takeout boxes from the insulated bag onto our kitchen counter before he cracks.

"So, who's the rose guy with the dope car?"

"Alex." I walk the rosebush into Mom's office. I leave it and the note attached to it on Stephanie's table.

When I come back into the kitchen, Leo gestures for me to continue. "Aaaaannd."

"He's a friend of Stephanie's niece." I pull two bottles of root beer out of the refrigerator, open them, and hand one to Leo. "We're going on a date during winter break."

"Oh wow. That was fast." Leo collapses on one of the barstools at our kitchen island in fake shock. "Sniff. Our little Koty is all grown up and going on a date."

"Shut up." I take a gulp of root beer. "We're coming to the restaurant for our date, by the way."

"Awesome. Hold up, is this an audition or a real date?"

"Honestly? I'm not sure. If the date goes well, Stephanie is going to see if Phil will do some screen tests with Alex after the crew comes back from vacation."

"I'm confused. So is Alex, like, genuinely interested in you?"

I kick the leg of Leo's stool. Root beer dribbles down his chin.

"Hey!" Leo wipes his chin and checks to make sure he didn't get soda on his white button-down shirt. "I'm not implying that you aren't dateable."

"Pretty sure you did."

"No, I just know that you are very careful about who you let into your bubble. This Alex guy must be something, based on the smile that was on your face when he was telling you bye."

"Stalker much?"

Leo kicks the leg of my barstool. "I was right there. I couldn't *not* see it."

"I agreed to let him pick me up here instead of meeting me at the restaurant."

"Wow. First, he's handing you flowers. Now, he's picking you up at your house. Next thing you know, you two will be at Lookout Mountain Park stargazing and . . ." Leo winces. "I'm making things weird, aren't I?"

"Yes."

Leo drains the rest of his root beer and lets out a burp. "Sorry. Gotta go. I talked my parents into giving me the night off for a change. Poor Aurora. Hashtag SorryNotSorry."

My heart soars. "In that case, you should stay. You know my dad always orders enough food for ten people. We can play video games or watch a movie or something since finals are over."

Leo drops his eyes. "Raincheck? I'm going to Lindsay's to watch a movie."

My heart plummets. "Oh. Okay. What movie?"

"Don't know. Don't care."

"Have fun, and don't do anything that I wouldn't do."

"Yeah, definitely can't promise that."

"TMI. Seriously."

It hurts my feelings, because Leo knows why I keep people at a distance—even the well-meaning fans who want to take a selfie with me or hug me.

"For the record, I'm working on my trust issues," I say. "I just move slower than most people, including you, apparently."

"And you should." Leo puts his hand on my shoulder. "Take your time. Don't rush into anything, Koty. Listen to your gut. If it doesn't feel good, don't do it. And I mean that for every stage from holding hands to kissing to . . ."

"And we're done here." I press the insulated bag into his chest. "Go have fun with Lindsay."

"While I still can," Leo grumbles while following me through the hallway to the front door.

"You couldn't get your parents to budge on the New Year's thing?" I don't want to do our annual McDonald-Matsuda New Year celebration if Leo is going to be up in Flagstaff on a romantic skiing vacation with Lindsay and her family.

"Nope." Leo punches the insulated bag a few times. "I had Mom turned to the Dark Side and Dad too almost, but Ojiichan wouldn't budge. *I'm almost seventy years old. I don't know how many more New Year celebrations I'll have with my family* . . . blah blah blah. Now we're all stuck at home doing the same old thing. Just like every other boring year."

My heart crashes into the earth, but Leo is oblivious.

"You're still coming over, right?" Leo throws an arm around my shoulder. "To save the night from completely sucking?"

"Well, I'm no Lindsay."

"That's okay. We'll have a *Kitsune Mask* marathon or something to make the night fun."

"Sure," I say.

"Ja mata ne," Leo says when we get to the front door.

"Later."

I close the front door behind Leo and rest my forehead against the cool wood.

"Honey?" Mom says from behind me.

I wrap my arms around Mom and say into her shoulder, "Please tell me this stage of life gets easier?"

"It will." Mom squeezes me in a bear hug. "Leo's right though. You do things on your terms, okay? If you need a little longer than average to build up a level of trust with someone, that's okay."

"I second that," Stephanie says on her way from the downstairs bathroom to Mom's office. "One step at a time."

I think about the tiny spark that I felt with Alex. Can we fan it into a flame? Will it ever burn out the deep-rooted feelings I have for Leo?

"One step at a time," I say.

Chapter

16

New Year's Day is the one day a year that Matsuda is officially closed. While most other restaurants in Phoenix are hopping, Ojiichan insists that the Matsudas honor their family's roots and traditions, whether his grandkids are on board with it or not. And this year, they're not. Early New Year's morning, Leo sends me a gif of himself wearing a coat and tie. A black cloud gif rains on his head.

LEO
Kill me now.

"Akemashite omedetō gozaimasu!" I greet Ojiichan with a *Happy New Year* when he opens the door later that afternoon.

Ojiichan pats the top of my head and says a lot of things back to me, but all my Japanese II brain can understand is Happy New Year. Though Mom and Mrs. Matsuda hug each other all the time, Mom gives Ojiichan a deep bow and the greeting her grandmother taught her when her mixed family used to go to the Akagi grandparents' home for O-Shōgatsu. Dad greets Ojiichan with his usual enthusiastic handshake.

After we all swap our shoes for guest slippers, we follow Ojiichan into the Matsudas' immaculate house, festively decorated for the holidays with bamboo, pine, and kagami mochi—two white rice cakes stacked on top of each other with a mandarin orange on top. I started calling it "Leo's Snowman" somewhere around first grade and it stuck.

During Season 11, Episode 12: "A Very Koty Christmas," seven-year-old me begged the department store Santa on camera not to forget Leo's house *again*. I told him that Leo was always good and that it was *my* idea to use "Mommy's special markers"—aka Sharpies—to draw designs on ourselves. We didn't know that those kinds of markers take a long time to wash off your skin. Mom— and a good portion of our viewers based on the emails—burst into tears and then gave me a quick lesson off camera about how not everybody celebrates the same. And also a reminder not to give Leo any more Sharpie mustaches in the future. Santa still didn't visit the Matsudas on Christmas Eve, but he did start delivering extra presents to my house that were never on my list. I had a complete meltdown years later when I found out that not only did Leo know about the "Santa Game" my family played, but he was Head Elf in Charge to Dad's Santa by shopping for some of those presents. I also learned that Leo's ability to both act and keep a secret are light-years ahead of mine.

As we come into their kitchen, Mrs. Matsuda pushes mute on the annual Kōhaku TV show from Japan that they record, since Matsuda is open all day New Year's Eve. Things must be bad. Leo's phone is more interesting to him than all the cute idol-group girls singing on TV. Ojiichan says something in Japanese that is hard and loud. In a synchronization that would make AKB48—still dancing away on TV—proud, the three Matsuda siblings sigh, put their phones on the coffee table, and say an unenthusiastic "Akemashite omedetō gozaimasu."

"You're not wearing your kimono this year, Jen." Mom hugs Mrs. Matsuda.

"We decided . . . not to this year." Mrs. Matsuda gives Mom an exasperated look that is half eye roll, half lip curl.

"Well, you all looked lovely at the temple this morning in your mom's Facebook post," Mom says.

"Smoke and mirrors," Aurora grumbles from the couch.

Aurora wears a University of New Hampshire sweatshirt over her black yoga pants, and her hair is pulled into a sloppy bun. Leo has his own passive-aggressive fashion going on. He still has on khaki pants, but has untucked and unbuttoned his dress shirt until his *Kitsune Mask* T-shirt underneath shows. Only Sasha has on her original Buddhist temple outfit, a fashionable polka-dotted dress, with her hair in a bun.

"There's my favorite trio!" As usual, Dad does not read the room correctly and plows forward. He plops down on the sectional between the scowling Matsuda siblings and grabs Sasha and Leo in a double-armed hug. "So proud of you kids. Sasha killing it at pastry school, especially with her manju-making. And Aurora being accepted into UNH and getting ready to start a whole new life this fall. And of course, Leo, our culinary entrepreneur preparing to take over the family empire."

Mom and Mrs. Matsuda share an eye-roll-lip-curl look of exasperation. It takes talent to hit everybody's pain points in one breath. Dad makes things slightly better when he digs in his inner coat pocket and comes out with three small, decorative envelopes. "One for you. One for you. And one for you.

"It's not much," Dad says, though I saw the crisp Benjamins that went into each of those envelopes. "But I hope you do something fun with it."

This is one New Year tradition that will never get an argument.

"Thanks, Mr. Doug. You are always so *supportive* of what I do," Sasha says, and the others echo her thanks.

Ojiichan pulls a decorative envelope out of the inner pocket of his blazer. "And I have something for my—"

"Currently favorite granddaughter," Aurora mumbles, and Sasha lets out a snort.

"Taihen datta ne." Ojiichan shakes his head, but the tiniest of smiles pulls at the corners of his mouth.

I accept the envelope decorated with this year's zodiac symbol on it with two hands, a thanks, and a deep bow.

My parents used to not let me accept Ojiichan's otoshidama, the Japanese New Year custom of giving the children in your extended family money in small, decorative envelopes. That is, until Mrs. Matsuda pulled Mom aside one year and begged her to allow me to accept it. She explained that because Ojiichan is estranged from his family back in Japan, and all four of my grandparents are gone, he truly thinks of me as his bonus granddaughter. Dad only agreed if "Uncle Doug"—who *loves* giving gifts—got to reciprocate, without commentary on the amount. So now Ojiichan is happy, Uncle Doug is happy, and all the Matsuda grandkids are happy. Win-win-win.

"Can we eat now?" Aurora says, looking at the time on her phone.

"Somebody's hangry today." Leo joins me in the kitchen area. "But I also second the idea."

Ojiichan places a tower of large, daintily decorated lacquerware boxes on the counter.

"Tah dah!" Leo breaks the tower down into three boxes, each layer filled with little bits of this and that—everything from shrimp with their heads still attached to candied sweet potatoes to pickled lotus to rolled, sweet omelets to other stuff I've never tried. "After helping make osechi for half of the Japanese community in Phoenix the last two days, I'm glad to finally get to eat one of them."

"I can't make a traditional osechi, because I can't find all the special foods, but I hope this is okay." Ojiichan is culturally required to be humble about the culinary masterpiece his family created, and we are culturally required to disagree.

Dad dips into our bag. "I'm planning on bringing a bunch of these babies back from my trip to Alaska this summer and smoking them myself, but until then—voila." Dad pulls the plastic wrap off our decorative platter to reveal smoked salmon slices, high-end crackers, a little bowl of caviar, and an assortment of vegetables.

As the parents continue to gush and thank each other for their food contributions, the oven timer goes off.

"Awwww yeah," Leo says, and my mouth waters at our Matsuda grandkids' New Year tradition.

Mrs. Matsuda shakes her head as Leo pulls two large baking trays out of the oven. They are filled with BBQ chicken wings, tater tots, and mozzarella sticks—all pre-made by someone whose last name is probably not Matsuda.

"You didn't forget your part of the feast, did you, Dakota?" Leo plates up all the deep-fried goodness onto their designated decorative platters.

"Bam." I put the box of chocolate-dipped Oreos next to Leo's plates. I didn't make the Oreos. I didn't make the chocolate dip either. I did, however, dip the Oreos into the chocolate and sprinkle them with fine, white, glittery sprinkles. "You're welcome."

"Life's short. Eat dessert first." Leo picks up one of the Oreos and crams the whole thing in his mouth. As he chews, Leo gives me two thumbs up. "You passed the test, Koty. You are allowed to stay and enjoy the Matsuda-McDonald feast."

I flick Leo in the arm hard, but he just laughs. Everyone receives a plate and a pair of chopsticks.

"Itadakimasu!" we all echo after Ojiichan, who officially starts the race to food coma.

We settle in around the kitchen and the open living room in duos and trios. I pull out my phone and take a quick picture. My plate is filled with lacy lotus roots, a shrimp with its head still attached, mozzarella sticks, tater tots, smoked salmon on bougie crackers, a rectangle block of non-decorative mochi roasted and covered in shōyu, and two dipped Oreos. And now a pile of kuromame.

"Hai, hai," Ojiichan says when Leo refuses his teaspoon of the black soybeans in sweet syrup. "You need them for good health and hard work this year. Our whole family needs good luck this year."

"The beans are delicious," Mrs. Matsuda says loudly. Translation: Eat the sweet beans and make your grandfather happy. *Now.*

We all eat the beans.

∂ ∂ ∂

"Sucka!" Aurora says when the Matsuda siblings finish playing janken—the Japanese version of Rock, Paper, Scissors—and Leo gets stuck washing the dishes. She high-fives Sasha. "Let's go upstairs, Sash."

"Why are you always Cinder-fella?" I nod at the pile of dishes that have to be done before we can start our ever-evolving Top 5 *Kitsune Mask* episodes marathon.

Leo lets out an irritated sigh. "I think the game is rigged."

"Here, I'll wash. You dry." I reach into the Matsuda's pantry and pull Leo's full-sized black apron off the back of the door. When I slide it on, it carries the scent of his soap mixed with whatever oily thing he was cooking the last time he wore it. It still makes me smile. "Glad you're getting a lot of use out of my New Year's present from what? Seventh grade?"

"Eighth. Because that's the fall *Kitsune Mask* came out." Leo digs through a drawer and pulls out a clean dish towel.

"Speaking of gifts." I dig through my family's bag and pull out the stained-glass window decoration of a nine-tailed fox I made for Leo.

"This is so cool!" Leo's dimpled smile immediately disappears. "I thought we weren't exchanging Christmas-slash-New-Year gifts this year so that we could put the money toward you-know-what."

I deflect. "Yeah, we totally aren't. I had such a fun time creating stuff with Mr. Tang that I went a little overboard. Like, everybody will be getting one for their birthday, Valentine's Day, Groundhog Day. . . ."

"Thanks. I love it."

Leo hugs me. It's a side hug instead of his usual frontal hug, but I'll take it. It's probably better this way.

"How about a little tuneage while we work?" Leo says.

"The Leo Mix?" I hold up my phone.

"Did you add Rayne Lee's newest song?"

"Uh, duh," I say, as my phone finds the Matsudas' Bluetooth speaker.

Leo does a goofy shoulder dance to the beginning of "Create Your Spark." Fueled by the dozen or so Oreos he consumed, Leo soon goes full ham. Mrs. Matsuda comes to investigate the thudding sounds coming from the kitchen—also known as Leo's attempt at performing the video's bouncy choreography—but wisely retreats without comment.

We are three-quarters through The Leo Mix and on the last few dishes when Rayne's breakout, slow-jam song "One Last Kiss" comes on. Leo bumps my shoulder as he does the single-single-double bounce pattern like Rayne does in the video. Water flies off the tray I'm rinsing and hits me in the eye.

"Hey!" I flick some suds at Leo in retaliation.

"Come on. You know you want to dance with me." Leo travels backward, never missing a beat in the dance pattern, to throw a used napkin in the trash.

Though I intended to retrieve a forgotten glass off the coffee table, Leo mistakes the drying of my hands as my acceptance of his dance invitation.

One step forward.

Since we're mimicking the choreography, I take Leo's hand like Rayne does to the guy in her video. A squeal rips out of my chest when Leo spins me around in a ballerina-like turn. We continue to dance hand-in-hand through the second verse and chorus until we get to the song's bridge. Leo attempts—and epically fails—to do Rayne's trademark vocal run into the stratosphere.

I lean into Leo until we are forehead-to-sweaty-forehead. We're both breathing hard, but when Leo looks directly into my eyes, blood surges to my face. The four slow snaps that go with this part of the song keep us connected, closer than we've been in a long time. Leo bites his bottom lip. I close my eyes.

Two steps forward.

Leo kisses me. Only it's not on the lips like I'd hoped. Just like Rayne does to the guy in her video, Leo kisses my hand and backs away as he sings along with the final chorus. Though he doesn't have Rayne's Lamborghini to peel out and leave me in the dust, it kind of feels the same anyway.

Instead of ending the song with Rayne's "One last . . . *kiss,*" Leo ends it with "What the . . . ?"

Caught in the motion-sensor lights, we can see Aurora sitting on top of the six-foot wall in their backyard. Aurora cranes her neck to see what's going on in the kitchen. That is, until she loses her balance. Her arms windmill before she falls off the wall and into the oleander bush below. She pops back up a moment later, brushing off her yoga pants. Aurora puts an index finger to her lips at us before turning and climbing back up on the wall. Like a tightrope walker, Aurora's shaky squat turns into a stand, with her arms out for balance. She takes a few steps down the wall before making a sharp left. Now, it's Leo's and my turn to crane our necks as Aurora walks like a cat down the communal wall, which divides their neighborhood into two.

"One of these days, Aurora's going to break her neck sneaking out her window like that," Leo says.

"Where's she going that she can't use the front door like a normal person?"

"Ten bucks says she's going to Jayden's house for his family's annual Snowball and Hot Chocolate Party." Leo sighs. "Aurora does get points for persistence and ingenuity. Meanwhile, my dating game is limited to texts, selfies, and one phone call each day. Woo."

"Sorry."

"It's not your fault. Even if you guys hadn't come over, I'd still be stuck here for New Year's instead of up in Flagstaff with Lindsay's family. Ugh! I wish Ojiichan's archaic traditions would just die."

I swoop around Leo to collect the final glass so he can't see the hurt on my face. He noodles around on his phone as I finish the last of the cleanup.

"Finally." I hang the apron back up. "Now we can get our marathon on. Which episode do you want to watch first?"

"Something from season two?" Leo continues to type away on his phone. With an agitated sigh, he looks at his phone one last time before putting it in his back pocket. "Anything that will help me escape this sucktastic reality for a while."

Two steps forward. Forty steps back.

Chapter

17

"How many Frappuccinos did you have today?" Nevaeh says via FaceTime the next day. "Put your phone on a flat surface please, before I upchuck."

"None. But I feel like I had four. How bad are the dark circles under my eyes? I couldn't sleep last night." My brain decided to give me the one-two punch of remembering everything going wrong with Leo, plus a heaping helping of anxiety over my date with Alex tonight. "Wait. What did you do to your hair?"

"Weeeeellll. I attempted an undercut, and it went horribly wrong." Nevaeh holds up a handful of rainbow-hued hair that used to be attached to their head.

"It looks like you cut the tail off a My Little Pony."

The top of Nevaeh's hair is still bleached blond with dark roots and turquoise one-inch tips, but when they pull it into a topknot, I see just how ragged the cut is underneath. I wince. It looks like the time Leo and I decided to give each other haircuts when we were six. Yeah, he looked cute with super short hair. Me with a pixie cut, though? Not so much.

"Tonight of all nights." Nevaeh lets out a frustrated sigh. "What if I shave it all off and start again?"

I tip my head from side to side. "That might be a little too Furiosa, especially if you leave your brows natural."

Tears well up in Nevaeh's violet-contacted eyes.

"Hey, hey, hey. Everything is going to be okay, Nev. Have your stepmom even up the bottom for you a bit, and then leave it alone. If anybody can pull this look off, you can. Remember the whole Sharpie tattoo trend that was popular for a hot second? All thanks to you."

This makes Nevaeh crack a smile. "True. People are used to me being provocative."

"Once the undercut grows out a little bit on the bottom, how about restyling the top part more like Leo's? Your skin tone is different, but your face shape is similar. I think you'd look good with it that way."

Nevaeh bites their bottom lip. "Yeah. Good call. Thanks for talking me down, Koty."

"Anytime, Nev. Now, back to me." I shuffle back a few paces so Nevaeh can see my whole outfit. I turn around in a slow circle. "What do you think?"

"Oh myyyyy," Nevaeh jokes but then immediately walks it back. "Stop scowling. You look great, Koty. But if you're feeling too far out of your comfort zone, then switch to your lower-heeled boots."

I slide off my knee boots and put on the tan ankle boots.

"For the record, you're allowed to push the envelope with your look too," Nevaeh says as they French braid their hair into a dramatic swoop. "And don't let anybody tell you how to dress your body."

"Can you be my stunt double tonight and go on this date for me?"

"No. Because, I have *plans* tonight."

"Spill!"

"Not yet. It might be something. It might be nothing. They're a cosplayer friend of Jax's who goes to the community college. We're getting together tonight as a group. If there's a spark, I'll pursue it. If not, I'll keep waiting until the right person comes into my orbit. Baby steps. You too, okay? We don't have to be as thirsty as Leo and Aurora. We have more at stake than they do and some still-fresh wounds, so we deserve to be a little more cautious with our hearts and the rest of our parts."

"Thanks. Fingers crossed for you tonight too."

"I gotta go. Got to fix *this*." Nevaeh points at the ragged undercut. "Peace."

I look at myself in my long mirror one more time. I put the tall boots back on.

o   o   o

"Irasshaimase!" Mrs. Matsuda says when Alex and I burst through the restaurant door after our mad dash through the rainy parking lot.

"I am so sorry," Alex says, shaking the water off the top of his hair. "I didn't realize my umbrella was completely dry-rotted. I guess that happens when you leave it in your car all summer long in Phoenix."

I shake off the permanently stuck, half-opened umbrella on the mat. "I'm sorry for you. At least I'm not soaked."

"I'll be fine." Water bubbles up through the cloth part of Alex's tennis shoes. At least his leather jacket doubled as a raincoat.

"Your usual spot, Koty?" Mrs. Matsuda says.

I nod.

"After you," Alex says, and lets me pass in front of him.

"How about some hot green tea to warm you both up on this rainy night?" Mrs. Matsuda gives me a look, which makes me wonder how much info she pumped from Mom last night about this date.

"Yes, please." Alex shivers.

I'm shivering too, but that's been happening since well before the rain started. "Thanks."

Out of the corner of my eye, I see Aurora prep a tray with the ocha on it. Leo sees her and walks even faster toward our table with his order tablet out. Aurora cuts him off.

"Hi, I'm Aurora, and I'll be your—"

Aurora's foot hits a wet spot caused by my malfunctioning umbrella. As her foot slips out from underneath her, Leo's hand swoops in to grab the tray of steaming ocha from her. Aurora grabs our table with two hands to steady herself as Leo makes a large arc with the tray. Somehow, the cups magically stay on the tray and the ocha inside them.

"Are you okay?" Alex says to Aurora.

"Nice save," I say to Leo.

"I'm fine," Aurora says as Leo puts the steaming cups in front of us. "You must be Alex."

"Dakota was telling me about you guys on the way over. And you must be Leo. Named after the inventor or the actor?" Alex says.

"The Ninja Turtle," Leo deadpans, and Aurora elbows him in the ribs.

"Ummm, okay. Dakota highly recommended your tonkatsu meal. The miso-katsu, right?"

"Yep, that's what I'm having."

"Me too, then."

"Any special instructions?" Leo says like he's waiting for Alex to be another version of Jake Yong.

"Nope. However you usually make it for Dakota is fine," Alex says.

"We will put that order in for you then." Aurora pushes Leo toward the kitchen. Unfortunately, we can hear Aurora clearly from the other side of the kitchen door. "The Ninja Turtle? Baka dayo! And stop hovering. Give them some space. That guy, though. Yum-my. You go, Koty."

I duck my head and rub my temples, trying not to burst into flames. Meanwhile, Alex stifles his grin by sipping his tea.

"So besides building things, what else do you like to do? For fun, I mean," Alex says.

I don't have that much downtime between school and the show, but I have to come up with something slightly normal-sounding, so I decide on, "Video games."

"Cool. Me too. Which ones?"

Since Lindsay came on the scene, Leo hasn't had much time or interest in playing video games with me anymore. I like video games, but I don't love them enough to play alone.

"This is completely embarrassing, but let me couch this with the fact that my parents won't allow any games where you are shooting another individual. It doesn't even have to be a human. Any kind of weapon pointed at another being is a no-go at my house." I lower my voice and whisper, "*Mario Kart.*"

Alex laughs, but not in a mocking way. "Hey, no shade from me. I like shooter games, but I'm not allowed to play them or other adult games when my little cousins are around, which is a lot. Therefore, *Mario Kart* is my game of choice most days. Because it's either that or *Minecraft.*"

"Now, I feel better about myself." I can feel the walls around me drop a few inches. "Stephanie said that you're a senior. What are you doing after graduation?"

"Not to brag, but I was accepted at all the state schools. All of them have offered me a scholarship to play ball for them. I'm also wait-listed for Duke University in North Carolina. I'm sure Ms. Stephanie has told you all about my family's drama, which sometimes borders on telenovela-level ridiculousness."

"No, not at all."

"Hmmm." Alex sits back in the booth. "Let's leave it at: My parents had a very contentious divorce, and the kids got to decide which parent they wanted to live with. Pretty much every holiday and birthday has been somewhere between Hot Mess and Do-I-Need-to-Call-My-Lawyer since then. Yeah, Duke is my Number One choice right now."

"Wow. I'm sorry."

I get it. I live in a bubble. Yes, my parents fight, but not often and usually over silly things like the correct way to load the dishwasher. And even though Leo's parents aren't as lovey-dovey, touchy-feely as my parents, they have their own way of showing their love for each other.

"What about you? I know you're only a sophomore, but any plans?"

"I might take a gap year." I leave out that I'm not dependent on either scholarships or my parents for when or if I go to college. "Or maybe travel or study abroad or at least go somewhere that isn't Arizona too. But I would be going to expand my horizons, not to run away from my present life."

Open mouth. Insert foot.

My face burns. "I'm sorry. That didn't come out right."

"No, you're right. I do want to escape from my parents. Their drama. I'd love to be Just Alex for a little while."

Alex drops his eyes. He fiddles with the edge of the tray that the shōyu and other spices sit on. I take a chance and put my hand over the top of his. I squeeze it. He looks back up at me.

"You're not the only one. I know a couple of people like that." I look at Aurora as she passes by our table with someone else's order.

"It's nice to know I'm not the only one."

Alex rotates his wrist until our hands are palm to palm. For the first time since my word vomit in the walk-in refrigerator with Leo after the Homecoming Carnival, I wonder if everything is finally going to be okay. That maybe I can have a real relationship, instead of a hormone-fueled misfire with my best friend.

Leo arrives at our table. "Two miso-katsu meals."

I don't move my hand away from Alex's. Leo clears his throat and holds the bowl of miso soup in the air, over its designated spot. I remove my hand from Alex's and place it back in my lap.

When he's done, I look up at Leo and smile. "Itadakimasu."

Leo gives me a head nod in return for my thanks-let's-eat.

"I'm going to attempt to eat with chopsticks, but could I possibly have a fork as a backup?" Alex says.

Leo delivers the fork without comment. We're halfway through our meal when Leo swings by again and interrupts our in-depth discussion about appropriate pizza toppings.

"How is everything?" Leo says.

"Great." I finish my ocha. "Tell him, Leo, pineapple on pizza is a crime against humanity."

"Pineapple on pizza is a crime against humanity," Leo's voice is flat. Which is weird, because he usually adds "Fight me" at the end of that declaration.

"Fine. You win." Alex throws up his hands in defeat. "What if we order Philly cheesesteak pizza then? Maybe take it over to Tempe

Town Lake for a picnic, and then go for a paddle boat ride at sunset?"

I'd be like bam. *I'm dead. RIP.*

"I'd like that, Alex," I say. Of course, I'll have to strategize with Stephanie beforehand about how to avoid the paparazzi. I'm used to being safe here, tucked in the back corner of the restaurant, with the Matsudas always watching for phones out. Every once in a while, somebody gets a picture on the sly, but most of the time, the Matsudas do a great job of reminding people to respect my family's privacy.

Mr. Matsuda has only thrown one person out of the restaurant and called the cops. That was a TMZ reporter right after the Great Homecoming Disaster last year who dared to both invade my privacy and stick a camera in Mr. Matsuda's face too. The silver lining from that cringey event was that Matsuda got a boost in traffic after "Daring Dishwasher Comes to the Rescue of Humiliated DIY Princess" ran the next week, complete with unflattering pictures of both of us.

"Might have to steal that date idea. For, you know, *my* girlfriend." Leo lets out a half-hearted laugh. "Would you guys like to try some of the chef's newest pickles? On the house, of course."

"As long as it doesn't involve natto, I'll try it." I turn to Alex. "Natto is fermented soybeans. It's stinky and slimy." I decide to skip the story about how Leo and I used to pretend to sneeze them out of our noses at each other.

"Not good date-food then," Alex says. "Sure, I'm game if you are, Koty."

"Can we have some more ocha while you're at it, please?" I notice that Alex's cup is dry too.

Leo gives us a nod and heads for the kitchen.

"Hey, watch it," I hear Aurora say from the other side of the swinging kitchen door when Leo bursts through it.

A moment later, Leo puts a small bowl of brown ovals between Alex and me.

"What is it? Water chestnuts?" I say, poking at one with the back ends of my chopsticks.

"It's ninniku no misozuke," Leo says and then looks over his shoulder. "I need to go help a customer. I'll be back with your ocha in a sec."

"On the count of three." I pick up one of the miso-something pickles easily, but Alex's pickle keeps slipping through his chopsticks. He finally puts it in his palm after dropping the same piece three times.

"One . . . two . . . three." I pop the pickle in my mouth at the same time as Alex does. Based on the look on his face, his taste buds register the slice of garlic at the same time mine does. Both of us swallow the piece of salty garlic and grab our teacups at the same time. Except they are still empty. My eyes stream. I put my hand over my mouth and focus all my attention on not gagging. Meanwhile, Alex is laughing and waving at his open mouth. Tears dot his kaleidoscope-colored eyes.

It's Aurora to the rescue. She slides two glasses of water at us. Alex and I chug.

"I am so sorry. These aren't meant to be served yet." Aurora picks up the miso-pickled garlic. "The chef just put them in this afternoon. These won't be ready for another month when they will be much much MUCH milder." Aurora refills our drained water glasses. "You know what you guys need?"

"A breath mint or seven?" I say before I drain that glass of water too.

"Ice cream mochi. On the house. Since Dakota is our favorite customer." Aurora gives Alex a flirty wink. "It's a ball of ice cream with a layer of pounded sweet rice around it. I promise, no garlic involved."

Alex nods. "I'd love some."

"Which flavor: Matcha, vanilla, or strawberry?" Tonight, I'm in no hurry to move this date along. "I always get matcha, but I like bitter green tea. Not everybody does."

"I'd love to try a strawberry one. Thanks."

Leo won't look me in the eye as he follows Aurora into the kitchen. Nor when he comes back out a moment later with somebody else's order.

No. He wouldn't.

"Here you go," Aurora says as she passes the mochi ice cream to us. "One ichigo—strawberry—and one matcha."

"This is so good," Alex says a few bites in. "Not gonna lie. Everything still has a little bit of a garlic taste to it, but I would get this again."

Leo still avoids eye contact when he slides our bill onto the table. Alex and I reach for it at the same time. His hand covers mine to keep me from pulling it to my side of the table.

"Stephanie told you I was paying, right? That this is technically an audition." I pull out my credit card.

Alex tips his head to the side and gives me a sweet smile. "Audition implies that I have to pretend like I wanted to be here with you, but I wasn't acting. Honestly, I'm not even sure I know how to act. The last time I was on any kind of stage, I was eight. I had one line in the Thanksgiving-themed class play, and I was so nervous that I threw up all over Mikayla Dutton. Yep, that was my first and last time on a stage. Mikayla still doesn't talk to me to this day."

A goofy smile pulls across my face too. I proceed to Level Two without getting Phil or anybody's approval. This is my life. My choice.

My heart revs. "Want to do a screen test together when the crew gets back?"

"Yeah." Alex nods. "But, if I flunk the screen test because I, say, throw up on you or something, could we still go to Tempe Town Lake for a pizza picnic? No pineapples involved."

"I'd love to." I make a mental note to buy Stephanie a second potted rosebush for her collection.

When Alex excuses himself to use the restroom, I hand my credit card to Aurora and take the opportunity to poke my head into the kitchen.

"Gochisōsama deshita, Ojiichan!" I yell my thanks-for-the-meal across the bustling kitchen.

"Hai, hai." Ojiichan loads a second bowl of steaming ramen onto Leo's tray. "Come back soon, Dakota-chan."

"I will." I hold the door open. Just as Leo is almost on me and directly in my line of sight, I say, "I want to try your garlic pickles again. When they're ready, of course."

Leo drops his eyes and halts.

"Sorry about that. If you want some heavy-duty Japanese mint gum, I have some." Leo balances the packed tray on his shoulder. It starts to tilt when he digs his hand into his apron pocket.

I grab the edge of the tray before a hundred dollars' worth of food hits the floor. "That's okay. I'll grab a mint from the bowl upfront."

"Hope you had a good time tonight." Leo is smiling, but his voice is weird. "Thank Buddha he wasn't another Jake Yong."

"For real, and I did have a good time. Maybe now that the rain has finally stopped, Alex and I can go stargazing." I give Leo a sassy wink.

A crease forms between Leo's eyebrows. I feel bad for half a second. The truth is that neither of us is going to be stargazing or anything else tonight. The restaurant is still nearly filled to capacity, and though I am definitely interested in getting to know Alex better, it's going to be a long time before I trust someone again. I start to tell Leo this, but Ojiichan barks something at him, probably, "The food is getting cold!"

"I gotta go." Leo straightens the tray and races away.

"Thanks for coming in tonight," Mrs. Matsuda says as we pass the cash register. "Be safe going home, Koty."

"Koty!" Aurora runs up to me. "I'm sorry about last night."

Mrs. Matsuda clears her throat. That's not enough to get Aurora off the hook.

"I should have at least seen if you and Leo wanted to sneak out to the Snowball and Hot Chocolate Party with me. Then we could all be grounded for two weeks together, but hey." Aurora shrugs. "I'll make it up to you sometime when I'm not here pushing the limits of child labor laws."

Mrs. Matsuda grumbles something in Japanese under her breath.

"Anyhoo, thanks for coming in. See you at school on Tuesday. Nice to meet you, Alex." When Aurora leans in to give me an uncharacteristic hug, she slides something into my coat pocket.

When we get to Alex's car, I slide my hand into my jacket pocket and finger the thing.

"I think Aurora is trying to tell me something." I pull a pack of heavy-duty Japanese mint gum out of my pocket.

We drive around town for a good hour, comparing musical tastes and chewing the entire pack of mint gum before the torrential rains come again. It rarely rains in Phoenix, but of course, it had to today. When we get back to my house, Alex parks between Phil's trailer and the dumpster. He turns off the engine, and we sit in silence for a few minutes listening to the rain.

I turn to face Alex, who has his hands on the steering wheel. "You wanna come over sometime and learn how to use the airbrush to do more detailed work?"

"Yeah. I'd love to paint a pinstripe on my car. I was too chicken to attempt it before."

My heart pounds so hard that I can't tell if the sound in my ears is my blood rushing or the rain hitting the roof of the car. A sweet love song plays on the radio with a Latin beat. Alex reaches out his hand, and I allow his fingers to lace with mine. Alex's thumb taps out the downbeat of the song.

"Do you like to dance?" I say.

"Sometimes. Am I a good dancer? That's debatable. The Mexican part of my melting-pot family always has dancing at their parties and get-togethers. Since I hit high school, my abuela keeps volunteering me as a chambelan for all her friends' granddaughters' quinceañeras. That's why I was so late to Vanessa's birthday party. I had a quinceañera before it. I barely knew the girl, but her family wanted a very traditional quinceañera. We're talking about an all-day event with fourteen damas and fifteen chambelanes, a special mass at church, and a reception that was bigger than most people's weddings. They were short on chambelanes, so Abuela volunteered me. So, short story long, if you need someone to do a vals—"

"I'm sorry, what? Balls?"

"Vals, with a *V*." Alex bends the *V*, but it still sounds like bahlz. "It's a special dance—usually with a waltz beat—that you do with your chambelan. I could probably do something like that with you at your Sweet Sixteen party."

Panic stabs my chest. "Wait. Stephanie never said anything about organized dancing on camera."

"Oh, I thought it was a given. We could come up with some choreography together if you want. I can also do a simple side-to-side step on the downbeat, if you prefer. I am happy to audition both of these dances for you next week."

"I can't wait to see them."

The porch light comes on, alerting me to the fact that my parents know we are back home. Thankfully, they don't come outside.

"I should let you go," Alex says, but he doesn't let go of my hand.

"Yeah, I should go." I don't pull my hand away either.

Alex leans toward me. He tucks a lock of my hair behind my ear. His fingertips travel down the length of my jaw. Half of me wants to run. Half of me wants to pull Alex in closer. When Alex leans in, my barriers instinctively come up. My hand shoots out to protect my bubble.

Alex freezes. "Not okay?"

My hand stays firmly planted in the middle of his chest. "It's complicated."

"Someone hurt you?"

"Like I said, it's . . . complicated."

Thanks to last year's Great Homecoming Disaster, the push and pull never stops. If you let people in, they will hurt you. If you don't let people in, you will still get hurt. Alex's heart pounds underneath my palm. I want my first kiss—first *real* kiss—to be right here, right now, and with Alex Santos. I do. Yet something doesn't feel right. Doesn't feel good. And even worse, my brain decides to pull up an image of Leo telling me that if something doesn't feel good, don't do it.

"Hey, it's okay." Alex sits back in his seat, and my hand falls away. "No pressure."

I clench my fists until my nails dig into my palms. I am so frustrated with myself and all the people who have turned me into this non-functioning version of a teenager.

"Really, Dakota. It's okay."

"No, it's not. Why can't I be a normal teenager and kiss you like I want to?" I probably should have put a filter on that. "I'm going to go before I humiliate myself even further."

"Hey, Dakota, for the record, you can kiss me. Anytime. Today. Tomorrow. Next week. Next year."

This guy is too good to be true. Though my heart still threatens to leave my chest, there is a new feeling with it. Usually, when somebody invades my bubble, I feel a contraction. Right now, there's an expanding feeling. I could . . .

"Night, Alex." I chicken out instead.

I unhook my safety belt and grab my purse, but when my hand hits the cold metal door handle, I pause. *Dakota?!?!? What are you doing?* Before I can chicken out a second time, I turn in my seat, put my hand on the side of Alex's face and lean into him. Time moves like molasses as my face turns and dips toward Alex's. I press my lips against his warm, full lips. His eyes open slowly as I pull away. A smile pulls at the corners of his mouth.

"Thank you," I say. "For everything."

"You're welcome, and anytime."

I slide out of the car and head up the walkway. Alex starts his car but waits until I'm on the porch with the front door unlocked. He rolls down the window and waves at me.

Now this feels good. Maybe this is exactly what I need to move on.

Chapter

18

"Hey, I'm going to have to bail on our plans to watch *Kitsune Mask* today." I slide my phone back into my pocket. "Something's come up."

"What? We are like three episodes behind now since last week was a double episode," Leo says as we drop our skateboards on the ground outside of school.

"I know. It's Phil. Now that everybody is back from vacation, our shooting schedule is cranking up. Plus, we're doing Alex's screen test today."

"So, this means you've finally found your Prince Charming for the party?" Leo ollies his skateboard up onto the metal rail of the steps in front of the school and slides down.

When we meet up again at the bottom, I say, "Maaaaaybe."

"I'm glad," Leo says and takes off.

When we get to the intersection where we break off, Leo stops again. "How was the big romantic picnic by Tempe Town Lake? Which, by the way, I am stealing for Lindsay's and my six-month anniversary. Presuming that she hasn't dumped me by then."

"Okay. We only got to do the pizza picnic part this time before there was some family emergency." I drop my foot to stop my skateboard. "Why? Something go sideways on Monday during your date?"

"Pfft. What? No." Leo pulls his jacket closer around his body even though it is unseasonably warm today. After a beat, Leo says in a quiet voice, "Guys and girls can be friends, right? Best friends, even?"

"Yes. You just have to set some guidelines, so things don't get weird."

"Weird like when your *friend* suddenly wants to make out in a walk-in refrigerator?"

And there we have it.

"First of all, we didn't make out. All I said was that I had feelings for you, and you noped me. Second of all, dude, why would you tell Lindsay about that?"

"First of all, I didn't nope you. It was a gentle let-me-think-about-it, followed by you ghosting me for a solid month. Second of all, it just kinda slipped out during our fight on Monday."

"Well that explains the weirdness at lunch for the last two days. Fine, I'll go eat by myself again. No biggie." My heart cracks, but I'm afraid of what will happen if Leo is given an ultimatum.

"What? No. That's not what I'm saying." Leo puffs his cheeks and lets out a frustrated breath. "What I'm saying is that if you and Alex—or somebody else—could be A Thing, then my problem with Lindsay would be a non-issue. Then everybody could be happy."

"I want you to be happy. I want to be happy too." I'm not sure if it's going to happen with Alex or not, especially if his family keeps interrupting our dates every five minutes like last time, but I want to give it a try. "So stop sabotaging my dates."

"It was a joke. I'm sorry. I hope it didn't ruin your date."

"Oh, believe me, it didn't."

Leo might go for quantity, but I'm going for quality. Thinking about Alex's soft lips makes me buzz.

Leo cringes. "TMI, Koty."

"I didn't tell you anything."

"Still too much. I don't want to know about Aurora's love life or yours either." Leo says with an overly dramatic shudder.

"Says the guy who inflicts PDA with Lindsay on us pretty much every day, everywhere."

"Sorry. I didn't know it bothered you so much. I'll dial it back. At least in public."

I don't want say it's okay, because Leo and I don't lie to each other. "You guys are going to get busted by Principal Docker."

"Too late. Yeah, it's going to be fun explaining to my parents why I have detention after school tomorrow. Especially when we have a huge retirement party coming in at five."

I snort-laugh. "I'm sorry. It isn't funny. But, yeah, it kinda is."

"Shut up." Leo gives me a gentle push. "Are you sure you can't come to the restaurant with me for five minutes while I deliver the news? Ojiichan won't kill me if you are standing there."

"I wish I could, but I'm in a hurry." I put my hand on Leo's bicep and solemnly wish him luck. "Gambatte ne."

"I still want to catch up on *Kitsune Mask* with you soon."

"Me too!" I yell over my shoulder.

o   o   o

Alex's silver Toyota is already at my house by the time I get home. So much for my plan of taking a quick shower and redoing my hair and makeup. I let myself in the house and rekey the alarm code. Alex's and Stephanie's voices echo down the hall from Mom's office. I place my skateboard in its designated spot in the hall closet and put my shoes in my cubby. Since nobody can see me from this angle, I do a quick pit check. I grab the Febreze out of its designated basket and quickly spray my socked feet. I give my pits a quick squirt for good measure too. I'm fixing my hair in the hall mirror when Stephanie pokes her head out of Mom's office.

Stephanie catches my eye. "We're in here, Dakota. Come on through."

I give my makeup one last check before heading down the hallway. Mom's office is slightly less cluttered than usual, but there are still rolls upon rolls of vintage wallpaper stacked up like fire logs on her desk.

"Hey, Alex. Glad you could change your schedule." My heart flutters when Alex looks up.

We do a weird dance of an almost-hug followed by an almost-handshake followed by both of us stepping back a pace and just sitting down without any kind of touching. Stephanie raises an eyebrow.

"Where's Mom?" I say.

"She and your dad both have eye doctor appointments this afternoon, so I'm running the audition on her behalf." Stephanie pours a splash of milk into a teacup for me before adding the rich, brown tea to it.

"Dakota's party is the last Saturday of April, right?" Alex looks down at the fancy tea set and then takes off his baseball hat. "Because if things go well, I hope to be playing in the All-State tournament the first weekend of May. Sorry, that sounds super braggy."

"It's not bragging. It's a fact." Stephanie hands a teacup and saucer to Alex. "You are a very talented baseball player, Alex. And, yes, the party is the last Saturday in April at Chez Versailles."

"In all its ridiculous chandelier and velvet glory," I say.

"Been there. For a quinceañera in August. The hand-painted porcelain urinals. Yeah, that was extra." Alex reddens. "Sinks. Hand-painted porcelain *sinks*. And, my audition is over. I'll show myself out."

Though I laugh, Alex stands up. When Stephanie gives him a look, he sits back down.

"Now then." Stephanie looks over the top of her retro purple glasses at Alex. "I will be grilling Mr. Santos here to determine if he is a worthy candidate to be your . . . *escort* sounds odd, but *date* sounds too pedestrian for something of this caliber."

"Chambelan de Honor?" I say having spent more time than I care to admit to researching the history of quinceañeras. "There really isn't a non-quinceañera equivalent, but if Phil and The Network get their way, we might as well be doing a crossover special with *My Super Sweet Quinceañera*. I'm talking ice sculptures in my likeness and a horse-drawn carriage that would make a Disney princess jelly."

When I laugh, but Alex doesn't, I make a mental note to insist that Phil should *not* include either of those things. Because he would if somebody waved enough money in his face.

"I would be honored to be your Chambelan de Honor," Alex says with the correct pronunciation. "Or whatever your equivalent is."

"It does require being on camera. A lot. Not as much as Dakota and her parents, obviously, but producers are going to expect you to be part of the narrative. And A Class Act Tuxedo Company would require you to do some call-outs for them wearing their new prom line."

Alex gulps. "How much talking do I have to do?"

"Some." Stephanie puts a hand on Alex's arm. "But we can practice beforehand and do some basic media training with you, if you are comfortable with it, of course. And . . ." Stephanie holds up a pile of papers written in legalese. "Your mom signs off on it. Sherri already told me she would, *if* you want to, Alex. But, you don't owe me anything as your mom's friend."

"Five thousand dollars would help pay for all the fees and parking and stuff that my scholarships won't cover." Alex nods his head.

I know this is a business, but it still bothers me. And yet, if Alex was on the fence about this, I would dangle that same carrot in front of his face to get him to change his mind.

"Come to the Dark Side, Alex. We have cookies." I pick up the plate of Cadbury biscuits and wave them in his direction. "Like for real. These *biscuits* are awesome."

"What if we film you and Dakota in the McDonalds' personal workshop today instead of the build's? We won't use it on the show. It would just be a test to see if you can block the cameras out."

"Okay, but remember, you two asked for it," Alex says.

"Fantastic." Stephanie grabs her phone and texts madly. A minute later, she reports back. "Phil and some of the camera crew will meet you both in the workshop in ten." Stephanie looks me over. "You don't need to change for today, Dakota. But you do need shoes."

"I left my work boots upstairs yesterday. Let me go grab them." I drain my teacup. Though Scared Me is fighting to come out, I say, "Do you want to see my room, Alex?"

Alex says, "Sure," just as Stephanie says, "No."

"We will wait for you down here," Stephanie says, pouring herself another cup of tea.

"Oh-kay. Back in a sec then."

It's more than a second. I don't change clothes, but I do fix my hair and makeup. And quickly brush my teeth. Because, you know, you should always be prepared. I clomp back downstairs to see that Stephanie has found a pair of work boots for Alex too.

"Ms. Stephanie said to meet her outside." Alex stomps around in the hallway. "I feel like Frankenstein's Monster."

"Sorry. It's a shop rule. And . . ." I reach into the hall closet and pull out two pairs of safety glasses. I put mine in my back pocket, but I step toward Alex and slide the clear glasses over his brownish-green-blue kaleidoscope eyes.

I'm in his personal bubble. He notices. The corner of his mouth pulls up. Though the voice urging me to run away is still there, it's quieter today. I stay inside Alex's bubble.

"If you wanted to give me a hug or something, I would be cool with that." Alex looks deep into my eyes but keeps his hands down by his sides.

My arms slide into the space between Alex's arms and his waist.

I look up and say back, "If you wanted to give me a hug or something back, I would be cool with that."

Alex's hands gently press on my hip bones first. When I don't pull away, his hands slide around my back until his arms encircle me too. I turn my head to the side so I can rest my cheek on his chest near his collarbone. Though my heart is racing and there is a part of me that still wants to run, I don't move.

"Thank you," I say.

"Any time. If you wanted to—"

"Let's go, guys!" Stephanie's voice echoes down the hall from the kitchen.

"Hold that thought." Especially if it was going in the same direction as mine.

I lead Alex through our house and out the back door to Dad's personal workshop. As usual, Dad's side looks like an episode of *Hoarders*. My side is as tidy as a working area can be. I slide my protective eyewear on.

"I grabbed some old, leftover boards so you can practice with low stakes at first." I slide open one of the bottom drawers in my twenty-drawer turquoise tool chest and pull out the small air compressor, hose, and the airbrush itself.

"First things first, what colors would you like?" I lean over and pull out a drawer before turning my attention back to the air compressor.

"Wooooow," Alex says about all the choices.

"There are some advantages to having a paint company as one of your sponsors. Pretty sure I have enough paint to graffiti all of Phoenix." I look over to where Phil stands, giving orders to today's camera operator. A scowl crosses his face. "Not that I would ever do that, of course."

"Don't mind us, kids," Phil says as Jordan the Camera Op suddenly stands right next to us.

What the actual Phil?

"Hey, you guys need to back up a little." I flick my hand at Jordan. "I only have two masks. OSHA rules."

So, I might be bending the truth a little bit. I'm not an expert on OSHA rules, but Dad does make me wear a mask every time I paint.

"Which do you like better?" Alex's smooth voice suddenly sounds squeaky and choppy. He holds up two gold paints.

"Both." I take them from him. "We'll use this one as the base color and this one as the accent color. First, what do you want to design?"

I lean in front of Alex to grab a pencil from my jar. Alex looks up at the camera and gulps. Sweat dots bead up on Alex's forehead even though the workshop is cold.

"How about something simple like your name?" I put my hand over Alex's and squeeze it. "Block letters or a fancy script?"

When Alex doesn't answer, I sketch out his name in block letters on a piece of old wood.

"Can you go plug in the air compressor over there for me?" I say when I'm done.

When Alex turns around to find the outlet, I give Phil and Jordan the Camera Op an irritated flick with my hands to back up even more. Phil rubs his temples. He whispers something to Stephanie.

"Now for a little latex. Safety first, friends," I mimic Dad, and Alex bites his bottom lip to contain his smirk.

Yep, that's a bingo square. It's one of Dad's most-used catch-phrases. I hand Alex a pair of latex gloves and slide on a pair myself.

"Let's fill the color cup with this one." I gently mix the paint. "Normally, you would need to thin your paint, but this one is made specifically for airbrushes."

I put the airbrush in Alex's hand and walk him through the process of filling it. With our face masks on and Jordan and his camera pushed back another few steps, I flip on the air compressor. The motor roars as the air pressure increases inside the tank. Once we hit the optimum pressure level at 30 PSI, the motor quiets so I can continue my lesson.

"Hold it like a pen with your index finger on the trigger." I position the airbrush in Alex's hand. "Remove the cap protecting the delicate needle. Let's practice on this piece of scrap paper first."

"Hey, I'm doing it . . . Oh no." Alex's brow wrinkles when the paint blooms on the paper and drips. He holds the airbrush out to me. "I'm messing this up."

"It's a double-action airbrush, so it takes a gentle touch." I spray a light coating of the matte gold paint on a piece of scrap newspaper. "The farther you pull the trigger back with your index finger, the more paint comes out. So start light. You can always add more layers, but once it's down, it's down."

I spray out a simple *A* outline on the newspaper and hand the airbrush back to Alex. Alex pulls the trigger too far and another huge bloom of gold paint forms. He lets out a frustrated sigh.

"That's why we're working on paper first." I put my hand over Alex's to steady it. "Try again. Light touch."

It takes several more tries for Alex to find the exact amount of controlled pressure he needs for the job. After he fills in my *A*, Alex freehands a *D* and then looks at me. He raises his eyebrows, and I bump his hip lightly with mine.

"Cut!" Phil yells. "Okay, guys, this is a TV show, not a silent movie, which means I'm going to need some kind of talking here. Witty banter. Flirting. *Something.* The only thing we're doing right now is curing people's insomnia. Can we have some kind of *spark* for the folks watching at home?"

"No, we cannot, Phil," I say.

"C'mon, son, this is a chem-test. I'm not asking you to quote Shakespeare."

"Alex, honey, you're doing great for your first time." Stephanie gives Phil some serious side-eye. "Think of it as practice. One day, you're going to be the MVP in a World Series game. Cameras are going to be in your face, expecting you to talk about how you led your team to victory. That's what we're preparing you for today. Channel that guy."

The wrinkle in Alex's forehead releases. He gives Stephanie a confident nod.

"Okay then, let's practice." Phil turns off my compressor and gestures for Jordan to zoom in for a close-up. "Both of you take off your masks and have a conversation. About anything. Your favorite TV show. What you had for lunch today. Your grandma's famous apple pie. I don't care. *Anything.* But show us a *spark* and wake Middle America up."

Alex lowers his mask around his neck, looks at me with deer-in-the-headlights eyes, and says stiffly, "My abuela's apple pie is meh, but her tres leches cake is the bomb."

"And." Phil rolls his hands at Alex to continue as Jordan steps even closer.

"Maybe you could try it sometime, Dakota." Beads of sweat appear on Alex's forehead.

I put my hand on Alex's arm. I've been doing this literally since birth, so it feels like second nature to me. I forget that most people find a video camera in their face unnerving.

I tell a tiny white lie as I cap the airbrush needle. "I don't know what that is."

"It literally means three-milks cake. It's kind of my family's go-to dessert for birthdays and holidays, at least for the Mexican half of my family."

"More," Phil says. "Just keep talking about the cake."

"It's a . . . uh . . . sponge cake . . . but then you . . . uh . . . poke holes in it with your . . . uh . . . fork." Alex clears his throat and puts the airbrush down. His voice is still unnatural but stronger when he says, "You top the cake with a mixture of sweetened condensed milk, evaporated milk, and whole milk until it seeps into the cake. Later, you decorate the top with whipped cream and fruit. I like strawberries the best."

"That sounds awesome. And I love strawberries."

Phil turns to Stephanie. "I got it! You know the footage we did of Tamlyn talking about strawberries from Glendale? Let's do a short segment with Alex's family. We'll have Dakota make tres leches cake with the grandmother and Alex. Middle America would eat that up with a spoon. Then Dakota can post the authentic family recipe on her social media. Perfect. Think your family would be on board with that, son?"

Alex wheezes and shoots Stephanie a panicked look.

"Stephanie, you're friends with Alex's mom. Work your charm. Make this happen," Phil says.

"It's his dad's side of the family," Stephanie says gently. "We aren't . . . close."

"Oh, okay." Phil turns back to Alex. "You could set that up for us, right?"

"I . . . uh . . . I don't know," Alex stammers. "I'm not sure Abuela would—"

"This isn't rocket science, son," Phil interrupts. He steps even closer to Alex. "All I'm asking you to do is make a cake on TV with your grandma and a pretty girl. In fact, we don't even have to shoot at your house. You get Grandma here, and we'll take care of all the details. Stephanie, what's Grandma's phone number? Let's have a conference call with her. I know we can talk her into it."

"Hey, I'm sorry." Alex slips off his mask and safety glasses and leaves them on the workbench. "I don't think this is going to work out."

"Alex, honey," Stephanie says as he brushes past her out the door.

"Wait!" I rip off my mask and safety glasses and rush after Alex. I find Alex in my backyard near the picnic table.

"I'm sorry about all that back there." I put a still-gloved hand on Alex's back. "I'm used to Phil. He doesn't get under my skin half as much as he used to."

"I want to do this," Alex says but doesn't turn around. "One day, I want to play professional baseball. They expect you to be able to talk on camera. Sometimes with no warning whatsoever. And here I am, I can't even talk to a cute girl while painting a friggin' sign. For the record, I would rather roll around naked in a garden of cacti than bring you over to my dad's house right now. Cake or no cake."

I wince, hearing Leo in my head. *I just need some breathing room. You suffocate me sometimes.*

"Hey, I'm sorry. You know what? Let's stop this. It's not worth it. I'll find somebody else to be my date." I shudder thinking about spending another evening with Jake Yong. "Can we still be friends, though?"

Alex turns to face me. "Of course. Can we keep going out even after you find the perfect guy for the party?"

"Yes! And you better come to the party. Maybe Stephanie's niece could be your date?"

"Would you save a dance for me?" Alex strips off his latex gloves and puts them on the picnic table.

I chuck my gloves on the table too before taking Alex's hand in mine. "Yes. Though, warning, my dance skills suuuuck."

"How about this to wake up Middle America? You're slow dancing with your Ken-doll date looking like a princess, when suddenly a handsome Latino guy cuts in." I let out a squeal when Alex suddenly pulls me into him. "He does a *spicy* but tasteful vals—because this is a family show and his abuela is watching—with America's DIY Princess around the ballroom. And at the end, after hundreds of hearts are broken, Mystery Guy hands the princess a single red rose, kisses her passionately—but again tastefully, because Abuela needs to be able to show her face at church the next day—and slowly backs away without a word until he disappears into the crowd. People would be talking about that for weeks."

"Yes! Yes! Yes!" The spark explodes in my brain. "This is *exactly* how we are going to save the night. Especially if I end up with a potato like Jake Yong as my date."

"I could teach you part of the last quinceañera dance I learned, because I could do that dance in my sleep. How about that? Could you fake that you'd never done the dance before so my credibility of being a strong lead would go up?"

My heart is pounding, and we haven't even started dancing. But it's an expansive feeling, not a contracted one. This feels good.

"Yes."

Alex turns me around but leaves his hands on my waist. "The first thing you need to know is this is not a typical *Downton Abbey* kind of waltz. Yes, you have the one-two-three-one-two-three, but there is also a lot of arm work. Cross your arms low in front of you, right over left." Alex's hands leave my waist and tuck into each of my hands. We are so close to each other that our personal space bubbles practically squeak. "You doin' okay? Because you need to loosen your hands up. A lot."

I release the knuckle-crushing grasp I have on Alex. I force myself to deepen my breath. Alex must be able to sense when the good feeling outweighs the bad because he suddenly twirls me out to the side.

"And . . . come back in." Alex gently tugs my hand until I roll back into him. And onto his foot.

I break away from him. "I am so sorry."

"Hey, that's what steel-toed boots are for." Alex shrugs.

"Pretty sure they're not."

"I like the jeans and boots combo. It makes my job easier. That way I'm not terrified I'm going to slip on the hem of your thousand-dollar dress and bite it in front of all your tías and tíos, which is immortalized on film by the official quinceañera videographer that your abuela spent too much money on. Not that I'm speaking from experience or anything. Much."

"Is it rude to say I'd like to see that video?"

"Yeah no, I'm not showing you that video."

"Can I have a redo?" I take Alex's hands in mine again. Gently this time. "I know I can get this."

"I swing you out," Alex talks me through the move. "I swing you back in. There you go. Much better. Now, let's try it with a waltz beat. One-two-three, one-two-three, one-two-three. You got it."

We twirl to the other side. I also finally learn how to do a basket turn without getting tangled and conking your partner in the head. My seventh grade PE teacher would be so proud.

"Now, we're going to do the *Downton Abbey*-ish part." As Alex turns me to face him, I can see Phil and Stephanie standing in the doorway of the workshop, but I keep that to myself. "One hand here. The other out to the side. As I step forward, you're going to step back."

It's a good thing we have boots on, because I am all over Alex's feet. But we get it. Sorta. As we set up to try again, I notice Jordan the Camera Op standing next to Phil, probably with the camera zoomed in on us.

"We're *not* using this footage, Phil," I yell his way after my turn goes rogue, and Alex has to grab me to keep me from doing a header into the fake grass.

"C'mon, you guys are adorable," Phil yells back. "Fans would eat this stuff up."

Alex looks like he's eaten bad potato salad. I shake his hand to make him focus on me again.

"You got this," I say.

"So do you. Want to try what you know so far with the quinceañera music?" When I nod, Alex slides his phone out of his back pocket and pulls up the song. He sets his phone on the picnic table. "The first thirty seconds are the intro to get us on the dance floor and into our starting positions."

Alex holds my hand, and we promenade to the middle of the fake grass in my backyard. Phil is filming us, but I block him out. Alex and I take the opening position. Alex's middle finger taps the downbeat on my hand until the music swells, and we step off.

Is it perfect? Nope. Is it better? Definitely. We have a couple of wobbles and stumbles, especially when Phil sends Jordan closer and closer, like he's a lioness stalking two gazelles at the watering hole.

"Gonna get an elbow to the nose if you keep standing there, Jordan." I give him fair warning before we start over.

We do several more tries and even add a little more choreography.

"You pick things up quickly." Alex turns his back on the camera.

"My brain right now . . ." I mime my head exploding.

"Maybe we should call it a day."

As we walk toward the back door, Stephanie jogs up next to us. "Hey, lookin' good."

"I wish that were true," Alex says.

"C'mon, I only stomped on your instep once this last time." I bump Alex's hip though I know he was referring to himself.

"Are we done for today, Phil?" Stephanie yells across the yard.

Phil raises his hand in affirmation. Stephanie herds us inside. Alex sits down at the kitchen table to take off his boots. I sit next to him and do the same.

"I should get going." Alex glances at the kitchen wall clock. "We're watching my cousins tonight while my aunt has class."

"A fun evening of *Minecraft* ahead of you then?"

"Yes, and probably fraction flashcards, and if I'm super lucky, books about cats with hats who sit on mats with rats."

"Sucks to be you."

"I complain, but honestly, it's not that bad. Everybody enjoys having their own fan club. Even if it is a fan club of two."

I put my hand on his knee and squeeze it. "Three."

Alex puts his hand over mine and squeezes it. "You gained a new fan club member today too. Though I am probably number one million."

"One million and seventeen," I joke, though if you count my Instagram followers, that number is probably pretty close.

"Would it be okay if I filmed you guys for Tamlyn and Doug? Here in the kitchen. Just the three of us."

"Are we going to live dangerously and dance without boots this time?" Part of me is totally serious.

"I think we'll be okay." Alex takes his phone back out of his pocket and pulls up the song.

Stephanie's smile gets bigger and bigger as our simple dance travels around the kitchen.

"Whoa." I put my hand on the kitchen counter to keep from colliding with it when Alex turns me out too far.

"Sorry," Alex says.

When he twirls me back toward him, my socked feet slip on the wooden floor until I slide up against him. Like, smack up against him. Like, so plastered against him that I can feel Alex's muscles through his shirt. This feels good. Safe. I don't move even though the song and our choreography continues without us. An undignified squeal escapes my lips when Alex suddenly dips me backward and lets me hang in a dramatic arch.

"Not sorry." Alex kisses my cheek.

My bottom foot slips from underneath me. Which wouldn't be the end of the world if I hadn't unintentionally done a leg-sweep on Alex at the same time. We end up in a pile in the middle of the kitchen floor.

Stephanie shakes her head as Alex and I crack up. "I'll meet you outside the front door in a minute, Alex. I have to get some clothes for your mom out of my car."

"Thank you, Ms. Stephanie." Alex sits up cross-legged on the floor. "For everything."

"My pleasure."

Alex rolls to his feet as Stephanie heads down the hallway. He offers me his hand and pulls me to a stand. I don't let go of his hand until we get to the front door.

"I'll keep working on my on-camera skills with Ms. Stephanie. Maybe I can reaudition in a week or two?" Alex dips down to tie his tennis shoes. "I want to do this event with you."

"And I'll keep working on my dance skills. I want to do this event with you too."

"So, goodbye?" Alex rocks back and forth on his heels. "If you wanted to kiss me goodbye, I'd be cool with it."

I loop my arms around Alex's neck and invade his bubble. As I lean in, Alex closes his eyes. And this time when our lips meet, it is a full give-and-take between the two of us. Alex pulls me even closer to him, stepping backward until he is sandwiched between me and my front door. So maybe there is a little bit of "octopus arms" going on. I promise not to bust on Leo about this anymore. Why am I thinking about Leo at a time like this?

Just as my concentration returns to the boy at hand—literally under my hands—the door suddenly opens, cracking Alex in the head. I stumble away from him as he rubs the back of his head.

"Are you okay?" Stephanie says with a bag of clothes against her chest. "You know what? Don't answer that. Please give these to Sherri."

Alex takes the bag from Stephanie with a nod. "Are you free Saturday, Dakota? Maybe we could try the Great Pizza Picnic Plan a second time? I promise to leave my phone at home."

Stephanie gives me a subtle nod to answer my unasked question. "Yeah, I'm free. Let's give it another try."

I stand on my front porch in my socks as Alex walks to his car. He gives me one last smile before driving away. My heart melts a bit. When I float back through the front door, I finally feel like I'm walking into something new—a new, rebuilt version of me. I can't wait to start this new chapter of my life.

Chapter

19

"We're going to have a redo on our last date," I babble at lunch the next day, after showing everybody Alex's and my dance video. Both Phil's version before I made him delete it and then the blooper one Stephanie took in the kitchen, including the fall onto the floor.

"Do we ever get to meet Prince Charming?" Nevaeh swipes one of the Oreos from my lunch.

"Already met him." Leo swipes an Oreo too, with the arm that doesn't currently have Lindsay attached to it. "He seems nice."

"Nice?" Nevaeh scoffs. "My poodle is nice. Going to need some better adjectives, Cinnamon Roll Prince. Or should I call you *Sin*-amon Roll Prince now that you have detention today?"

"Ha ha." Leo looks up at the cafeteria's ceiling for inspiration. "According to Aurora, Alex is 'Kakkoii ne!'—only said much louder and at a dog-whistle pitch."

"But what do *you* think?" Nevaeh presses.

"He's polite to servers and makes Koty laugh. If she's happy, then I'm happy." Leo shrugs. "If you want to come back to the restaurant on Saturday, Koty, I will pay more attention this time and give a detailed review on Monday."

"Thanks, but I'm ready to fly solo now," I say.

The bell rings and everybody groans. Leo and I have US History class together right after lunch. For the first time since he and Lindsay officially became a couple, Leo's right behind me.

"Koty, whatcha doin' next Monday?" Leo jogs up next to me. "Want to have a Matsuda Monday with the mom units so we can catch up on *Kitsune Mask*?"

"Nothing, I think, and yeah, I would love to. I thought that was your and Lindsay's Date Day?"

"Well." Leo rubs the back of his neck. "The detention news yesterday kinda started a domino effect, which included Lindsay's parents checking her grades a little closer since her midterms weren't up to the usual standard. It was the number of missing assignments last quarter despite the many 'homework sessions' we had on Matsuda Mondays that put the final nail in the coffin."

"Wait. Lindsay was attached to you like a barnacle during lunch, so it's definitely not over."

"It's not over, but it's cut back, at least outside of school. Now I'm on dating lockdown until spring break—or until all my grades come back up to at least a B. Meanwhile, Lindsay might be on dating lockdown until graduation. At least I get to keep my phone. Lindsay has to turn hers in as soon as she gets home, with the exception of twenty minutes right after dinner, which, of course, I'm usually working. So. Not. Fair."

"I'm sorry," I say truthfully. "If you are in social-life lockdown, are your parents going to let you come over to my house on Monday?"

"Of course. You're my dude. Not my girlfriend."

That truth bomb still hurts, but not nearly as much as it used to.

"Then I will *suggest* to Mom that she invite your mom over on Monday to watch that new chick flick they were talking about at the New Year party. Once they get talking, that should buy us at least two episodes. We should get pizza too."

"Yeah, just like the old days."

I nod even though I'm not the Old Dakota anymore. I'm the rebuilt version. The one who can love her best friend without being in love with him.

0   0   0

"I'll meet you in the workshop, honey." Mom jogs up the hallway in her yoga attire and her phone in hand. "I know I promised to help you with the electrical part of the dollhouse project today."

"It's fine. No rush. I want to get a snack first." I reset the alarm on the front door.

"We can work on the dollhouse project while Dad finishes our laundry. But then we need to pack and get to bed. Our flight leaves at six thirty tomorrow morning."

"What?" My backpack, and my heart, hit the floor with a thud. "I have a date this weekend. Remember? I cleared it with Stephanie."

"Yes, but that was *before* we got the call from the head of The Network this morning. HGTV is sending us to Prince Edward Island this weekend. We'll shoot with *The History Makers* in Charlottetown all day Saturday, and then swing up to Cavendish on Sunday to do a quick shoot at Avonlea Village before taking the red-eye home. Stephanie already called in your absences for tomorrow and Monday. I sent you a text about all of this at lunchtime." Mom looks down at her phone and grimaces. She pushes a button on her screen, which makes my phone ping. "Sorry. I got distracted and forgot to push send. Here are all the details."

"Mom, I don't want to go to Canada."

"Duly noted. However, the History Channel *begged* HGTV to borrow us for a crossover special because none of their teams are willing or able to go to Canada on such short notice. So guess who's going to suck it up and take one for the team?"

"I hate my life."

Mom pulls me into a hug, which I don't return. "C'mon, Koty. It will be fun. Ridiculously cold, so pack layers, but fun. You'll finally get to fulfill your dream of going to Avonlea. Remember that Halloween when you were ten and you asked me to spray your hair red for the night? You were so annoyed with Leo because he refused to go trick-or-treating as Gilbert."

Season 14, Episode 6: "Koty of Avonlea." Also, the only time Leo has been on TV with me. It's also the only time a Ninja Turtle of similar namesake has been on TV with me.

"Still hate my life."

"Tough cookies. Be a professional." Mom swats my butt before she goes upstairs. Halfway up the stairs, she stops and turns around. "Also, I talked to Jen. She and Leo are coming over on Monday night. You'll have to fill me in on our way to Prince Edward Island about why exactly Leo had to beg to come with her. Something about detention. You're not a part of that, right?"

My brain gives me an unsolicited image of Leo and Lindsay making out in the hallway.

"No, definitely not."

"Good."

"Mom, I don't want to do the electricity today. I want to talk to Alex instead."

"Probably a better plan. We'll reschedule for next week. As long as you are packed with lights out by nine, I don't care how you get things done."

"Nine?!"

"Nine. Your call time, Miss McDonald, is four a.m."

I hate my life.

Chapter

20

"I miss you too," I say to Alex during our video chat on Monday. "Let's have a redo this weekend. Come over to my house. We need to practice our dance. Among other things."

"Sure. Let me check one thing first. I'm supposed to be at my dad's this weekend."

"We could practice at your dad's house."

"Mmmmm, I'm not sure that's such a great idea. Ricky is on Dad's very last nerve right now. Then again, maybe if you came over, it would get Abuela off my back. By the way, she has binge-watched the last two seasons of your show so far."

My heart contracts. For the most part, I don't care what strangers think of my show, as long as they aren't ugly about it. But what if I don't pass this audition? What if Alex's grandma doesn't think I'm good enough? For once, I care.

"I would be lying if I didn't say I was jealous of your plans tonight." Alex takes off his baseball hat and runs his fingers through his sweat-flattened curls.

"Of watching TV with Leo? We've been best friends since we were little kids. *Just* friends." With the exception of the misfire in the walk-in refrigerator after the Homecoming Carnival.

"I know. I'm ridiculous. I just don't want to share you."

That bothers me. Yes, everybody likes to be wanted, but I'm used to everybody wanting a piece of me. And sometimes I don't want to share *any* of me with *anybody*.

"Sorry, that sounded stalkerish." Alex gets into his car and throws his backpack to the side. "I had a bad day at practice. I have no idea what we are doing in physics class despite going for extra tutoring. And I miss you. Physical you. You bring a sense of calm in my family's ongoing hurricane-level storm. I wish you were here."

I contemplate ditching Leo and asking Alex to pick me up, but I'm tired. After being "on" all weekend in Canada, my well is empty. I'm allowed to set boundaries, even with the people I care about the most. Of course, repeating what my therapist says and actually doing what she suggests are two different things.

What do you want, Dakota, right now? I hear Dr. Berger's soothing voice in my head.

The doorbell rings, breaking me out of my thoughts. "Pizza!"

"What?" Alex says.

"I've got to go. The pizza is here. Can we chat later tonight?"

Alex's face saddens as my barriers come up.

You're going to disappoint people, Dakota. But sometimes you need to put your oxygen mask on first before you can help others.

"Sure. Bye," Alex says.

I feel like such a jerk. I text Alex a gif of two otters hugging. He immediately texts back a gif of a toddler boy kissing a toddler girl.

"Koty! The Matsudas are here," Dad yells up the stairs.

Out of habit, I check my look in the mirror. I probably should have washed my hair earlier today when I got up at the crack of noon. I pull it up into a messy bun. I also realize that I'm wearing the Dakota McDonald Halloween costume: Ripped jeans, black cami, and an unbuttoned plaid flannel button-down. All this costume needs are work boots, bedazzled safety glasses, and for me to say "Hot dam!" a few times. It's too late to change. All my other clothes are either dirty or in a giant pile in the bottom of my closet anyway. Whatever. It's only Leo.

I bound down the stairs, my heart feeling lighter, but my barriers still halfway up. I don't want to talk about Alex. I don't want to talk about Lindsay. I just want pizza, some yōkai butt-kicking, and to hang out with my best friend.

"One double pepperoni with green peppers and onions for the kids." Dad hands over the top pizza box to Leo, who stands at the bottom of the stairs. "One artichoke, feta cheese, spinach, and mushroom pizza for the ladies."

"Why, Mom, why?" Leo shakes his head in disgust.

"Oh hush," Mrs. Matsuda says.

"I've got everything set up in the theater for us, including a big box of tissues. You know, in case we need some therapeutic crying. I hear Hugh Jackman brings down the house in this one."

"That would be my cue to take my lonely meat-lovers pizza and head to the man cave. Ladies." Dad does a dramatic, flourished bow. "Please enjoy Hugh Jackman."

"Oh, we will," Mrs. Matsuda says. "Especially on the giant screen."

"Gross, Mom," Leo says.

"Ignore my son." Mrs. Matsuda links her arm through Mom's, and they walk off toward our home theater room.

"Go set up upstairs, and I'll be there in a second," I say to Leo.

Leo's foot pauses on the bottom step. He looks over at me.

"What?" I say.

"Nothing." Leo takes the stairs two at a time.

o   o   o

I push my bedroom door open wider with my socked foot.

"So, we're gonna be all *fancy* tonight?" Leo teases as I put the tray down on my desk. "Mom isn't here. Therefore, table manners are optional."

"Fine." I leave the plates and glasses on the tray and hand Leo his bottle of root beer. "Do NOT spill on my new bed."

I put my root beer bottle on my bedside table and belly flop onto my queen-size bed. A few of the dozen pillows I have bounce to the floor. Leo moves the smallest one off the top of the pizza box before sliding down onto the floor to sit next to it. He leans his back against the foot of my bed.

"You're going to get a crick in your neck down there." I scuttle to the foot of my bed and sit up cross-legged.

"Nah, it's fine," Leo says as Jay Yoshikawa's face fills the TV screen on my dresser. Leo sighs.

"Suit yourself," I say, though Leo used to sit on my bed all the time.

I know we are at a new place in our friendship, but part of me wishes we could go back in time. Back to when we could sit on my bed and play Uno and snort-laugh at silly memes, and everything was normal and not weird or questioned. I shake my head. Boundaries and barriers.

"Stop hogging the pizza," I say.

By the end of the first episode, the pizza is gone, and Leo is rubbing his cramped neck.

"Seriously, you can sit up here." I drain the last of my root beer. "When I redesigned my room recently, I wasn't thinking about you."

"Um, ow." Leo closes the pizza box. He puts it on my desk along with his phone.

"You know what I mean. I thought our Matsuda Mondays were officially over. No need for two beanbags in here anymore."

"Are you saying you miss Matsuda Mondays?" Leo gives me a flirty pout through my mirror. "That you miss me?"

I let his words hang in the air until he turns around.

"Yeah," I say quietly. "I do."

Leo launches himself at my bed. I have to hold on to keep from being knocked off the end. First by Leo's bounce and then by the series of pillows being aimed at my head.

"Hey!" I grab a pillow and whack him back.

"Hey, hey, hey!" Leo holds his arms up around his face after he runs out of pillows.

"You deserve it, butthead."

"Butthead? Are we six?" Leo drops his arms.

While he's distracted, I whack him upside the head with my pillow. He continues to laugh until the dimple in his still slightly chubby cheek comes out. This is my best friend. This is my Leo.

Instead of whacking him a second time, I drop the pillow into my lap. "Keeping it real. I do miss you. A lot. I miss us. Like a younger version of us, back when we were two friends playing Uno until one in the morning while consuming an entire Costco-sized bag of Sour Patch Kids. Except I never want to see Sour Patch Kids again. I was so sick."

Leo chuckles ruefully. He's the one who barfed all over the back seat of the Matsudas' minivan on the way home that night.

"Keeping it real. I miss you too." Leo picks at the threads in the knee of his jeans.

"Yeah, but you have Lindsay now."

"So? You have Alex."

"That's different."

"How?"

"Because Alex goes to a different school. Therefore, you don't have to stand there and watch as somebody else slowly steals your best friend away." And, I probably should have put a filter on that.

We sit in silence. Leo continues to pick at the threads until the whole knee of his jeans rips wide open.

"I know what that feels like too, Koty, okay? But I get what you're saying. It must hurt worse to have a front row seat to it every day."

I can't lie to Leo. "Yeah, it does. And I'm sorry. I don't want to be that jealous best friend. I want you to be happy. Honestly, I do."

"I want you to be happy too. Can I tell you something?" After a beat, Leo continues, "I love Lindsay. But I always feel like I'm on guard with her. Like, I'm two steps away from completely losing her because her parents hate me. Okay, they don't hate me. They hate that I am distracting their daughter and damaging her GPA. I'm worried that Lindsay will finally get tired of always being second place to my family's restaurant and go find somebody else less complicated and with more free time."

Leo looks up at me. His watery eyes stab me deep in the heart.

"I can't do anything about the Lindsay situation, but know that Alex isn't stealing your best friend away. I know we're both changing, but I will always make room for you."

"Thanks. And I'll try to be a better friend too. Even after I'm out of dating jail. Also, know that whatever happens with Alex, I've always got your back."

The cement block on my chest finally lifts. Especially when Leo scoots back until he is leaning up against the left side of my bed's headboard, like old times.

"Can you throw me a pillow or two from your ridiculous collection?" he says, a smile returning to his face.

I slide off my bed, scoop up all the pillows, and throw them back on the bed.

"Cue up the next episode. I'll be back in a sec," I say.

"Hey, Koty, keeping it real. You're cute, but not when you've got a huge chunk of green pepper stuck in your teeth."

I pick up the pillow closest to me and aim it at Leo's head. And then I check my teeth in the mirror on my way downstairs to the kitchen.

o   o   o

"Ahhhhhh." Leo stretches out on my bed and tucks his hands behind his head. "This is nirvana. No waiting tables. No cleaning. My future girlfriend on a giant TV and my BFF bearing candy. Can this night get any better?"

I drop the half-empty bag of mini Twix bars between Leo and me on the bed and climb up beside him. Just like old times.

"Nope. Also, you may have to drive your mom home tonight. I heard our moms cackling when I passed the theater room."

"Good. Mom deserves some fun with her BFF too. And hopefully, now we'll be able to watch all three episodes before Mom realizes what time it is."

I start the next episode and put my iPad back on my bedside table. The opening strains of the *Kitsune Mask* theme song fill my room. Leo and I do our usual dance until half of the pillows are back on the floor again. Leo digs into the bag of candy and hands one to me before taking one for himself.

As the night rolls on, my barriers come completely down. I needed this too. Though part of me wishes Alex was here, I know it would be something completely different. Like, I don't think we would be taking bets on which of her signature fighting moves Jay is going to use on the yōkai of the week to defeat it. Or commenting on the awkward relationship Jay has with Pizza Guy Eli, who she is majorly crushing on.

"Oh, for the love of . . . just kiss her, Eli!" Leo yells at the TV. "Baka dayo!"

"It's called romantic tension," I say through a mouthful of Twix. "Ten bucks says they get their first kiss—first *real* kiss—at the end of this season. The writers are going to milk the romantic tension between the two of them for as long as possible before the payoff. Then, you can swoon."

"Pfft." Leo crams another Twix in his mouth. "Let's watch the last episode with the lights out."

If that sentence had come from Alex, it would have a totally different meaning. Like a romantic tension kind of meaning. Meanwhile, Leo's objective is to scare the crap out of us because the next episode happens in a haunted house. We haven't gone to an actual haunted house since we were thirteen, when I conga-lined behind Leo with my eyes firmly closed, which kind of defeats the purpose of going to a haunted house in the first place.

"If that doll Jay found at the end of the last episode suddenly comes to life, I'm out." I have never been a doll girl. Even my beloved dollhouse was home to a herd of ponies, not a family of humans.

"It's fine. You can hold my hand if it gets too scary." Leo rolls off the bed. "After I pee."

"Gross, and no."

"I'll wash my hands first."

"Do we have to watch it with the lights out?" I say when Leo gets back from the bathroom.

He flips off the lights. "Yes."

Blinded by the lack of overhead lights, Leo's palm grinds into my thigh as he climbs over me to his side of the bed.

"Ow, watch it," I say.

At minute two of the episode, the doll comes to life. Leo offers his hand. I push it away. When the doll opens its mouth to show a row of sharp metal teeth, I grab his whole arm.

"Don't look." Leo puts his free hand in front of my face.

I close my eyes when I hear the doll's teeth gnashing together. Jay yelps in pain.

"Welp, I'm out." I say.

"Wait. It'll be over soon." Leo pulls my head against his shoulder.

Leo's hand stays cupped behind my head. The doll takes a few more bites out of Jay, based on the sounds coming from the TV. I wince every time she yelps in pain. At least until Leo's thumb gently starts to stroke the skin behind my ear. I slowly melt into his shoulder even as the action continues to ratchet up on the screen. Leo's thumb suddenly freezes, but he doesn't push me away. He lets my forehead stay on his muscular shoulder. The soft cotton of Leo's long-sleeved shirt brushes against my lips. In the low light, I can see Leo's breathing quicken as Jay races against the clock to defeat the yōkai controlling the doll. Despite the horror going on in Jay's world, my little bubble with Leo feels safe. It refills my well. Even if I couldn't hear the creepy music swelling, I can feel the tension building in Leo's body.

"KUSO!" Leo jumps so much at whatever happened on the screen that the top of his shoulder cracks me in the chin. "Sorry, Koty. You okay?"

I rub my thumb across my lower lip, which collided with my upper teeth. No blood comes off. "Yeah."

I don't let go of Leo, but I do watch Jay destroy the yōkai. Leo lets out a tired sigh and flops back like he's the one who had to kitsunebi—Jay's signature move—the yōkai himself. Leo turns his head to look at me. He tips his head to the side until our heads touch. If he rotated a little more, our lips would touch. My stomach is a knot of contradictions. I have no right to be in his bubble, but he's also not pushing me away. It feels good, so we rest in comfortable silence.

"Koty?" Leo says as he reaches across my body.

I close my eyes expecting his lips on mine. Instead, I get a light in my face when Leo turns on my bedside table lamp instead. I wince.

"I am so weirded out right now." Leo thankfully clarifies, "By the show. That episode was wild. Can we watch cat videos for a while to clear my brain?"

"Sure." I look around my room for my phone. Then I realize I left it downstairs in the kitchen next to the refrigerator when I was getting the root beers out.

"Here, we can do it off the tablet." Leo's arm brushes against my chest as he reaches across me to grab the tablet off my bedside table. He colors. "Sorry."

I have no words. At least ones that wouldn't make things even more awkward between us. Leo pulls up YouTube but keeps it on the tablet instead of casting it to the TV. We both sit up. Side by side with less than a centimeter between us, but *not* touching.

"Awwww, that one looks like Maru," I say to change the energy of the room.

We watch a good fifteen minutes' worth of cat videos in the low light of my table lamp. I glance at Leo. His eyelids fight to stay open. Finally, his head falls to the right until it rests on my shoulder. A small snore escapes his lips. I push the hair off Leo's forehead and lean over until my lips are a fraction of a millimeter above his skin.

"I love you," I whisper.

I'm going to pretend whatever nonsense he mumbled back was, "I love you too."

Just as I am beginning to nod off too, Mrs. Matsuda yells up the stairs, "Leo! It's time for us to go."

"Leo? Koty?" Mom says, and the sound of booted feet echoes up the stairs.

"Leo." I gently shake him. "My mom is coming."

"What time is it?" Leo, with his eyes barely open, wipes the side of his mouth with his hand. "Sorry, Lindsay."

"Dude." I shove him.

"I mean Dakota."

Leo scoots off the end of my bed. He has his shoes back on by the time Mom cracks open my door after only one knock. Leo yawns and picks up the tray.

"Honey, you don't have to do that," Mom says to Leo.

"Habit." Leo balances the tray on his shoulder so that he can slide his phone in his back pocket. In one swoop, he collects the empty root beer bottles and empty Twix bag and heads out the door.

"I'll get the pizza box." I jump off my bed.

Mom gives us a weird look. Maybe because Leo has bedhead? I race out of the room before Mom can ask why my bed is so disheveled and my pillows are all over the floor.

I follow Leo into the kitchen. My phone still sits face-up on the counter. Leo can see as well as I can that I have ten texts from Alex and three missed calls. Leo rinses out the root beer bottles before putting them in our recycling bin. He's reaching for the pizza box when my phone goes off again.

"Shouldn't you get that?" Leo says.

"I'll call him back in a minute." I don't want to come out of my Leo Bubble. Not quite yet. For both of us.

"So, is Alex going to come at me now?" Leo whispers, half-serious.

"No, I told him we were hanging out." My phone lights up with yet another message from Alex. "He's got some family drama going on at home right now. That's all. I'll call him back in a sec."

"We should get going," Mrs. Matsuda says, and we follow the moms back to the front door.

They do their usual "we need to do this more often" speech as they hug each other.

When Mrs. Matsuda leans in to hug me next, she says in a stage whisper, "I like Lindsay, but I like my Koty-chan better. A lot better."

"Mom!" Leo says.

"Oyasumi," *Good night*. Still deep in the Leo Bubble, I don't think twice about hugging him. A full, frontal hug this time.

Leo doesn't hug me back. The bubble begins to dissipate as

reality sets back in. Once he gets his mom out the door, Leo stops and turns around. He steps back into me.

"Oyasumi."

Leo gives me a full, frontal hug back. That's something that hasn't happened in a long time. Something that makes the conflicted knots in my stomach even tighter.

As the Matsudas drive away, my phone goes off again.

"Dakota, it's almost midnight," Mom says. "Go to bed."

ME

Mom is on me because it's so late. Chat tomorrow right after school?

ALEX

Oh, okay. Sure.

ME

Night.

ALEX

Miss you. Night.

When I crawl into bed fifteen minutes later, I pull the pillow Leo was using closer to me. It smells like Leo's shampoo mixed with chocolate. I wrap my arms around it and pretend like Leo is still here. Tomorrow can be complicated. Tonight, I'm going to stay in the Leo Bubble because it feels good here.

Chapter

21

Lindsay slides into her seat—my old seat—in Japanese class, interrupting Leo's and my heated debate about the Top 5 worst yōkai. Leo drops me like a hot potato.

"You okay, babe?" Leo says to Lindsay, concern etching his face. "You didn't answer any of my texts this morning."

"Yeah, Mom and I had a big blow-up during breakfast, so that made both of us super late, but good news." Lindsay laces her fingers through Leo's. "We can have our date on Friday. Valentine's Day is on."

"Oh," Leo says.

"It's not on?"

"Maybe?" Leo pulls at the collar of his shirt with his free hand. "Bree, the lunchtime waitress, quit yesterday. She was the one who was supposed to work for me Friday night since Aurora will be in California with the winter drumline."

"But it's our first Valentine's Day."

"I'm sorry, Lindsay."

"Why does this always have to be so hard?" Lindsay collapses over her desk with a dramatic sigh.

Leo's plea telegraphs over the top of Lindsay's back to me. *Help me.*

I shrug and shake my head side to side.

"It's going to be okay, babe." Leo strokes her hair. "We'll celebrate Valentine's Day on Monday when I'm off."

Lindsay looks up. "Do you know what I had to do to get Mom and Dad even to agree to Friday? We aren't supposed to be going out at all, remember? So could you try a little harder on your end, please? I can't do this by myself all the time."

The bell rings, trapping me literally in a front-row seat to Leo and Lindsay's teenaged soap opera.

I have never been so glad to see Iwate-sensei in my life.

"Minna," Iwate-sensei says to get our attention. "Before we get started today, does anybody have their second installment for the Japan trip?"

Leo wisely takes the opening and bolts. After Jax turns in his check, Leo hands Iwate-sensei a bulging envelope with two hands and a small bow. Iwate-sensei says something serious to him that is way above everybody else's language level before turning to us and dumbing it down.

"Mina-san, okane o motte konaide kudasai." Iwate-sensei makes an X with her forearms while telling us not to bring cash like Leo did. She picks up Jax's parents' check and opens her hand to it. "Sensei ni chekku o kudasai."

I pull my check out of my wallet as Leo sits back down.

"Have you ever done a cashier's check?" Leo says. "My parents were . . . too busy to go to the bank with me yesterday."

I presume he's talking to me and not Lindsay who is still flopped over her desk between us. I shake my head.

Lindsay sits up. "I wish you weren't going this year. It would have been more romantic going together senior year."

"Yeah, I know, but I already made the deposit for this year's trip. If you'd given me a heads-up sooner that you liked me, I wouldn't have made the deposit," Leo lies. Or maybe he's not.

They are still problem-solving Valentine's Day when I get back from paying Iwate-sensei.

"I bet you and Alex are doing something romantic for Valentine's Day." Lindsay's voice has an edge to it.

"Yep, super romantic. Alex is modeling tuxes for me. And my parents. And Phil. And the entire crew. If we're lucky, Alex and I might get to steal a romantic moment over corn dogs from Sonic on the way home. Woo." Though this is a distinct possibility, I'm going to try a little harder now to make sure my first real Valentine's Day does *not* go this way.

While Iwate-sensei finishes up the Japan trip prep, I send Alex a text.

ME

Sure you're okay about Friday? It's not exactly a romantic way
to spend Valentine's Day.

ALEX

Unconventional but memorable.

Lindsay only shuts up about Valentine's Day when Iwate-sensei threatens her with detention. That adds lightning to the black clouds already thundering over her head. I bolt for the door as soon as the bell rings.

Leo slides in across from me at our lunch table a few minutes later with a sigh. "I'd like to thank you for, if not making me look good, at least not making me look as bad back there."

"You're welcome." It comes out more as a question than a statement.

"So what are you doing for Valentine's Day for real?"

"Why?" I pop open the box with my tuna sandwich in it.

Leo pulls out one of his sad PB&Js. "Because I want to steal your idea. Or at least put my own spin on it."

"Hate to disappoint you, but Alex is going to Tucson for the weekend for his cousin's wedding. Friday night corn dogs might be it."

"We could team up and pretend that celebrating Valentine's Day on the seventeenth is like the next big thing in Hollywood. We're not late. We're ahead of the curve. Yeah."

"Alex has a game on Monday. And even if he didn't, bringing your BFF on your Valentine's Day date is a really bad idea."

Leo lets out an exasperated sigh.

"Go back to your original date idea." I flash back to the only part of my date with Jake Yong that didn't completely suck. "The whole cook-for-her-and-then-look-at-stars thing. Throw in a single rose. Maybe some strawberry-flavored ice cream mochi to stay on theme.

Boom. Valentine's Day saved. There is one special thing that girls love. No, I can't tell you. It would be breaking Girl Code."

"What, Koty?" Leo leans in. "You're allowed to share insider information with your BFF. I'm desperate here."

I lean closer and look side to side before whispering, "Ojiichan's garlic pickles."

Leo flicks me in the head.

I laugh even harder. "Dude, I am absolutely the last person you should be taking dating advice from."

Leo sits back and crosses his arms. "Yeah, but at least you get it—what it's like working in the family business and all the social-life-killing baggage that comes with it. If Alex were in my shoes, you wouldn't be mad at him for working on Friday. We'd celebrate on Matsuda Monday, and everybody would be happy. No drama or guilt trips necessary."

Leo bites his bottom lip. He's said too much. Way too much.

"If I were Alex," Leo adds, dropping his eyes.

Because we always tell each other the truth, I go with, "Yeah, if you were Alex. But you're not."

"Yep, definitely not."

The energy is so off at our table that when Lindsay arrives with her tray, she looks at me and then Leo.

"Did I miss something?" Lindsay sits down and wraps her arm around Leo's back.

"No." Leo's lips brush against Lindsay's temple.

"Don't be baka, Leo. Of course she'd love it," I say, and when Leo looks rightfully confused, I add, "Leo wants to come over to your house on Monday and make you dinner for a belated Valentine's Day. I suggested that he cook for your whole family. That way, maybe they'd let you guys go stargazing or something after dinner for a little bit."

Lindsay's lower lip quivers. She throws her arms around Leo. "That would be the most romantic thing anybody has ever done for me."

"You deserve it and a whole lot more." As Leo hugs Lindsay back, he mouths "Thank you" over her shoulder to me.

I shrug.

"Wait until you see my gift for you!" Lindsay squeals.

"Gift?" Leo's panicked look probably mirrors mine.

Nevaeh drops their tray of cheese pizza on the table with a thud and sits next to me. "Valentine's Day is such a made-up, BS holiday."

"So, your coffee date with Jax's college friend went that badly?" I say.

Nevaeh scoffs. "I'm not looking for a hookup. I'm looking for a relationship."

I put an arm around Nevaeh's shoulders and give them a squeeze. "Hang in there, Nev. The perfect person is out there for you. Be patient."

"Yeah, we can't all have that perfect partner in their life since, you know, birth." Nevaeh cuts their silver-lined eyes at me. "Some of us have to work harder than that."

Chapter

22

I don't know what other people learned in school on Friday, but I spent the whole day second-guessing my Valentine's gift for Alex. Especially after Lindsay rolls into Japanese class with a giant gift basket for Leo. Like, you could cart a baby elephant around in that thing.

"Did I miss that today was your birthday?" I tease Leo.

Leo pulls at the collar of his shirt. "Wow, babe, this is . . ."

"Extra," Jax says, and I silently agree with him.

"Hey, I brought chocolate for you guys too." Lindsay pulls a box filled with Hershey's Kisses out of her backpack and gets up to distribute them to our classmates.

"Movie tickets, some headphones, Flamin' Hot Cheetos, and oh look, some Sour Patch Kids. *Yum yum.*" I poke through the basket as Leo turns redder and redder. "What's in the tiny gift bag?"

"Dakota!" Lindsay yells from across the room. "That's private!"

As Jax and I both crane our necks to see inside, Leo peeks into the tiny, sparkly red gift bag. He quickly closes the bag and puts it deep in his backpack.

"What did you buy Alex for Valentine's Day?" Leo rolls up his sleeves, trying to release some heat before he spontaneously combusts.

"I didn't."

"I thought you guys were officially a thing."

"Um, I think so. I don't think Alex is dating anybody else at his school. Also, I didn't buy him anything. I made it."

"Of course you did." After a beat, Leo adds, "How many power tools did it require?"

"Shut up." But because he knows me so well, I add sheepishly,

"Two. Three if you count the sanding drum attachment on the Dremel."

"Do we get to see it, or is it *private*?"

I pull up the picture on my phone.

"Wow, Koty, that's amazing." Leo blows up the picture of the license-plate-sized sign I made that says SANTOS, #7, and the year in different-sized but coordinating fonts. I debated how to sign my work on the back for *hours*. Finally, I just signed my name like I do on all my fans' requests. Well, unless someone sticks a body part in my face. That's a hard no from me.

"Sugoi!" Iwate-sensei does a double-take when she sees the enormous basket on Lindsay's desk. She picks up the tag that reads in size-72, glittery Papyrus font, I LOVE YOU, LEO!

So extra.

"Matsuda-san, you know that in Japan it is a newer custom that all men who receive chocolate on Valentine's Day must reciprocate the gift on March 14 for White Day. Only, you must give a gift two to three times greater in value than what you received." Iwate-sensei pats Leo on the shoulder. "Gambatte ne."

I laugh at sensei wishing Leo good luck on that. Leo shakes his head.

o   o   o

Even though Nevaeh and I prod him at lunch before Lindsay arrives, Leo won't tell us what's in the bag.

"C'mon, we're BFFs. I'm dying here," I try again when we are alone after school.

Leo skateboards down the street with the ridiculous gift basket in his hands, but he won't budge.

"I know. It's a man thong," I tease.

Leo stumbles off his skateboard. "First: Wrong. Second: Ew. Third: Nobody needs that visual."

"Then what is it?" I jump off my skateboard so I can retrieve Leo's skateboard from the grass since his hands are full. "Maybe I should buy one for Alex."

"No, you should not."

"It's that bad?"

"It's not bad or good. It's . . . thought-provoking." When I press him further, Leo snaps at me, "You're suffocating me again, Dakota."

I put my hands up. "Oh-kay, I'll get out of your business. Happy Valentine's Day."

"Yeah. You too." Leo's voice sounds flat, and his shoulders slump as he rolls away.

o   o   o

Nevaeh will be proud. I brought a purse with me tonight. Mostly, it's so I could carry Alex's gift inside it. *If* I give it to him.

"Looking good, Alex," Stephanie says when Alex comes out of the changing room with the first of the four tuxes on.

"Come over here, son." Phil hails Alex from across the large tuxedo store, which is closed tonight for our invasion. After we signed autographs and took selfies with the owners, of course. "Dakota too."

I leave our makeshift hair and makeup station and smooth down the black-and-white, retro, A-line party dress I'm wearing. I carry the ridiculously high, peep-toe, black patent leather heels in my hand as I walk across the store.

"Still think I should be wearing a tux too," I say when I join them.

"Please don't start with that again." Phil rubs his temples. "A Class Act Tuxedo Company wants a good-looking boy in a tux. That's what they're going to get. Everybody is going to do their job with *happy* faces, right?"

I do jazz hands around my fake smile. Phil shakes his head and walks away.

"Is it cringe to admit that Ms. Stephanie had to give me a crash course on modeling yesterday?" Alex takes my highly manicured hand and gives it a kiss. "I mean, really, how hard is it to stand in one spot? It took me three hours to get it down, but here I am, looking like James Bond and ready to be your Ken doll."

"I'm sorry. I should have warned you that I come with a lot of social-life-killing baggage."

Alex shrugs. "It's worth it."

"We're burning daylight here, people!" Phil yells across the store. "Lights up. Alex on set. Now."

"The sun went down twenty minutes ago, Phil," I say to yank his chain. Stephanie hushes me.

Mom and Dad leave Stephanie in charge as they celebrate an unromantic Valentine's Day with the owner of A Class Act Tuxedo Company and her husband at a restaurant down the street.

"Remember, no fig-leaf poses, okay?" Stephanie straightens Alex's classic white bow tie on a white shirt combo.

Alex removes his clasped hands from the front of his crotch. "I feel like I should be serving you tea and crumpets in this outfit."

"Not gonna lie, it's a little *Downton Abbey*, but I like it," I say.

"Alex!" Phil yells.

Alex leans in to kiss me, but Stephanie shoots out her arm like a traffic guard. "We're working right now."

"Yes, ma'am." Alex winks at me and jogs to the makeshift set.

Stephanie's crash course in modeling works, even if Alex is a little stiff at first. I pull up The Alex Mix on my phone, and Stephanie hands me a mini speaker—which suddenly appears out of the Magic Handbag—to Bluetooth it through.

"That's it! And turn. Turn. Look back over your shoulder," Stephanie calls from the side of the green screen set somebody built for tonight. I bite my lip to stifle a laugh when Stephanie mirrors Alex's poses like a true stage mom. "Alex, BMW called, they want you to be in their next print ad campaign."

"They did?" I say as a huge smile lights up Alex's face.

"What? No. We're pretending. Or vision-casting, if you prefer." Stephanie mimes taking off the jacket and throwing it over her shoulder. "What's that? Alex Santos was named MVP of this year's World Series. Why, yes, he'd love to walk the red carpet at your blockbuster movie premiere. You want him to wear a suit from Armani's new collection? Sure. He could do that."

I take some stills and video of Alex before he moves on to Look #2. I load up the best picture on Instagram. He'll be flattered, right? What do I call Alex though? He's not my boyfriend officially. "My Valentine" sounds too elementary school. "My friend" sounds too generic. "My love"—yeah, we aren't there yet. My manicured finger hovers over the share button.

I'm still debating what to do with the picture when Phil sends Alex to put on Look #3. Alex takes a detour on the way to the changing room.

"For you, my . . . Dakota." Alex presents me with the faux red rose that was his coordinating prop during Look #2. He kisses my cheek before zooming away.

I close the app without posting. I don't want to make things even more awkward than they already are. The one million and twenty-six people who follow me on Instagram will have to make up their own story about how I spent my Valentine's Day. I still want to humblebrag, though, so I send the picture to Nevaeh.

NEVAEH
blink blink Woooooow.

"Where's Dakota?" Phil says when Alex is on Look #4, a white dinner jacket paired with black pants and a white shirt. Very retro and classy. "She better not be eating in that dress."

I put the powdered sugar doughnut hole down and slip away from the tiny craft services table set up in the back. Stephanie walks backward in front of me while touching up my lipstick and brushing powdered sugar off the front of my dress.

"You're doing great, Alex. That last set in particular is gold," Phil says. "See if you can pull something like that out of Dakota for me. Please. So we can all go home."

Good thing we're not near the craft services table, or Phil would be getting a doughnut hole upside his head. I climb onto the make-shift stage. Stephanie hands me the ridiculous shoes. Suddenly, I am eye to eye with Alex.

"Well, hello." Under the intense lights, Alex's eyes look even more like a kaleidoscope. My heart flutters, and I can't contain my smile, especially when Alex leans in to kiss my cheek.

We do a little bit of our choreography to shake things up. I do some solo shots too, to include in my headshot portfolio—on the odd chance that I want to continue in the business after the show officially ends.

"And a couple of Alex by himself in Look Number Four," Phil says.

I wobble on my heels toward the edge of the stage. Toby, aka the guy who holds my ladder, puts out his arms. Sadly, I'm more likely to fall off my heels than my ladder. I accept his help off the stage. I slip off my shoes and hand them to Stephanie.

Dad announces his return to the tux shop with a "Looking good, Alex!"

"You look good too, honey." Mom air-kisses my cheek because we're both adulting tonight and wearing lipstick. She nods at Stephanie, who is posing on the side again. "Every time I think I know everything about Stephanie, she surprises me."

"Me too."

"I think Alex has got this modeling thing down." Mom nods her head. "Now, if we can get him to talk on camera."

"Stephanie's working on it with him. At this rate, Alex will be Miss Congeniality by the end of the season."

"And that's a wrap," Phil yells. "Good work, everybody."

"So. Hungry." I eyeball the craft services table.

"Me too." Alex suddenly appears behind me and greets my parents.

"What do you say, Alex? You, me, and a romantic dinner of corn dogs from Sonic?" I take out my borrowed diamond-and-pearl earrings and hand them to Stephanie, who puts them in a little robin's-egg-blue box.

"I hate to be the one to rain on your parade, but you need to stay on set, Dakota." Stephanie digs in the Magic Handbag and swaps the tiny jewelry box for makeup-removing wipes. She hands a wipe to Alex. "Unless you want Phil to pick the shots, because A Class Act Tuxedo Company's new prom campaign launches tomorrow morning."

"Why does the universe hate me so?"

"A tad dramatic, don't you think?"

"Don't worry, Dakota. Go change, and I'll meet you back here in," Alex looks at the expensive watch that doesn't belong to him. "Ten minutes for a romantic Valentine's Day dinner. The special tonight is doughnut holes."

"Works for me."

o   o   o

"Tah-dah!" Alex waves his hand at the floor when I come back out, in what I hope is a cute girl-next-door look. "A romantic dinner for two."

In the back corner of the tuxedo shop, while a dozen people rip apart the stage, pull up cables, and go over footage and pictures, Alex has created an oasis for us. I'm pretty sure that our picnic blanket is the tablecloth off the craft service table, but whatever. I place my purse next to Alex's small duffel bag. I kneel down next to a trio of paper plates filled with strawberries, doughnut holes, and cheap pretzels. Two bottles of seltzer water round out our dinner. Alex puts his phone in the center of the blanket. A candle video with slow jams playing in the background helps muffle some of the banging coming from the front of the store.

"Wow! Thank you for all of this. This is the best Valentine's Day date I've ever had." It is also the *only* Valentine's Day date I've ever had, but Alex doesn't need to know that.

Before I can chicken out, I dig in my giant purse and pull out Alex's present wrapped in a simple layer of red tissue paper.

"Happy Valentine's Day," I say.

Alex nods his head as he unwraps the gift. He flips the sign over and runs his index finger over where I signed my name. "Nicely done, Miss McDonald. You are a girl of many talents. I love it. And I have something for you."

Alex digs a tiny red bag out of his duffel bag. My brain decides to pull up an image of Leo and his "thought-provoking" tiny red bag.

"Is this something *private*?" I have to ask.

"I guess. Other people might not get it," Alex says.

After checking where both my parents and Stephanie are, I cautiously put my hand in the bag. I raise an eyebrow at Alex. When I pull it out, it's a palm-sized stuffed otter on a keychain. I can't decide if I'm relieved or disappointed.

"It's . . . cute. Thank you."

"It reminded me of you. Like how you are always sending me otter gifs. But now I feel bad, especially as you *made* this sign for me."

"You made me a picnic, so I think we're even."

We keep our kiss both brief and G-rated because our privacy is only a fantasy here in the corner.

"Can we have a redo on my thank-you kiss later when there aren't so many eyes on us?" I say.

"Yes, if you can talk your parents into letting me take you home."

"But that's out of your way, and you have to leave super early tomorrow morning for Tucson."

"Worth it."

Though I don't post about it or even humblebrag to Nevaeh about it, my first real Valentine's Day date is pretty nice despite the dozen or so other people on the date with us, including Stephanie, who walks over to our picnic corner after the rest of the store has finally been put back together.

"Shhh, we'll make copies of these ones for your mom." Stephanie shows us some of the best shots on her phone. "For her birthday."

"She'd like that." Alex wipes the fingers that have been feeding me strawberries on the craft services tablecloth/picnic blanket and scrolls through the photos on Stephanie's phone. "Could I give this one to Abuela? Pretty sure my abuelito owned a tux just like this back in the day. She'd love it."

"Consider it done. Also, Dakota, I talked your parents into letting you ride home with Alex after all." Stephanie, our fairy godmother, points at Alex. "Do *not* make me regret that. Also, I highly recommend that you leave right now. Doug and Tamlyn only need about ten more minutes before we're all done. Leave the mess. I'll clean it up."

Though I'm immediately on my feet and ready to roll after a quick "Thanks," Alex says, "We can't let you do that."

It shaves another five minutes off our already ticking clock, but I follow Alex's lead and help him clean up the area. I decide not to mention that this is another first for me tonight.

o   o   o

We hit every red light on the way home. Come on, Universe! Throw me a bone here! As soon as the Toyota comes to a full stop in front of my house, I pop my seatbelt and thank Alex like I've wanted to all night.

When we finally break away again, Alex continues to stroke my cheek with his thumb. "I really like you, Dakota. A lot."

I wince, partly because of the blinding headlights of Dad's truck coming through the back window of the Toyota, but also because I'm pretty sure that the script is supposed to say, "I love you, Dakota" and that my next line is, "I love you too."

But this is reality. Plus, the last time I mistook intense like for love, it bit me. Hard. I decide to stick with the truth. "I really like you too, Alex."

Chapter

23

"I thought your Wednesday afternoons belonged to Alex now," Aurora says when she arrives at Matsuda passive-aggressively late, even though everybody knows we all get out of school at the same time.

"They do. We're meeting after dinner tonight though." I add one last cherry blossom to the Specials board and step back to survey my latest work. "We're done with the choreography finally. Every minute when there is a hole in both of our schedules at the same time, Alex comes over to rehearse. Wait, does that even count as dating?"

"Is there kissing involved?" Aurora says.

"Maaaaaybe," I say, and Aurora laughs. "Why does dating have to be so hard?"

"Girl, I'm feelin' ya. At least next week is spring break. Not that that means much when you're a Matsuda. Next year though, when I'm at UNH"—Aurora slides her sunglasses from her head back to her face—"I'm going to Rocky Point or whatever the New Hampshire equivalent of Rocky Point is. Sun. Fun. Absolutely no working."

Once she flies the nest, I don't think Aurora is ever coming back to Phoenix. I'm surprised by the tears suddenly pricking my eyes. Yes, Leo is my BFF, but Aurora has always been part of the package deal. Last summer, everybody changed. Everybody moved on. And now, everybody is leaving me behind. What happens when Leo leaves for college too?

I turn on my heel and grab a wet towel. I scrub the table Leo already cleaned until I can get my emotions in check. Meanwhile, Aurora flops into another booth with a weary sigh and types away on her phone.

"Hey, while I'm waiting on Leo to finish with the trash, you want to give me your two cents on which dress I should wear to my birthday party?" I sit down at my favorite booth. "We're not going with the original designer—Royce Cantrell—after the whole sweatshop in Vietnam controversy."

"Uh, yes. I'll be back in a minute with both snacks and an expert opinion." A few minutes later, Aurora slides into the booth with two glasses of melon soda and a bowl of himemaru arare, my favorite kind of deep-fried rice crackers. "You okay, Koty? You seem off today."

Part of me wants to lie or at least deflect, but I don't. "I'm going to miss you next year."

"I'm going to miss you too." Aurora pops one of the rice crackers into her mouth and pulls out her phone to return a text.

My face must say it all because when Aurora looks back up, she puts her phone in her back pocket. Hot tears prick my eyes again.

"I'm going to miss you too, Koty." Aurora wraps an arm around my shoulders and pulls me into her until the tops of our heads touch. "Hey, I'm the one who's supposed to be getting mushy here. Senior year is almost over. As long as I show up for school every day after spring break, I can pretty much coast over the finish line to graduation. But there are two things before graduation that I can't wait for—prom and your party. And it better be ridiculous like only the McDonalds know how to do ridiculous."

I sniff and wipe my eyes on my sleeve. "Oh, it is. Especially if we can get who I want for the musical guest."

"Exactly. I mean, who else has a 'musical guest' at their birthday party? Like, use your Spotify playlist like everybody else." Aurora gives me a tight hug, and I bank this moment in my memory. "Show me the dresses before somebody comes in and interrupts my five minutes of free time this week."

I push the glasses of soda farther back on the table and slide the colored sketches of my Top 5 dress choices from their folder.

"Starr Shibutani offered us dibs on one of her new dresses from her upcoming 'Fashion Forward' line. You know, the one that partnered specifically with factories that pay their garment workers living wages." I know I'm bragging, but Aurora doesn't care. "Of course, she'll take one of these and customize it especially for me, but these are the basic designs for her fall-winter formal line, which will run at Macy's."

"What if you do several wardrobe changes throughout the night? That way, you could let your sister from another mister borrow this one for prom." Aurora taps a finger on the sketch of the short, icy-blue one with a silver overlay. "This one would look great with my skin tone."

"My party is the weekend after prom, though."

"I promise not to spill anything on it."

"Says the girl who has ketchup spots or something on her shirt." Leo slides into the booth across from us. He pops one of the rice crackers into his mouth and crunches away.

Aurora looks down. "My favorite shirt!"

While Aurora races to the bathroom, Leo pulls her full glass of melon soda to his side of the table and takes a swig. He pops a few more rice crackers in his mouth before turning the sketches around. Leo moves the pictures around, ranking his choices.

"Why this order?" I say when he's done.

"Color, shape, and most importantly, functionality. The purple one is pretty, but not really your style. You prefer an understated elegance like the white one, or maybe the rose-gold one," Leo says with confidence. When I give him a surprised look, he elaborates. "I used to watch a lot of *Project Runway* with Lindsay when we were still allowed to date. Well, more listened to than watched, if you know what I mean."

I put my hands up. "TMI."

"As soon as this quarter's grades come in on Friday, we hope to finally be released from Dating Jail." Leo grabs another handful of rice crackers and crams them in his mouth. "Maybe all four of us could do something over spring break, like play miniature golf. If you and Alex are getting serious, then he should know that your awesome BFF is part of the package deal."

I scoff. "He knows. But I would like it if you guys could be friends too."

I'm thankful that Aurora returns before Leo can cement a date for what will undoubtedly be the most awkward double date in history. Aurora pulls the sketches back to her side of the table. She rearranges the order, still putting the icy blue one first.

"Not that one. You're going to see Koty's banged-up legs." Leo moves the icy blue one to the fifth-place slot.

"Stop riding your skateboard until after the party." Aurora moves the icy blue one back to the first-place slot.

"It's not from skateboarding. My knees are bruised from laying tile in the build's downstairs bathroom with Dad. He can do it for about fifteen minutes while the cameras are rolling, but it's too hard on his knees for much longer than that. Dad won't let anybody else do it, so he's micromanaging me through the process. On the plus side, if Ojiichan buys me a few matching tiles, I can replace the cracked ones in the restaurant's bathroom. I am now Koty, Queen of Tiles."

"Hmm, Ojiichan's seventieth birthday is coming up soon." Leo taps his chin with his index finger. "Maybe we could surprise him. And by *we*, I mean *you* because Aurora and I have no building skills."

"Because *our* dad never has time to teach us any." Aurora waves her phone at us. "Speaking of Dad, he said to tell you the romance writers are coming in tonight."

"He couldn't poke his head out the kitchen door and tell me that?" Leo says and then puts on a cranky-old-man voice. "Kids these days. Always on their phones."

"You know that phone is his baby," Aurora says.

"Yeah, he deserves it. Dad is the most overqualified dishwasher in Phoenix."

"Your dad gave up a lot to keep Ojiichan's dream going," I add.

"Well, I hope he doesn't expect to hand the Matsuda torch to me, because I'm moving to New Hampshire full-time come August, even if I have to get a second part-time job on top of my work-study one. Besides, being Favorite Matsuda Child is Leo's job." Aurora stands up and looks at the sketches one more time. She pulls out the middle one—the long, rose-gold one—and holds it up next to me. "This one. This one is all Koty."

Leo grumbles as Aurora walks away, already on her phone to Jayden, no doubt. "I'm Favorite Matsuda Child because Sasha is gone, and Aurora sets the bar so low I could trip over it and still be the favorite."

"She does have a point." I lower my voice. "I know it's not my business—but keeping it real—I've overheard our dads talking in the man cave. About what happens after you leave for college too."

"No pressure or anything." Leo sits back in the booth. He puffs out his cheeks and blows out a frustrated sigh. "And then there's the whole Number One Son thing. Before you go off on me about the patriarchy, it's a Japanese thing, not an American thing."

"Yeah, not changing my mind."

"Agreed, but all three of us are Number One Sons. There is a lot of Japanese-style baggage that comes with that, even when your mom is a white American. Which means at some point I'm going to have to make a difficult decision about the future of Matsuda. But not today." Leo nods at the front door as a party of five comes in. "Today, I need to focus on making that last Japan trip payment."

"Speaking of difficult, you're going to have to let your parents know about the trip sometime. You can't just dip for three weeks this July and hope they don't notice you're gone."

"I don't know. That works for me," Leo jokes as he slides to his feet. "Again, if I can't make the final installment, it doesn't matter anyway. We'll cross that bridge when we get to it."

"Leo, that is not a good plan."

As Leo flits off to take care of customers, I look at the sketches one last time. The purple one is fun, a little sassy, and—Leo's right—not me at all. Nevaeh encouraged me to push my fashion boundaries for this event. Though I agree about not going with the safest choice, I'm not sure a dress with a slit way up one side is right for me either, especially on TV. I don't need any more memes created about my social gaffes. Thanks.

When Leo passes by my booth with his customer's order ticket, he stops for a second to pull the rose-gold one back to the top.

"You'd look pretty in this one. Very princess-y," Leo says, tapping it with his middle finger. The same finger that flicks me in the arm after the compliment.

I look at the rose-gold gown. The neckline is a little lower than I would normally like, but some of Stephanie's magic tape will keep the fabric securely attached to my skin. The bottom part flows out wide, but it doesn't have a train for Alex to trip on. I could pull this dress off, especially if I pile up my hair like the model in the sketch and add a tiara for some extra bling. Nevaeh made me promise that there will be some tiara action happening because, "Come on, how many times is a tiara appropriate in your everyday life?" For normal people, that is. Nevaeh's hoping that my tiara will start a new trend at school, especially as tiaras are not officially banned headgear. Yet.

I pull out my phone and take a picture of the rose-gold dress. I text it to Mom and Stephanie at the same time.

ME
Order this one from Starr please.
> **STEPHANIE**
> Perfect choice, IMO. Next up: shoes! I'll start a new file for
> you ASAP.

ME
Uggggggh. Start a tiara file too please.
> **STEPHANIE**
> You got it!

After all, I did promise Aurora that this party would be ridiculous, like only the McDonalds know how to do ridiculous.

Chapter

24

With the amount of negotiating I'm required to do just to go to Alex's Senior Night baseball game, I should work for the State Department.

"It's one high school baseball game," I argue with my parents. Again.

"Please? It's Senior Night," Alex says as we all crowd in the kitchen after Alex's and my latest dance rehearsal. I even ditched the work boots for two-inch heels to practice in tonight. I am working my way up to three inches. Progress!

"Maybe, but you absolutely cannot go to a party afterward. Whether there are parents there or not," Mom says.

"Mom!"

"Honey, I know you think we are being unreasonable about this, but we just want to protect you." Dad throws an arm around my shoulders. "It's not like asking to hang out with the Matsudas. You're fair game out in the bigger world. We don't want you to get hurt."

"Yeah, but not ever facing that potential danger hurts too. And since I started dating, now I see how much I've been missing out on."

"We know, Dakota." Mom shares a pointed look with Dad. "Boy, do we know. We live this life too, remember. And for a lot longer than you have."

"I promise, we will not go to any parties after the baseball game," Alex says. "The most dangerous thing we'll do is get double scoops of ice cream instead of singles. Please, Mr. and Mrs. McDonald. It's a special night for me. Please let me share it with Dakota."

I won't say it out loud, but I can fill in the rest of his thoughts from a previous conversation.

"If you could be Switzerland and sit between the Santos and Gordon sides of my family on Senior Night, that might keep everybody on their best behavior." Alex had pretty much begged me after our—as predicted—completely awkward spring break double date to Golf Land with Leo and Lindsay. "Also, if I could use you as my excuse for why I can't go out for dinner with them afterward, I would owe you forever. That will cut down on the passive-aggressive behavior from whichever parent I *don't* choose. I did promise Abuela that I would bring you over for a visit soon. Just the three of us. I know the unnecessary drama between my parents grinds on her too."

"I don't know, Doug," Mom says, bringing me back to the present.

"I will agree to it, young man, but only if you listen to Dakota one hundred percent. If she doesn't feel safe or people are acting inappropriately to her, you will get her to safety immediately and call me." Dad takes off his bifocals and gives Alex the full Evil Santa glare.

"I'm not a member of the royal family, Dad. The scariest thing that might happen is that I get brain freeze from too much ice cream."

Dad crosses his beefy arms. "Those are my conditions."

"Yes, sir," Alex says.

I grab Mom's hand. "Mom. Please. Everything is going to be okay. I promise. Let me come out of the McDonald Bubble for a little while and be a regular teen. A regular teen who wants to support her boyfriend at one of his last high school games before he leaves for college."

As soon as the word "boyfriend" comes out of my mouth, I regret it. Alex looks at me. We haven't had that conversation yet.

The idea hangs in the air for a few more beats before Mom says, "Okay, you can go."

"Thank you, Mrs. McDonald. Mr. McDonald. I promise you won't regret it." Alex throws his arms around me and lifts me off the ground. That is until Evil Santa clears his throat. Alex places me gently back down on the wooden floor. "Toning it down, sir."

Dad grumbles and wanders off to his man cave.

0   0   0

"I'm not kidding, Dakota Rae," Dad lectures me for the hundredth time. Today. "Keep your phone close by. If things start going sideways, you call me. I'll be there in three minutes."

"I think it might take a little longer than three minutes." The drive over was forty-five minutes.

"No, I timed it from Chucky's Sports Bar and Grill around the corner yesterday."

"Dad!"

"Where I will be enjoying all-you-can-eat Happy Hour hot wings until after the game." Dad pulls up to the curb of Desert Bloom High School. "Text me when you are in the car with Alex. And stop rolling your eyes at me, young lady, or I will turn this truck around right now."

"We're all going to be fine, Dad. I promise. Go enjoy your hot wings." I kiss Dad's cheek. "Look, there's Alex's Mom."

Probably. I've never met Mrs. Santos, but who else would be wearing a baseball jersey with a giant bedazzled 7 on it. Of course, she can't see me through the pickup's tinted windows. I jump out of the truck and follow the light crowd toward the baseball field.

"Dakota! Yoo-hoo!" Mrs. Santos yells.

Instinctively, I put my shades back on and pull my baseball cap down lower.

"Hi, Mrs. Santos. Thanks for inviting me to the game," I say quietly, hoping that she will take my lead and lower her voice.

She doesn't. "Look at you, Dakota! That jersey looks perfect on you!"

Once we got the official okay from my parents, Mrs. Santos insisted on making me a Desert Bloom High School Scorpions baseball jersey with a giant 7 and SANTOS on the back. I am thankful that Alex talked his mom out of bedazzling mine.

"Derek is holding our seats inside," Mrs. Santos says. "But first, a picture."

"No," is my conditioned response, but Mrs. Santos already has her phone out.

"Not even for Alex's Senior Memories book? Next to the tuxedo pictures you sent us. What a precious birthday gift. Thank you." Mrs. Santos looks ready to burst into tears.

I can't take the credit for that, or the picture Alex's abuela is getting next month for her sixtieth birthday, but I know better than to bring that up. "You are very welcome."

"Alex was over the moon that you were able to come support him tonight. Please, let's take a picture."

You wanted to be out here in the bigger world, Dakota. Time to own it. Alex's and my relationship is about to go public anyway. It's not like I can stop everybody who might want to take my photo with their cell phone tonight. I might as well "control the narrative" as much as I can.

I slide my sunglasses off and lean into Mrs. Santos.

"Here, my arms are longer." I take Mrs. Santos's cell phone so that I can set it up at the optimum selfie angle for me. If I'm going to control the narrative, I'm going to make sure that the small pimple on my right temple isn't part of it.

"Sherri!" echoes across the area until we turn around. A white woman wearing a matching bedazzled jersey walks toward us. Two little girls wearing SANTOS-bedazzled T-shirts and huge, burgundy-and-gold bows on their curly blond hair fight over who gets to hold the poster with a giant picture of Alex's face on it, until their mom snatches it out of their hands. The older one jumps at the poster, which is now over her mom's head. The younger one has a meltdown in the middle of the sidewalk.

"Where's Ricky?" Alex's aunt says to Mrs. Santos.

"In his room. Possibly until the next decade. Lord, grant me patience with that child." Mrs. Santos leans down and coaxes the younger cousin into her arms. "Lily, are you going to be a cheerleader tonight, or does your mommy need to take you home?"

"Cheer-weeder." The little one wipes her snotty nose on her arm.

The older one tugs on my jersey until I look down at her.

"Are you Alex's girlfriend?" she says.

"Ummmm. I'm a girl, and I'm Alex's friend, so, yes?"

"Of course you are, Dakota." Mrs. Santos puts the other little girl down. "Alex has had lots of girlfriends. You are the only one he's ever let me make a jersey for, even if he insisted on the boring version."

My insides push and pull. I don't like it when somebody else hijacks my narrative, but I also appreciate that someone can clarify the facts for me.

"Alex is texting me." Mrs. Santos waves her phone at us. "It's time for family pictures."

"If you can point out where you want me to sit, I'll wait in the stands." I put my sunglasses back on.

"Oh no, sweetie. Alex wants you to come too. He wants you to be in one of the pictures since you can't go to prom with him in April."

"Wait. What?"

"You're going to be in New York for an award show or something? At least that's what Stephanie told him when he ran his prom-posal idea across her."

It's hard to be annoyed with Stephanie when this is literally her job. I guess I should thank her for saving me the potential embarrassment of Alex spending a lot of time and money and then me turning around and rejecting him. Even if we weren't going to New York, I'm not ready to be that open. At least at my birthday *extravaganza,* I have my friends, Stephanie, and the crew looking out for me. I would be a wide-open target at Alex's prom. My stomach clenches and I force the *SNL* skit out of my head.

"Hey, baby!" Mrs. Santos yells when our group rounds the corner and finds a professional photographer set up for the team.

"Mooom." Alex rubs his temples. "Where are Dad and Abuela?"

"How should I know?"

"But it's my turn next."

Mrs. Santos puts her hands out to her sides like "And?"

"Never mind. We'll do candid shots later with the family instead. Maybe."

"Santos, you're up." The coach waves him over.

"Oh no, we're doing this. I'm going to celebrate my baby. Even if *other* people aren't responsible enough to get here on time." Mrs. Santos smooths her bedazzled jersey over her generous curves.

"SANTOS!" The coach yells.

"Coming, Coach." Alex looks back at us and lowers his voice. "Can we not do this right now, Mom?"

"Then stop complaining and take the blessed picture." Mrs. Santos hands me all her gear and walks two steps behind Alex. "And I'll be happy."

The photographer does a couple of shots of Alex by himself, plus a sweet one of him and his mom. Either Alex is a better actor than he lets on about, or whatever the photographer said pulls a genuine smile out of him.

"Dakota, baby, come over here." Mrs. Santos waves at me, and I jog over.

She steps out of the frame and grabs the gear from me. I step into the frame and do my standard pose next to Alex.

The photographer lowers his camera. "How about you loosen up there a bit, sis. This isn't the red carpet."

I turn into Alex and link my arm through his. I hit another red-carpet-worthy pose, again maximizing the angle of my head to minimize the view of the pimple on my temple. The photographer is obviously not impressed by my red carpet training. He shakes his head.

"How about this?" Alex takes the opening move to our dance.

"Now we're getting some life into this picture," the photographer says.

Egged on, Alex swings me out and then back in again. A squeal rips out of my lungs when Alex suddenly lifts me off the ground and spins me around. The photographer keeps shooting long after my tennis shoes hit the packed earth again.

"Do I know you from someplace?" the photographer says when

we finally leave the area so another baseball player can take his turn. "You look familiar."

"No," I say as Alex starts to out my identity. "I'm nobody special."

"Yes, you are," Alex whispers as we walk toward his family. "Very special."

Alex's little cousins immediately attach themselves to his long legs. It takes both moms—and the bribe of kettle corn—to pry the girls off Alex.

"Good luck tonight," I say as his loud family walks away. I rock back and forth on my heels. "Would a good-luck kiss be out of place here?"

"Not at all." Alex looks around. "We only have a minute or two, but let's find a more secluded spot."

Alex laces his fingers through mine, and I jog with him to the side of the building. When we get to the most visually obscured area, Alex throws his arms around me and spins me around a second time. Both my hat and sunglasses fly off thanks to centrifugal force, but I don't care. This time when I float back down to the earth, I leave my arms wrapped around his neck.

"Good luck." I glance around before I give Alex a G-rated kiss.

"How can I go wrong? I've got my lucky charm tonight." Alex pulls me in tighter and kisses me deeper. At least until we hear whooping behind us. Alex smiles, but I can practically hear the clanging of my barriers coming up. Three guys in Scorpions baseball uniforms jog by us, harassing Alex as they go.

"Ignore them. I do." Alex leans down and scoops up my hat and sunglasses. "At least now they have solid proof that you exist."

"I should go." I scramble to get my hat and sunglasses back on. "Make your Mom proud tonight."

"Pretty sure I could just stand on first base, and Mom would burst into tears." Alex squeezes my hands. "Now my abuela, she knows her baseball. She even played on her high school's softball team back in the day. Make no mistake, when we go visit her, she will have my favorite tres leches cake along with notes on my performance tonight."

"Good luck." I lean in and kiss Alex one last time.

"Good luck to you. You're the one who has to be Switzerland. I'll meet you out front after the coach releases us tonight. Then, ice cream." Alex puts up two fingers. "Two scoops because we are living on the edge tonight."

I feel like such a baby. "I'm sorry."

"Don't be. We could go pick up garbage on the side of the road for our date, and I'd still look forward to it."

"SANTOS!" the coach yells when he comes around the corner. He puts a hand on Alex's back and pushes him toward the field. "Save it for later. We have a job to do."

At first, I was worried that I wouldn't be able to find Alex's family in the stands. Yep, not a problem. Just look for the thundercloud. I shuffle down the heavily bedazzled and decorated side of our row until I get to the other half of the row, who look like they just left their corner offices.

"Hi, you must be Alex's abuela." I stick out my hand to the black-haired woman wearing a pantsuit and strand of pearls. "I'm Dakota."

"I know. We've been watching your TV show." Abuela Santos firmly shakes my hand. Her son, who is talking to somebody on the phone, reaches over and does the same.

Mr. Santos leans down the row when he gets off his business call. "Where is Enrique, Sherri?"

"He opted to stay home," Mrs. Santos says.

"You let him stay home alone?" Abuela Santos says with alarm.

"He's twelve. He's fine," Mrs. Santos snaps.

"He should be here to support his brother."

"Well, it's too late now."

The still-light crowd goes wild as both teams take turns on the field warming up. It's an unseasonably warm late afternoon in Phoenix, but our bleacher row threatens to freeze over. I pretend like I don't notice Alex's parents repeatedly checking out what the other is doing.

I have a lot of gifts, but singing is not one of them. When we stand for the national anthem I slide my cap off and mumble-sing the words. Abuela Santos is a better singer than the soloist who cracks the money note.

"You have a beautiful voice," I say when we sit back down again.

"Thank you. Alex does too. I wish he would come back to church and sing with us again like he did when he was little. Back when he still lived at home."

"¡Mamá, no empieces!" Mr. Santos says, like they've had this discussion a million times.

The game starts, and everyone's attention turns to the field where Alex plays first base. Thanks to my dad and a gym class unit, I know the basics of baseball. Unfortunately, I would rather lay tiny pieces of tile in my dad's intricately designed pattern for three hours than watch it. At least, in the end, I would have something to show for it. I fake my way through the game, clapping when Abuela Santos does and adding a "Go, Santos!" to whatever she yells. I'm not sad when the older cousin, Sabrina, who is as bored as I am, climbs into my lap with her mom's iPad. We play a couple of rounds of Candy Crush before she's tired of that too. I have never babysat anybody in my life, so I'm at a loss.

"Ummmm. Want to take silly pictures?" I pull out my phone and open the app.

"Yes, Alex and I like the doggy face." Sabrina snatches the phone out of my hand and swipes to the dog-face filter like a pro.

While we wait for Alex's turn to bat, Sabrina and I do the dog face, a bubbly mermaid, swap faces, and even do the femme fatale one before Abuela Santos taps my leg with her perfectly manicured hand.

"It's Alex's turn," she says.

Sabrina isn't happy when I take my phone from her. I flip the camera around to take a few pictures of Alex and some video.

"Oh oh oh!" Abuela Santos levitates off the bench as the ball Alex smacked sails back toward the outfield.

"Awww!" Our whole row says in unison when the other team catches the ball, and Alex is out.

Somewhere around the halfway mark of the game, they stop for

Senior Night. Alex's parents—going in opposite directions down the bleachers—head down to the field. You could drive a Mack truck through the gap between them as they wait on the side with all the other senior parents, along with a few grandparents and siblings. When the guys come off the field, Mr. Santos steps up to his son first, giving him a short, tight handshake pulled into a hug. You can read Mrs. Santos's annoyance all the way over here. When it is her turn, Mrs. Santos gives Alex an overly demonstrative hug and kiss on his cheek. The seniors take the field, and the announcer gives a quick bio about each of them. I clap politely.

"Get ready to cheer for Alex," I say to Sabrina, who is playing Candy Crush on the iPad again.

"Number Seven, Alejandro Santos, Jr." Alex hooks his elbows with his parents and walks down the middle of the field. Someone hands Mrs. Santos a flower. "Alex is the son of Alejandro Santos, Sr. and Sherri Gordon-Santos. First baseman for the Scorpions for the last two years, Santos boasts a batting average of .352. Next fall, he will attend Duke University in North Carolina and major in business."

Abuela Santos's "Qué?!" blends with my "What?!"

In tandem, Mr. and Mrs. Santos snap their heads to look at Alex. Unfortunately, it's probably that *WHAT?!* picture that the professional photographer gets before the announcer moves on to the next player. I have to give them credit, Alex's parents keep it together until the ceremony is officially over and they are back in the stands, again coming from opposite directions.

"Why didn't you tell me about this, Sherri?" Mr. Santos leans forward and hisses down the row.

Mrs. Santos wipes at her eye makeup and hisses back, "Because I didn't know about it, Alejandro."

"I thought he was moving back home with us and commuting to ASU," Abuela Santos says to her son.

"No, he was going up to NAU. They offered him a bigger scholarship," Mrs. Santos says. "I never thought he was serious about Duke."

"Did you know?" Abuela Santos looks at me, deep wrinkles forming on her forehead.

Mr. and Mrs. Santos stare at me too. The fight or flight response that once saved my cavewoman ancestors from sabertooth tigers kicks into overdrive. My heart races, and my chest tightens. I tuck my shaking hands under my thighs.

"No." My voice squeaks. I take a deep breath to steady my voice. "No. I knew he applied to Duke and was wait-listed, but I didn't know that he'd gotten in."

I'm not sure if I wish Alex would have shared this truth grenade with me before the game or not. And then there is the whole "Now what?" with our relationship since he has one foot out the door.

"Oh, we are going to have a *family meeting* about this after the game," Mr. Santos says, punctuating his sentence with a swear.

Derek, who has wisely been seen but not heard the entire game, leans in. "Hey, watch your language. This is a family event."

"You don't get to lecture me, *Derek*. That is your name, isn't it? I can't keep up with all of Sherri's *boyfriends*."

Derek stands up. Mr. Santos stands up. I fumble to get my phone out of my pocket. I am so out of here. Before my shaking fingers can pull up Dad's contact, Abuela Santos says something sharp in Spanish and jerks her son by the hand until he sits down again. It takes both Mrs. Santos, who is red-faced and teary, and her sister to get Derek to sit back down.

Sabrina looks from one man to the other and says in a gleeful voice, "Oooooh, somebody's gonna get a timeout."

I'm not the only one who laughs.

"Hey, man." One of the other baseball dads sitting behind us puts his hand on Mr. Santos's shoulder, and leans into him.

Whatever he says calms Mr. Santos down. Mr. Santos sits quietly with his hands in his lap for the rest of the game without further commentary. Derek lasts for about another ten minutes before he informs Mrs. Santos loudly that he will wait for her in the car. My shaking finger hovers over Dad's contact icon. Abuela Santos must notice because she puts her hand on my back and leans into me.

"I'm sorry," she whispers, and I nod.

I'm not going to say it's okay, because it's not. It's raw and heated and emotional. I don't like any of the above. I'll give it five more minutes. If I can't get the sound of blood surging in my ears to stop, I'm out. My phone buzzes.

> **LEO**
> OMB! They're having a Kitsune Mask panel at Hebi Con this August. Wanna go?
>
> **ME**
> Can you get off work again after being gone for 3 weeks?
>
> **LEO**
> If Ava Takahashi is coming . . . I will find a way. I wonder if she signs body parts. Then I can get a tattoo of it.
>
> **ME**
> No. Just no. I'm talking from experience here.
>
> **LEO**
> Life-size poster?
>
> **ME**
> Yes.
>
> **LEO**
> Question: Do I siphon money off my Japan trip fund now or wait to buy a ticket the weekend of the con?
>
> **ME**
> Neither. You let your BFF buy the tickets now as an early birthday present.
>
> **LEO**
>
>
> **ME**
> C'mon! It won't be the same if we don't go together. This way, I have a wingman, and you get The. Best. Birthday. Present. Ever.
>
> **LEO**
> *twisting my arm* Okay. Alex won't mind?

My heart clenches. Will Alex even be here in August, or will he already be thousands of miles away, starting his new-and-improved, drama-free life in North Carolina? And where does that leave us?

ME
It's fine.

I do a quick search online to find the complete boxed set of *Kitsune Mask* so that I can have Ava Takahashi sign it at the con. I'll save it until New Year's when I can give it to Leo as the perfect present. I slide deep into my bubble, thinking about the con and Leo's face when he goes full fanboy over Ava Takahashi. My heartbeat slows, and my hands steady. I'm finally feeling peaceful again when Sabrina suddenly launches herself at me.

"BYEEEEEE!" Sabrina yells into my face before giving me a big hug.

"Oh, hey, yeah, sorry. Bye." The game ended without me noticing.

Mrs. Santos has a passed-out Lily draped over her shoulder. She reaches her hand back for Sabrina. "Come on, baby. Let's get you home."

Sabrina attaches herself to my arm instead. "No. I want to stay with Dakota."

"Ummmmm." I know how to break off stuck tile. I do not know how to break off small children. "I'm going out for ice cream with Alex after the game."

Womp womp. Wrong answer. Just as Sabrina turns to her aunt to whine about how she wants to have ice cream with Alex too, Abuela Santos turns to her son and says, "You said Alejandro was coming home after the game. I made a tres leches cake and everything."

"He is," Mr. Santos says definitively.

"He's not," Mrs. Santos says, her voice rising. "Alex is going on a date with Dakota as *he* planned."

I pull my baseball cap down lower and curl in on myself. The whooshing in my ears starts again. I close my eyes and attempt to pull up an image of Leo meeting Ava Takahashi.

"Hey! Stop it!" I look up to see a scarlet-faced Alex standing on the other side of the fence. His hands clench into fists at his sides.

Tears well up in Sabrina's big brown eyes. "Don't be mad, Alex."

"He's not mad at you, Sabrina." I stand up and take her by the hand. "Or me. Let's go wait for Alex out front."

My heart continues to pound as Sabrina and I make our way down the bleachers, but I also feel a surge of power. I'm not retreating from the situation. I'm choosing to walk away. There's a difference.

To their credit, Alex's parents—still standing a Mack-truck width away from each other—don't say a word when Alex finally jogs over to us a while later with his bag slung over his shoulder. He plops down on the curb between Sabrina and me even though he's still wearing his white baseball pants.

Sabrina stops digging in the pothole at her feet and looks Alex squarely in the eyes. "Are you still mad, Alex?"

"Yes, but not at you." Alex's voice is gentle as he reaches over to fix the lopsided bow in Sabrina's hair. "Thanks for coming to my game tonight. Did you like meeting my . . . girlfriend, Dakota?"

"We took doggie pictures together." Sabrina snatches the phone out of my hand.

When I unlock my phone for her, a text from Leo fills my screen.

LEO
I love you!!!!! 🖤 🖤 🖤

Shoot me now.

"That is *not* what it looks like," I say as Sabrina goes into my camera roll to find one of the silly pictures I saved of the two of us. "Leo is thanking me for getting us tickets to an anime con this fall."

"Uh-huh," Alex says as Sabrina goes past our last silly picture, landing on the one that Leo and I took on Wednesday of us making *Kitsune Mask*–inspired "fox fingers" next to our faces, which are way too close to each other for platonic friends. Like, Leo's still slightly chubby cheek is pressed into mine because he's smiling so big.

I snatch the phone back from Sabrina. "I'll send our mermaid one to Alex so you can see it anytime you want."

Alex's aunt pulls up to the curb and lowers the passenger side window. Lily continues to snooze in her booster seat in the back.

"Great game tonight, Alex," Auntie yells out the window. "We are so proud of you, baby. I know you have plans tonight, but let's have a family celebration soon. Come on, Sabrina, we need to head home."

Of course, Sabrina is not on board. "I want to spend the night at Aunt Sherri's."

"Not tonight, baby. We can get you a Happy Meal on the way home for a late dinner, though."

"C'mon, BriBri." Alex stands up. When Sabrina doesn't follow, he scoops her off the ground, swings her around, and throws the giggling little girl over his shoulder.

Alex's aunt rolls down the back window after Alex gets Sabrina hooked into her booster seat. Sabrina blows us kisses out the window as they pull away. When Alex turns back around, the smile slides off his face.

"You are not going to North Carolina," Mr. Santos says.

"It's too far away, baby," Mrs. Santos says and then balks at agreeing with her ex-husband.

Abuela adds something that also doesn't sound supportive, only in Spanish. Alex looks at me. I don't know what to say. I don't know if I've even been a part of the picture long enough to have earned an opinion.

"I would miss you," I figure is a safe bet.

But instead of comforting Alex, his eyebrows furrow even more. "Would you?"

The texts from Leo.

"Let's go get some ice cream and talk about it." I don't want to air my dirty laundry in the middle of a high school parking lot.

"I'm sorry, but your date is going to have to be rescheduled." Mr. Santos pulls out his phone. "I'm happy to pay for a Lyft to take you home, Dakota."

"You don't get to dictate Alex's life, Alejandro," Mrs. Santos says. "He chose to live with me for a reason."

The sound of blood rushing in my ears returns as the argument heats up. I jump to my feet and pull out my phone. Nobody notices when I walk toward the front of the school while texting Dad.

ME
Change of plans. Can you pick me up?
> **DAD**
> Everything okay?

ME
Sorta. I'm fine. Family drama happening.
> **DAD**
> Be there in five.

"Dakota!" Alex runs up next to me. "Hey, I swore I would call your dad if people were acting inappropriately. I didn't realize it was going to be my own family. Let me drive you home. We'll even hit Culver's drive-through for a double scoop in an attempt to save this date from being a total dumpster fire. And I want a rain check."

"So, you believe me about Leo now?" I have to ask because I don't want to get my hopes up for a rain check if it is never going to happen.

"Do I have a choice?"

"Yes. I told you about Leo pretty much on day one. We're best friends, but that's it. You met his girlfriend. You saw how they are together. It's a wonder we didn't get kicked out of Golf Land for the amount of PDA that was going on between them."

"I know. It's just hard because he gets so much more of your time than I do. There you go—the truth. I'm jealous of your best friend and wish he wasn't a guy. Especially a straight guy."

"While we are being honest with each other, when were you planning on telling me about North Carolina?"

"Once I finally decided on whether I was going or not. As of right now, I'm about ninety-nine percent ready to hit the commit button. Tonight." Alex waves his hand back toward his family, still arguing on the sidewalk. "For obvious reasons."

"What about us?"

Alex slides off his baseball cap and runs his hand through his hair. Air puffs out his cheeks as he thinks. "You could come to North Carolina to visit me."

I cross my arms and give him a skeptical look. "Do you remember who my parents are and how much negotiation it took just to come to this game?"

Alex winces. "Or I could come to visit you in Phoenix. Could I stay at your house? Otherwise, there would be a lot of drama." Alex gestures behind him at his family. "Exhibit A."

If Leo and I aren't allowed to watch *Kitsune Mask* in my room anymore, somehow, I doubt my parents are going to sign off on Alex staying at our house. But we don't have time for an in-depth conversation about it right now. I can see Dad's truck waiting at the stoplight.

"There's my dad," I say instead.

"That was fast."

"He was eating hot wings around the corner."

"I can practically see the walls up around you right now—again, courtesy of my family—but can I hug you before you go? Truth: It's more for me than you. We're all coming back to Mom's house for a *family discussion* about my college plans."

I step into Alex and wrap my arms around him tight. My life is complicated, but at least most of the drama comes from people *outside* my own family. My home, especially my room, is my fortress of solitude. Now with his younger brother back home and sharing his room, Alex doesn't even have that.

Alex leans in to kiss me but aborts that idea when my dad pulls up right next to us with the passenger-side window down. Evil Santa's glare could weld metal together right now.

"Thanks, Dakota. I'm sorry about tonight." Alex gives me one last squeeze before backing away. "I'll text you later, and we'll set up our next dance rehearsal."

"And dinner. And maybe a movie at my house."

"I'd like that." Alex looks back over his shoulder at his family and lets out a dramatic sigh. "It's going to be a long night."

Evil Santa's glare doesn't lessen even after I'm tucked safely in the truck.

"I knew this was a bad idea," Dad grumbles.

"It wasn't a bad idea. The plan was good. It's the execution that went sideways."

"Did the paparazzi capture it? Do we need to prepare a statement?"

It was Senior Night. Everybody had their phones out. "No, at least, I don't think so."

"Hmmm. I think you and Alex should stick to home dates for a while." Dad cuts somebody off in traffic in his rush to put his princess firmly back in her tower.

"Why? Then it means they won." I have to grab the roof handle of the truck when the person Dad cut off returns the favor.

Dad lays on the horn. "Dakota Rae, you are not an average teen. You know our life has some unique challenges. We're going to have to set better ground rules if Alex is going to be a part of your life."

Can Alex even be a part of my life? Can anybody ever be part of my life? Will I have to hide for the next five years until people forget who I am, or move abroad to escape this golden cage? When do I get to be me?

Chapter

25

"Here's my address." A senior who hasn't said three words to me all year in art class suddenly thrusts a slip of notebook paper at me when the dismissal bell rings. "I'm so excited about coming to your party."

"Great." I look down at the paper to double-check what her name is. "Shayla. I'll add you to the list."

I put down my HB pencil and take the paper from her. Shayla leans in like she's going to hug me. Uh, no. We are nowhere near that level of friendship. I duck to avoid her hug and throw her piece of paper into my backpack with the fifty or so other people's deets I received today. All thanks once again to Nevaeh and their social reach.

Yesterday, Phil informed me that three hundred of my closest friends *must* come to my birthday extravaganza next month. If Shayla wants to fill one of the two hundred slots still available after I invited the Matsuda siblings, Nevaeh, everybody in the Japanese Culture Club, and a handful of genuinely nice people from my other classes, I couldn't care less.

"You are so awesome." Shayla bounces on her toes.

"Thanks. Glad you can come."

I pick up the HB pencil and go back to my sketch. Shayla takes the hint and swarms out of the art room with the other twenty-five people in our class.

"Something on your mind today, Dakota?" Mr. Udall says from his desk at the front of the room.

"No, sir. Just enjoying the quiet." I take a deep breath. Something about the smell of oil paint and pencil shavings is more relaxing to me than lavender. "Plus, I'm behind on this assignment."

Mr. Udall appears at my elbow. "As always, Dakota McDonald takes my simple assignment and—"

"Overcomplicates it?"

"I was going to say refines and elevates it." Mr. Udall pulls up a stool next to mine and slides my sketchbook toward him. He flips through my last couple of sketches before closing the cover and resting his hands on top of it.

"That bad, huh?" I say.

"Quite the opposite. Did I overhear you telling Beth today that you aren't doing your calligraphy project in pen and ink? Why? You don't like that medium?"

"No, I love pen and ink. In fact"—I dig in my backpack and pull out my latest purchase—"I'm hand addressing all my closest friends' invitations for the party."

Mr. Udall cracks open the highly decorated wooden box and dramatically takes out the glass-nibbed pen like he's discovered an ancient Mayan artifact. "Ah, and you have a bottle of glittery gold ink too."

"I know, I'm overcomplicating a simple task." The other criticism I've heard multiple times in my school career bubbles up. "And I can't follow directions."

The corners of Mr. Udall's deep brown eyes crinkle. "Dakota, understand that it's the can't-follow-the-directions, off-the-chart creative people like you who change the world."

"Yeah, can you talk to my sixth-grade English teacher? Pretty sure she'd fight you on that."

Though Mr. Udall laughs, I'm still salty about that C- on my report card. I spent twenty hours *building* a historically accurate replica of the barracks the Wakatsukis lived in during WWII, instead of regurgitating those same facts into a paper during our unit on *Farewell to Manzanar.* Dad and the principal talked Mrs. Henry out of the zero she originally gave me for not following the directions. Still, the D I received on that major assignment wrecked my English grade for the quarter, especially when I refused to redo the assignment to specifications, even though it would have meant a higher grade.

"What's the intention of this piece of art?" Mr. Udall taps the closed sketch pad. "Because, let's be honest, you don't need *another* A+. What's the heart behind the art?"

Emotions swirl inside my chest. While most people are celebrating spring and Easter, here in the McDonalds' Alternate Universe, my family is lost in time. Over spring break, we put on sweaters and did a photoshoot for *Better Homes and Gardens*' October issue. Last weekend, we previewed the cringetastic, canned part of what will be our last show in May. Tomorrow, Mom's going back in time to 1942 to shoot a special crossover show with *The History Makers* about the Akagis and life in Phoenix during WWII. Some people don't know where they are. I don't know *when* I am half the time. I shake my head to come back to the present.

"My intention?" I chew on the inside of my lip and think. "I want to create something physical that my parents can hold on to after I leave for college that reminds them of me every time they see it. The heart behind the art is to thank them for giving me all the tools—literally and figuratively—I needed to create that successful life outside of the TV world and away from them too."

"You don't want to have your own show?" Mr. Udall quirks an eyebrow at me.

"Not a network show, no. Besides, I already have a show. The spin-off digital series on the HGTV website. Maybe one day I'll have my own YouTube channel or something. That way, I can do the projects that are close to my heart, versus what will prominently feature the sponsors' products. Remember"—I point at myself—"can't follow directions."

"Sounds like you already know what you want to make." Mr. Udall opens my sketch pad to a clean page and slides it back across the workbench to me. "I have a staff meeting in thirty minutes, but you're welcome to stay until then. Don't overthink it. Start sketching. Let it flow."

As Mr. Udall walks away, I knead my gum eraser and stare at

the blank page. My brain finally sparks. And just like how I discovered the exact shade of red to paint the yakisoba booth, I add a little bit of this to a little bit of that until I finally come up with the perfect design.

"What do you think?" I show Mr. Udall my crude design as he herds me out the door twenty-five minutes later. "I wish I could use our laser cutter at home, but Dad insists that he has to be present when I use it, which would ruin the surprise. Maybe I could try burning it by hand?"

"Hmmm." Mr. Udall strokes his silver-flecked beard. "Usually, only the seniors in my advanced art class get to work on the laser cutter as their final project. But as your dad *donated* pretty much all the equipment in our school's Industrial Arts program, Mr. Ledbetter and I might be able to make an exception."

I cringe. The considerable donation of state-of-the-art tools and equipment was made to our school in honor of Dad's sixtieth birthday, and as part of the bigger, nationwide trade school initiative Dad's been a part of for years. Dad specifically picked Cholla Vista High School because he knew I would be coming here the following fall. Then I turned around and chose Visual Arts as my elective. Even Leo, who loves a good power tool, let him down, choosing Game Design over Industrial Arts.

"If you can get the final design drafted and inked by Friday, I'll see what Mr. Ledbetter says." A conspiratorial smile lights up Mr. Udall's face. "Don't worry. I'll make sure he says yes. Can you stay after school one day to run it through the laser cutter? This design looks too complicated to complete in one class period."

I look down at the rough sketch for my newest sign:

赤
城
AKAGI HOUSE
Tamlyn Akagi-McDonald & Doug McDonald

"I need Iwate-sensei to double check my kanji first. Also, I'm not sure I like this Goudy font for the English part." I scribble a note to myself on the upper right-hand corner of my sketch. "I want to see what other classical-style fonts are out there. Or maybe I'll come up with my own twist on one. I know, don't say it. Plus, I should probably add the date on there somewhere too."

Mr. Udall holds the door open for me. "Dakota, let's talk about you joining my Advanced Art class next year. Maybe getting you on a path toward a degree in industrial design or something that will help you blend your artistic eye with your advanced technical skills. You're going to do big things, kiddo. I take that back. You've already done big things. You're going to do even bigger things, kiddo."

A warmth spreads in my chest because Mr. Udall can see it, even if I can't just yet. Life beyond Dakota McDonald, child star and DIY Princess. He sees Dakota McDonald, the visionary. The Dakota who is not only praised, but makes bank for her won't-follow-the-directions big ideas.

o   o   o

I think about Mr. Udall's words all the way home. I was going to take a gap year, but maybe I want to go straight to college now after all. Maybe Mr. Udall can help me find a college that fits my goals versus one that makes me look the best in *People* magazine. I take the front steps of our house two at a time.

"Mom? Dad?" I yell through the house after I set the alarm. "Stephanie?"

"Unless you want three hundred teenagers showing up at *your* house, Phil, then you better get the brass to cough up some more money for a new venue." Stephanie's voice travels down the hall from Mom's office. "I'll keep working on my end. You work on yours."

I knock on the open door of Mom's office. "Everything okay, Steph?"

"No. It is not." Stephanie bangs her fist on the table so hard that her teacup rattles on its saucer. "Chez Versailles caught on fire this morning. Between the smoke and water damage, there is no way that it can be renovated and back up to code in one month."

My stomach drops. I know I've whined and complained about this ridiculous party, but the idea has grown on me. And if I'm totally honest, it feels like the final step in shedding the DIY Princess version of Dakota.

"What are we going to do?" As much as I have joked about it, I don't think Nevaeh throwing me a pool party with pizza at their house instead is going to cut it.

"Doug and Tamlyn are there right now talking with the building inspector to see if we can work some Hollywood magic and make it into a plotline. They hope to find some new sponsors to help rebuild at least parts of Chez Versailles quickly. Meanwhile, I've spent all day calling around for a possible backup venue." I can hear the weariness in Stephanie's voice. "Between it being prom season, the beginning of wedding season, and the Phoenix Phoodie Phestival the following weekend, locations are already booked. We may have to move the venue out of town. Is Globe too far?"

"Yes! I know my party is important, but not drive-to-Globe important." My heart squeezes at the thought of HGTV trying to make the ten friends who come in the limo with me to Globe look like the three hundred they expected. *And here's a shot of the* empty *dance floor.*

"I can spin this. Let me think about it." Stephanie closes her eyes and rubs her temples. "I know. How about we make it a 'secret location event'? It's so top secret and exclusive that attendees will meet at . . . Matsuda, let's say, and then chartered buses take them to the event. There you go. Boom. Situation solved."

"Phil is going to sign off on chartered buses for three hundred teenagers?"

"Oh, the production insurance nightmare that would be. Don't worry. I will figure it out." Stephanie stands up and collects her teacup and saucer. "This is going to require another cuppa and many biscuits. Would you care for some?"

"I'll have something later. I want to change first."

"Okay, and come try on these shoes so I can get them out of the office. I want to get one thing checked off my massive to-do list today."

I'm just heading back downstairs when the front door slams. To say that Phil is in full freak-out mode would be the understatement of the century. He slams the door to Mom's office too for good measure. Even with the door closed, the language coming out of Phil's mouth would make a pirate blush. Raw. Heated. Emotional. Welp, I'm out.

Dr. Berger says when things start to get messy, and I feel out of control, to come back to the things that ground me. The things that make me feel confident, proud, and secure. I grab my work boots and safety glasses out of the hall closet and tiptoe down the hallway and out the back door.

⌀   ⌀   ⌀

I take a deep breath and turn on the video camera.

"Hey, guys, thanks for tuning in to *DIY with Dakota*. A lot of you have been asking what my next project is. Today, I'm ready to reveal it." I step in front of my build, and in one dramatic flourish, I pull the cloth off the top of it. "Tah-dah! But wait, there's more."

I step out of frame for a moment to flip a switch. The lights in the dollhouse mansion come on. I pick up the camera so I can do a close-up of all the rooms.

"This dollhouse is for some special friends of mine. I hope it brings them as much joy as the dollhouse my mom made for me when I was five." I dig in my back pocket and pull out a parting gift. I even signed it. I tuck the plastic pony into one of the doll beds and pull the handmade, tiny blanket over the top of it. "Take care of my friends, Pinkie Pie."

I turn off the lights.

Later, I'll edit out the small sob that sneaked out of my chest. After almost six weeks—and a lot of hot-glue-gun burns, and accompanying swearing because of those burns—I'm ready to release my industrial design, or maybe it's better to call it "functional art," into the world. But not until I take a few pictures to show Mr. Udall. That's why I am so far behind on the calligraphy project. I was too busy racing to finish the dollhouse in time for Raising Hope Women and Children's Shelter's tenth anniversary gala tomorrow. Maybe I can use this project as part of my portfolio for my college applications? Mom walked me through the electrical part, but all the work is mine. I pull the sheet back over the dollhouse.

I yelp when I turn back around. Alex leans in the doorway with his backpack slung over one shoulder.

"Just so you know, your front door was unlocked. Also, Ms. Stephanie almost impaled me with a high heel shoe when I let myself in. She's a little stressed today."

"I thought we were getting together on Friday." I leave the video camera in the Fab Lab. I still need more close-up footage of the dollhouse before I edit it all together.

"I couldn't wait until then." Alex's voice lacks its usual playfulness.

I secure the workshop and lead Alex into my backyard. "Let's talk out here where we can have some privacy. Stephanie is freaking out because we may have lost our venue today. But don't worry. Stephanie and her Magic Handbag are on it."

Though Mom gets on me every time I do it, I crawl on top of the picnic table instead of sitting on the attached bench seat. I tap the table.

"Uh, is that going to be able to hold both of us?" Alex says.

I catch myself before I say, "Leo and I sit on it all the time." Instead, I go with, "I made it. It's stable."

Alex still looks doubtful, but he crawls onto the table beside me. We turn and sit cross-legged facing each other.

"Wait. I have an apology gift from Abuela." Alex rotates his upper body until he can dig something out of his backpack. He puts a red, plastic container between us. When he pulls the lid off, a sweet, milky smell wafts out. "Abuela was so embarrassed by how my parents acted at the game that she's trying to bribe you into giving the Santos side of the family a second chance with an extra big slice of her famous cake."

I drag one of the whole strawberries decorating the top through the pile of whipped cream and pop it into my mouth. "Yum. I want to eat the rest of this, but I also don't want to go into the kitchen to get a fork. If you wanted to stay for dinner, maybe we could share this for dessert?" I drag the other strawberry through the cream and eat it. "Never mind. I'm not sharing this, but you can still stay for dinner."

This pulls a small smile out of Alex. "That's fine. I have the rest of the apology cake at Mom's house. Unless Ricky ate it while I was gone, which is a possibility."

I put the lid back on the container and put it behind me. When I turn back, Alex has his hands open and resting in the space between us. I put my hands in his. We sit in uncomfortable silence for what seems like an eternity.

"I officially committed to Duke," Alex says. "Now, my entire family is disappointed with me. Yay."

My insides jumble with the news. "Oh."

Alex's shoulders droop. "And you too. Awesome. Batting a thousand today, Santos. Well, at least you are taking it better than I thought you would."

"How did you think this was going to go?"

"Maybe a few tears. A declaration of undying love?"

"From you or from me?"

"Ow."

I can practically hear the whoosh of the barriers flying up around me. I take my hands back. "What if I was the one leaving for Duke? Would I get a few tears? A declaration of undying love?"

Alex chews on his bottom lip for a minute before answering. "I would miss you. But if your family was as messed up as mine, I would understand why you wanted to leave."

"I understand why you want to leave. I was at the game, remember?"

"That's not what you are asking, though, is it?" Alex drops his eyes. "The reality of the situation is this: I can't *let* myself fall in love with you. Because if I do, then I won't want to leave Phoenix."

"Got it. Plus, I'm a sophomore, and you're a senior. We should have known this relationship had a limited shelf life from the get-go." I slide my legs off the table. "Thanks for not dragging it out any longer than necessary."

"Dakota, wait." Alex grabs my arm to keep me from retreating. When I look down at his hand, he immediately removes it. "I'm sorry."

About using me or breaking my heart? I decide to go with the less painful of the two.

"We were originally going to go with an actor anyway. I mean, this is reality TV. You can still be my dance partner if you want. Play your role, collect a paycheck, and then we'll go our separate ways. No harm. No foul."

"Why can't we still hang after the party? I'm not leaving until August."

"Because the longer we do this, the harder it is going to be to say goodbye."

"You say that, but I've noticed that you've yet to say the L-word either. Even on Valentine's Day." When I don't immediately answer him, Alex scoffs. "Of course, it's the other L-word."

"It's not Leo," I say, though the Leo Situation definitely makes things more complicated.

"Yes, it is. It's always been Leo. It's always going to be Leo. I guess it's a good thing I'm leaving then."

"IT'S NOT LEO. IT'S ME." I lower my voice a few decibels before the whole neighborhood knows my business. "You don't know what it's like not being able to trust anybody. I have my parents, Stephanie, Nevaeh, and the Matsudas. That's it. Everybody else just wants a piece of me. And when I fall for their flattery and am gullible enough to give them a piece of me, then they turn around and stab me in the back or break my heart. Every. Freaking. Time. Once people get their fifteen minutes of fame or their fat paycheck from the tabloids or the power trip of being the one who knocked that diva Dakota McDonald off her pedestal, then they're done with me. So, no, I'm not going to let myself fall in love with you either because you might hurt me too. You know what? Congratulations, you already have."

Alex's face is as white as if I had crammed the tres leches cake into it.

"Did Austin Webber hurt you at Homecoming?" Even though Alex's voice is gentle, That Boy's name still impales me. "Like beyond the embarrassing part of the video?"

I can't stop the hot tears burning my eyes.

"Yes, I saw the video." Alex drops his eyes. "The original one. The one *SNL* took and warped into a parody with the rubber chickens. And I may have even felt smug at the time about some spoiled, arrogant little TV princess getting her comeuppance. But now I know the real Dakota McDonald. She's amazing. And she didn't deserve it. Any of it. I hope your parents sued his."

I let out a sarcastic laugh because that's not what happened afterward, despite what the tabloids reported.

"Austin's family moved to New Mexico to escape the negative press." I'm not lying. I'm repeating bad information.

"Good, now I won't have to find Austin and give him a beatdown." Alex puts one hand out, palm up, between us. "I'm sorry I hurt you. I'll do whatever it takes to get off that long list."

No, he won't. And it would be unfair to ask him to because this is reality, not reality TV.

I put my hand on top of Alex's, palm to palm, but our fingers both stay open. My phone pings. And then again. And then multiple times.

"Sorry." I wipe my eyes on the sleeve of my shirt and pull my phone out of my back pocket. When I unlock the screen, I find five texts from Leo and one from Aurora. Before I can read them, Leo calls.

"Leo, if you are calling to fanboy about Ava Takahashi being at Hebi Con again, I'm going to seriously kill you."

"Dakota!" Leo barks at me. "Do *not* read Aurora's text. Delete it right now."

"Why?"

"Just delete it."

"Fine." I tap on it and see I'm so sorry, Koty. The best defense is a good offense on top of the hidden picture.

"Did you delete it?" Leo says frantically.

"Oh no." Alex shows me the screen of his phone. "Vanessa says it's all over school. My school."

"Kuso," Leo swears, obviously overhearing Alex.

"I gotta go. I'll call you back later." I hang up on Leo and open Aurora's text and the attached picture. Then I pour salt into the wound by enlarging it so I can read the tabloid article under the picture of Alex and me kissing in our Valentine's Day oasis. Because Alex is eighteen, there is no bar across his eyes. Being with me made him a target for the vultures too.

> If these walls could talk indeed! It seems our favorite DIY Princess, Dakota McDonald, has not only rebounded from her freshman year heartbreak but now she's found love yet again, this time with a tuxedo model. An anonymous source close to the *If These Walls Could Talk* camp told us that Alexander Santos (18) was a last-ditch effort to find Dakota, known for her diva behavior, a date for her over-the-top sixteenth birthday bash being filmed in late April. A trained Latin dancer, Santos was brought in as arm (and eye!) candy, but during one of their many private lessons, young love bloomed. We can't wait to see Dakota and Alexander take a twirl on the dance floor at her upcoming Sweet Sixteen party. Here's hoping the *ITWCT* team battens down the hatches before our young starlet takes the dance floor, so there are no more unfortunate poultry-esque wardrobe malfunctions this time.

"I'm sorry, Dakota. You know this 'anonymous source' wasn't me, right? Because, if I was going to start a rumor about myself, I would at least get my own name right. Dakota? Are you okay?"

Blood rushes in my ears, but even then, it's not loud enough to drown out the mocking roar of laughter in my head.

o   o   o

That Boy tells me how beautiful I look as we slow dance at Homecoming. He's a senior. I'm a lowly freshman. I'm thrilled that he even talks to me in art class, much less wants me to go to Homecoming with him. Leo is skeptical of the match. I ignore him. Leo's salty that he can't go because of work. That Boy talks me into ditching my bolero jacket, even though I might get busted at any moment for breaking the dress code rule about no bared shoulders. That Boy's hand slides the spaghetti strap of my dress off my shoulder. . . . That Girl—his ex—told me in the bathroom that she's not mad at me for coming to Homecoming with That Boy. They broke up months ago. That Girl says that the rumors about me aren't true. I'm actually cool. That Girl says I should come dance with them. In the center. In the circle. Nah. That's not for me. The tabloids would have a field day if they caught wind of me dancing with That Girl and all her cool senior friends—underwear flashing both accidentally and on purpose. "Maybe later," I lie and hide in the bathroom stall for a good ten minutes. I return to That Boy. "You owe me," That Girl says to him before walking off. It's nothing. She's just jealous. Let's dance. Slow. He pushes the spaghetti strap off my shoulder. That's the cue. That Girl. That Girl's friends. Phones hit record. That Boy picks me up and swings me around. My short dress rides up in the back, over my butt. They laugh. They film. It creates a perfect storm. I grasp at my now too-loose bodice. My strapless bra shifts. One of my silicone "chicken cutlets" falls out the side of my dress. The crowd roars and pulls out their phones too. That Girl picks up the chicken cutlet and throws it at her friend—the one who's allowed to go to Rocky Point with them after graduation if she helps That Girl get the footage for the tabloids. I scream at That Boy to put me down as the epic game of Chicken Toss continues. Finally, my feet hit the floor again. My hand presses to my lopsided chest. I wait for the floor to open up and swallow me. A hundred people film it all. "Leave her alone!" Nevaeh peels off their black-and-silver fringed jacket. They wrap it around me. "We're leaving." That Boy races after us. Apologizing. Swearing that he had nothing to do with That Girl's plan. Don't be mad. It's all a joke. I can't catch my breath. I can't speak. My newish friend Nevaeh drives us to a place we both know. Aurora bursts out the front door of Matsuda. Leo two steps behind. I burn with shame. Nevaeh recounts the story. The wound opens wider. I shake harder. My chest burns, desperate for more air. Leo opens the car door. He takes a knee. "Koty, are you okay?" His voice cracks. His eyes are wide with fear. The dam breaks. "NOOOO!" The sob stuck in my chest explodes out. Tears flow freely. Leo's strong arms pull me to a stand and encase me. Protect me. But it's too late. "I'm sorry." He repeats over and over. "Why didn't I listen to you, Leo?" I hold on to him for dear life. So many cameras. So many people laughing at my humiliation. So many people cheering my fall from such a high pedestal. Celebrating the way I smash into a million pieces. Celebrating how I turn to dust under their stomping feet. Mrs. Matsuda's face white as chalk when she pulls me away from Leo. "Dakota? Are you okay?"

o   o   o

"Dakota? Are you okay?" Mrs. Matsuda's voice deepens into Alex's.

I release my body from the hunched ball I've become. I use every trick and technique Dr. Berger has taught me in the last year to come back from the edge. To pull all the millions of pieces back in until I am whole again. Bruised and battered, but back in one piece.

"I'm getting Ms. Stephanie." Alex scrambles off the picnic table.

"Wait. I'm okay-ish." The tightness in my chest decreases by ten percent.

Alex reaches out to hug me but stops himself. Worry flashes behind his kaleidoscope eyes.

"You can hug me. In fact, I would like that." I slide off the table and wrap my arms around Alex's waist.

Alex's arms encase me. He sways us gently until all the pieces of me return one by one.

"I'm sorry about the tabloid," I say.

"It's not your fault. Ms. Stephanie warned me that it could happen since I'm technically an adult." Alex pulls me tighter into his bubble. "Also, people at my school have been trying to ID you since the baseball game. Now the truth is out."

"Why does everything have to be so hard?" I step back from Alex. "When do I get to fall in love with someone who both loves me back *and* is going to be here for the long run?"

"I'm sorry. I mean that from the bottom of my heart. I hope I don't look back one day and kick myself."

I scoff. "I hope you do."

"Okay, I kind of deserved that. How about, I hope *you* look back one day and remember me fondly. That I was the guy who helped make your Sweet Sixteen perfect. So perfect that the haters had absolutely nothing to say."

"The haters always have something to say. And if they don't, they'll make stuff up about you, *Alexander.*"

"True." Alex puts his forehead against mine. "Will you trust me?"

I don't want to pretend that a few words and a well-timed hug are all it takes to earn my trust. I've been burned before. Badly.

When I don't answer, Alex says, "Will you give me Leo's phone number?"

"Why? Please don't start drama with my best friend."

"No drama, I promise. If we're going to make this Sweet Sixteen perfect, I'm going to need Leo's help. Leo and his sisters and Nevaeh too. Anybody else who should be on the ultraexclusive Team Dakota?"

"Would it be weird to say my Visual Arts teacher?"

Alex wrinkles his nose. "Maybe a little. But we want Ms. Stephanie and Leo's parents on backup too. Maybe your teacher could play on the B-team with them?" Alex pulls me in tight. "Trust us. Let us show you that there are people in the world who love you just the way you are."

I let the words hang.

"Yeah, I said it, McDonald. I love you." Alex pulls me in tighter. "There. Are you happy? You broke me."

"I don't want to break you."

"I don't want to break you either."

"But in August—"

"Let's deal with August five months from now when it is, you know, August. Until then we'll take it day by day. Okay?" Alex kisses me gently. "You got this. And if you don't, you know who to call."

I know Alex is talking about himself, but based on the sadness that crosses behind his eyes, Alex knows I'm still going to call Leo too.

Chapter

26

I talk my parents into letting me stay home from school for the rest of the week to give the buzz a chance to die down. I go see Dr. Berger twice. I come back to the things that ground me. The things that make me feel confident and safe. I sketch and ink the AKAGI HOUSE sign with the font I designed to turn in to Mr. Udall on Monday. Though I bow out of the Raising Hope Tenth Anniversary Gala, Stephanie reports the fundraiser she helped plan makes over a hundred thousand dollars. She insists that women like her sister—mothers who need shelter after escaping abusive relationships—appreciate the little things that make their new reality less scary, like a dollhouse for their children to play with. Instead of wearing an expensive dress and a fake smile, I spend the evening at home finishing the dollhouse video and posting it.

True to his word, Alex assembles Team Dakota, which included calling Leo. Six people get booted off my party list after Aurora reports they revived the "Bok bok!" meme of me. I presume it's the one where I have one hand on my lopsided chest and my other hand has a rubber chicken photoshopped into it. Nevaeh helps me pick out the perfect tiara, and sends me every wombat video ever created on the planet. Leo hand-delivers our takeout dinner order from Matsuda every day promptly at five and dissects an episode of *Kitsune Mask* with me over root beers. And Alex insists that we keep our dance practice date on Friday after school.

"Once more. I messed up that part in the middle." I hike up my skirt poofer—according to Stephanie, it's technically called a crinoline—and sit down on the kitchen floor to adjust the strap on my bedazzled, three-inch heels. "And thank you for not laughing at my outfit."

I sent Nevaeh a selfie before Alex arrived. Their response to my cinched T-shirt and jean shorts combo mixed with my bedazzled heels and skirt poofer was MY EYES!!!!

"You look beautiful no matter what you wear." Alex, red-faced and sweating, flops down on a barstool at our kitchen counter. "And so what that you turned left instead of right. It's okay. We're the only two people who know what the choreography is supposed to be. Trust that I'm going to make you look good no matter what happens."

I flop on my back to catch my breath. Sweat drips down the sides of my temples and pools in my ears. I should have put my hair up. "What if I totally wipe out in these ridiculous shoes?"

"Then I will"—Alex slides onto the floor next to me like he's stealing home plate—"make it look intentional. And—" The skirt poofer creaks a little when Alex rolls over and does a high X-shaped push-up over top of me. He lowers himself and kisses me. When he pushes back up a moment later, my head is still spinning. "Do something to make them forget all about your fall."

"What fall?" I ignore the skirt poofer's protests and tug at Alex's shirt until he lowers himself back down.

"Well, this is all kinds of awkward," Leo's voice suddenly echoes through my kitchen.

Alex laughs, but my face burns. In one smooth motion, Alex rolls to his feet and pulls me to a stand. I yank the skirt poofer back down.

Leo clears his throat and holds out the insulated bag. "I have your order."

"Thanks." I take the bag from Leo. "Have time for a root beer?"

"I don't want to interrupt Alex and your"—Leo rotates his hands around—"whatever that was."

"Dance lesson," I say.

"Riiiiiight."

"Says the King of PDA." I hand Leo a root beer. I pat the barstool until he sits down.

"You're lucky your mom went into her office after intercepting me at the front door." Leo takes a chug of root beer. "I mean, she won't even let us watch *Kitsune Mask* in your room anymore."

I give Leo a *DUDE?!?!* look. Yes, it's true, but he didn't need to say that in front of Alex, especially because Alex has *never* been in my room.

"Dakota, I'm leaving." Mom walks into the kitchen while putting in her good pearl earrings. She does a double-take at the amount of food boxes I've pulled from Leo's bag. "Oh dear, Doug forgot to cancel tonight's order since he and I have a business dinner with *The History Makers*." Mom pops a gyōza in her mouth. "No worries. Now I don't have to cook tomorrow either."

"About that." Leo pulls several folded bills out of the back pocket of his jeans. "Mom said you overpaid us, even with your usual generous tip."

Mom pushes Leo's hand back. "No, we didn't."

Leo holds it back out. "Mom will kill me if you don't take it, Ms. Tamlyn."

"Okay, I officially received it from you." Mom takes the bills out of Leo's hand. She folds them and tucks them into the pocket of Leo's button-down shirt. "This is me donating to your car fund. Thanks for helping make this challenging week bearable for Koty. For us. I don't know what we'd do without you, Leo."

I know Mom didn't mean that as a slam to Alex, but I can see the hurt in his eyes. The not-good-enough kind of pain I unfortunately know too well.

"Hey, Mrs. McDonald, could Dakota possibly come to my All-State competition next month? They announced the teams today. Guess who is playing first base?" Alex says.

"Congratulations," I say, as Mom says, "When is it?"

"The first weekend in May." When I don't immediately say yes, Alex adds, "You don't have to sit with my family."

"That's our final episode," Mom says. "We'll be doing some live, remote parts mixed with the already canned stuff like we are doing with the birthday episode. I'm sorry, Alex."

Alex's shoulders slump. "Oh. Okay. Of course."

Mom's phone buzzes. "That would be your dad outside. I've got to run. We won't be out too late, Koty. Also, don't forget: Stephanie wants an answer on hairstyles by Monday. Are you staying for a while, Alex?"

"No, I promised Abuela that I would go to Good Friday mass with her tonight." Alex looks at his phone. "I need to leave in about five minutes."

"Okay, and Leo? Are you sticking around for a while?" Mom says it more like a request than a question.

"Mom, I'm fine," I say.

"I can stay and keep Koty company for a little bit," Leo says.

"Thank you. You're such a sweetheart, Leo."

I give Mom a look that I hope telegraphs *Moooooom!*

Mom's phone buzzes again. She gives our trio one final, concerned look before kissing my cheek and telling us good night. Everybody drinks their root beer in silence until the front door closes.

"Wow, thanks for throwing me under the bus there, Ms. Tamlyn." Leo rolls his eyes. "Yeah, I'm not sticking around as your chaperone. I'll let you two get back to *dance practice*."

"Thanks." Alex puts his arm around my waist.

"Wait. I want to show Leo our dance. Stephanie and my parents have seen it, but we need someone who is hypercritical."

"Thank you, Dakota," Leo says sarcastically.

"And since Aurora isn't available, that job falls to you, Leo. If I look baka, tell me now so I can fix it."

Leo sits back down. "Okay, but you asked for it."

Disappointment creases Alex's face, but he immediately replaces it with a smile. I start the music on Alex's phone. We take our opening position.

"Stop smirking, Leo," I say as I promenade around Alex. I get it. I look, if not ridiculous, at least not like my usual self.

"I'm not," Leo insists, before putting a hand up to his mouth to camouflage his smirk.

Though it isn't in the choreography, when Alex turns me to face him after the promenade, his fingertips slide down the side of my face. Alex's kaleidoscope eyes hypnotize me and pull me deep inside his bubble. Electrical bursts flood my system as Alex holds me firmly but gently, leading me around the makeshift dance studio in between our kitchen and living room. I trust him even when he suddenly changes the choreography on me, like putting a slow dip after the bridge of the song.

A squeal sneaks out of my chest when Alex whips me back up to standing. While there was a kiss in the original choreography, Alex changes that too. I accept his brief peck on the cheek as usual, but as I start to walk away, Alex turns me back into him and kisses me a second time. For real. Like, an I-wish-I-hadn't-insisted-Leo-stay kind of a kiss. We move through the rest of the song completely in sync and in our own drama-free bubble.

A huge smile lights up Alex's face as the song ends. "See, there's no right or wrong choreography to this song."

My knees feel like Jell-O. Meanwhile, Leo picks his chin up off the floor.

"What do you think?" My heart continues to slam around in my chest. "Honestly."

"That was hot." Leo's cringe makes me laugh. "They may have to bump up the rating on your show after this number."

"I vote we keep the new additions to the choreography," I say.

"See, trust me." Alex laces his fingers through mine. "We're going to do everything in our power to make sure this event is flawless. Right, Leo?"

"You're not expecting me to follow that, are you?" Leo says.

"Of course not." Alex's laugh has an edge to it. "But you know what has to be done."

Leo groans.

"What has to be done?" I say.

Alex's phone rings with "Abuela" coming up on the caller ID. Alex sighs. Yeah, we should have taken Leo up on his offer to leave earlier. Then again, having Leo here made me take this project to the next level. As he always does.

"I better go." Alex collects his things, and I walk with him to the front door.

When I turn to punch in the code to disarm the door, Alex pushes my loose hair over my shoulder and plants a kiss on the back of my neck. He adds several more kisses to my cheek, my jaw, and finally, my lips.

"What has to be done?" I press, knowing that Alex is trying to distract me.

"Trust us," Alex says as he backs out the door. "That's all I'm going to say."

"Hmmm." I raise an eyebrow at Alex.

After resetting the alarm, I deposit both my heels and my skirt poofer on the stairs. I uncinch my T-shirt and use the hair elastic to create a high ponytail. As I pad barefoot back to the kitchen, I see Leo sitting in the middle of our sectional playing on his phone. With a Jay Yoshikawa–style warrior cry of "Kitsunebiiiiiiiiiii!" I vault over the back of the couch. Leo's phone flies out of his hand when I land next to him.

"Yeah, no more soda for you tonight, Koty." Leo retrieves his phone and tucks it into his back pocket.

"Spill, Leo. What has to be done?"

Leo crosses his arms. "Nope. Not breakin' Bro Code."

I scoot up close to Leo and poke him. "But BFF Code trumps Bro Code."

Leo moves farther away from me. "Not gonna happen."

I poke him again in the side. Right where I know from experience that Leo is extremely ticklish. Leo continues to dodge and deflect my pokes, but soon he runs out of couch.

"We could have done this the easy way, Matsuda, but now . . ." I crack my knuckles.

Leo mimes a yawn before flicking me in the arm. When I start to flick him back, my bracelet snags on the button of his shirt, unbuttoning it.

"Hey, stop trying to undress me, McDonald."

While he's distracted, I grab Leo in a headlock and give him a noogie of sixth-grade proportions. Leo breaks my grasp easily, but his hair continues to stick up at weird angles. I screech when Leo leans forward to return the favor. Except when I reach my hand back to scuttle away, I hit the ottoman part of the sectional instead of the couch. The ottoman slides out at a ninety-degree angle. Leo grabs my waist. But even Leo's cat-like reflexes can't defy gravity. We tumble down into the narrow gutter between the couch and the ottoman.

"Owwww." I rub my head where it hit the floor.

Leo releases my waist and props himself up on one elbow. He looks down at me.

"Hey, you started it. Before you hurt yourself for real, I will break Bro Code. Alex made me promise that I would dance with you at the party."

"That's it? Bro Code is so weak sauce." I tuck my hands behind my head and look up at Leo. "Of course you'll dance with me. We'll grab Aurora, Nevaeh, and the whole JCC crew. That way the focus isn't all on you. We'll get them to play Rayne Lee's 'Create Your Spark,' and you can go full ham like you do in the restaurant when it's empty. I'll make sure Phil cuts to a commercial break first, of course."

"No, Alex wants me to do a slow dance with you. On camera."

"Why?"

"To, and I quote, 'make Dakota forget about Austin for good before she spends her whole life afraid of guys.'"

I scoff. "I'm not afraid of guys. Okay, sometimes. But those ones are creepers. Like why would I want to see a picture of your junk? Gross."

"Not those idiots, he means the real guys in your life, like me."

"I'm not afraid of you. Pretty sure I just kicked your butt."

Leo rolls his eyes. "You know what he means, Koty. Between Alex leaving at the end of the summer and me Friend Zoning you in the walk-in refrigerator—"

My face burns. "You told him about that?!"

"Yeah, because I thought you already had."

"Why would I do that?" I sit up, even though the narrow space becomes even more crowded.

Leo sits up too. After we untangle our limbs, he says, "Because Alex asked me point blank, 'What did you do to break Dakota's heart?'"

I put my hands over my burning face. "Kill me now."

Leo pulls my hands away from my face. "And you know what he said after I told him? 'Don't break Dakota's heart a second time.'"

I'm not sure if I should be flattered or horrified that my current kinda-sorta-not-really boyfriend can see a future where I'm getting dumped by another guy for the second time.

"All I said was, 'When do I get to fall in love with someone who both loves me back *and* is going to be here for the long run?' I'm not sure how that translated to 'As soon as you leave for Duke, Alex, I'm going to steal Lindsay's man.' Because I'm not."

Leo lets go of my hands. "I'm sure Lindsay will be relieved to hear that."

"She still thinks I'm a threat? I thought we'd worked that out at Golf Land during the world's most awkward double date. Like, Alex is mine. Leo is yours. Move on, sister."

"Let's say she's *concerned* because we will be celebrating Tanabata in Japan together."

I wince. After all, last summer's Star-Crossed Lovers holiday was the spark that ignited this whole mess to begin with.

"Speaking of, shouldn't you be raking in the tips right now instead of hanging out with your dysfunctional BFF?"

Leo shrugs. "I wanted to stay. Plus, Ms. Tamlyn likes me best."

"I'm fine, Leo. You still need to make the final payment on the Japan trip, so go make the bucks." I stand up and then reach down to pull Leo to his feet. "Besides, I want to practice my part of the dance some more. Alex says it's fine, but I don't know. I don't want to look baka."

Leo doesn't let go of my forearms even after he's on his feet again. "You don't look baka."

"Ha ha," I say sarcastically.

"For real, Koty. I mean, fall-off-the-couch girl, that's my Koty. I don't know who that other girl was dancing with Alex though." Leo looks down. "And if she's going to stay for good after the party is over."

I quirk up an eyebrow.

Leo clears his throat and pulls his hands back. "I should go."

"Wait." I lean in and button Leo's shirt. I pat his chest when I'm done. "Okay, now you're back in Cinnamon Roll Prince mode."

Leo looks me in the eyes as he unbuttons the button again. "Maybe it's time for him to disappear too."

I turn on my heel and bolt for the front door. Once we step out on my front porch, I expect one of our occasional, swoop-in-swoop-out kind of platonic hugs. But I'm wrong. Leo steps into me and wraps his arms around me.

"I promise, Team Dakota is not going to let you down." Leo's breath is warm against my neck. It sends a tingle down my spine. "*I'm* not going to let you down."

"I know," I whisper back. Though I should probably keep the words as Mr. Inside Voice, the truth tumbles out of my mouth anyway. "Sometimes, you are the only thing that makes this reality bearable."

"Same." Leo gives me a tight squeeze before letting me go. "We've always made a great team, Spider-Gwen."

"Yeah, we do."

The buzzing continues in my body as I watch Leo walk away. Once he's tucked inside the minivan, Leo rolls down the passenger window. Though I wave, Leo pretends to shoot spider webs at me.

"Dork!" I yell, and Leo throws a mocking kiss back at me before driving off.

When do I get to fall in love with someone who both loves me back and is going to be here for the long run?

Chapter
27

"Tadaima!" Leo yells when we enter Matsuda the following Friday after school. When there is no reply, he yells a second time, "Ojiichan?"

"Maybe he's taking out the garbage or something?" I hand my skateboard to Leo to put in the back with his.

"Yeah," Leo says, though a worried line crosses his forehead.

While Leo is in the back, I dig my phone and a small Bluetooth speaker out of my backpack. I pull up Rayne Lee's slow jam, "One Last Kiss." After much discussion, this is the song that Leo and I—and okay, Lindsay—decided that Leo will use to fulfill his promise to Alex.

"One song. That's it," I told Lindsay via text earlier. "I swear. Then Leo is yours."

All I received back was a passive-aggressive *LOL*. Yeah, somebody is not happy with me. Join the club. The club also includes three more people who were kicked off the party list today after Aurora overheard them trashing me during concert band.

This dance is not going to be as highly polished as Alex's and my dance. If I can get a simple step-touch on the downbeat for four minutes without Leo passing out, then we're going to call it a win. Which is sad, because I wish everybody could see the goofy, raw, Cinnamon Roll Prince version of Leo that I get to see. The one currently dance-walking out of the kitchen with a small tray on his shoulder while humming "Create Your Spark."

"Why's your dad here?" Leo puts two glasses of melon soda on the table next to the Bluetooth speaker and nods at the front door. "And why is he with my mom? This can't be good."

Dad wears his emotions on his sleeve, which is why America loves him, even when he's completely cringetastic. Santa is not happy.

"What happened?" I say when Dad holds the front door open for Mrs. Matsuda.

Dad scrunches up his face. "You want the good news first or the bad?"

"Daaaaaad."

"The good news is that we can still have the party at Chez Versailles. The bad news is that we have to bump the party back one week."

"But that's prom." I don't want to ask Nevaeh and Aurora to have to choose between their final prom or my party. Maybe they could do half and half.

"No, Koty-chan," Mrs. Matsuda says. "The other way. They're delaying the party until May first."

"But that's our last show," I say at the same time as Leo says, "But that's the Phoenix Phoodie Phestival."

Phestival weekend is like Black Friday to the Matsudas. It's the thing that keeps them afloat during the broiling summer months when traffic is extra slow.

Mrs. Matsuda nods her head. "I know."

"Since the two final shows are already in the can, Phil says we can swap them. Akagi House is finished, so doing the live parts there a week early is no problem," Dad says. "Tamlyn and Stephanie are working overtime to make the switch—at least appear—flawless."

Ojiichan comes out from the back, wiping his hands on his black apron. Mr. Matsuda follows two steps behind him with some kind of car piece in his hands.

"I'm afraid it's not going to work, Doug." Mr. Matsuda holds out the piece. "The food truck needs too much work, and we just don't have the funds right now or the time to get it up and running. I'm sorry."

Dad sighs. "Thanks for trying, Kenichi."

"I'm sorry, Dakota." Mrs. Matsuda puts a hand on my arm. "I wanted so much for our whole family to come to your party."

"There has to be another way," Leo says.

My stomach sinks as reality sets in. I fall into my favorite booth. "That means Alex can't come either. He won't be able to make it back in time after the game on Saturday night."

"He could skip the game," Leo says.

"No, Leo, he can't." Plus, it wouldn't be fair for me to ask him.

"Let me look at the food truck, Kenichi." Dad crosses the restaurant in a few strides. "Tell me what you need. I'll find it. I can call in some favors. Or maybe one of our sponsors can loan us a truck, or we can hire some extra servers for you or something."

"Doug, we can't let you do that for us." Mr. Matsuda shakes his head.

"Let's talk about this in the kitchen, please." Mrs. Matsuda herds Dad and Mr. Matsuda toward the kitchen. After both men are through the door, she looks back over her shoulder at Leo and me. "Don't worry, okay? We're going to figure this out."

"Taihen datta ne." Ojiichan pats my head and tells me things are tough before following the crowd into the kitchen.

That breaks me. A sob of desperation sneaks out of my chest.

"Hey." Leo slides in beside me and puts an arm around my shoulders. "Don't give up yet. Trust us. Let Team Dakota put our heads together. We'll come up with something."

"I'm sorry." I wipe my eyes on my forearm, leaving a smear of eye makeup behind. "I know it's just a birthday party—nothing to cry over. Everybody is going to forget all about it ten minutes after it's over. I don't know why I'm being such a baby about this."

"Because it's more than a birthday party. It's the end of the Mc-Donalds' Alternate Universe."

"Was that supposed to make me feel better?" I sniff. "Because now I feel even worse."

"Sorry. Ugh." Leo's voice is tight. After a beat he adds, "I wanted one night. One night to be a normal teen."

"As usual, Cinder-fella has to work while everybody else goes to the ball. I promise I'm going to make this up to you somehow." I tip my head to the side until it touches Leo's. "I know. As soon as we get back from Japan, I want you to start training me. That way, junior and senior year, I will be your stunt double. I will fill in for you every Homecoming, prom, Valentine's Day, New Year's Eve, JCC event that doesn't fall on a Monday, or any other normal teen event that you want to do. You always give up so much of yourself for everybody else. It's not fair. Let me do something for you."

Leo pinches the bridge of his nose to keep his emotions bottled up inside. I don't press him for an answer. Instead, we sit in a pained silence. I take a deep breath and come back to the things that ground me. The person who grounds me.

"Hey, Leo. Now would be a great time for one of your idiotic ideas." I turn my head and gently tap it against Leo's. "I mean the more outrageous, the better. Just let 'em fly. Because once you give me the spark, then I can expand it into an awesome plan. As I do."

Leo sniffs and taps my head gently with his. "As *we* do."

Chapter

28

We're out of time. The jury is still out on whether this plan is brilliant or idiotic. It doesn't matter. Reality is about to collide with the McDonalds' Alternate Universe in T-minus ten minutes and counting.

Early Saturday morning, I weave through the makeshift Matsuda booth to the back where Dad's delivery truck is doubling as the prep kitchen/storage unit for the weekend. I can feel the side-eye from the other vendors. The ones grumbling about how Matsuda magically got a prime location at the Phoenix Phoodie Phestival this year instead of their usual fringe spot—which is a fraction of the buy-in cost—right in front of their restaurant.

When pressed by the Matsudas—who were as shocked by the sudden switch as everybody else—Dad shrugged and said, "I called in a few favors."

"Leo?" I peek into the back of the truck. "I brought you Thai iced tea. The kind with the boba at the bottom. Your favorite."

I put our drinks on the floor of the truck and climb into the back. Leo's bagged tux and washbag hang inside the truck's door. Near the back of the truck next to the giant coolers, Leo stands with one hand against the wall.

I put my hand on Leo's back. "You okay?"

"Yep. Yep. Perfectly fine. Just give me a minute." Leo's voice doesn't match his words.

Even in the low light of the truck, I can see the redness creeping up his neck. His back continues to expand and contract rapidly under my hand.

"C'mon, Leo!" Leo yells at himself. "Time to man up. Stop being such a baby."

"Hey." I turn Leo around to face me. "Having anxiety does *not* make you a baby. Mine comes in a different flavor, but I know exactly how you feel."

"I want to do this. For you. For me too." Leo takes a deep breath. "Is The Network still balking at the last-minute change in the lineup?"

"Well—" I can't lie to Leo, but I can give him the stripped-down version of Phil's tantrum. "Don't worry about Phil. Plus, Stephanie ironed everything out with The Network and with A Class Act Tuxedo Company. Alex already did the sound ups and other obligations. As long as you are on camera tonight wearing the tux and standing on your own two feet, the contract is fulfilled and you get fifty percent of the modeling fee. Hey, they're the one getting the two-for-one deal here. They should be thanking me."

"That would make my last Japan trip payment and give me some spending money." Leo takes another cleansing breath but still lets out a frustrated sigh. "Why does my heart still feel ready to explode out of my chest? Ugh! I will not pass out on live TV!"

"The tabloids would love that. Unlucky in love DIY Princess kills another relationship. Such a bad kisser that her latest boyfriend—stolen from a frenemy during a vicious catfight in the girls' bathroom—is rushed to the ER."

"I'm not your boyfriend."

"I'm also not a bad kisser, for the record. However, facts don't exactly matter with the paparazzi. So, who are we going to let tell this story today? Them or us?"

"Us." Leo's voice is barely more than a whisper.

"If you start feeling overwhelmed or woozy"—I stick out my hand—"hold my hand and picture yourself going 'Kitsunebiiiiiiiii' on some creeptastic yōkai. Or Phil. Or both, whatever makes you feel better. The paparazzi will be so distracted by the hand-holding that they'll forget whatever bumble came before it. If you're desperate, hug me. I'll take that as an SOS. Then I'll make a scene so you can escape for a while. Okay?"

"Thanks, Koty."

"No, thank you. Only a best friend would do this."

"Seriously, I wouldn't do this for anybody else but you." Leo rubs a hand on the back of his neck. "I think this officially makes us even for the Soccer Ball versus Front Tooth event."

"Eeeeeh, we'll see." I tug Leo into motion. "Drink your boba tea."

We sit on the floor of the delivery truck, sipping our drinks, and swinging our legs like we're six, not now both officially sixteen.

"So, Alex is cool with all of this?" Leo points at the tux bag with his boba tea.

"Does he have a choice?"

"I guess not."

Leo doesn't need to know the rest of the conversation Alex and I had last Sunday night when he celebrated my real birthday with my family. Specifically, the stargazing part afterward in my backyard, when I told Alex that I *didn't* expect him to give up his dreams for me. Now or in August. That we would just take things one day at a time until the clock runs out. My heart still stings from the truth.

I give Leo the CliffsNotes version instead. "I care about Alex, but the reality is that our relationship was doomed from the start."

"Wow, aren't you the Queen of Romance."

"He's leaving for college soon, and I have two more years of high school. It's not going to work after August." I blink back the tears. "It still hurts though. Dude, reality sucks. How about you? Did you and Lindsay get everything worked out yesterday? Is she still coming to the party tonight?"

"Who knows?" Leo lets out a sarcastic laugh. "This party isn't turning out how we planned *at all*."

"No, it definitely is not." I throw an arm around Leo's shoulders. "But everything's going to be okay. I got my BFF and our friends and a tiara that would make Miss Universe jelly. We'll have fun no matter what happens. I promise."

Leo hops off the back of the truck and offers me his hand. "Time to start what might be our most baka idea ever."

Even after my flip-flops hit the asphalt, Leo doesn't let go of my hand. Phil signals to Jordan to start filming. The red creeps up Leo's neck as we walk over to his part of the booth. Props to Mom for seeing Leo's distress. Though Phil hasn't given her the signal, Mom intercepts Jordan and begins her scripted monologue early.

"Today, we're in downtown Phoenix for the twelfth annual Phoenix Phoodie Phestival." Mom turns on the full Tamlyn Akagi charm and talks to the lens like it's a trusted friend.

Meanwhile, Leo's hands are shaking so much that I take the white piece of fabric from him and tie it around his forehead.

"Okay, okay. I need to get into the zone now." Leo walks over to the handwashing station. "I plan on working nonstop from nine a.m. until two forty-five."

"Stephanie said to remind you that she will pick you up at the Circle K on the corner at three. Then you can take a quick shower at my house and presto-change-o, Clark Kent becomes Superman."

"I'm more Arthur Curry becomes Aquaman."

"We live in the desert, Leo."

"Yes, but movie Arthur is half Asian too. Well, Pacific Islander. Representation matters."

"Okay, Aquaman, be sure to apologize to the shrimp before Ojiichan cooks them today." While Leo scrubs his hands, I pull the twenty dollars in small bills out of my pocket and tuck them into his tip jar.

"Koty." Leo points at the tip jar when he returns to his station.

"What? I'm priming the pump." I lower my voice. "Because I'm not going to Japan without you this summer."

I expect Leo to smile, not suddenly get a deer-in-the-headlights look. I look back over my shoulder to see Jordan the Camera Op and Mom. I let out a nervous laugh.

"You'll see that Dakota's build from the Homecoming Carnival is getting another outing this weekend." Mom walks behind the build and puts a hand on Leo's back. "Just like Dakota has followed in her family's footsteps, so has her longtime friend Leo Matsuda. At sixteen years old, Leo is an accomplished chef, taking after his grandfather, Nagoya-born chef Masao Matsuda. Today, Leo will be making yakisoba, a popular street festival food in Japan. Want to learn more about Japanese festival food? Watch the first two episodes of Season 13 when Team McDonald did a build in Japan. So, what exactly goes into yakisoba, Leo? I see you have some cabbage and noodles."

Mom continues to pat Leo's back and ask him leading questions about his process. Though his voice is squeaky and his words choppy at first, Mom's calming energy helps Leo get through the interview without his heart going *Alien* out of his chest.

"Cut." Phil slides off his headphones and takes Mom's lapel mic from her. "Dakota, let's do a couple of sound ups for your Instagram video series. One outside the tent area and one inside with Leo. If we could get a little bit of something about how excited you are about Leo being your date, you know, some kind of *spark*. That would be nice."

"Phil, I'm going to go," Mom says. "I need to extract Doug from the Fudge Brothers' tent before he samples too much of their product. Meet you in about fifteen minutes, Koty."

I walk with Phil and Mom to the front of the tent, where Mr. Matsuda is hanging the chalkboard sign listing today's limited-menu specials.

"Can I add some drawings?" I ask Mr. Matsuda, and he hands me the bag of chalk markers.

"That would work too," Phil says more to Jordan than me. "Start outside the booth and then focus in on Dakota as she finishes the drawing. Then we'll follow her back over to Leo to say goodbye until tonight. Maybe a *spark* or two. Dakota, if you want to talk about your upcoming trip to Japan with Leo and plug his booth, that's okay for Instagram."

"What trip to Japan with Leo?" Mr. Matsuda's voice carries through the tent.

"Ummmmm," I say.

"Or whatever trip you were just talking about." Phil holds up the lapel mic Mom had on.

"Please leave that part out, Koty." Mrs. Matsuda shares a pointed look with Leo. "For now."

"Fine. We're not covering the trip anyway, so it's irrelevant." Phil hands me the lapel mic and slides his headphones on. He signals to Jordan the Camera Op. "Okay, we're set."

I hold the chalk marker up to the board, but nothing comes out. Mr. and Mrs. Matsuda continue to talk in hushed Japanese until Mrs. Matsuda finally grabs her husband by the elbow and leads him behind the delivery truck. For half a second, my old drawing of a pile of poo comes to my mind. Nope. Well, yes, but nope. I draw a picture of a squid on a stick instead. Its panicked facial expression pretty much sums up how things are going this morning.

I slap a smile on my face and fix the squid's expression before standing up.

"Hey, guys. Thanks for tuning in tonight for my Super Sweet Sixteen *Extravaganza*. Before I start getting ready, I stopped by our family friends'—the Matsudas'—booth here at the Phoenix Phoodie Phestival."

I walk back under the giant red-and-white striped tent Dad sweet-talked somebody into letting us borrow for the weekend.

"Ooh, what do we have here? Looks like eldest sibling and future famous patissier Sasha Matsuda created some of her famous manju—Japanese sweets—especially for this weekend's event."

Phil emphatically points in Leo's direction.

"And, gonna give a high five to my friend and middle Matsuda sibling Aurora who is rocking the cash register this weekend. And finally, we have Leo—my BFF and date for tonight—who is creating his signature dish, yakisoba. If you are coming to the festival this weekend, do not miss this booth."

Phil pretends to yawn. Rude.

"Hey, Leo." I put my hand on Leo's shoulder so that he'll look at me instead of the camera. "Which tux from A Class Act Tuxedo Company did you end up choosing?"

Leo's mouth opens, but nothing comes out. A redness shoots up from his collar. Phil lets out an annoyed sigh. Whatever, Phil. Even Aquaman needs an assist from Wonder Woman occasionally.

"Wait. Don't tell me." I put my hand up. "I want it to be a secret."

Leo raises an eyebrow because he knows as well as I do which one he chose. I put my elbow out. Leo taps his elbow to mine.

"Tune in at five p.m. Pacific Standard Time, eight p.m. Eastern and find out. Dakota out. Peace." Not only do I steal Nevaeh's outro, but I steal their hand sign too.

"Cut," Phil says. "What was with the funky chicken arms?"

"I didn't want to contaminate Leo's hands."

"Go take a couple of selfies with Leo and post them. *Sparks*, please. I'll get the other footage to Stephanie to post as soon as I can."

"Gotcha, boss."

When I turn back around to face Leo, I give him an eye roll and an I-may-puke face. It makes Leo smirk, and I snap a picture. I add a squid emoji and a location pin to it and load it up.

Even though the whole Matsuda family finally signed the appearance release so they could be on camera, I still ask Leo, "Can I take a selfie with you?"

"If you must."

I step behind the yakisoba booth with Leo. He doesn't smile.

"C'mon, we're trying to boost your tips here." I wince. "I'm so sorry."

"Don't be. And Mom already knew. She and I kind of had a kitchen sink argument yesterday after my whole thing with Lindsay, and the truth about the trip came out along with a bunch of other stuff. We wanted to get Dad on board with the idea first before we broke the news to Ojiichan."

"Wait. Where is Ojiichan? He went to buy a ginger ale half an hour ago."

"I don't know. If he's not back in five, I'll go look for him." Leo cranes his neck to look over the light but steadily increasing crowd. "Ojiichan's probably doing recon at the Wisteria Village Café booth.

Yeah, we see your melon pan and Olympic skaters signing autographs and raise you manju and selfies with America's DIY Princess."

"I don't know, the speed skater with the gold medal around his neck was pretty hot. I mean, somebody should go do further research on the competition and report back."

Aurora raises her hand. "I volunteer as tribute."

"Traitors, both of you," Leo says.

"Then let's fight fire with fire." I step into Leo and hold my phone up.

This time I get a genuine smile. The hearts start racking up two seconds after I post it. I'm happy to be a sell-out if it means more traffic at the Matsudas' booth.

"Welp, here's hoping that this year's festival is lit, because Dad and Ojiichan are not going to be on board with the Japan trip if we don't make bank this weekend. Also, as of yesterday, Sasha has officially reclaimed the title of Favorite Matsuda Child."

"Don't want it!" Sasha yells from behind her manju display table.

Mr. and Mrs. Matsuda come back out from behind the delivery truck. They don't say a word to each other. All the Matsuda kids wisely duck their heads and busy themselves. I feel so bad for Leo. Everything I do to make things better for him always seems to make things worse.

"I gotta go," I announce to the tent. "Gambatte, Team Matsuda!"

I head toward the Circle K, where I'm meeting up with Mom and Dad. I see Ojiichan coming back the other way with a can of soda in his hand.

"Daijōbu, Ojiichan?" I ask if he is okay when we intersect.

"Hai, hai." Ojiichan barely makes eye contact as he passes me by.

"Gambatte, ne!" *Good luck,* I yell to his back.

His head dips a little, but he doesn't stop his shuffle down the street.

Chapter

29

To say that my fans liked the selfie with Leo would be an understatement. Part of me feels bad for Lindsay, especially if she reads the hundreds of comments saying what a cute couple Leo and I make. I even comment: *Thanks, but we're just BFFs.* It doesn't help the speculation.

"Dakota!" Dad yells up the stairs, "The camera crew is here."

"She'll be down in a minute, Doug," Mom yells down the stairs before bursting into my bedroom. "Here's the tape. Stephanie just left to pick up Leo. I feel like this day has flown by us. That's enough tape, honey."

I smoosh the fabric of my dress against the double-sided fashion tape attached to the skin on my chest. I do some jumping jacks. I shimmy my shoulders around. Everything seems secure. I add another piece of body tape anyway.

Mom turns me around and sniffs. "I wish your grandparents, especially Obaachan, were here to see this. I know they would be so proud."

"Hey, hey, hey, no crying," I say to both of us because I'm getting misty too. "Jonathan will kill us if we ruin his work before the party."

"Today has been such a rollercoaster of emotions. I'm happy. I'm sad. Relieved. Hopeful. Remorseful. Ugh." Mom dabs at her eyes with a tissue. "I want to think about tomorrow. I also don't want to think about tomorrow."

"How about we sleep in tomorrow?"

"Agreed. I vote for a complete PJ Day. Maybe binge-watch something *not* on HGTV? Order in pizza?"

"Sounds perfect." I adjust Mom's tasteful, vintage marcasite tiara, which Nevaeh finally talked her into wearing. "Can I tell you a secret? And this absolutely cannot get back to Phil."

Mom raises an eyebrow.

"I'm looking forward to the party," I confess. "Having Leo and Aurora and Nevaeh and all my peeps from the Japanese Culture Club to celebrate with me means a lot. Yes, this party is completely extra, but a part of me wants to spoil my friends a little to say thanks for all the unnecessary drama I've put them through because of our family's business. My only regret: that I can't drive the Mustang I'm going to pretend to be surprised to receive at the party tonight. At the end of this semester, after I pass Drivers Ed . . ."

"You're still not going to be driving it," Mom says.

"But it's my car."

"If you can drive clean with no accidents or tickets for a year, then we will hand over the keys to the Mustang to you on your seventeenth birthday. Until then"—Mom takes the sunglasses off my dresser and slides them on—"Mama is going to break it in for you."

Yeah, we're going to revisit this conversation later, but for now I say, "You give the woman a tiara, and suddenly she thinks she deserves a convertible."

"Dakota Rae!" Dad yells up the stairs. "Now!"

o   o   o

I take my time coming down the stairs. Dad's face lights up like this isn't the fourth time we've filmed my grand entrance.

"Look at my little girl." Dad's voice does genuinely break.

I spin around slowly. Dad gets misty for real this time.

"I wanted to give you something, Koty. Something special from me."

Dad digs in his tux's coat pocket and pulls out a small turquoise box. Dad pauses with the closed box on his palm so Jordan can get a good shot before he opens it.

"Aw, it's beautiful, Dad," I say as Dad puts the small diamond solitaire on a gold chain around my neck.

"Cut," Phil says. "Start at the foot of the stairs again. Come on,

Dakota, this is your first piece of real jewelry. You're a grown-up now."

"Yeah, talk Mom into giving me back my Mustang. *That* will make me burst into tears."

Phil lets out an irritated sigh. "Can we just film the pickup, please?"

I swish the bottom of my gown around in true diva fashion and stomp back to the stairs. We do three more versions before I can do a take that doesn't include snickering and/or sarcasm. To Phil's disappointment, no tears are shed.

"Dakota, go wait in your Mom's office, please," Phil says after checking his phone. "Leo is here."

"We're not getting married. It's not bad luck for him to see me before the event."

"Please, for me."

"Fine." I check my tiara in the hallway mirror before I swoosh into Mom's office. "I want my phone and something to drink."

"Dakota Rae," Dad says in a stern voice.

I grumble, "Please."

A few minutes later, I hear Leo's heavy feet running up the stairs and the water running. Stephanie appears in Mom's office a minute later with a bottle of sparkling water.

"I couldn't find your phone, your Highness." Stephanie flops down on her chair and rubs her temples.

"Everything okay?" I say.

"We're behind schedule. Good thing Leo isn't as high-maintenance as you are."

I slide the bottle of sparkling water across the table to her. Stephanie accepts it with a nod.

"Warning: Something is going on with Leo's grandfather," Stephanie says. "According to Leo, Grandpa has been feeling under the weather all day. Jen just texted me that they are closing the booth down early because he started throwing up. Sasha will bring Aurora to the party as soon as they get everything packed up and take Grandpa home."

"Oh no!" I sit up straight. "What about tomorrow? Leo's Dad can cook too, but not at Ojiichan's level. This is going to mess everything up. The Phoenix Phoodie Phestival is like Black Friday for the Matsudas."

"I know. Jen said not to tell Leo because he'll worry. She wants him to have one night for himself."

But I always tell Leo the truth, even when it hurts.

As usual, Stephanie reads me like an open book. "If things get serious, Dakota, I will let you know immediately. I promise. Now then, what's next? Ah, yes, flowers."

Stephanie is off and running again. Meanwhile, I close my eyes and steady my breathing. I hear Leo thud down the stairs a moment later.

"Here. Take this. No, turn it around so the name is on the out-side." Stephanie's voice echoes down the hallway. "Go stand outside and pretend like you just arrived in your car."

"Can we pretend I rolled up in a convertible and not the Matsuda mobile?" Leo says.

"Oh look, poof, it's a Ferrari. Enjoy. Now go. And a big smile when Dakota answers the door. I'm talking The Full Dimple, got it?"

"Got it."

The front door opens and closes before Stephanie comes to fetch me. She tucks an errant curl back into the cascade of them tum-bling down my back, including the hair that I was *not* born with. Whatever. They can take their hair back after tonight, but they're going to have to pry the tiara from my cold, dead, perfectly mani-cured hands.

"Here's your mark, Dakota." Phil points down at the piece of blue tape on the floor. "Start here and come back to here."

"Got it."

"Sparks, *please*," Phil pleads. "Quiet in the shot."

When I open the front door, Leo looks up. My heart forgets its purpose for a moment before it *ka-thuds* back into rhythm.

"You look ah-mazing," I gush.

Leo's sweet smile turns into The Full Dimple. I know Jordan is on full zoom. Because I would. That's some good TV right there, I'm tellin' ya.

"These are for you." Leo holds out the long, white box. He opens it so the folks watching at home can see that it contains a bouquet of sixteen blush-pink, long-stemmed roses. "Happy Birthday, Dakota."

Leo's hands are vibrating, so I put my hand over the top of his to steady the box. "Thank you, Leo."

When I step back to let him through the door, Leo grabs my hand. I lead him to the blue tape. At the designated mark, Stephanie stealthily leans in to collect the flowers.

"You look . . . wow . . . like a princess." Leo twirls me around. The Full Dimple doesn't disappear.

"Yeah, I'm not giving this tiara back. Pretty sure I'm wearing it to school on Monday. Nevaeh and I are going to start a new fashion trend."

"And cut," Phil says.

"Once more from the top?" I say.

"No, that was perfect. Now *that* had a spark. Keep up the good work." Phil checks his phone. "The limo will be here in five. We'll do some footage of that and then meet you at the venue."

"Wait. Where's Aurora?" Leo pulls his phone out of his pocket with his free hand. "We can't leave without her."

"We can and we will. Sorry. The live, pre-episode teasers begin at four thirty, whether we are ready or not."

"Your mom texted that they are running behind schedule, so Sasha will drop Aurora off at Chez Versailles," Stephanie says, the flower box still tucked under her arm.

Leo's eyebrows furrow.

"Don't worry." I squeeze Leo's hand. "The party officially ends at eleven, but we have the limo until one. You. Me. Aurora. Jayden. Nevaeh. And as many JCC peeps as we can cram in. We'll get burgers from In-N-Out or go wherever Aurora wants."

"Well, that won't completely go to her head," Leo jokes.

"Want a root beer while we wait for the limo?" I say as the crew heads out the front door to set up.

"Only water in that dress, Dakota," Stephanie says as she follows after them.

"Water is fine for me too," Leo says.

When I turn to leave, Leo stays attached to my hand. I stop. "You okay?"

"I'm worried about Ojiichan."

"Yeah, me too." I squeeze Leo's hand. "Want to send him a full-length shot of you? 'Cuz, when I opened the door, I was like, 'Who is this guy and what did he do with my best friend?'"

Leo genuinely laughs. "You have to be in the picture too."

A warmth spreads in my chest as Leo reaches out to caress my hair. At least until he says, "Is this your real hair?"

"Yes. Well, part of it is at least."

"Aurora is going to be so jelly." Leo looks at his phone. "Why won't she text me back?"

"You get some water." I let go of Leo's hand. "I think I left my phone upstairs in my purse. Be back in a sec."

I swoosh up the stairs to find my retro, beaded purse, courtesy of my mom's closet. I pull my phone out and see I have a series of texts from Aurora. My heart sinks into my stomach as I read through them. The last one has an emphatic plea.

AURORA

Please, Koty. Don't say anything to Leo. There is absolutely nothing that he can do about it. Let him have a night to remember. If we go to the ER, I'll let you know. Until then, tell Leo Ojiichan has an intestinal bug.

ME

That's a lie.

AURORA

No, it's me giving you bad information. I'm still coming to the party. I promise!

"Dakota, the limo is here," Dad yells up the stairs.

Though my heart is torn, I plaster on a smile. Things get a little easier when I find Leo and Dad standing near the front door together, sharing a joke and a selfie.

"You ready?" Leo says to me.

"Yeah." I can't lie to Leo, so I give him the part of the truth that I don't feel icky about. "Aurora texted. She'll be there soon."

Leo shakes his head. "Aurora and her twenty-seven-step beauty routine."

"Wait. Let me fix this." Dad adjusts Leo's rose-gold bow tie. "I'm so glad you're sharing this day with us, Leo. Don't get me wrong, Alex is a nice guy, but I'm glad you're the one helping us end this chapter in our history. The Matsudas have been such an important part of our journey. You. Your parents. Your sisters. Your grandfather. All so special to us. Don't know what we'd do without you guys."

Dad gets misty, and this is a one-two punch to my gut. Tears well up in my eyes. Real ones.

"I'll be outside." Dad quickly beats a retreat out the front door.

"Phil's missing out." I flap my hands in front of my eyes to dry them. "Look, Dakota McDonald has emotions. Who knew?"

"I knew, you giant marshmallow." Leo pulls me into a side hug. My tiara stabs him in the head. "Ow. You are a danger to others tonight."

I sniff and bounce on the balls of my feet, trying to pull my armor back on. "I will not cry on live TV. I will not."

"I will not pass out on live TV. I will not." Leo mimics me before putting out his elbow. "How long do you think Phil would let us live if we did like a shuffle or disco arms or something goofy down the sidewalk to the limo?"

I shrug. "He's the one who insisted on some sparks."

Phil nods as Leo and I promenade out the front door and down the front steps to the sidewalk. His jaw drops when Leo and I suddenly turn to face each other, do-si-do, and chassé hand in hand all the way to the limo. When the driver opens the limo's door, Leo twirls me around like a ballerina and dips me back. Leo pauses, looking at my lips. My eyes instinctively close when Leo leans in. I'll admit it. I'm as disappointed as viewers are going to be that Leo only kisses my cheek.

Chapter
30

The limo driver rolls down the partition when we arrive at Chez Versailles. Toby, aka Break-Dakota's-Fall Guy, sits next to the driver.

"Phil says to stay put," Toby says over his shoulder. "They'll have the live feed up in a moment. Also, he says absolutely no more square dancing."

"Square dancing is so thirty minutes ago. How about the robot?" Leo illustrates his choice. "Or like, one, two, three—*bam*, mic drop?"

"Speaking of mics." Toby holds out a small silver box, and Leo reluctantly retrieves it. Inside are two small lapel microphones. "Hide Leo's beside his boutonniere. Yours is going to have to go . . . um, yeah."

I cram the mic down my cleavage and clip it to my bra. I pull the fabric back up and adjust The Girls. Leo cringes.

I shrug. "Where else am I supposed to put it?"

"I feel like a secret agent with this on." Leo picks up the corner of his lapel and drops his voice deep. "I have eyes on the package. Cover me. I'm going in."

"Hey." Toby waves frantically at us. "Your mics are hot."

Leo gulps.

"Get ready for the door to open," Toby says as the divider rolls up.

There is a quick *knock-knock* before the driver opens the door. I hope they have Leo's mic turned down, so viewers don't hear his gasp for air. Or mine, when I slide out of the limo to find that HGTV asked—or maybe straight-up paid—a bunch of people I vaguely recognize from school to show up early with signs and balloons and bubbles. Phil gives us a halt sign. Leo anchors himself to the rose-gold carpet leading into the venue. I hit a rose-gold-carpet pose and then a second version as people—including people way too old to be partygoers—take our picture. Leo wavers a little, but he stays on his feet. Phil gives us the signal to proceed.

Leo continues to crush my hand as we walk into Chez Versailles.

"Happy Birthday, Dakota." I'm sure Phil has ordered the camera to zoom in tight on Mom's glistening eyes as we join my parents.

"Hot dam!" Dad says.

Viewers get a special treat along with their bingo square for Dad's catchphrase. Tonight—for one night only—the HOT DAM! beaver is wearing a tiara on the screen instead of a hardhat.

My parents smother Leo and me in a group hug.

"And, we're out," Phil says. "In twelve minutes, we do the cake spot. Warning: Mics will remain hot."

Jordan lowers his camera, but my parents don't let go of us. Like for thirty seconds. It's getting awkward, even for me.

"Guys. Love you, but you need to get out of my bubble," I say from inside Mom's rib-crushing hug.

Mom breaks the McDonald huddle. "We'll leave you to your friends."

As my parents walk away, Nevaeh, Jax, and all of our JCC peeps crush in. Well, except for one. Leo cranes his head looking for Lindsay.

"Does our Cinnamon Roll Prince clean up nice or what?" Nevaeh loops their finger around until Leo turns in a tight circle for them.

Egged on by Nevaeh and our JCC peeps, Leo does a few male model poses until he cracks up.

"Group selfie!" Leo digs his phone out of his pocket, and we all crowd in.

"Give me your phone." I put my purse, with my phone still tucked inside, next to the marble fountain that we start posing on. "You and Nevaeh first."

Stephanie rushes by with her clipboard. "Leo Matsuda, you fall in that fountain, and I will kill you with my own bare hands."

Leo hops down, but Nevaeh continues to walk on the edge. As they always do.

I thought Jax wanted to be next in line for a picture, but when he gets to Leo, he says, "I have a surprise for you. Look who was able to come after all."

The small crowd parts, and Lindsay walks through it. A conflicted smile crosses Leo's face. My heart ices over.

"My parents are still mad at us, but they reconsidered about tonight." Lindsay hugs Leo before turning to me. "Happy Birthday, Dakota."

"I'm glad you were able to come," I say, though I step backward to avoid her hug. "Thanks for letting me borrow Leo. I'll give him back to you soon."

"Give him back?" Leo says with a strained laugh.

"We're walking. We're walking." Phil swoops in behind us and herds Leo and me toward the smaller of the two ballrooms. "We start filming in ten seconds."

"Oh wow!" Leo picks up one of the hundreds of dainty pastries and confections filling the room. "Wait till Sasha sees this."

"Speaking of Sasha." Mom walks into frame carrying a lacquerware tray that I'm pretty sure came from the Matsudas' house. Mom places it on the only open spot on the table. "She sent over a special gift for your party, Dakota."

I look down at the steering-wheel-sized tray filled with a fluffle of manju rabbits. A couple of them perch up on the side of the tray, holding a tiny banner written in Japanese. Mom steps to the right so that Jordan can get a close-up.

"Can you read it?" Mom says, and I lean in closer.

"O-something-something-way-above-my-kanji-knowledge omedetō gozaimasu." I look at Leo for help. "I'm guessing that says Happy Birthday?"

"Yes. Otanjōbi omedetō gozaimasu," Leo says, and then makes me repeat after him to "make Iwate-sensei proud."

"I will forgive you, Sasha, for impaling these poor bunnies in the name of art."

Phil stands behind Jordan. He holds up his clipboard and points emphatically at it. It has the sponsor's name scribbled out in huge letters.

"Look at all these macarons and cannoli. I'm not sure what this chocolate work of art is, but I'm going to have one later. Sweet Lil Something Bakery has outdone themselves."

I follow Mom past the chocolate fountain over to a five-tier cake that would eclipse most people's wedding cakes. The bottom layer has a bunch of rose-gold ribbons coming out of it.

"What are these?" I say, genuinely surprised. I was there the day we taste-tested Sweet Lil Something Bakery's cakes. We had so many that I almost barfed in the car on the way home. But we didn't talk about this.

"Everyone has been so generous to us that we wanted to share the love." Mom steps back into frame. She has a pile of gold paper wristbands in her hand. "Twenty-five lucky party-goers will get to pull a ribbon that has a number charm attached to it. Whatever number they draw is the order in which they get to make a trip to the prize table."

Jordan pans over to the table Mom is gesturing at. It is covered with everything from an iPhone to a Coach bag to palettes of designer-brand makeup to a pair of front-row concert tickets in a protective plastic box, and more over-the-top, excessive, embarrassing, overkill prizes. Some of this swag came from sponsors, but I also suspect that "Uncle Doug" had a hand in it. From the conspiratorial look on Leo's face, I have to wonder if Leo was Head Elf in Charge on this project too.

"That is definitely . . . *something*." Before anybody can stop me, I snatch the wristbands off Mom's palm. "I can't wait to give these out."

Phil emphatically shakes his head no, while Jordan chases after me.

"One for you. One for you. One for you." I hand them out to my JCC peeps. I'm sure these weren't the people Phil already hand-picked. Undoubtedly, he chose people from my school who look like they model for *Seventeen* in their spare time. I'm choosing the people who chose me, even when they didn't have to. Even when I ruined their Homecoming last year with my wardrobe malfunction. Even when I am weird or extra or just awkward.

"One for my VIP, Nevaeh. And one for my best friend, Leo." I wish I could say that I'm mature enough to immediately put a gold wristband on Lindsay too. But I'm not.

After a telling pause, I add, "And one for Lindsay. Thank you for helping my best friend take a step forward this year."

Okay, nobody else in America knows what I'm talking about, but Leo does. He nods. Message received.

"And we're out." Phil snatches the rest of the wristbands from my hand. "I didn't say you could give those out."

I hold up my index finger. "Nor did you tell me I couldn't."

Phil lets out an exasperated sigh. "We're going to let the rest of the partygoers inside. Stay close to the ballroom doors so we can do another live spot in fourteen minutes."

"Gotcha." After Phil leaves, I turn back to Leo and Lindsay. "If you guys want to have a moment, I don't need Leo for another ten minutes or so. Give me your mic, though. And keep things PG, because cameras are always rolling whether you see them or not. Sorry. That's the downside of being my friend."

A conflicted wrinkle forms between Leo's eyebrows, but he hands me his mic. When Lindsay reaches out for his hand though, Leo crosses his arms.

o   o   o

As ordered, I stand near the door next to the gift table. *Your presence is your gift* was printed at the bottom of my invitations, but Phil insisted that we include a piece of paper that clearly stated a gift wasn't necessary; *however,* a donation to the Raising Hope Women and Children's Shelter would gratefully be accepted. I know it's a ploy to downplay the criticism we are rightfully going to receive after all the excessiveness from tonight leaks out, but if it helps Raising Hope buy the new cribs they desperately need, I'll take one for the team.

I thank people as they drop off envelopes into a locked, gilded cage. I greet the people I actually know by name, duck a few hugs, and give head nods to people I'm not sure even go to my school. It wouldn't surprise me if the tabloids sent a few moles to dig around for a hot scoop. I push on the bodice of my dress to check that it's secure.

Exactly ten minutes later, Leo arrives. Solo.

"You and Lindsay okay?" I mouth at Leo. He shakes his head. "Are *you* okay?"

Leo shrugs and puts his hand out for the mic. His hands vibrate as he reattaches the mic behind his boutonniere.

"Oh, wow. Ugh." I say when a collective laugh goes up in the ballroom. On the large screen above the stage is a picture of me in pigtails wearing kid-sized, bedazzled safety glasses, and wielding a hammer mid-strike.

"I remember that girl." Leo steps in closer to me. "She's the one who seconded my baka idea to build a tree house in my backyard even after her dad—who is a professional builder, mind you—said mimosa trees were not strong enough for tree houses. Yeah, should've listened to Mr. Doug on that one."

As if on cue, the next picture is a same-age version of Dakota, only with a cast on her arm and holding Leo's stuffed cow, Mr. Ushi. If you know where to look, you can see the *I'm sorry. ~Leo* written near my wrist.

The crowd has another laugh as a picture of me in Japan wearing a yukata comes up. There are a series of photos, including someone handing me a squid-on-a-stick and my genuine reaction to it.

Leo leans into me. "We are definitely going to have a redo on that one in July."

My stomach tightens. If Ojiichan ends up in the hospital tonight, Leo is not going to Japan with me. His final payment to Iwate-sensei due next Friday would go to his family instead.

"We go live in thirty seconds." Phil suddenly pops up behind us. "You will walk straight through the crowd, greeting your adoring fans, of course, but do not stop. Take the stage. Do your thanks. Tamlyn will insist that you come outside . . . blah blah blah. If you could somehow find some emotions, that would make my night."

"How about I do-si-do around the car?" The surprise is only going to be a surprise to the people watching at home, because I may have bragged shamelessly about my new car in Japanese class once or twice or thirty times already.

"Absolutely not."

"How about a dab? Too dated?"

"No."

"How about . . . Kawaii desu ne!" I cup my chin in a V between my hands.

"No."

"Leo and I could do a chest bump."

Phil rakes a hand through his hair. "This is going to be a disaster."

Leo takes a deep breath and offers me his arm. Somehow, we make it to the stage without either of us slipping, tripping, or passing out. All of my body parts—including my stunt hair—stay put. When we get to the stage's steps, Leo pulls up short. His eyes are as big as saucers. Beads of sweat dot his brow.

"Thank you, Prince Charming." I remove my arm from Leo's. "I'll take it from here."

People will undoubtedly criticize me later for hogging the spotlight, but what I see—and what the reality is—is that my best friend may pass out if I keep pushing him. Instead, I play into my role and do a royal wave as I climb the few stairs up onto the stage.

I look out at the audience. This is it. This is the end of the McDonalds' Alternate Universe. This is me closing the door on the last sixteen years of my life, and opening a whole new one as Dakota McDonald, average teenager and future industrial designer/functional artist. I find Nevaeh in the front row. They give me a nod.

"Thank you, everybody, for being here tonight." I look down at the JCC members huddled around the front of the stage next to Nevaeh. "Thanks to those of you who have always accepted me for who I am." The collision of High School Dakota with DIY Princess Dakota is jarring, but I look directly into the camera as I was coached to do. "And a big thanks to all our viewers at home for tuning in for one last trip down memory lane with us. You've been with me since literally my birth and watched me grow up. Tonight, HGTV wanted to send me off with a bang. . . ."

Cue Mom.

"Wait, wait." A spotlight follows Mom as she swishes to the middle of the stage in her retro Hollywood starlet gown. "I know you want to get back to your friends, Dakota, but before you do, your dad and I have a special gift for you." Mom looks directly into the camera. "But it requires that you come outside."

The crowd hoots as I follow Mom off the other side of the stage. I'm sure Leo was supposed to come with us, but he still has a death grip on the handrail at the other side of the stage. I see Nevaeh out the corner of my eye heading toward Leo. Situation handled.

When Mom and I get to the doors with the curtains drawn across them, I have my next line.

"Where's Dad?"

Mom nods at the hotel employees who rip open the curtains, while employees on the other side open up the giant sliding doors. There it is—my customized, retro-inspired, cherry-red Ford Mustang convertible. My gasp is authentic. Leaning into his nickname, Dad sits in the driver's seat wearing a Santa hat and sunglasses.

"Hot dam! It looks like Santa came early this year," Dad says, and the tiara-wearing beaver makes another appearance on the TV screen.

"This car is sick." I deliver my line with complete sincerity.

Dad slides out and holds the car door open for me. "For America's DIY Princess."

I hope Jordan doesn't pan to the audience right now. Quite a few people are rolling their eyes. I probably would too in their shoes.

I tuck my skirts around me and slide across the leather seat.

My bedazzled fingertips skim across the retro-style dashboard and caress the state-of-the-art sound system. The passenger door suddenly opens.

"This car is sick." Leo slides in next to me. He's still pinkish, but The Full Dimple Smile is genuine. "I'm thinkin' . . . You. Me. Road trip?"

"Yeah, not so fast. Safety first, kids." America marks another bingo square, as Dad holds up the car keys. "Dakota has to finish Drivers Ed first. And you two on a road trip together?" Dad crosses his arms. "I don't think so, bud."

"Daaaaad." I play the role of a spoiled princess to perfection.

But also, just watch me. After I have *a lot* more practice driving on the interstate, then we'll take "Lightning" on a road trip. Maybe to San Diego for Comic Con? Or Los Angeles for the *Kitsune Mask* movie premiere one day? Baby steps. I look over at Leo. We are so there.

"And we're out," Phil says. "Thanks, everybody. Please go back inside and enjoy the party. Dakota, seventeen minutes."

Though most of the crowd goes back inside, a few members of the JCC stick around. Nevaeh sprawls across the hood of my car like a supermodel while Jax takes their picture.

"Anybody seen Aurora?" Leo checks his phone. "She should have been here by now."

"She's probably inside." Nevaeh slides off the hood of the car and adjusts their tiara. "You guys take a breather. I'll find Aurora. C'mon, Jax."

"Too bad Mr. Doug took the keys with him," Leo says when we are alone. "We could have taken this sweet ride for a spin around the parking lot."

"I don't have a full license yet."

"Yeah, but I do." Leo waggles his eyebrows.

"So, for real, you want to go on a road trip with me sometime?"

"Uh. Yeah. Like you have to ask me that. How about San Diego the summer before senior year?" Leo throws his hands up in the air with double "fox fingers" and whoops. "Comic Con, here we come!"

The McDonalds' Alternate Universe might be ending tonight, but I can still see into the future. Leo and I flying across the desert with the top down and our matching, limited-edition *Kitsune Mask* T-shirts on. Me, sweet-talking event organizers into gifting us special passes for the *Kitsune Mask* preview screening. Leo fanboying all over Ava Takahashi as she signs his T-shirt. Leo and I smacking each other with two of the pillows from the mountain of decorative ones in our hotel room. Leo and I. Together.

I can practically hear the squeaking-brake sound effect as all the wheels fall off my fantasy. Okay, so there are some major stumbling blocks with this plan. But we're the Dynamic Duo. We can make anything happen.

The party goes on inside without us. Even the hotel staff doesn't realize we are still sitting out here, because they turn off the lights. It's not exactly dark because of all the ground lights, but we can see the stars in the inky-blue, early-May sky. It would be kind of a romantic moment if Leo's girlfriend wasn't waiting for him inside.

"Are you okay, Leo?" I put out my hand to stop his answer. I dig my mic out of my bodice, and we throw both of them in the glove compartment before continuing. "I mean about everything. The party. Your anxiety. Lindsay."

"So-so, so-so, and . . ." Leo sighs. "One step forward. Two steps back."

"Is it because of me, Lindsay's parents, or the restaurant?"

"All of the above."

Not only do the wheels fall off my road trip fantasy, but the whole idea disintegrates into dust and blows away. I take a deep breath and pull on my armor so I can do what I have to do.

"Tell Lindsay that after tonight, I'll get out of her way. Like, eat lunch at a different table, move to a different seat in Japanese class, and start watching *Kitsune Mask* by myself. I will completely disappear so that you two can get on with your life together without me always butting in and making things weird and complicated."

"What if I don't want you to disappear again?" Leo looks up at the stars in the cloudless sky. "Yeah, we needed some personal space earlier this year to figure things out. To experiment solo a little bit. But now I want us to come back together like we always do. Like I always want us to."

"You wanna go play Spider-Man and Spider-Gwen on the monkey bars with me?" I pretend to shoot webs out of my wrists.

I laugh, but Leo doesn't. A serious look crosses his face.

"Koty, there's something that's been digging at me. Honestly, for a while now."

We sit in silence for several more heartbeats until I can't help myself. "What, Leo, what?"

"Alex, Lindsay, and even Nevaeh keep seeing us as a couple. The first two, I can chalk up to jealousy, but Nevaeh?" Leo turns in his seat and gives me a probing look. "Am I missing something?"

I'm scared to answer that question truthfully, so I deflect. I blow on my bedazzled nails and buff them on my designer gown. "Yes, you are."

"I'm serious, Dakota." Leo puts his hand on my arm. "Could I do something as an experiment? Something that will answer the question for me once and for all?"

"Yes, you can kiss me, if that's what you are asking." My insides tighten, fearing that I'm wrong. Again. "I hope that's what you were asking, or this night just got even more awkward. And that's saying a lot."

"Really?" Leo squeaks and then clears his throat. "I thought maybe that boat had sailed, since, you know, Alex and all."

"Nope. Unfortunately, it's always been there. Whether I wanted it to be or not."

"So, to make sure that I heard you correctly. Before I potentially ruin our friendship for good, I could kiss you right now, and you wouldn't knock my left front tooth out."

"Leo."

"Yes?"

"Stop. Talking."

Leo and I lean in at the same time. We both tip our head to the same side. And then both course-correct to the other side. Always a pair. Always in tandem. Leo's warm fingertips rest on my cheek and gently guide my head to the right as his head tips the other way. I don't want to close my eyes. I'm afraid that the sparks I'm feeling—the ones currently sending electrical bursts to the pit of my belly—will disappear. I'm afraid that after the test concludes, Leo won't feel the same way I do. I'm afraid that I will spend the rest of my life knowing *exactly* what I'm missing.

As soon as Leo's warm, soft lips meet mine, I know the risk is worth it. No matter what happens next, I will always remember this birthday kiss. It will be the measuring stick for all future kisses. One tentative press of Leo's lips against mine turns into a second kiss, and then a third. Each one becomes braver and bolder. I kiss Leo back with all the pent-up energy I've been carrying around since last summer. Since Tanabata. Since living inside of Leo's Friend Zone became unbearable. This was never on Stephanie's hundred-point party planning list. There is no plan B if Leo shatters my heart tonight. I can't bear to hear his truth if it doesn't match mine. I can't live without my best friend. I also can't live with *only* being Leo's friend.

When the memory is burned into my mind for forever, I lean away. Leo pulls me back.

"Liar!" Lindsay's voice cuts through me like sharp glass. "Both of you! Liars through and through. You say one thing and then turn around and do another. Over and over and over. I am so done."

"Lindsay, it's not—" I stop because, yes, it is *exactly* what she thinks it is. I slump back in my seat. "Shouldn't you go after her?"

"Why? She's the one who broke up with me. Twice," Leo says, but his hand is on the door handle. "I don't want to hurt Lindsay. I don't want to hurt anybody."

"I see." I guess the experiment is over then.

"Hey, you two." Stephanie comes up behind the car. "Your mics are malfunctioning. Phil says he can't hear you at all."

I lean over and remove the mics from the glove compartment.

"Can you hear me now?" I say into mine before burying it in my bodice again.

Stephanie, doing her best secret service impression, puts a finger on the earpiece in her left ear. "Yes, he can. And he says you are on in less than two minutes. So, let's go."

Leo and I scramble out of the car. Stephanie grabs Leo's arm as he passes in front of her. After shining her cellphone's light in Leo's face, Stephanie digs around in the Magic Handbag and pulls out a baby wipe. She cleans the lipstick that has migrated off my lips onto Leo before giving him a little push toward the ballroom.

"Dakota. Here. Now." Stephanie digs in her handbag and pulls out a tube of lipstick. A sly smile pulls across Stephanie's face as she touches up my still-tingling lips. "Try to keep this on *your* lips, okay?" When I start to leave, she adds, "And, I'm sorry about Lindsay. Phil wouldn't listen to me."

Farther behind Stephanie, I see Jordan the Camera Op. He drops his head and goes in a side door.

"How much of that did Phil get?"

Stephanie lets out a sigh. "More than you would probably like, even if the audio was bad on it."

They turned off the lights on purpose. Phil wanted a spark. A fire races through my veins. Phil set me up and I fell for it—hook, line, and sinker.

Chapter

31

This time when Leo and I enter the ballroom holding hands, things feel the same and yet totally different. Stephanie follows a few steps behind us. The auxiliary light in my face lets me know we're live again. The results of the experiment will have to wait a little longer. If they come back negative, I'm going to ask for a redo. Preferably somewhere a little more conducive to our experiment. Like my room.

I expect to park Leo on the edge of the stage again, but this time he doesn't release my hand. The DJ lowers the music as we take the stage. I accept the mic from him and come center stage. Though I can hear his breath quicken, Leo's face stays more of a light tan this time instead of pink. I close my eyes and order High School Dakota to the back seat again. After a deep breath, DIY Princess Dakota takes the wheel.

"Hello, Phoenix! You guys having a good time?"

There is a sudden snickering from the audience, followed by mocking laughter. Stephanie swoops into the audience. I hope they have Leo's mic muted, or our show just got a mature rating for language. The jerk with the rubber chicken in his hand winces as Stephanie drags him toward the door by his earlobe. Half a second later, two security guards grab another troll. Their buddy makes a run for it, but Mr. Udall and Iwate-sensei's WWE-worthy tag team maneuvers leave the troll sprawled out on the floor trying to catch his breath.

Blood rushes in my ears. I won't let them shake me. I won't let them penetrate my armor this time. I won't let them win.

I turn to Leo. He pushes up his sleeves. I shake my head at him. This is my fight.

Leo mouths, "Kitsunebiiiii!"

Since I don't have Jay Yoshikawa's magical sword, I adjust my tiara instead.

"Anybody else?" I cross my arms and wait. I stare out into the audience and let the awkward silence sink in. "Because if the trolls and moles and agents of chaos are finished, the rest of us would like to get back to enjoying our evening with the people we love instead of stirring up hate."

There's some murmuring from the crowd. Cell phones are out. The show's not over yet.

Nevaeh's two-fingered, high-pitched whistle startles the crowd. "We love you, Dakota!"

I find Nevaeh in the crowd and blow them a kiss. "Love you back, my friend!"

Jax is the one who starts the "Ko-ty! Ko-ty!" chant. Not everybody is on board. I see several people duck out of the ballroom. When Leo's voice joins Jax's chant, I stop caring about what other people are going to say about my party tomorrow. Tonight, I want to create a perfectly imperfect memory for Leo and Nevaeh and all the people who will continue to be a part of my life long after the TV show and even high school are over.

"Thank you!" I interrupt the chant until people quiet down again. "Now that we're ready to move on from the drama, I have a special guest tonight. You've seen her burning up YouTube for the last year, but here she is to sing her first number-one hit and last summer's favorite slow jam: Rayne Lee!"

Leo, Aurora, and Nevaeh kept their promise. People gasp when Rayne Lee—wearing her trademark bedazzled school uniform, which wouldn't pass any school's dress code—struts on stage. Rayne Lee exudes confidence or arrogance, depending on who you ask. I've seen the tabloid stories about her. We've even been gossiped about on the same page multiple times. Apparently, both of us are dramatic and difficult to work with. Or we are both empowered, opinionated teen girls trying not to get steamrolled by the industry. Again, it depends on who you ask.

"It's truly my honor to come to Phoenix tonight to sing for America's DIY Princess." Rayne stands next to me. Her long nails sparkle against her bedazzled purple microphone. "I grew up watching your show with my grandparents in Fort Lee, New Jersey, and like millions of viewers from around the world, I feel like your family is an extension of my own. Dakota, I have a confession. I may have bedazzled a pair of safety glasses when I was ten and gone as you for Halloween." Based on the good-natured laughter, I'm guessing that Phil cued up a photo of Rayne wearing the costume for the audience. "It's all love, my sister. But from one diva to another, I'm gonna need you to get off my stage."

Rayne turns so the audience can't see her and mouths to me, "Play along, okay?"

I raise an eyebrow but nod. As I leave stage right, Rayne puts a hand on Leo's arm to stop his retreat.

"Wait. Not you though." Rayne exaggerates looking Leo up and down. "Definitely not you."

As Rayne croons the beginning embellishment of "One Last Kiss," Leo looks ready to spontaneously combust. Rayne bumps Leo's shoulder with hers during the first verse in an attempt to get him to move with her. But he doesn't.

"You got this, Cinnamon Roll Prince!" Nevaeh yells from the base of the stage.

The crowd hoots when Leo turns to face Rayne. She puts a hand on his shoulder. At first, I'm worried that Leo's knees are buckling, but then I realize he's wobbling on the downbeat. Rayne notices too and gives Leo a nod of encouragement. By the first chorus, Leo leans into the single-single-double pattern. He's only dancing at about 50 percent, but this is still huge. Just like in the video, when Rayne sings about holding hands with her former love, she laces her fingers with Leo's. I don't think she expected him to spin her around in a ballerina-like turn, but that's what's in the video we've watched a million times. It's what was in *our* choreography of this song.

Yeah, I can't compete with this. When they get to the bridge of the song, Rayne does her trademark vocal run into the stratosphere, before leaning into Leo until they are forehead to forehead. Quite a few people in the audience do the four finger snaps along with Rayne and Leo during the dramatic pause in the song. When the chorus kicks back in, she kisses Leo's hand before turning on her heel and strutting away like she does in the video.

Instead of sliding into her Lamborghini and peeling out, though, Rayne pulls me back onto the stage. As she starts the final chorus about waiting to find the love of your life, Rayne connects me to Leo. The audience loses it—I can hear Nevaeh's ear-splitting, two-fingered whistle—as Leo wraps his arms around me. We throw out our original choreography and simply sway side to side. Just two best friends dancing with a popstar and three hundred other people in the room, and yet still somehow in their own bubble.

"One last . . . *kiss*," Rayne sings from the edge of the stage.

Leo picks me up and swings me around. And this time, when my feet touch the ground again, he doesn't kiss my forehead or my hand or my cheek. Instead, Leo kisses me on the lips in front of ALL. OF. AMERICA.

"Happy Birthday, Koty," Leo says when we break away.

"Best. Birthday. Ever." My lips say though I doubt Leo can hear me over the roar of the crowd.

"Are they not the cutest?" Rayne says, returning to center stage. She gently herds us toward the side. "But for real, you guys need to get off my stage. Because I brought some friends along for this next number."

As Leo and I exit stage right, Rayne's twenty or so "friends" wearing similar school uniforms take the stage from the left—though I'm pretty sure nobody but Rayne is actually, you know, *in* high school. The bumping bass line of her newest song ignites the JCC squad, who bounces around in a group, with Jordan the Camera Op filming it all.

"YES!" Phil says, letting me know that my mic is no longer hot. "More of *that*, please. And nice save with the trolls."

"Speaking of trolls." I'm about to rip Phil a new one when Stephanie storms our trio. Though her eyebrows furrow, Stephanie says calmly, "I need Leo for a moment."

"Fine. But I want him back in ten," Phil says.

Stephanie puts a hand on Leo's back and guides him toward a quiet corner. I crane my neck to see what's going on. My stomach falls to my toes when Leo suddenly clamps a hand over his mouth. He rips off his mic and runs for the door.

"Where do you think you're going?" Phil grabs my arm as I start to go after Leo.

"What's going on, Stephanie?" I say as soon as she returns.

"Leo's grandfather has appendicitis." Stephanie hands Leo's mic to Phil. "The Matsudas are all in the ER, and doctors are prepping Grandpa for emergency surgery before his appendix bursts. Sasha is here to pick up Leo."

"He can't leave. We're in the middle of filming!" Phil says.

"I gotta go."

Phil steps in front of me. "You can't leave *your own* party. We've still got the birthday cake and presents part to do."

"I. Don't. Care," I say loud enough that camera phones rotate my way. Stephanie steps to the side to block their view.

"Get over here." Phil drags me by the arm to a secluded spot behind the stage. "Look, I'm sorry about Leo's grandfather. I am. But we have a job to do here. What's gotten into you? It's like you're trying to tank tonight's show. Let me tell you, young lady, that is *not* going to happen. We are going to pull a three tonight if it kills me. And it just might."

"Is that why you sent Lindsay over? To boost ratings?" I yank my arm out of Phil's. "I don't care if we hit three million viewers tonight. Protecting my best friend is a hundred times more important to me than my ratings bonus."

"What a selfish little—" Phil takes a deep breath and hisses through his teeth. "I know this is a hard concept for an 'it's all about me' teenager to understand, but this show is a group effort. If we do well tonight, you get a ratings bonus, and I get a promotion to executive producer next season. And then I *never* have to work in the field with bratty, entitled teenagers ever again."

"Hey! You don't get to talk to Dakota like that." Stephanie gives Phil a look that might actually melt his face off. "I will consult with *the talent* and her parents, and we will inform *you* how the rest of tonight is going to go."

Stephanie puts an arm around my shoulders and leads me toward the green room. I quiver with rage. Meanwhile, Phil throws his clipboard on the carpet, stomps around, and drops a couple of F-bombs. I hope somebody got that on camera, though it would undoubtedly get redirected at me: "DIY Princess Has Epic Tantrum at Her Birthday Party, Causing Production to Revolt."

"Dakota?" Dad stands up when Stephanie and I burst into our makeshift green room.

I slump down on the couch next to Mom. "Leo just left the party with Sasha."

Mom waves her cell phone at me. "So I heard from Jen. I'm sorry, Dakota. You and Leo looked like you were having so much fun together."

"Yeah, Leo and Uncle Doug are gonna have a little man-to-man chat about that kissing part."

"Doug!" Mom says.

"Later, of course." Dad sits next to me and wraps his hand around mine. "Masao is going to be fine, Koty-Kat. People have their appendixes removed all the time."

"But what if something happens to Ojiichan, and I was too busy giving away designer handbags to people whose names I don't even know? I would never forgive myself."

"I understand, honey. More than you know." Mom's eyes glisten. "When my dad was hospitalized for the last time, I chose to fly back to Phoenix the next morning instead of taking an overnight flight from New York City. I have regretted that decision ever since. I never got to tell my dad goodbye."

"Tamlyn, Masao has appendicitis, not the end stages of lung cancer," Dad says gently.

"But Masao is no spring chicken either," Mom says.

"I don't know what to do, Mom. Part of me wants to race to the hospital to be with Leo, because he's always been there for me. But if I leave, it will mess up everything here. I don't want to hurt you guys or Stephanie. Though Phil can currently kiss my—"

"Dakota," Stephanie interrupts. "Hot mic."

Phil can listen in if he wants to. He doesn't get a say in my decision.

"What do I do, Mom?"

My parents look at each other, then at Stephanie, and then back at each other.

"I don't know." Mom wraps an arm around me and pulls me against her. "But whatever you decide, I will support it. This wouldn't be the first time a show's gone sideways on us."

"What? When has there ever been a problem that I couldn't fix?" Dad says.

"Got it, Phil," Stephanie barks into the tiny walkie-talkie mic on her shoulder. "What do *you* want to do, Dakota? Because Phil wants you back on set."

All the unknowns swirl around in my head until I am dizzy. I don't know what to do. I need Leo here to spark an idea so that I can build off of it. The green room's TV is on mute, but Rayne's energy pours through the screen as she travels around the stage. Rayne gets a lot of crap thrown at her too from the media and on-line trolls, yet here she is shining bright. Her spark is contagious.

"Can you stay long enough to thank Rayne Lee? She's a genuine fan of yours." Stephanie points to a pile of merch sitting on a side table, including a T-shirt and a CD.

My mind flashes to Leo and Rayne bouncing side to side on the stage. When his fear melted away, and he showed the world what I get to see every day. The Real Leo. I grab the CD and a gold metallic Sharpie off the table.

"I'm on my way," I say into my cleavage.

I'm out of breath, but I slap the CD and pen into Phil's chest and make it to the side of the stage just as Rayne finishes "Create Your Spark." Sweat flies off Rayne's forehead as she punches the air above her head on the final note. Based on the number of people now crushing the front of the stage, I think Rayne made some new fans tonight.

Rayne continues to bow and throw kisses to the screaming audience as I take the stage. My smile may not be authentic, but the commitment behind it is.

"Is she awesome or what?" I yell into my handheld mic. "Thank you, Rayne Lee. You have made this birthday one to remember. Thank you from the bottom of my heart."

"From one diva to another, it was my honor." Rayne mock curtseys at me.

"There is one thing before you go."

I hand Rayne my microphone. She quirks an eyebrow at me as I reach up and unpin the tiara. I pull the tiara—thankfully with none of my stunt hair still attached to it—off my head.

I say into her bedazzled microphone, "My reign might be coming to an end, but yours is just beginning."

After I get the tiara pinned on her head, Rayne does her best Miss Universe impression, including over-the-top, fake crying. I accept her hug. Meanwhile, Phil raises his clipboard, which says CAKE on it in big black letters, and taps it like a woodpecker.

"While I send Rayne off, I hope you guys will head into the other room for dessert by Sweet Lil Something Bakery. Then we'll give away some prizes," I say, and Phil nods at me. "Don't forget to try some of Sasha Matsuda's adorable rabbit-shaped manju."

So Phil won't smack me with his clipboard, I link my elbow with Rayne's and walk off the stage with her. As we pass Phil, I grab the CD and Sharpie.

Once we are tucked away from the crowd, Rayne puts her hand on the tiara. "I'm guessing you want this back?"

"No, for real. I want you to keep it. I mean, where am I going to wear it after tonight?"

Rayne's laugh sounds like little tinkling bells. "I'm sorry about the Halloween picture. Phil insisted that it was funny, but I don't know."

"No, it's fine. Because one day I'm going to be *you* for Halloween. So, be sure to wear the tiara and remember Leo and me fondly when you accept your Grammy one day."

"Speaking of . . . where'd your boyfriend go? I wanted to say thanks. At first, I thought he was going to pass out on me, but then he nailed it. He's a good dancer."

"He's not my . . . it's complicated."

Rayne crosses her arms. "It's complicated, or are you two *making* it complicated? Because clearly I'm seeing something that you aren't."

"Probably more of the latter."

"Then stop making it harder than it needs to be. Listen to your heart."

"You want to write that in Sharpie across my forehead to help me remember it better?"

"How about I write it on the CD instead?"

"Would you be offended if I gave it to Leo to cheer him up?" I say as Rayne takes the CD and Sharpie from me. "His grandfather was rushed to the hospital tonight. That's why he left so suddenly."

"To: Leo," Rayne says as she writes on the paper insert. "Listen to your heart. Create your spark. Much love, Rayne Lee." She signs her name with a flourish in both English and Korean characters before putting the CD back in its case.

"He's going to love it."

"You too, Dakota. Listen to your heart." Rayne pokes me in the chest gently with her bedazzled index finger. "And send me your contact info so the next time I'm in Phoenix, we can hang."

"Yes!" And I do feel a spark—a genuine one. "I will take you to my favorite Japanese restaurant, Matsuda. And if things aren't busy, you might even see a certain waiter dancing along to your song. Seriously, Leo was only at fifty percent tonight. You haven't seen him go ham."

"You got it."

"Dakota." Stephanie puts her hand on my arm. "I'm sorry to interrupt, but you need to take this. It's Leo."

Rayne squeezes my arm before walking away with Stephanie.

"Talk to me, my dude. How's Ojiichan?" I say.

"Not good." Leo's voice wavers. He clears his throat and hardens his voice. "They were prepping him for surgery when his blood pressure spiked and his heartbeat became irregular. Until he is stable, they can't do the surgery. But if they don't do the surgery soon, his appendix might burst, and that's also life-threatening."

I can see Leo in my mind, raking a hand through his hair as he lets out a frustrated sigh.

"I feel so helpless, Koty."

"I'm sorry. I wish I could be there with you."

After a long pause, Leo whispers, "Yeah. I wish you were too."

My heart smashes into a million pieces.

"Dakota, now." Phil snatches Stephanie's phone out of my hand, grabs me by the elbow, and drags me toward the cake room.

"Hey!"

When we get there, he shoves a microphone in my hand. Mom and Dad stand to the side of the cake. Though there is a convincing smile on her face, Mom's knuckles are white from the death grip she has on the cake table. Dad, however, is not a good actor. They could do a whole show on his flubs, cringey dad jokes, and genuine-if-inappropriate comments. Santa is anything but jolly now, especially when Phil pushes a microphone into his chest too. With the camera rolling, we have no choice but to move forward with this pointless display of consumerism at its worst.

"I know I'm not going to be able to hit the high note like Rayne Lee, but I hope you'll all join me in wishing Dakota a happy sixteenth birthday," Dad says.

As the room echoes with voices singing "Happy Birthday to You," my eyes fill with tears. Phil beams. I'm not breaking down because my friends—and two hundred other acquaintances and strangers—are celebrating me. I'm breaking down because I would happily trade all of this for one matcha ice cream mochi with a tiny, used birthday candle, and Leo's tenor voice adding vocal embellishments to the song to make me laugh on a random Tuesday.

"Thank you," I say at the end, with sudden clarity about several things in my life. I look around the pin-quiet room. "Thank you for all of your support over the years. Thank you for your support tonight." I look directly into the camera. "Though you didn't get to see much of Leo in the twenty years *If These Walls Could Talk* has been on the air, he's been the one constant in my life since our moms put us in Toddler Time together fourteen years ago. Family lore says that our friendship got off to a rocky start when I clocked Leo upside the head with a backhoe because he interrupted my build in the sandbox. What can I say? I've always been a diva."

As the room chuckles, I look at Mom. She gives me a nod. "Anyway, Leo's grandfather collapsed today at the Phoenix Phoodie Phestival and is in rough shape. The Matsudas are private people, so that's all I'm going to say. I hope you will understand why I have to leave."

I'm pretty sure all of America heard Phil's "WHAT?!?!"

"Don't worry. I'm leaving you in good hands." I walk over to a slack-jawed Nevaeh. "My friend, the incomparable Nevaeh Cooper. Nevaeh, if you could do the prize drawings for me, I would owe you for forever."

Nevaeh snaps their mouth closed and gulps. They adjust their tasteful pink tiara and take the mic from me. "Oh, I got you, Koty. You take care of our Cinnamon Roll Prince, and I will take care of the party. As I do."

I hug them. "As you do."

Mom takes the microphone from Dad. "Don't go away. After the next commercial break, we have a special event for our viewers at home. In fifteen minutes, Doug and I go live to answer all your burning questions."

"We will?" Dad says, and Mom elbows him hard. "Yes, we will. Can't . . . wait."

"Be sure to use #GrowingUpWithKoty so we can see all of your questions."

Dad looks at Mom with slight horror and a lot of confusion in his eyes. When I'm off camera, I dig the mic out of my bodice and slap it on top of Phil's clipboard. He doesn't try to stop me. I swish out the door to find Stephanie already there, my purse in one hand and her car keys in the other.

"I can't stay at the hospital," Stephanie says as we rush toward the parking lot. "But I'm happy to drive you there."

"What about Phil? Maybe you should call me an Uber or something instead," I say when we get to Stephanie's car. "I don't want to mess up future jobs for you because I'm 'being a diva.'"

"You need to stop saying that. Being a diva is asking for exactly forty-three blue roses and a bathtub filled with freshly expressed goat milk. Insisting that people honor your boundaries and priorities is called being an empowered woman. Don't worry. Nevaeh and your parents have this. Okay, Tamlyn has it. Doug needs a few minutes to switch gears, but he's always authentic and fun. That's why he's 'America's Dad.' You focus on Leo and his family."

I slide into Stephanie's car and tuck my skirts around me. A warmth expands in my chest because this feels, if not exactly good, then at least right. "Thanks, Stephanie. For everything."

"You're welcome." Stephanie fires up her car. "Also, Phil can say I'm 'difficult to work with' or whatever he wants. My work speaks for itself. Plus, I know your mom will give me a glowing review."

"We don't deserve you."

"Sometimes, I have to agree with you. Like, pick a pair of shoes already." Stephanie gives me a wink. "But tonight is not one of those times."

Chapter

32

When we pull up to the hospital fifteen minutes later, I can see Leo and his Dad coming out the front door of the ER. Leo, with a black bag over his shoulder, follows his dad around the corner toward their minivan. At least now I know why Leo hasn't answered any of my last few texts. I slide my phone back into my purse next to Rayne's CD.

"Give Grandpa Matsuda my best. And call me if you need anything." Stephanie's phone rings.

"Thanks, Steph," I mouth at her as she answers her phone. She raises a fist of solidarity.

I walk across the parking lot toward where the Matsudas are parked. Mr. Matsuda isn't normally a yeller, but you can tell by his body language that he is so done with Leo.

"It's like I don't even know you anymore," Mr. Matsuda says, along with something in Japanese I don't understand.

"I'm tired of being Favorite Matsuda Child," Leo says, and now I know he's flustered.

Speaking in Japanese isn't a challenge for Leo, but it's not his first language. And like how Ojiichan reverts back to Japanese when he's angry, excited, or surprised, Leo reverts back to English, especially when his feelings are raw or when he's in trouble.

"You're not the favorite. I love all my children equally."

"You don't treat us equally. That's why Sasha left. And Aurora can't wait to leave."

"And you too? So, now you're planning to run off to Japan for the summer with your girlfriend?"

"It's a three-week class trip, Dad, with my teacher, classmates, and Dakota. Lindsay isn't even going."

I stop behind the Matsudas' van. The official conclusion of the experiment breaks my heart, especially because I thought it was going to go a different way.

"We can't afford to hire another server while you're gone, Leo. Even at minimum wage, it will sink us. And that's presuming that Ojiichan is going to be able to cook again."

Leo slumps down on the curb next to the van and drops the black bag between his feet. "I know, okay?"

"I'm sorry. Being Number One Son is hard. I get it." Mr. Matsuda runs a hand through his hair like Leo does. "I want to give you more freedom, but can you stick it out a little bit longer? For the family? For Ojiichan?"

Leo lets out a defeated sigh. "Yes."

"And stop sneaking around. No more skipping seventh period. Just wait. Those days are coming, but not yet. We need to have part two of The Talk first, but I'm not doing that tonight in the middle of a parking lot while my father fights for his life. I don't have the bandwidth right now, or a cucumber."

"Fine. It's not an issue anymore anyway." Leo holds his head in his hands like he's trying not to explode.

"Okay then." Mr. Matsuda puts a hand on Leo's back. "Let's put the family first."

Instead of comforting Leo, it ignites him. "We always put the family first, that's the problem. Why can't we be a normal family? Why can't I have one night off to be normal?"

"How is any of this—" Mr. Matsuda gestures at Leo, who is still in his tux—"normal? We're not the McDonalds. We don't live in a world of smoke and mirrors and sound bites. The McDonalds' fantasy is about to come to an end, and then what? Meanwhile, the Matsudas' feet have always been firmly on the ground. We know how to work hard."

Leo jumps to his feet. "And how's that working out for us, Dad? Oh right, Ojiichan is in the hospital. The walk-in refrigerator is nearly dead, and we don't have the money to buy a new one. Sasha and Aurora are willing to drown in school loans to escape this life.

My girlfriend dumped me because my life is 'too complicated.' I broke my promise to my best friend and ditched her tonight on live television. And now I'm going to have to bail on going to Japan, the one thing *I* wanted. So, excuse me if I want to escape into the McDonalds' Alternate Universe for a little while. At least life there doesn't suck twenty-four-seven like it does out here in the real world!"

"Hey." I decide to out myself before I hear anything else about my family I don't want to know.

"Kuso!" Mr. Matsuda flinches. "I'm going to go back inside now. I'm sorry, Dakota, only family members are allowed back in the ICU. Thank you for coming. I'll let my father know you were here. Go back to your party. You know what? Take Leo with you."

Mr. Matsuda adds some kind of directive or lecture or something in Japanese aimed at Leo, who thumps the black bag and answers tersely, "Got it."

I sit down next to Leo, a frothy sea of pink and rose gold flaring out around me. My fantasy world of smoke and mirrors colliding with Leo's harsh black-and-white reality.

"You okay, Leo?"

"Fan-freakin'-tastic." Hurt flares behind Leo's eyes. "How much of that conversation did you hear?"

"Weeeeelllll." I cringe.

Leo hangs his head. "Somebody kill me now."

"Why? It's no secret that I live in an alternate universe. My birthday cake tonight probably cost more than Sasha's car. I get it. We're ridiculous and extra and out of touch with reality."

"I'm sorry you had to hear it, though."

"Not gonna lie, it hurt my feelings. And it's going to make things weird when you guys come over, because now I know what your dad really thinks of us."

"Yeah, and now it's going to be weird for me too, because you know that I know that you know."

We sigh in tandem and slump lower on the curb.

"You want to know what else I really didn't need to know? The real reason you and Lindsay both skipped seventh period the other day." I pretend to dry heave. "And thanks to your dad, I will never be able to look at a cucumber the same way again."

"Kill me now." Leo cups his hands over his face. "But while we are keeping it real. Nothing happened, okay? Lindsay's mom came home early."

I put my hands up. "Please stop talking. I know we don't lie to each other, but we also don't need to share every bit of truth with each other either."

"Agreed." Leo flips the key ring in his hand. "C'mon, I'll take you back to the party, but I can't stay. I have to take a load of stuff and the cashbox back to the restaurant first for my dad. Again, Favorite Matsuda Child. No, that's not true. I volunteered because all those tubes and wires coming out of Ojiichan were freaking me out. Ahhh. I need to man up."

I put my hand on Leo's knee. "Hey, you're allowed to be scared. I am too."

"What if—" Leo's voice breaks.

"No. Don't go there. Everything is going to be okay."

When Leo looks at me, his eyes are wide and watery. "But what if it isn't?"

Leo's breath hitches, and my eyes start to fill with tears. I can't imagine a world without Ojiichan in it. Would there even be a restaurant without Ojiichan in the kitchen? Would Mr. Matsuda go back to being a chemical engineer? Would Mrs. Matsuda take a job as a translator somewhere else? Would they move away? Would Leo finally have the freedom from the family machine that he and his sisters have wanted so badly? And what about me? Would I know how to go on in a place without both my best friend and first love? But this isn't about me.

"Then I will hold your hand." I wipe underneath Leo's eyes with my thumbs. "Or wipe your tears. Or do something dorky to make you laugh. Or bring you a root beer. Or watch *Kitsune Mask* with you for hours on end to take your mind off things. Or do whatever it takes to bring you a moment of peace until things eventually become okay again."

Leo takes a deep breath. "Thank you, Koty. For everything."

"That's what best friends do. That is what I will always do."

Leo stands up. He offers me his hand and pulls me to a stand too.

"It's only nine, not midnight, but I guess the magic is over." Leo slides off his tuxedo jacket. "Back to my sucktastic reality. At least I have my wingwoman with me."

Leo chucks his jacket at me. Except I don't have Leo's cat-like reflexes. The jacket collides with my chest and hits the ground. Leo scoops it off the ground and wraps it over my shoulders instead. A second later, he stuffs the cummerbund and bow tie into the black bag.

I tip my head to the side as Leo untucks and unbuttons a few buttons on his tuxedo shirt. "I kinda like the Cinnamon Roll Prince look better anyway."

"Good. Because now that all the smoke and mirrors are gone, I need a miracle."

"Working on it." I slide into the passenger side of the van.

Chapter

33

I've got nothing. *Nothing.*

Leo flips on the lights at Matsuda and locks the door behind us. I follow him into the kitchen.

"My brain desperately needs some glucose to work with," I say when Leo comes back from putting the cash in the safe. "I haven't had anything to eat since the smoothie at the nail salon this afternoon."

Leo unbuttons and rolls up his sleeves. "What do you want?"

"You don't have to cook for me. Just some rice crackers and ocha are fine. Besides, I'm supposed to be the one taking care of you."

"You are. You're here." Leo washes his hands in the sink. "Besides, I like living in the McDonalds' Alternate Universe. It's peaceful there. Well, not when Alex is there, but the rest of the time."

"You're jealous?"

Leo scoffs. "No."

"Are you sure?"

Leo slides on Ojiichan's full, black apron and ties it around his narrow waist. "Okay, yes. And you? Are you . . . were you jealous of Lindsay?"

"Yes. But I wanted you to be happy. To be able to take a step forward in your life. To finally get out of the suffocating bubble I live in. Of course, how thirsty you and Lindsay were was excessive." I mime octopus arms, and Leo laughs.

"So, you're saying you forgive me for the pickled garlic incident then?"

I punch Leo in the shoulder. "I knew you did that on purpose."

"Did it work?"

"Nope. Not at all, thanks to Aurora's gum."

"Kuso."

I follow Leo into the walk-in refrigerator where all the weekend's food sits in haphazard piles. He squats down and rummages through a box. I hike up my skirt poofer and squat down next to him.

"Whatcha want, Koty? Preferably something with a lot of vegetables in it, because we currently have about three hundred pounds of pre-cut vegetables going to waste in here." Leo takes the lid off another box, and a sweet smell wafts out. "Unless you'd prefer dessert first. We also have a crap ton of manju at the moment."

"Yaaas. I've been wanting one of these all day."

"Me too."

Since his hands are clean, Leo picks out a manju rabbit. He feeds me a big bite before popping the other half into his mouth. The sugar hasn't even hit my bloodstream yet, but I can feel the wheels in my brain creaking into motion.

"You have a little . . ." Leo leans in to wipe the corner of my mouth. His warm fingers stay on my face and fan out until they caress my jaw. Leo leans toward me, his eyes closing.

"Oh!" I jerk to a stand as an idea explodes in my brain. "Oh oh oh!"

"You okay?" Leo raises a confused eyebrow at me. "Leg cramp?"

"I've got an idea. A big idea. You make us some omelets while I start making phone calls." I rub my palms together. "This is going to be the Dynamic Duo's biggest plan yet."

"Wait." Leo grabs my wrist to keep me in the refrigerator with him. "I need to tell you something."

I turn back around, but my brain is going in a hundred different directions. "Yeah, what's that?"

"I love you."

"I know." I give Leo a sassy wink. "And you haven't even heard my great idea yet."

"No, Han Solo, like, for real." Leo puts the manju box back down and steps into me. "I know my timing is terrible, but it's the truth."

"Wait. Are you saying the kiss experiment from earlier tonight was a success? Because I would be happy to test that—"

Leo leans in and interrupts me in the best way possible.

"I love you too," I say several minutes later. "Both Old Leo and New Leo."

Leo's fingertips gently caress the side of my face like he's looking at me in a completely different light.

"I love Old Koty." Leo kisses my right cheek. "But this girl right here . . . I don't know who she is." Leo kisses my left cheek. "I definitely want to get to know her better though."

"It's about time." I pull Leo closer to me until his spark warms me from the inside out.

It only takes a few more stolen minutes inside the Matsudas' walk-in refrigerator before my fantasy solidifies into reality. Leo and I share our truth one kiss at a time. We have always been better as a team. We will always be better as a team. We can do anything as a team.

Chapter

34

"Gooooood morning, Phoenix!" I say when Nevaeh gives me the signal. "Thank you from the bottom of my heart, America, for your love and support last night. We're not out of the woods yet, but there isn't anything that Team McDonald can't fix with the right tools, a little elbow grease, and a lot of heart."

Nevaeh follows me under the tent to Ojiichan's griddle. Leo stands behind it with his happi coat on, his feet firmly planted, and his arms crossed. His sisters in matching outfits and stances flank him.

"Okay, Team Matsuda, are you ready for day two of the Phoenix Phoodie Phestival?" I say, and the trio nods in unison. I step to the side. "Mom and Dad?"

Mom and Dad have on Mr. and Mrs. Matsudas' happi coats with the restaurant's name written in white kanji characters down the black lapel part. Not going to lie. Santa looks a little goofy with the white fabric around his forehead. Undoubtedly, we—especially Dad—will get flamed for "cultural appropriation" later, but it's not about us today. We, along with Nevaeh and Stephanie, are simply cogs in the Matsuda Machine. None of us have a food handler's certificate, though, so the Matsuda siblings are in charge of the actual cooking. Sasha is the boss, Leo is head chef, and Aurora is just opinionated.

"Ready to do our part to help out our dear friends, the Matsudas," Mom says from their station behind the cash register.

Over one hundred tiny rabbit manju, each in its own packaging, sit in fluffles on ornate cupcake stands borrowed from Sweet Lil Something Bakery.

I glance over at Sasha. Aurora's makeup skills cleverly mask the two hours of sleep Sasha got last night while prepping all the manju for today.

"In that case"—I slide on Ojiichan's oversized happi coat and tie the fabric around my forehead—"it's time to work."

As planned, Nevaeh zooms in on the large donation jar on our table—already primed with some cash from our new Wisteria Village Café friends. Then Nevaeh zooms out to find me behind the table with a special guest wearing a ridiculous tiara.

"If you get down here in the next forty-five minutes," I look over at Rayne, who gives the camera a thumb-and-index-finger heart. "Rayne Lee will be here signing autographs and taking pictures before she flies back to New York City. You saw her perform last night at my birthday party. Now, here's your chance to meet her in person."

"But no body parts though, people, because that's weird," Rayne says.

"And gross."

Rayne throws an arm around my shoulders. "Rayne Lee and . . ."

"Dakota McDonald out. Peace."

"I'll get this up on your social media ASAP." Stephanie takes the phone from Nevaeh. "Then, I'll give it a push on the show's channels." As usual, she can read my mind. "Don't worry, Dakota. We broke a three last night. Phil is ecstatic. Keep on keeping it real. Fans love it."

"Do you think the tiara is too much?" Rayne says after Stephanie leaves.

"Never." Nevaeh adjusts the pink tiara still perched on their colorful, short-haired head.

Rayne fingers the tiara my stylist insisted she could keep, especially if she wears it in public and tags her company on Instagram.

"I know I'll get slammed for it, but I don't care. A Pop Princess needs a tiara when she's doing promo pictures with a Cinnamon Roll Prince. But first"—Rayne pulls Nevaeh next to her for a selfie—"I think tiaras should be the next fashion trend, don't you?"

My video probably hasn't even hit the internet yet, but the crowds are already picking up. There's a tingling in my chest, warning me that this is dangerous. I'm exposed out here, especially after last night. Aurora's laugh refocuses me. The people who I love and trust the most are around me. I can put Ojiichan and his most treasured possessions—his family and his restaurant—first for one day.

"Can I get a picture with my favorite DIY Princess?" I hear from across the tent.

With a nod of encouragement from Stephanie and a Fujifilm Instax pulled magically from the Magic Handbag in his hand, Alex walks toward my station. Conflicting emotions swirl around in my head until I feel dizzy. I look over at Leo. He and The Full Dimple are clowning around with Rayne Lee. I don't even feel stabby about it.

Even Alex's simple "Hey" makes me feel guilty. We agreed earlier that we would take our relationship one day at a time, but that was before Leo's truth came out. I can't go forward with Alex, just like I can't go backwards with Leo.

Alex and I stand there in an awkward silence, which feels like years.

"I saw the footage of your official dance with Leo this morning on YouTube," Alex says.

"Everything last night . . ." I mime an explosion. "I'm sorry. I feel like I wasted your time."

"Please don't ever think it was wasted time, Dakota." Alex takes my hands in his. "Because I don't."

"Alex, I—"

My heart clenches when Alex steps close to me. It gets even worse when I see somebody in the rapidly increasing crowd with their phone out, pretending like they aren't taking pictures of us. Alex drops his head to whisper in my ear.

"Just because we aren't endgame, Dakota, doesn't mean we weren't right for each other at the time. In another time or another place, maybe we would've even been perfect for each other." Alex hugs me tight. "But that's not how the stars aligned. So starting now, I'll be officially hanging out in your Friend Zone."

A weight lifts off my chest. I don't care if I make it on the front page of the tabloids next week or not. I stretch up and kiss Alex's cheek.

"Thank you. I know the perfect girl is waiting for you in North Carolina. In your whole new, wonderfully uncomplicated life as a baseball-player-slash-tuxedo-model."

Alex throws his head back and laughs. "Can I still take a picture with you though? Otherwise nobody is going to believe that I was your almost-date to the infamous Sweet Sixteen party."

When I nod, Alex stretches out his arm as far as it will go to take the picture.

"Here, let me do that for you." Rayne takes the camera from him. "I'm going to have to come back to Phoenix more often, Dakota. All your friends are so fun and down-to-earth and, you know, real."

I look over at Leo's station. I don't know what Rayne said or did, but Leo is bright red and Aurora and Nevaeh are howling with laughter. Rayne takes our picture. While we are waiting for the camera to spit out the picture, Rayne looks Alex up and down.

"Hiiiii, I'm Rayne. Dakota's new friend. And you are?"

Alex puts out his hand. "Alex Santos. Dakota's . . . friend and former dance partner."

"Don't forget tuxedo model," I say.

And that's how Rayne Lee missed her flight, and we ended up on the front page of the tabloids the following week together: "Teen Divas Brawl over Tuxedo Model at After Party."

Smoke and mirrors and sound bites. That's what we do. And that's what's going to save the day. And hopefully, save the Matsudas' restaurant too.

"Ii yo. Daijōbu da." Ojiichan grumbles, pushing Mr. Matsuda's helping hand away and telling everybody that he's fine.

"Yep, he's back to normal," Leo says.

Ojiichan lightly baka slaps the back of Leo's head as he hobbles past us to his bedroom. Mrs. Matsuda carries in a small overnight bag and sets it on the kitchen counter.

"Where are the girls?" Mrs. Matsuda says.

"Asleep," Leo says. "Sasha didn't even make it to dinner."

Which definitely made our new-and-improved Matsuda Monday even better. Especially when Aurora retreated with her pizza to her parents' room so that she could FaceTime with Jayden. Leo fixes the throw pillows, which fell off the couch during our marathon kissing experiment after dinner. I rub my index finger across my lips. Yep, still feeling the sparks.

"We all deserved a day off after this weekend." Mrs. Matsuda puts a glass of water and some pills on a decorative tray. "What a weekend."

"I got Ojiichan into bed." Mr. Matsuda pokes his head into the kitchen. "I'm heading upstairs to sleep for the next three days."

"Ms. Tamlyn said Koty could stay until ten if I wanted her to." Leo looks at me and then his dad. "I want her to."

"There's more pizza if you want a midnight snack." I open up the top box of pizza, which nobody has touched, because who puts artichokes on pizza?

Mrs. Matsuda wraps her arms around me. "Thank you, Koty-chan."

"It's just gross pizza."

"No, for everything." Mrs. Matsuda fingers the tiny, *tasteful* tiara on my head, which Nevaeh insisted that I wear to school today. She shakes her head but doesn't comment. Meanwhile, Nevaeh and I have a bet going on how long it takes for a "No Tiaras" rule to be added to the official school dress code.

"Mom, should they have let Ojiichan come home so soon?" Leo's voice is tight.

Mrs. Matsuda pulls Leo into our hug. "We're going to keep the restaurant closed for the next week. Possibly longer. Right now, let's focus on Ojiichan."

Mrs. Matsuda breaks away from us so she can hand Leo the tray. "How about you deliver these to Ojiichan? He wanted to talk to you."

Leo gulps but accepts the tray. Leo is only two steps out of the kitchen before he gestures for me to follow him.

"Konban wa, Ojiichan," I greet him after Leo pushes me through the door first like a human shield.

"Dakota-chan, my bonus granddaughter. Thank you for the picture." Ojiichan's bruised hand shakes as he puts the sketch I did of Leo this afternoon on his bedside table.

"Here are your meds, Ojiichan." Leo holds the tray until Ojiichan gets all four pills down.

"Dōmo." Ojiichan leans back against the headboard of his bed. "Leo-kun, we need to talk. Your father says that you have been secretly saving up money all year to go on a vacation with your girlfriend."

"Ugh. No. It's a class trip to Japan with Iwate-sensei and twenty of my classmates." Leo looks at me. "*And* my girlfriend. The one whose series of awesome ideas helped me make it happen."

"Ah, I knew this would happen." Ojiichan picks up a small photo frame on his bedside table. It's a faded picture of Ojiichan as a much younger man sitting next to an attractive woman with long, straight hair. A chubby-cheeked baby sits on her lap. "At the Homecoming Carnival, I saw Koty-chan looking at you. My Michiko-chan looked at me the same way when I was a young man. I thought, 'Oh, this boy is in big trouble.'"

"Um, ow, Ojiichan," I say.

Ojiichan laughs and gestures at Leo. "This boy is in big trouble because he does not think with his head."

Leo cringes. "Seriously, Ojiichan?"

"I know because I was the same." Ojiichan puts his weathered hand over Leo's and pats it. "I would give anything to have just one more day with my Michiko-chan."

Ojiichan's eyes are watery as he places the picture back on his nightstand. Leo sits on the side of the bed and puts the tray on the nightstand too.

"Ojiichan. I need to tell you the full truth. I want to go to the Matsuda Manju shop while we are in Nagoya. Mio-san, your great-niece, has been talking with Sasha for several months now. First, about wagashi, and then about our families. You don't ever talk about your sister, and according to Mio-san, her grandmother never talks about you. Without them, I feel like there's a part of me that's missing."

"Hmmm" is all Ojiichan says.

"So can I go? To visit Mio-san at the Matsuda Manju shop?"

After an eternity, Ojiichan sighs. "Hai, hai."

Leo throws his arms around Ojiichan. Though Ojiichan winces in pain at first, he wraps an arm around Leo. With his free hand, Ojiichan gestures at me to come to him. When I sit down on the other side of his twin bed, Ojiichan pulls me into a hug too.

"Do not lose Koty-chan," Ojiichan says when we break away.

Though I'm sure Ojiichan meant while we are in Japan, Leo takes my hand. "Nope. Never again."

EPILOGUE

"Do *not* lose your passport. Either of you." Mrs. Matsuda grabs Leo and me in a double-barreled, rib-crushing Mom Hug. When we break away, her eyes are misty. "Ah, it seems like yesterday that I was the one telling my parents goodbye and stepping onto a plane to Japan."

"Mom, you were gone for five years." Leo takes pity on his mom and kisses her cheek. "I'm going for three weeks. You guys are going to be so busy that you won't even miss me."

"True." Aurora breaks out of the crowd of JCC family members sending off their high school students this morning. "Post lots of pictures so I can live vicariously through you, since I will have absolutely no life while you are gone."

"Now you can be Favorite Matsuda Child," Leo teases.

Aurora rolls her eyes. "Pass."

"Oi! Leo-kun! Dakota-chan!" Ojiichan yells from behind the wall of Matsudas. They part so Leo and I can take a knee in front of his grandfather's chair.

Ojiichan pulls a plain envelope from his light jacket's pocket. "Please deliver this to my sister in Nagoya when you visit the manju shop. She may not accept it, but it says all I want to say. What I need to say."

"I will." Leo takes the envelope. "I have a good feeling about this, Ojiichan."

"We will see."

"Mina-san!" Iwate-sensei is probably already regretting her decision to take this over-caffeinated, sleep-deprived herd of cats to Japan for the next three weeks. "Ikimashō!"

Leo and I return to our respective families to retrieve our backpacks.

"Thank you for coming out so early. We appreciate it," Mom says to a trio of teen girls swarming her and Dad. "If we could have a moment of privacy as a family, then we would be happy to take a few pictures or sign autographs."

"Of course, I'm sorry." The tallest girl grabs her friends by the elbows, and they shuffle off to the side as a clump. They wave at me as they pass. "Hi, Dakota!"

I wave back. I still don't love people so close to my bubble, but I'll cut these girls some slack. One wears a pink tiara that matches the one currently sitting on Nevaeh's multi-hued, space-bunned head. All three have on edamame-green T-shirts with "Matsuda" written in kanji and the new logo I designed for the restaurant. Part of me is annoyed that somebody ripped off my design and is making counterfeit T-shirts from it. Another part of me is willing to take one for the team if it means Matsuda stays busy—even with their continued limited hours—while Leo and I are gone on our first of what I hope will be many adventures together.

Mom and Dad smother me one last time, repeating all the warnings they've been giving me for the last month.

"Okay, okay, I love you guys too. I gotta go." I can see Leo waving from the end of the security line. "See you at the end of the month. Send me pictures from Oxford and Alaska."

I don't want to stop to chat with the fan girls, but I make myself do it anyway.

"Thanks for coming out." I take the Sharpie from the tallest girl and sign everybody's copy of *Seventeen,* which has Rayne wearing an even more ridiculous tiara on the cover and an interview with me somewhere in the middle.

After a quick selfie with the girls, I jog over to the end of the line. Leo laces his fingers through mine. The girls continue to stare at us.

"Can we give them a little fan service?" I whisper.

Though I can see the red creeping up from the collar of his new

Kitsune Mask T-shirt, Leo looks over at the girls—with their phones out—and waves at them. The tallest one just about swoons into the floor when Leo leans in and lightly presses his lips against mine.

"Wait!" Sasha runs up to us and shoves a little white box into my hand.

"Thanks for giving up your summer plans for me, Sasha," Leo says.

"It needed to be your turn." Sasha hugs him before backing away. "Enjoy your vacation, because Aurora and I are tagging you two back in come August first."

Thanks to Rayne Lee, not only is Matsuda popping, but so is Sasha's small manju business. I rub my index finger over the gold foil printing on top of the dainty box that reads MATSUDA MANJU, PHOENIX LOCATION. While the line moves along at snail speed, I open up the box.

"They are sooooo cute!" Two little manju bunnies sit in a nest of shredded paper, snout to snout. Two signs impale them. "I can't read it."

"Kokoro no koe ni mimi o katamukete," Leo says, pointing to the one on the right first. And then pointing to the one on the left. "Supaaku o tsukutte."

"Yeah, I still don't understand."

"Nihongo de." Leo lightly chastises me for not speaking in Japanese. He's threatened to pretend like he doesn't know me in Japan if I don't at least attempt to put my two years of Japanese to use.

"Wakarimasen." I tell him I don't understand.

Leo turns the professionally printed tiny signs around.

"Listen to your heart. Create a spark." Leo gives me The Full Dimple Smile.

"Wakarimasu." *I understand.*

Author's Note

I officially joined the Fujimura family in 1993 and have been on a cross-cultural adventure ever since. Though I never taught English in Japan like Leo's mom, I have spent almost every summer in Japan with my kids for over fifteen years. Food is my love language, so I enjoy spending time in the kitchen with my mother-in-law and Japanese friends learning new dishes. I may struggle to conjugate verbs, but my Japanese food vocabulary is solid. I apologize in advance if you now have a sudden craving for yakisoba and manju. #SorryNotSorry

Since this book spends a lot of time in a restaurant, you won't be surprised to hear that my family once owned a small restaurant and that I was the lunch waitress. I got that job not based on my skill set but because my dad needed a new waitress ASAP. I am a huge fan of Japanese food—and moonlight as The Obento Lady at Arizona-based anime cons—so you can connect the dots to see how Leo Matsuda came to be. Meanwhile, Dakota was inspired by YA author friend Kara McDowell's book *Just for Clicks* which is also about a teen who lives in the spotlight (fashion) and is desperately trying to figure out her reality. Mix that with my favorite HGTV show, *Fixer Upper* (Chip and Joanna!), and my love of historic houses, and you'll see how the Akagi-McDonald family came to life. Though I take my research very seriously, I occasionally bend some of the facts to make my fiction flow better or as a wink to certain people in my life. For example, Akagi House is loosely based on the Petersen House in Tempe, Arizona. Be sure to look for the lovely stained-glass window in between the first and second floors.

Finally, this one goes out to the next generation of biracial Asian teens in the US and around the globe looking to see themselves represented in more YA books. *Faking Reality* and my other contemporary YA books, *Tanabata Wish* and *Every Reason We Shouldn't*, are only one specific lens on the bigger experience of being a multiracial

Asian teen. You may see your family in my books. You may not. If you don't, I encourage you to take a look at the running list I keep on my website (www.sarafujimura.com) of other YA books featuring biracial Asian main characters and/or love interests. It is still an incredibly short list. Please help me add to it, because every teen deserves to see themselves on the bookshelf.

I hope this book brings you inspiration as you find *your* new reality in the post-pandemic world. Listen to your heart. Create your spark.

Acknowledgments

As always, though my name is on the cover, I have a huge team who helped me take a wild idea out of the ether and solidify it into book form.

Thank you first and foremost to the immediate and extended members of the Francis-Fujimura family. I wouldn't be inspired to write the stories I do without you.

Diana Gill and Rebecca Angus for sparking this new idea and then tag-teaming with Susan Chang (Tor Teen) and Ann Rose (Prospect Agency) to bring it to life despite being in the middle of a pandemic. Here's to even more creative adventures together!

Sara Van Acker (a real-life Stephanie!) for sharing her immense knowledge of TV production and how Hollywood magic works.

The strong, talented, awesome Kolland women: Kimber, Brooke, and Mikayla for their power-tool knowledge, fact checks, cheerleading, and "Everybody needs a Leo" comment. Also, I concur.

The Constandse-Strait family, especially Carrie and Vanessa, for your longtime friendship, peek into blended Mexican American family life, and the excuse to make tres leches cake in the name of research.

Hilda Serrano for not only making my hair look great, but for the deep-dive into all things quinceañera.

Wonder Twin for helping me find the story I didn't even know I had in me and alerting me to the dangers of "chicken cutlets."

Patrick Canfield, Saraciea Fennell, Anneliese Merz, Lesley Worrell, Melanie Sanders, Christa Desir, Heather Saunders, and the whole Tor Teen team for bringing this story to life.